# Stephania

# Stephania

BY ILONA KARMEL

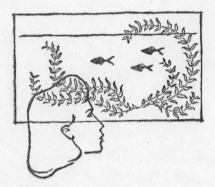

HOUGHTON MIFFLIN COMPANY

BOSTON The Riverside Press Cambridge

TO
ARCHIBALD MACLEISH

# CHAPTER I

THE ROOM IS SPACIOUS and full of light. Even on the most gloomy days it seems to be bright and cheerful because the walls are painted warm yellow and the floor, covered with grass-green linoleum, is shiny like a mirror. It is a pleasant, a cozy room, and were it not for the three beds one would never think it just a hospital room — Room Number Five, Ward Two, in the Institute for the Handicapped in Stockholm.

Still, the beds are there, undeniable, huge and massive, real hospital beds, even if the bright green covers adorned with the gray pattern of polkadots try to hide their true character. But the bedside tables are again pleasant and homelike — of brown maple covered with something that looks almost like pink marble. Three vases, all identical, all empty, stand on the tables, and next to them three books, also identical, lie looking fresh and untouched in their shiny black covers. BOOK OF PSALMS AND PRAYERS, the golden letters read.

White charts are fastened on the bed frames — like visiting cards on apartment doors. The chart on the bed next to the window is empty still, and the bed also is empty, covered with immaculately fresh linen like a house that waits, all scrubbed and painted, for new inhabitants. The charts on the two other beds are covered with sharply rising curves with black and red signs. "Thura Svenson" is written upon one, "born 1932." And underneath in much bigger letters, as if the words were of much greater importance than those dealing merely with accidents of age and birth, it says — INFANTILE PARALYSIS. "Maria Nilsson" — the second chart says — "born 1913," and again the big letters underneath announce — FRACTURE OF THE LEFT LEG.

The empty bed had belonged to Fru Hernruth, the wife of the police superintendent in Göteborg, who had left this morning. Last evening, as hospital custom dictated, she had invited her roommates to a coffee party. Drinking coffee in the evening was illegal in Ward Two. There was no official prohibition, but Sister Gudrun, the head nurse, was of the opinion that coffee was too exciting for the patients, unhealthy for both their nerves and hearts. Sister Gudrun's opinion was a law for everybody in the ward, or rather for almost everybody — not for Fru Gustavsson the head maid. Looking with a conspiratorial air at the door, Fru Gustavsson whispered that a good cup of coffee had never yet done harm to anybody. And before she left she smuggled into the room a thermos bottle filled with freshly brewed, strong coffee.

The party turned out to be a real feast: there were two kinds of pastry, small tarts, and a chocolate cake which Thura thought was better than any she had ever tasted. But Fröken Nilsson was of a different opinion. "If I were the wife of a police superintendent, I would have sent for the cake to Paris Pastry, or at least to Eriksson's," she said, as soon as the door had closed after Fru Hernruth, "but of course, she had to get them in the cheapest place in the whole of Stockholm."

But Thura, remembering that Fröken Nilsson had had three helpings of the chocolate cake and had put a whole lot of tarts into her cooky box, said nothing. Fröken Nilsson murmured something about the chocolate cake tasting like soap, not a speck of butter in it, and then they both lay silent, looking at the empty bed.

For it was a special, a privileged bed; it stood right under the Venetian window and without sitting up you could see out of it the drive, the park and far away even a part of the street.

"Well . . ." Fröken Nilsson cleared her throat, "I wonder, I've been wondering all day long, who's going to get that bed now." Again Thura did not answer, but Fröken Nilsson, unperturbed, went on. "I should have gotten it last time, after Fröken Brig left. I've been longer than anyone else in this ward. But then, I'm not married to the police superintendent. I'm just plain Fröken Nilsson, so, of course, I have to stay in my dark corner. All right, all right. I'm used to that. But now, I wonder, I just wonder . . ."

"I wonder too," Thura said, and stopped, horrified by her own audacity. Still she kept looking straight into Fröken Nilsson's face. For a moment they gazed at each other, coldly, hostilely almost — Fröken Nilsson, once pinkish and blond, now faded and heavy, her features submerged by spongy layers of fat, and Thura, so thin and pale that although she was sixteen she looked just like a sick child. Her thin pale face weary but eager — a sick child's face.

[ 2 ]

At last Thura gave in. She felt a little guilty, but only a very little. For even if Fröken Nilsson had been there longer than she — and not so much longer either, just two months — still Fröken Nilsson could sit in her wheel chair and look through the window as much as she wanted. Thura could never sit in a wheel chair; she could hardly raise her head, and all she could see from her bed was a tiny square of the window. But, Thura sighed longingly, if she could ever have Fru Hernruth's bed then she could see the whole window and the sky and the chestnut and fir trees, and perhaps even the smoke from the trains passing on the nearby track.

Yes, it was true that Fröken Nilsson could sit in her wheel chair, but to get into it was not an easy thing at all, especially if you weighed a hundred and eighty pounds and had your leg in a plaster cast up to the hip. Fröken Nilsson, therefore, had good reasons, very good reasons, indeed, when she asserted her right to the privileged bed. For then she would not have to miss all those important events taking place in the drive. Then she could see the old patients going home, the new ones coming. She could watch the crowds of visitors pouring out of the red bus. Last week, when she sat in her wheel chair at the window, one of them, a tall blond fellow, a really good-looking one, waved at her. She hoped to see him on the next visiting day, but, of course, everybody was too busy to help her to get into the wheel chair and so she had missed him. But, most important of all, she could see Doctor Liliencrona, the handsome Doctor Liliencrona, in whom Fröken Nilsson, as everybody in the ward knew, was passionately interested. And so the bed under the window opened new vistas, unlimited possibilities. "Yes," Fröken Nilsson said, "we shall see who gets the bed. Everything depends on Doctor Ström."

Fröken Nilsson wanted to add something about Thura being Doctor Ström's darling, but at that very moment the door opened and Doctor Ström came in. "Good morning!" he exclaimed, already on the threshold. "Good morning, ladies, or rather good afternoon. Time passes so fast here you never know if it's morning or afternoon."

And in his white coat, as always unbuttoned and too long for his short square body, with the tails flying behind him, Doctor Ström walked into the room.

Everybody liked Doctor Ström, and the ladies in the ward used

[ 3 ]

to say he looked like a poet, so pale and delicate, and with that little mustache.

"So, everybody is fine?" Doctor Ström said. He came to Thura's bed, lifted the blanket and uncovered her feet. They were tiny and shapely feet, but bony and covered with a withered greenish skin, which here and there peeled off in big patches, like paint falling off the wall. Doctor Ström passed his fingers over Thura's toes as if they were the keys of a piano. Thura screamed and everybody burst into laughter. During each of his visits Doctor Ström pretended to be tickling Thura's toes, and every time, Thura made believe it tickled so terribly she just couldn't stand it.

"You see," Doctor Ström said now. "And here she tries to tell me that she has no feeling in her toes, the little scoundrel. None at all." Doctor Ström, imitating Thura, raised his voice to the highest possible pitch, and at that Thura and Fröken Nilsson burst again into laughter. "And now let's have a look at your hand. I've heard good news from the physiotherapist, very good news."

"Oh yes," Thura answered proudly, "it's three inches now." She clenched her teeth as if she were going to lift an immense burden, and slowly raised her hand a few inches above the blanket.

"That's the girl." Doctor Ström stroked Thura's face and then walked over to Fröken Nilsson. "And how's the diet, Fröken Nilsson?"

Fröken Nilsson grasped with both her hands a wooden handle which hung above her head, suspended on two converging iron bars, and she hoisted herself up, slowly, laboriously. She looked like a drowning man struggling out of the water.

"The diet's fine, Doctor, it's my leg which is not fine, not at all."

"My dear Fröken Nilsson." Doctor Ström stretched out his arms in a gesture of resignation. "We are doing what we can, but you must help us. You must lose weight, the more of it the better, otherwise your leg will never be able to carry you. You see what I mean?"

"I do," Fröken Nilsson answered obediently, although she saw nothing. A diet was one thing, and a fractured leg another. If he had only taken better care of her, if he . . .

"Good-bye, ladies, see you tomorrow," Doctor Ström said, and he was at the door before Fröken Nilsson woke up from her meditation and exclaimed, "Doctor — just a moment, Doctor . . ."

"Yes?"

"It's about the bed, Fru Hernruth's bed, I mean . . ."

"Yes," Doctor Ström repeated. "What about it?"

"I . . . we've been wondering who's going to get it."

Doctor Ström looked at the bed, then at Fröken Nilsson.

"Stephania," he said. "Stephania."

"What?"

"Her name is Stephania. Ste-pha-nia," he repeated in a slow, sad singsong, as if the strange, outlandish sound of that name was an explanation, a justification of the wrong that was taking place. "She's Polish," he added, although that was hardly relevant. "Goodbye everybody, good-bye."

"So," Fröken Nilsson snapped, "now you see." She had forgotten all her grudges against Thura. The common injustice had brought them together again. "And how do you like *that?*"

"Oh, isn't that exciting, Fröken Nilsson?" Thura said. "She's Polish, and what a beautiful name . . . Ste-pha-nia." She pronounced it sadly, singingly, exactly as Doctor Ström had. "I think it's perfectly fantastic, just too marvelous." Out of her two years in high school Thura had brought a few of those exaggerated teen-age expressions. Coming out of her pale, parched lips, in the monotony of the hospital room, they sounded out of place and they strangely disturbed Fröken Nilsson.

"So what if she's Polish? We have a couple of Poles at home, at Eskilstuna. They always get drunk and then they fight."

Thura said, "Perhaps she's young, Fröken Nilsson. I just have a feeling she will be my age."

Fröken Nilsson rang the bell. "Would you help me to get into my wheel chair, please," she asked the nurse. The nurse pushed the chair to the bed, and stood leaning on it with all her strength. Fröken Nilsson grasped the wooden bar, raised her huge buttocks, and like an acrobat swung herself into the chair, dragging the leg in the heavy cast behind. "Ugh," she sighed. The chair creaked. She wheeled silently out of the room, still indignant.

Right after lunch Fru Gustavsson rushed into the room, the mop and the duster in her hand.

"Is *she* coming?" Thura whispered.

"Is Sister Gudrun coming?" Fröken Nilsson asked.

"She's here already," Fru Gustavsson answered. "You should have seen the fuss she raised in Room Three: she found an orange peel on the floor there. And of course it was my fault. As if I had time to walk from one patient to another and peel oranges for them," and Fru Gustavsson angrily passed the mop over the floor.

She was just about to leave when the door opened and Sister Gudrun came in. She was very tall, Sister Gudrun, strong and solidly built; but somehow at first sight of her one could not resist the impression she was composed of nothing but her uniform. The white hospital coat began right under her chin and reached almost to her feet; it covered her all over with wide impersonal folds which transformed her whole figure into one mass of white starched linen. Even her face looked as if it were a part of the uniform; so colorless and thin-lipped that only the three small carefully combed curls that stuck out from underneath the cap seemed to be really hers.

"How is everyone today?" Sister Gudrun asked. She looked around and her eyes stopped at the empty bed.

"So Fru Hernruth is gone," she said. "I guess you must have had quite a party yesterday."

"Well . . ." Fröken Nilsson muttered.

"All right, all right; drink as much coffee and stay awake as late as you want to." Somehow Sister Gudrun would always find out what took place in her ward.

"But then don't come to me and tell me that you can't sleep in the night, that you must have sleeping pills."

Nobody answered, until at last Fröken Nilsson gathered all her courage and said, "I don't think it's right for a stranger to get the bed under the window again."

"What? What stranger?"

"That Stephania."

"Who told you that?"

"Doctor Ström. Didn't Sister know about that?"

"No. So that's something else new." Sister Gudrun once more looked at the empty bed and left the room.

Fröken Nilsson, Thura and Fru Gustavsson looked at each other. Wasn't that strange? Sister Gudrun had always been the first to know about a new patient.

"Did you see her face?" Fru Gustavsson whispered. "She thinks she is as important as the Professor himself, and now even Ström doesn't tell her who's coming into the ward."

"Yes," Fröken Nilsson nodded absently. Usually she took great

[ 6 ]

interest in Fru Gustavsson's quarrels with Sister Gudrun, but now something else occupied her mind.

"Why didn't he tell her Stephania was coming?" she pondered aloud. "There's something queer about that whole story, something very queer, I'm telling you!"

CHAPTER 2

LIFE IN A HOSPITAL moves according to unchanging, constantly recurring rules. Every event has an exactly defined function, and takes place in exactly the same manner until, in the perpetual repetition, it becomes part of a pattern, indispensable, and of a profound, almost ritual significance.

There is the ritual of the inspection visit — when the long line of white figures passes from one room to another, the Professor talking on at the top of his voice, the assistant doctors murmuring respectfully, and, at a proper distance, the blue-and-white flock of nurses whispering timidly. There is the ritual of bedmaking when Fru Gustavsson stands on one side of the bed, the student nurse on the other, while the room fills with the sharp scent of rubbing alcohol, and white clouds of talcum hover in the air. Another ritual is afternoon coffee, called coffee although only tea is served, when shiny brown rolls are passed from one bed to another. But the most important of all is the arrival of a new patient; more solemn, more exciting, because of its rarity. Though in the course of their two years in the hospital Fröken Nilsson and Thura had seen many new patients come, the ceremony of their arrival was always the same.

It begins with a noise behind the door, a murmur of voices, the brisk steps of Sister Gudrun, and the slow, hesitant steps of the newcomer. There is always a knock — which signals Sister Gudrun's rapid check to be sure that everything looks tidy and neat — followed by the entry of the new patient and her companion. Patients never come alone: there is a husband or parents or at least a friend. They tiptoe in softly and stop in the middle of the room; the men clumsily turn their hats in their hands and the women, usually more at ease, cover their confusion with too broad a smile. They murmur their names in faintly audible voices and stand helplessly looking at the walls and the window. At last, with a swift glance at the beds, one of them suddenly says, in a high, relieved voice, "Look at that bedside table: it's maple, exactly like the one we have at home." It is always a comment about the tables, or about the linoleum — "It's so green and cheerful" — or the bedspreads — "They look so cozy, with the lovely polka-dot pattern." Thus they cling to homelike objects, the only familiar details in this room of impersonal beds, peopled with strangers in white hospital shirts.

The new patient usually stands alone, a little apart from those with whom she came, not belonging to their world any longer, and not yet initiated into the new one. Fröken Nilsson and Thura always look at her with a mixture of sympathy and condescension. They try to guess whether she is quiet or talkative, complaining or patient. They look at her dress very carefully, remembering each detail of color, buttoning and pleat.

It is because of the dress that the whole ritual of arrival has importance. Though it would be simpler to take the new patient directly to the bath, and leave her clothes in the storage room, she is invariably shown to her room first, and Fröken Nilsson and Thura always see her dress. Later, after the operation, when the newcomer lies on her bed groaning, horrified by the unfamiliarity of her aching body, they can say: "You'll be all right, dear, you'll be going home soon in that lovely dress of yours." And the dress, for Fru Hernruth (or Svenson, or Carlson, or whoever else it may be), becomes a link with the outside world — a proof that her body has not always been helpless, filled with fear and pain.

And then the new patient goes with Sister Gudrun to take a bath, while her companions wait in the room. They make a few attempts at conversation, uttering jerky sentences, but at last, ashamed of their good health, of the ease with which they move their bodies, and the fresh air lingering in their clothes, they fall silent. Then the newcomer returns, as feeble as if her strength had been stored away with her clothes, supported by Sister Gudrun. Her shapeless robe creates a gap between her and the people she came with, but to Fröken Nilsson and Thura she has become an ally.

[ 8 ]

It was just such an arrival that Fröken Nilsson and Thura now anticipated. The former waited impatiently, outraged by the loss of the bed under the window, but Thura was eager and excited.

Wednesday morning had passed without Stephania's appearance. It was a morning which their suspense made long and tiresome. "She's not here," Fröken Nilsson said to Doctor Ström when he came in on his evening visit. She pointed to the empty bed under the window. "Perhaps she has changed her mind?"

"No," Doctor Ström said slowly, his eyes following Fröken Nilsson's pointing fingers. "No, she will never change her mind; not Ste-pha-nia," and he left the room without having tickled Thura's toes.

Then Thursday came and the hours moved slowly. It was raining outside and the drops pounded rhythmically against the window. Nobody came. Thura, who had been raising her head whenever there was the sound of steps behind the door, grew anxious.

"How do you like that?" Fröken Nilsson exploded at last. "First she says she's coming, and then she doesn't show up at all," she said, as if Stephania had failed to keep a definite appointment with her. Fröken Nilsson felt angry. The tension was too much for her.

And then, late in the afternoon, when Thura had given up hope, suddenly, without any preparation, without the sound of voices or the shuffle of feet in the hall, the door opened. Sister Gudrun came in and said, "Here's our new patient."

In the great excitement Fröken Nilsson forgot to use her bar when she sat up. Thura, a strange wave of joy and fear passing through her body, raised her head. They looked at the door, and the first thing they saw was flowers, huge garish flowers decorating a hat, forcing themselves into view, growing as if upon a hill. For the head of the girl — she could not be more than twenty — was too big for her small deformed body and looked as if it had been pressed onto her shoulders, which were hunched as if she were constantly shrugging them. She walked into the room slightly sidewise and turned from Fröken Nilsson to Thura as if challenging them with her distorted back, exhibiting to them the whole grotesque deformity of her body.

There was a long moment of silence. Everybody, even Sister Gudrun, felt at a loss. The ritual had been violated. No men clumsily turning their hats in their hands stood in the room, no

[ 9 ]

vaguely smiling women. Not a word was said about the maple bedside tables, about the linoleum, or the polka dots on the bedspreads. Alone and silent, the hunchback stood in the middle of the room — and grinned. Yes, she grinned: a faint and somehow mocking grin.

"Well," Sister Gudrun said at last, "this is Fröken Ackermann, Stephania Ackermann. Did I pronounce it correctly?"

"Perfectly," the hunchback answered. Her voice was sharp and very loud.

"And that's Fröken Nilsson and our little Thura."

"Very glad to meet you," the hunchback said indifferently. She bent her head slightly and it made her shoulders look higher, even more grotesque.

"You're going to have the bed under the window," Sister Gudrun explained, emphasizing the last words. "The doctor arranged it so you'd have a bed under the window."

"Thanks. But it doesn't make any difference to me where I sleep." "Sleep" — she said, as if the bed in the hospital were nothing but a piece of furniture in which you only spent the night. She walked toward the bed and put a small suitcase on the table. It was made of alligator, as Fröken Nilsson noticed right off, with a golden monogram engraved upon it. Stephania opened the suitcase, took a purse out of it, and without a word began to walk toward the door.

"Where are you going?" Sister Gudrun asked, so surprised that until Stephania stood on the threshold she was tongue-tied.

"To the telephone."

"But . . . you have to take a bath first."

"I took a bath just before I came here."

For a moment Sister Gudrun was speechless. "But that has nothing to do with taking the bath here. Everybody must take a bath here."

"If you insist." Stephania shrugged her huge shoulders and her head almost vanished between them.

Sister Gudrun cleared her throat impatiently. Who did that Stephania think she was? First she had come in late, then she started arguing about the bath, and now she kept her waiting.

"We must hurry, Fröken Ackermann," she said. "It's getting late."

"Would you wait a moment please," Stephania said, to Sister

Gudrun, whom even the doctors would not dare to keep waiting. "I just have to take my things out."

"You don't need anything. Everything has been prepared." Sister Gudrun pointed to the hospital shirt and to the white bathrobe lying on the bed.

Stephania looked at them, passed her fingers over the rough fabric.

"You don't expect me to wear *that?*"

"They are for you, and my dear Fröken Ackermann, you must hurry; it's really getting late."

"I'm coming. Just let me take my things." Without asking for permission, Stephania took a nightgown out of her suitcase. And what a nightgown! Fröken Nilsson looked and Thura stared, and even Sister Gudrun forgot what a great hurry she was in. It was light blue, soft and shimmering, with lace everywhere, around the neckline, the sleeves, even around the hem at the bottom. As she hung it over her arm it rustled softly.

"It'd be a pity to wear a gown like that in the hospital," Sister Gudrun said. "Why doesn't Fröken save it for later?"

"I couldn't wear *that*," Stephania said, pointing to the shirt on her bed. She took out a blue silken robe. "Let's go," she said, as if it were she who had been obliged to wait for Sister Gudrun.

"Well, she's quite something," Fröken Nilsson snapped when the door closed. She looked at the rejected hospital shirt. " 'You don't expect me to wear *that!*' " she mimicked. "A princess! They are good enough for everyone except her. Did you see how she was trying to impress us with that nightgown, holding it in her hand for half an hour so that everybody could see it? She can't impress me. . . . I've seen as good and better things in my life. That" . . . hunchback, Fröken Nilsson wanted to say, but at the last moment she checked herself. No, it wasn't the right thing to say. After all, it wasn't Stephania's fault she was a hunchback. Still it was strange to have someone like that in the room. Fröken Nilsson had seen all kinds of people in the hospital, some with polio, like Thura, others with broken legs, still others with club feet. Once they even had brought in a girl who had her whole arm off. But a hunchback was something different. In bed, the others looked exactly like other people, but a hunchback was always a hunchback. She could never hide it. In a way Fröken Nilsson felt sorry for Stephania. A young girl — and so awfully

[ 11 ]

deformed. But what a show-off! Impudent, that was it, just impudent.

"We're going to have quite a time with her, I can see that," she said.

"I think she's wonderful," Thura answered. "And do you know, it doesn't bother me a bit that she's a hunchback." And then, lowering her voice, as if she were talking about a secret, Thura added, "Did you see her nightgown? I'm sure it was the most expensive silk."

"Of course not. It was just rayon, or something like that," Fröken Nilsson said captiously.

"Even so . . . I *do* think she's fascinating."

Perhaps Thura said those words so loudly and with such emphasis in order to deafen the slight but persistent voice of disappointment that was rising in her.

Yes, the newcomer was wonderful, but how different from that Stephania for whom Thura had been waiting for two long days. The other Stephania was shy, and very lonely, and helpless just like those people about whom Fru Gustavsson used to tell her — people who had gone through all kinds of horrible things during the war, and who now came to Sweden with nothing but the shirt on their backs, without a penny in their pockets. Thura wanted to take care of that Stephania exactly as Fröken Nilsson had taken care of her in the beginning. Whenever you want something and you don't know how to say it, just explain it to me, please, she would have told the imaginary Stephania, who of course hardly knew any Swedish at all. And then, since the other would have been very poor, she would have shared with her all the cookies that Mama would send her from home, and would have bought magazines for the two of them. But how could you even dream of offering a cookie or a magazine to someone who owned an alligator suitcase and wore nightgowns of expensive silk (for it certainly was not merely rayon)? How could you ever try to help Stephania, who had told, no, had commanded, Sister Gudrun to wait for her?

Still, Thura did not have the slightest doubt that Stephania *was* wonderful. "You know," she said to Fröken Nilsson, "she is different from anyone I've ever known in my life."

"Pooh . . ." was all Fröken Nilsson said.

In the huge, blindingly white bathroom the new patient stood glancing curiously at Sister Gudrun.

[ 12 ]

"Well," Sister Gudrun said, and to overcome an uneasy feeling of uselessness, straightened out the bathmat, "why doesn't Fröken start undressing?"

"I'm waiting for you to leave."

Sister Gudrun stepped closer. "Fröken Ackermann, I wish you would understand you're in the hospital now. I'm here to help you and . . ."

"I don't need any help." Stephania was smiling faintly when the door closed behind Sister Gudrun.

The bath felt good. Lying on her belly, the water touching her in continuous warm ripples, Stephania sensed with relief how the weariness moved through her body, gathered into a heavy lump in her feet, and then slowly dissolved somewhere in the water. What a day it had been — she thought. First the shopping and preparations — that alone would have been enough to make anybody tired. But the worst thing was that comedy of leave-taking — the affectionate good-byes at her boardinghouse. It was like a pilgrimage — all those people coming into her room. First the maids; with them at least you knew what they had come for — to remind you about the tip. But why on earth did the boarders have to come, one after another, each pretending to be so sorry she was leaving. "We're all going to miss you," the architect said; and the medical student: "The place won't be the same without you." It certainly wouldn't, Stephania thought, because they would all be so relieved once she was gone, so happy that now someone of their own kind would come; healthy, someone they wouldn't have to be ashamed of, who would make a good partner at a dance and look pretty at a cocktail party. But they had to pretend: they were so solicitous, so worried about her; the two sisters from next door insisted on bringing her to the hospital.

"You can't go alone," they said.

"I'm going to stay there alone, aren't I?" she told them. Still they wouldn't leave her alone, but called a cab for her and gave her flowers. It looked like a funeral.

"I am waiting here for you," Sister Gudrun said with emphasis.

"All right, all right, I'm coming." And smiling again Stephania got out of the bathtub.

Stephania returned from the bathroom and walked straight over to her bed. She hung the towel on the rack in the back of the bedside table, put the soap into the drawer, and folded the silk robe on the chair. She did everything quietly, without hesitating for a moment, not like a newcomer at all, but like someone who found herself in a place familiar for years. Then she lifted her suitcase and put it on the bed, and started unpacking. First came a mirror in a silver frame, then a bottle of perfume, slender, shimmering with warm gold, and then a photograph of a young girl, rather short, but fragile and graceful, dressed in a light evening dress and with flowers in her hair.

"Isn't she lovely," Thura said. "Who is she, Ste —" Stephania, Thura wanted to say, but at once corrected herself: "Who is she, Fröken Ackermann?"

Stephania looked at the picture. "It's me," she said simply, as if there were no difference between the slender figure in the picture and her present self.

"You mean that's you?" Fröken Nilsson exclaimed.

Stephania turned to her abruptly. "Yes, it's me," she said, and without another word went on unpacking. She took out another picture, this time of a man, or rather a boy, with a pair of skis on his shoulders. There was nothing but sky behind the tall figure, and the skis cut it with two sharp straight lines. Everything about him was like that, sharp and straight — his lean face, his gaunt erect body.

The two pictures stood on the bedside table facing each other. Fröken Nilsson and Thura looked at them. Fröken Nilsson wondered who the boy could be; he looked like a movie star, handsome, very handsome indeed. And Thura thought how strange it was that Stephania put her own photograph on the table. Usually you did it only with pictures of those who were far away, or even dead, so that you wouldn't forget what they looked like. Was the girl really Stephania? Once more Thura glanced at the picture. Yes, it was the same face, the same sharp thin nose, small lips, the eyes framed by the straight brows, and very long lashes. Suddenly both Thura and Fröken Nilsson thought with surprise, as though they had discovered something strange, that the face of the hunchback was beautiful — perhaps too severe, so dark and proud, but still very beautiful.

After dinner — there was beef stew and rice pudding for dessert — Sister Gudrun came to fill in Stephania's chart. "How do you spell your name, Fröken Ackermann?" she asked.

"S, T," Stephania began. She pronounced every syllable sharply; the S had a hissing unpleasant sound in her mouth.

"When were you born?"

"November the second, nineteen-twenty-seven."

"Where?"

"In Cracow. That's in Poland."

"I know where Cracow is," Sister Gudrun said with dignity. "We have sent some of our nurses there to train personnel for the Polish hospitals."

Stephania said nothing, and so Sister Gudrun asked: "Your home address?"

"What do you mean?"

"The place where you live, where you lived before you came to the hospital."

"I lived in a boardinghouse. Is that what you mean?"

"No. I mean your home address, the place where you always live, you see?"

"I don't have a home address," Stephania said. Her face was tight-lipped, angry.

"But what about Poland, about Cracow? You must have a home address there?"

"No."

Sister Gudrun sighed. She left the second line of the chart blank, although it was quite against regulations. Then she looked at the third line, where on Fröken Nilsson's chart the big letters said "Fracture of the left leg," and on Thura's "Infantile Paralysis," sighed again, and left it blank too.

"Well, I guess, that's all," she said, and left.

Stephania nodded, and when Sister Gudrun left she sat still looking at the chart. ROYAL INSTITUTE FOR THE HANDI-CAPPED, the inscription on the top of the chart read. Handicapped, didn't it sound lovely? Not crippled but handicapped. Well, let them call it what they wanted. The main thing was she was here. It certainly wouldn't be too easy to get used to this place. not with these two in here. The way they gaped at her when she came in, especially the fat one! What was her name? Stephania raised her head and looked at the chart on the bed opposite her. Nilsson, of course, she should have known that. All Swedes were Nilssons or Carlssons or Olssons. They did not have enough imagination to find decent names for themselves. But this Nilsson

[ 15 ]

was quite a specimen. She had literally opened her mouth when she saw Stephania coming into the room. And the little one was completely awe-stricken. Well, that's what you get, my dear, you're a hunchback, nothing short of it, and the sooner you get used to it the better for you.

Her mouth felt dry. I must have some water, she thought, and jumped out of bed. She reached for her robe, hesitated, and then walked to the washstand in nothing but her nightgown. With something that was almost like joy she saw her reflection in the big mirror. The shiny silk clung to her body, to the bulging curves of her back. Fine, now they could see exactly what it was like. Slowly she paraded through the room. Were they staring at her? With a quick, unexpected gesture, she turned back. Of course, they were, and now they felt ashamed; the fat one instantly pretended to be reading a magazine. She stopped at the washstand. Now she was turned with her back to them, now they could look. Just go ahead . . . she did not mind, not at all.

She filled the glass and began to drink. The water was luke-warm; Stephania grimaced, emptied the glass into the sink and walked back to her bed.

Fröken Nilsson turned on the radio. Accordion music — that was exactly the kind of music you'd expect her to choose. The little one began to hum. Stephania pressed her head into the pillow, but the sounds of the polka still penetrated into her ears.

> *I'll dance with you on midsummer night,*
> *I'll give you two roses*
> *One red and one white,*

the sleek voice sang.

Now Fröken Nilsson was humming too. Stephania sat up in her bed.

"Could you turn the radio lower, please?"

"Certainly," Thura hastened to assure her.

"Well, if you want me to," Fröken Nilsson said, and she looked at Thura triumphantly as if saying, You see. What did I tell you?

It was just like Ström to put her into a room like that, Stephania thought. As if she had not told him. "I want to room with people who are in the same boat I am," she had said to him. What did she mean by that, he had asked; people who faced the same problem of a physical handicap? He had a real talent for putting things

[ 16 ]

nicely and neatly across. Yes, she had answered, that was exactly what she meant . . . people crippled as badly as she was, so they wouldn't pity her. She was sick and tired of pity, of people staring at her, or pretending not to stare, of everyone who felt sorry for her. "At least in the hospital I want to be just like everybody else," she told him.

Nothing was easier, he promised. There were many people in the hospital who would be glad to change places with her. She would not only be in the same boat but better off than they were. And now, after all that talk, he had put her in here, with these two. There couldn't be much the matter with them. The fat one was definitely bursting with health; the very way she ate, and talked. . . . The little girl, no; she was rather pale and quiet, and she had to be fed at dinner, but still, she too seemed perfectly happy, kept humming to the radio and chattering by the hour. God, the way they were glancing at her.

The first thing she must do tomorrow was to ask Ström to transfer her to another room, to a place where people were quiet, where they were really sick, too preoccupied with their own pains to pay any attention to others.

Stephania raised her head.

"What time does the doctor come tomorrow?" she asked.

"Usually around ten," Thura answered eagerly. "Except on Tuesdays and Thursdays. They're operation days so he comes later; sometimes eleven or twelve. But tomorrow is Friday, and so he'll be here at ten sharp."

"Thank you," she said, and lay down to show that for her the conversation was finished.

"You are very welcome, to be sure," Thura said politely. And then she added the words that she had been repeating to herself all the time she had been waiting for Stephania: "Whenever you want to know something, please don't hesitate to ask me — us." She corrected herself in order not to be unfair to Fröken Nilsson. "We know a lot about the hospital; we are the old-timers, as Doctor Ström calls us."

"What?"

"The old-timers. You see we have been here longer than anyone else. Fröken Nilsson two years and two months, and I a little over two years."

"Oh," Stephania said hopefully, "so you'll be going home soon."

[ 17 ]

"No, of course not. How could I?" And delighted to be the one to introduce Stephania into the secrets of hospital life, she began. "You see, I've had polio, and I'm paralyzed."

"But you're better, aren't you?"

"Sure, I am, even the Professor says so."

"So you can walk now?"

"Walk?" Thura repeated, as if not understanding quite what Stephania was talking about. "No, of course I can't walk. But I can lift my hand, the right one. Let me show you." And Thura, flushed with excitement, raised her hand. "Do you see?"

"Y . . . yes . . ." Stephania murmured. She could not understand anything. What was she talking about . . . her hand? Did she lift it at all? "I don't follow you, quite," Stephania said. "Did you say you could lift your hand?"

"Yes, three inches."

"And how long did you say you've been here?"

"Two years. Two years and three weeks. I came in August, 'forty-five. And the doctor said that when I go home I'll be able to move both hands. That will be wonderful."

"Oh. And when are you going home?"

Again Thura was surprised. "How should I know that?" she said. "The doctor has never told me."

"You mean you never ask him?"

"Why should I? When the time comes he'll tell me."

"He sure will, don't you worry about that. They don't keep you here one day longer than necessary. Often not even as long as that. Sometimes they make you go before you can even stand on your feet." Fröken Nilsson at last seized the opportunity of entering the conversation.

Again Thura felt guilty about keeping Stephania for herself. "Fröken Nilsson has a fracture of her left leg," she explained, in the tone in which one speaks about a title or position of someone who is too modest to mention his own importance himself. "Four fractures, two in her thigh and two beneath the knee. Is that right, Fröken Nilsson?"

"Yes, it is."

"But it will heal. It just takes time."

"It certainly does," Fröken Nilsson agreed. "Two years, and here I am still in bed and still with that horrid plaster on my leg."

"And what does the doctor say?"

"Nothing. I even don't listen to what he says. They all just talk and talk and nothing comes of it. Talking, that's all they can do, all those doctors and professors." Fröken Nilsson fell silent. She was afraid she had gone too far.

The door opened. The little blond student nurse came in and asked if Fröken Nilsson would like to go to Room Three. Fröken Ostrom had just finished knitting the cutest little jacket one could imagine: it was for her nephew — all blue with tiny rocking horses knitted into it. Yes, Fröken Nilsson wanted very much to see it. The Sister brought in the wheel chair, helped Fröken Nilsson to get into it. "Good-bye," Fröken Nilsson waved, as if she were setting out on a long journey.

"Why doesn't her leg heal?" Stephania asked.

"I don't know exactly. She had an infection after her last operation, you see, she's had three of them. But once it was almost all right, and then the leg broke again. The doctor says she's too heavy and has got to lose weight," Thura whispered as if afraid that Fröken Nilsson, although she was in the next room, could still hear her.

"Well, why doesn't she lose weight, for Heaven's sake?"

"She loves to eat. Last time when Fru Hernruth invited us for coffee she had three helpings of chocolate cake."

"Good Lord!" Stephania said, and she lapsed into silence. So these were the people Ström had said would be glad to change with her any moment. Of course they would, they would exchange with anybody. They would be satisfied with everything as long as they had their beef stew for dinner, and accordion music, and cute little jackets to admire. That Fröken Nilsson certainly did not wish for anything more. And the little one . . . well, with her it was different . . . paralyzed, completely paralyzed. Again she glanced at the chart — Born 1932 — so she wasn't even sixteen yet. Yes, the little one had it hard. But the way she hummed and chattered so cheerfully, as if she had nothing in the world to worry about. . . . Strange — no, there was nothing strange about it; luckily for her she wasn't clever enough to see what had happened to her. Stephania raised her head, glanced at Thura; for a moment their eyes met — Thura smiled shyly, invitingly. Stephania hesitated, smiled back and hastily turned her eyes away.

I'll have to get used to them, she thought; at least the little one's not too bad. And Fröken Nilsson — well, probably most of them around here are like her, or even worse. No, she decided, there was no use talking to Ström.

CHAPTER 3

IN THE HOSPITAL, day starts quite differently from the way it does in the world outside. There, in the distant world of the healthy, a rigid demarcation line exists between the night and the morning. Day begins suddenly, in a single sharply distinguishable moment — with the jarring, compelling sound of the alarm clock, with the bright rays of light let into the room through the window from which curtains are pulled by one impatient gesture. But in the hospital night leaks into day, slowly, imperceptibly, until, before you know when and how, it dissolves into it. Day and night are interwoven. There is no rush, no hurry. The people in their beds languidly turn the pages of magazines, make a few stitches in their needlework, talk, and now and then, lulled by the monotonous murmur of voices around them, fall into a vague, lazy half-dream.

Then after lunch the rest hour comes; the curtains are drawn. Greenish twilight floods the rooms, and it is as if night, all the time quietly waiting to reappear, has come back. And the day never quite does disappear from the night; it persists in the muffled steps of the nurse in the hall, in the sound of bells rung by those who cannot fall asleep. Darkness, the dense solid darkness that fills the nights of those tired after a long day of work, never enters the hospital room — there is always light in it, the cool bluish shine of the small lamp above the door, that changes the darkness into gray dusk.

At midnight, the night nurse, Sister Ingeborg, a hypodermic syringe of penicillin in her hand, carefully opened the door of Room Five. She slid towards Fröken Nilsson's bed. Her hand, always cold, as if the weariness had drained it of all blood, touched the soft warm flesh of the sleeping woman's face. "Fröken Nilsson, wake up, the injection."

[ 20 ]

The soft murmur woke Stephania up. She sat up and passed her hand over her eyes. For a moment, which seemed very long to her, she sat motionless, unable to grasp where she was, what that darkness faintly dispersed by the blue light meant; the muffled sounds, the white figure standing opposite her. Slowly the objects around her began to acquire shape: first the outlines of beds, then the squares of the tables. Her eyes looked at them blankly, but gradually she started to put them into order, to unite all the details into one coherent picture — into the hospital room. Still she did not move, and as before the things around had slowly become distinguishable in the darkness, so now the events of the last day began to emerge out of the vague maze of her mind and assemble into a pattern. Until, at last, she remembered everything: her arrival, Sister Gudrun rustling with her starched clothes, Fröken Nilsson, little Thura. . . .

In the bed opposite her Fröken Nilsson, still half asleep, muttered plaintively. "It's penicillin. It's good for you, dear," the nurse persuaded her. Her whisper had a choked, asthmatic sound. She must be very old and tired. A flashlight flickered; its long pale ray looked like a ribbon tying the white figure to the bed. The nurse lifted the blanket. The mass of flesh, shapeless and dullcolored, sprawled in the faint shine. The hand of the nurse raised the syringe, held it for a moment suspended in air, and then suddenly, insidiously, struck it into the passively expectant flesh. "Oh," Fröken Nilsson whined, but without conviction, as if only performing a habitual duty.

Stephania stared, a strange exciting fear rising in her. It seemed impossible that the needle would ever emerge from the huge heap of flesh; it had to get lost there, like a pebble in placid bottomless waters. But there; the nurse held the syringe, with the sting of the long pointed needle, back in her hand. "So, it's all over," the tired voice whispered. Fröken Nilsson did not hear. Already she was breathing evenly, fast asleep, just as she was lying, with her bare buttock upward. The nurse covered her and walked to the door, the beam of her flashlight moving before her, now like a leash on which she was led out of the room. She opened the door. A broad strip of light penetrated into the room from the hall. Then the door closed, and again everything was darkness and silence.

Stephania lay down and closed her eyes, but sleep would not come. It was hot in the room. Her body seemed to be imprisoned by the blankets tucked in on both sides of the bed, deep under the mattress. Impatiently she pulled them out. Now it was better; she could move at least. The cover fell upon the floor, but she did not bother to pick it up. Then she lay quiet again, impassive, letting all that had happened that day flow through her, come to her from somewhere, effortless, all of itself:

*I'll dance with you on midsummer night*
*I'll give you two roses*
*One red and one white,*

the refrain of the polka obstinately sang in her ears. Little Thura who could lift her hand . . . how much? three inches, after two years. She remembered how that woman, Fru . . . Gust . . . yes, Fru Gustavsson they called her, had fed Thura at dinnertime, a napkin as big as a towel spread over the bed, two pillows put under Thura's head to support it. Once she started talking to Fröken Nilsson, and for a long while she sat holding the fork with the meat on it high above the girl's mouth. Thura lay with her lips parted, like a puppy waiting in vain for a bite from a child that was teasing it. She could not move at all: two years in the same room, the same bed, in the same position.

Fröken Nilsson moved, mumbled something, and smacked her lips noisily. Even in her dreams she must have been thinking of food.

Stephania felt more and more awake. What time could it be? She looked at the luminous dial of her watch. It was only twelve. Back in the boardinghouse the radio in the living room was still playing. The two blond sisters that lived next to her were now walking home, clinging to their beaux. The two spinsters from the third floor were beginning a new rubber of bridge. The young architect who drank was trying in vain to fit his key into the lock. And outside, the streets were only now filling with people. In the broad square of the Store Plan crowds streamed out of the movies. Long lines of cabs waited in front of the Opera and the Concert House. A sudden and great longing seized her — for the noise of the crowded streets, for the garish mosaic of the colorful lights, for all the confusion of voices, steps, car horns and tramway bells.

She struggled out of entangled sheets and blankets, and jumped out of the bed. Carefully she pulled up the window shade, listening anxiously to the grating sound. But no one woke up. She

[ 22 ]

pulled the shade a little higher still, and looked out. The drive in front of the hospital was completely deserted now. The tall arc lamp threw its light on the fir tree; the branches shone with a young transparent green. Farther away the highway ran in an endless serpentine. It must have been raining in the evening. The wet pavement glittered with the swift reflections of the passing cars. A darting light, and now again . . . and again . . . She could almost hear the soft whistle of the speeding machines: car rushing after car, carrying the people to the city, from the city. Twelve o'clock! The night was only beginning for them. And when they drove, late August air flew through the open windows, warm, smelling of rain, of leaves, of city smoke, and from time to time cut sharply by the sudden gust of the cold wind.

Stephania moved close to the window. Her cheek touched the pane. The glass felt cool and pure. She sighed.

Behind the highway the houses stood, big, heavy quadrangles, darker than the air of the night, their massive bodies punctuated by the brightly lit windows. They looked like blocks of dominoes, black with the light points engraved in them. But farther away the houses merged into one with the sky and the night, and the glittering windows seemed to be incrusted in the dark air.

Next to the hospital, just opposite the wing where her room was, stood a small house, probably a building for the employees. In one of the windows the shades were not pulled down: she could see the room, the people in it. A man, his face hidden behind the paper, sat on the sofa, a woman bent over some needlework in the armchair. Then the woman got up; her tall figure passed by the window and vanished. She returned after a while with a tray in her hands. The man took a glass from the tray, drank slowly, then he got up and put his arm around the woman.

They stood so for a moment, and then the woman freed herself in a reluctant languid gesture, and began to take the cover from the sofa. They must be using the living room as a bedroom, too. The man stood waiting. Then he walked toward the window. Suddenly the shade fell down and covered the window, blotting out from her view the room and the people within. It was as if they had discovered her, the intruder, the eavesdropper, and had quickly shut her out of their life by the impenetrable wall of the window shade. For a moment thin streaks of light were still flowing from underneath the shade. Then they also disappeared. For

[ 23 ]

these two the night began now. Were they asleep already? Or were they still talking, lying close to each other, their voices softened by the darkness?

Stephania felt cold. She should have lain down, but still she did not move. The dark window opposite reminded her of something — of what? — She did not know herself. And so she stood waiting until the vague sounds and shapes surging in her should assume form and meaning.

And then she knew. It was a few days ago, just before Barbara and Thadeus had left for Göteborg. Late in the evening she went into their room to pick up a book she had left there. The light was still on; she walked in. Barbara, dressed in her nightgown, was lying on the bed, uncovered, the blanket pushed aside. Under the thin fabric her belly rose in a curve. Thadeus' hand was resting on that roundness. They smiled. When she came in Thadeus said, "Your sister has just been trying to persuade me that she can feel the baby moving already. In the fourth month; how do you like that? A prodigy, that's what it must be."

"But it *does* move. I really can feel it, here, you see." And Barbara took Thadeus' hand in hers and moved it a little higher. Thadeus said, "You've just eaten too much, dear." And then they smiled, but that time not at her, only at each other.

That smile suddenly separated her from them, like the shade in the window from these two in the house opposite. "Come and have a cigarette with us," Thadeus said, but she only took the book and left.

What were they doing now? Perhaps they had just returned to the hotel. The light was still on in their room, and they sat and had the last cigarette before going to bed.

Suddenly she felt like smoking. It was strictly forbidden; that was one of the first things the nurse had warned her about — but who cared? She opened the drawer, groping in the darkness, took out the lighter and the cigarette case, and walked out of the room. The hall was empty. In the light of the big lamps, made even more glaring by the balls of frosted glass around the bulbs, the stone floor glittered coldly. She passed the long row of doors, all with numbers upon them, all closed — "Washroom"; here it was.

Inside she lit the cigarette and stood inhaling the smoke deeply, greedily. Footsteps sounded in the hall. Quickly she hid herself in the toilet. She wanted to close the door, but there was no lock,

[ 24 ]

and so she pulled the cover down over the seat, and sat smoking and looking at the monotonous pattern of white tiles.

The door of the washroom opened. "Is anybody in here?" the voice of the nurse asked.

"Yes," Stephania said hesitantly.

"Do you need any help?" And, without waiting for the answer, the nurse walked into the booth. "Oh," she whispered, "you . . . you . . . can't possibly smoke here. It's not allowed . . . never." Horror made the wrinkles in her face look like furrows; the protruding, too white, artificial teeth gave her a voracious expression.

"I didn't know it was not allowed." Stephania hastily took one puff more and hurled the cigarette into the toilet bowl.

"Please, flush it down, I'm afraid that somebody may see . . ."

"Don't worry." Stephania pushed the handle and walked out.

She was trying to fall asleep when the door opened again. The nurse stood on the threshold, the light of her flashlight directed like a reflector on her bed. Now she will spy on me for the rest of my days, Stephania thought, and aloud she said, "I'm not smoking. You've nothing to worry about."

The nurse murmured something and left.

Somewhere a bell rang.

A train rattled heavily on the track.

The night dragged itself on.

CHAPTER 4

SLOWLY THE HOSPITAL was waking up. The murmur of voices, the squeaking of doors opened and closed. The echo of feet hastening through the hall penetrated into the room, still quiet, still submerged in vague dusk. They lay no longer asleep, not quite awake yet, and listened: the hurried, energetic steps — that was Sister Gudrun coming; the heavy tramping of big boots — Lasse, the fat orderly, was walking over to the service room; and at last the swift pit-a-pat of high-heeled shoes meant that Fru Gustavsson was there, that the day had started in earnest.

[ 25 ]

After a while Fru Gustavsson came in, already in her white hospital coat and in soft rubber shoes, but with her cheeks still red with the crisp, cool morning air. She was a good-looking woman, Fru Gustavsson, not too young any longer, but plump and dimply — a doughnut, Willy the news vendor called her. Her big hands, all red and wrinkled from constant soaking in water, were wide and strong — good capable hands, for which lifting even the most aching and feverish body was the simplest thing in the world.

"Good morning, Fröken Nilsson, good morning, little Thura," she exclaimed now, with that peculiar accent of hers, stressing the first word, as if to emphasize how very good the morning was. She came closer to Stephania's bed, looked at the chart. "Good morning, Fröken Ackermann, and how are you today?" she asked.

"Good morning." Stephania opened her eyes reluctantly.

"So this is our new patient. Welcome, welcome. And let me tell you just one thing, dear Fröken. You could not have gotten into a nicer room, with nicer people. Good patients, nice people — the two always go together. Don't you think so?" And without even waiting for the answer she left Stephania and moved closer to the window. "Children" — Fru Gustavsson called all her patients that — "but it's stuffy in here! Let's open the window. There's enough fresh air for everybody." She lifted the shades, opened the window, and rushed out to bring all the patients in Rooms Two, Three and Four the news that it was a good day and that there was plenty of fresh air for everybody.

After a while she came back with three utensils in her hand, made of shiny metal, immaculately polished and very much like frying pans.

"Bedpans, ladies, who wants a bedpan?" she intoned in the voice of a street vendor, "one for Thura, one for Fröken Nilsson, one for Fröken Ackermann. . . ."

"No, thank you," Stephania said, "I can go out."

"That's excellent." Fru Gustavsson looked greatly impressed, as if Stephania had boasted of a most unusual accomplishment.

"And what about you children, are you ready?"

"Yes," Fröken Nilsson and Thura answered.

Then, "Thank you," Fru Gustavsson said politely, taking the full bedpans. She walked out of the room and returned with the wash-basins, also of silvery metal, also immaculately polished.

Fröken Nilsson washed herself, spilling the water around, huffing and puffing noisily. Fru Gustavsson put the basin on Thura's bed and began to wash her. "First the left hand," she said in a slow singsong, wiping Thura's lifeless hand with the wet washcloth, "now the right one, now the face." Thura smiled. She liked the feeling of warm water on her face; it was refreshing and gentle — like a caress. And she liked to watch how skillfully and swiftly Fru Gustavsson moved her big hands. It would be nice to be able to move her own hands like that one day, or at least the right one.

Fru Gustavsson knelt in front of the bed, and began to comb Thura's hair. "Does it hurt?" she asked.

"No, not at all," Thura answered her, although often the comb would sharply pull the tangled hair. Thura would never admit it; she enjoyed the sudden pang of pain; or the silent endurance of it was the expression of her gratitude to Fru Gustavsson.

"So, now we look all nice and clean," Fru Gustavsson announced, and tied Thura's hair with a piece of white tape. All the patients in Ward Two wore their hair that way — a common fashion dictated by necessity. Fru Gustavsson picked up the basins, stopped for a moment, pretending she was going to drop them right onto Thura's bed, and accompanied by piercing "ohs" and "ahs" and "for Heaven's sake, my dear!" left the room.

"Isn't she wonderful?" Thura asked.

"Yes, she's all right," Fröken Nilsson agreed. Everybody, even she, was very fond of Fru Gustavsson.

"You really are lucky to be on her side," Thura said to Stephania. "I wouldn't be on the other side even if they gave me ..." Thura hesitated, unable to find a great enough temptation which she was willing to resist in order to stay on Fru Gustavsson's side.

"The other side is Sister Gudrun's," she added.

"And what's wrong with the other side?" Stephania asked.

"She's horribly strict, Sister Gudrun," Thura whispered back. "And it's all because she's an old maid."

Stephania burst into laughter. "How do you know all that?" she asked.

"Fru Gustavsson says so."

And that was how Stephania was introduced into the complex politics of Ward Two; how she learned about Fru Gustavsson's and Sister Gudrun's sides. Legally, so to speak, there was nothing like Fru Gustavsson's side. Officially, Sister Gudrun was the head of the whole ward, the only recognized authority there. But Fru

Gustavsson had been there for fifteen years longer than Sister Gudrun herself. She had started her career with dishwashing, advanced to the status of a scrubwoman, and now she was simply everything and everywhere. "Everywhere except where she should be," Sister Gudrun, who strongly resented Fru Gustavsson's infringement on her rights, would often remark sarcastically. But there was nothing Sister Gudrun could do about it. Even Professor spoke about "Fru Gustavsson's side," and all the patients came to her with their pains and worries.

The two sides, that of Fru Gustavsson and that of Sister Gudrun, were like two countries, neighboring but different, and not always on the best of terms with each other. By a mysterious process of natural selection Sister Gudrun's side was the seat of all the well-behaved patients, of those who endured all pains and adversities without a word of complaint, never asked for a sleeping pill, never drank coffee late in the evening, and whose visitors obeyed the rules and never stayed in the room one minute over the appointed time. Fru Gustavsson's side, on the other hand, was the improper, the bohemian part of the ward. There no one realized the harmfulness of drugs, coffee was smuggled in of an evening in camouflaged thermos bottles, the radio played during the rest hour, and the lights were never turned off on time. The two sides treated each other with hostile and contemptuous politeness. A constant net of intrigues and gossip was spun in the green and yellow rooms of Ward Two.

After breakfast two nurses from the laboratory — the blood-sisters, as they were called — came in, to take blood samples for analysis from Stephania; one from her finger, the other from her arm. Hardly had they left when Fru Gustavsson came in. Quick, quick! they were calling for Fröken Ackermann from the X-ray room. Stephania got up; in spite of Fru Gustavsson's haste, she quietly stopped before the mirror, fixed her hair, and slowly walked out.

Shortly after she returned Doctor Ström came in for his morning visit.

"Good morning, Doctor," Stephania exclaimed, waving at him.

As if he were coming especially for her, Fröken Nilsson thought, shocked by such familiarity.

But Doctor Ström really behaved as if he had come to see no one but Stephania. He passed Fröken Nilsson and Thura with nothing but a brief good morning, and walked directly to the bed under the window.

"So here I am," Stephania announced, and she smiled again. "All prepared, Doctor. X-ray taken, blood analyzed."

Sister Gudrun started. Fröken Nilsson raised her head. Their eyes met — too surprised to be indignant. It was the law of the hospital, one of those unwritten yet immutable laws, that no patient should ever talk about his treatment with the doctor. X-rays, blood analysis, injections, all those were highly technical matters, sacred, and inaccessible to the uninitiated layman. The treatment of the patient had to remain a strictly private affair between the doctor and the nurse.

Doctor Ström plucked at his mustache with embarrassment, and glanced at Sister Gudrun, as if asking her for forgiveness for his protégée's infringement of the rule.

Stephania imperturbably looked from one to another. Her lips — painted much too red for the hospital — smiled again. "So when shall we do it, Doctor?" Sister Gudrun moved; her starched coat rustled impatiently.

"Do what?" Doctor Ström asked.

"The operation, of course. After all, you know what I have come here for."

"I know," Doctor Ström said severely, and then he added those strange words which startled Fröken Nilsson and Thura: "But you know too, don't you?"

"Exactly. That's why I asked you when are we going to do it."

"Next week, Tuesday. Sometime in the afternoon, I guess."

"Tuesday?" Stephania lifted herself higher in her bed. "But today's only Thursday."

"On Friday Ward One has the operation room. Then the weekend comes. Monday the Children's Ward. . . .."

"But that's ridiculous. I don't want to waste four days for nothing."

Sister Gudrun looked at her watch. "Fröken Nilsson has been complaining of a strange pricking in her knee," she interrupted. But Doctor Ström seemed not to have heard her. He came closer to Stephania's bed and, looking straight into her face, began: "Before you came here I had warned you that it was not going to be a matter of weeks, nor of months, but of years. You agreed to that. didn't you?"

[ 29 ]

"Yes, I did."

"So please remember that, and next time don't make an issue about a few days. Do you see what I mean?"

There was a long moment of silence. Until at last Stephania said, "Yes, but I can't agree with you. I cannot," she repeated in a dead stillness. "I'm going to be here two years, or more, if necessary, but only just as long as necessary, not a day, not an hour longer. I'm not going to waste my time. I've wasted enough of it. You know that, Doctor, don't you?" She pronounced the last words as if accusing Doctor Ström of something. "If you want to you can arrange to have the operation on Friday, even if it is the day for Ward One."

"I can't. And I don't want to." It was the first time Fröken Nilsson and Thura had seen Doctor Ström really angry. "And besides, could you remember another thing, please? It's not going to be an operation. Just a preparation for an operation. The operation will come much later . . ." He hesitated for a moment, and added, "If it ever comes."

"It'll come, Doctor, don't worry. But let's not quarrel about terminology. Call it a preparation if you like. So I have to wait?"

"Yes."

"Well." Stephania smiled and shrugged her shoulders. The hunch jerked in a grotesque gesture of malicious indignation.

"So we are not going to give her any anesthetics?" Sister Gudrun asked, just to remind the doctor that she was still there and that she also had something to say.

"Oh, yes, anesthetics. . . . I've not quite thought about that. I guess we might as well. . . . I want the cast to fit really tight. We've got to keep her completely quiet while we put it on. . . ."

The law was re-established. Now they talked as they always did, as if the patient were not there at all. But Stephania again ignored the custom.

"I think you'd better give it to me if you want to keep me quiet," she said.

Doctor Ström walked over to Fröken Nilsson's bed, talked to her for a while; then he looked at Thura's hand and left. On the threshold he stopped and his voice was much milder now as he said to Stephania, "So on Tuesday. Don't worry. You'll see how fast the four days will pass."

And so they moved on, the hospital days — strange days, shapeless somehow, with nothing happening that could help Stephania to measure the time, to distinguish between morning and evening, between day and day. Time dragged, as if the clocks in here were different from those outside, as if one hour in the silent yellow room comprised many of those in the world outside. But when the evening was there at last, and she tried to think about the day, it would vanish suddenly, as though it had never taken place; there was nothing to retain from it, nothing to remember. The long hours escaped somewhere like water leaking through spread fingers.

Plunged into that confusion of shapeless time, Stephania struggled to bring some order into it by dividing the day into clearly defined sections, by creating a rigid work schedule:

From eight to nine: morning toilette, breakfast.

From nine to ten: reading the newspaper.

From ten to twelve: letter-writing. Then lunch, then reading again until dinnertime. Still the whole evening was left empty, and the many hours of reading dragged on, long and tiresome.

"What do people do here all day long?" she asked Thura at last. It was on Saturday morning. Fröken Nilsson was outside visiting her friends, but Fru Gustavsson was in the room mopping the floor. Thura hesitated. No one had ever asked her a question like that.

"Well," she said at last, "they read, they knit, they visit other rooms. Wouldn't Fröken Ackermann like to meet some of the other patients?"

"No."

"What about some needlework?" Fru Gustavsson suggested hopefully.

No, Stephania did not care for needlework either.

She did not ask anyone for other suggestions. Instead she added reading German books to her afternoon schedule and ordered a few special magazines.

She was slowly getting used to her roommates. Their constant chatter did not disturb her any longer. It was like the sound of a train passing next to one's house hour after hour, day after day, until one stops noticing it at all. To her they became like pieces of furniture, just as inevitable, just as insignificant. She hardly ever talked to them, merely answered to their good morning and good night, and that was about all.

During his Friday visit Doctor Ström asked, "Are you getting used to being here, Fröken Stephania?"

"I am," Stephania said.

"That's fine."

Stephania smiled. She said. "I'm getting used to the fact that I'll never get used to it, Doctor."

Doctor Ström gave her a prolonged glance. "I see," he said slowly, "I see; but you'd better find some other aspect to get used to."

Stephania did not answer. She only continued to smile.

As soon as she left the room Fröken Nilsson said, "Did you hear what she told him, Thura? Can't get used to being here. Everybody else can, but not her, of course. We'll live to see many surprises, Thura, from your Stephania. Just wait . . ."

And almost immediately something happened that made Fröken Nilsson glance at Thura triumphantly, for on the same day Sister Gudrun came in saying: "Your friends from the boardinghouse called."

"Friends?" Stephania drawled.

"Yes, they asked when they can come to see you."

"Never," Stephania said quietly. "Tell them I can't have any visitors."

"But of course you can. Tuesday . . ."

"I don't want any."

And when Sister Gudrun looked at her, startled, Stephania repeated. "I don't want to see any of them, Sister. Will you remember that, please?"

Sunday passed, slightly different from other days because there were eggs and bacon for breakfast, and dinner was served at three instead of six. Then on Monday, during his afternoon visit, Doctor Ström said to Sister Gudrun, "So tomorrow we take Stephania."

"What time?"

"I guess around three. After the patient from Seven."

Sister Gudrun busily put it down in her notebook.

"Until tomorrow," Doctor Ström said to Stephania.

"Yes," Stephania answered, and she smiled that queer smile of hers.

Then she said something so shocking and so incredible that neither Fröken Nilsson nor Thura could trust their ears that they heard right.

[ 32 ]

"Don't be afraid, Doctor." Yes, that was exactly what she said, she, the patient, to Doctor Ström, to the same Doctor Ström, second only to Professor in his knowledge and authority. Without a word Doctor Ström left the room.

There was a long moment of silence. At last Thura said, "So tomorrow is your 'great day,' Fröken Stephania." Because that is what in the Institute they call the operation day, the "great day" . . . they say it the way grownups sometimes speak to children about birthdays or other solemn events. The operation is the baptism of the newcomer, because only at the time when, unconscious and helpless, the newcomer is laid on the white table; the moment when the mask or the transparent liquid in the hypodermic transforms him into an object, passive, insensible, submerged in the thick darkness of dreamless sleep; only then does he really become a part of the hospital.

Everybody in the ward knows when and for which one the "great day" is coming. And when the patient passes through the hall, nurses, patients, and orderlies stop him and say: "So tomorrow is the 'great day'!"

"Yes," the one questioned answers, and blushes like someone upon whom a sudden and unwonted honor has been conferred. "I hope it won't be too bad."

"Of course not, why should it?" they, the initiated, answer; and they look at him with eyes slightly mocking and slightly condescending, as women look at young girls whom they introduce into the secrets of their femininity.

The patients differ. Some are brave, some timid; there are those who confess their fear openly, and others who are afraid to admit it. But all of them ask the same questions, the frightened ones, immediately after they have heard the news about the "great day"; the others in the evening, when the lights go off — when darkness frees them from fear of ridicule.

"Tell me," they say, "how is it, that . . . that . . . anesthetic?" And they add hastily that they are not scared, of course, it's just from curiosity they would like to know. "How is it, do you feel any pain when they cut into you?"

"No, you feel nothing, nothing at all," answers the old-timer, someone like Fröken Nilsson, who has gone through a number of operations.

"Nothing." There is something horrifying about the word. It

[ 33 ]

is like ceasing to exist for a few hours; it is like . . . .like being dead.

Suddenly all of them, the brave and the timid alike, wish that there would be something left, a flicker of pain, a great pain, even. But nothing, they think, nothing . . . that is strange.

Then there remains the other question, and they struggle with it. They don't want to say it aloud, but at last they give in and ask: "And does it ever happen that you don't wake up at all, that you die without knowing it?"

"No," the old-timers say, "no one's ever died here. Not as long as I can remember."

They feel reassured, but not completely. Far into the night they toss in their beds, and some get up and say they're going to the bathroom, but everybody knows they call home and listen once more to the familiar voices.

Then, in the morning, Fru Gustavsson comes in with the white shirt, a clean shirt prepared especially for the occasion, and the whole room listens to the sounds in the hall, until at last Sister Gudrun comes in and says: "Well, now we're going." She always says "We," as if to show that she is willing to share in the fear and pain.

And now Stephania's "great day" came. On the eve of it Sister Gudrun, as the custom was, had offered her sleeping pills, "So that Fröken would not be nervous," she said.

No, Stephania was not nervous. She did not want any sleeping pills. "Aren't you afraid of the anesthetics?" Fröken Nilsson asked, at last. She had already prepared all the answers, and waited impatiently for Stephania to say: And tell me how is that . . . anesthetic?

"No," Stephania said, "not at all." And in the night Thura heard her breathing deeply in quiet healthy sleep.

The "great day" began. In the morning Sister Gudrun came in to remind Stephania that she was not allowed to eat anything. The orderly did not leave the glass of water on her table, and Willy, the newspaperman, did not even offer her any chocolate or fruit. He, also, knew that it was Stephania's "great day."

All day long there was the noise of stretchers rolled down the hall to the elevator, then the heavy clatter of beds in which the patients, their operations over, were brought back. Thura and

Fröken Nilsson lay and listened. Their watchful, experienced ears absorbed the vague muffled noises and dissected them, peeled out the particular sounds — steps, voices, ringing of the telephone — and out of them, like children building a whole picture out of the parts of a jigsaw puzzle, they slowly reconstructed the events taking place behind the closed door of their room. "Now they are calling for the patient from Three," Thura said. "Now they're bringing her down . . . now back." And again, the patient from Seven was taken down. "You come after her," Thura explained.

"I know," Stephania nodded. She was very quiet. There was nothing to make such a fuss about. It was not her "great day" yet, anyhow. A preparation for an operation. But her "great day" would come, too.

"The one from Seven has been an awfully long time downstairs," Thura said, looking at the watch.

"It must be a hip," Fröken Nilsson, who knew the timing of all operations, answered.

Lunch was brought in. "Fröken Ackermann cannot have anything," Sister Gudrun warned. Stephania watched Fröken Nilsson swallowing a second helping of vegetable omelette. She did not feel hungry, but there was a queer hollow feeling in her stomach. She looked at the watch. It was almost two.

"Soon Sister Gudrun will be here with morphine," Fröken Nilsson said suddenly.

Stephania raised her head. "You mean they give morphine here before the operation?"

"Don't worry, it doesn't hurt, Fröken Stephania, just a little prick," Thura consoled her.

Stephania laughed. "Don't worry, little Thura," she said. "I'm not scared." She put away the book she had been reading. Now she, also, lay with her eyes fixed on the door, listening, waiting.

The telephone rang. Two orderlies passed in the hall. The heavy clatter of a slowly rolling bed could be heard.

The door opened and Sister Gudrun, the needle in her hand, came in. "How about a little morphine, Stephania?" she asked. Her voice was almost friendly, and she called Stephania by her first name.

"Me . . ." Stephania smiled, and said slowly, "Oh, I don't mind. After all, if it's necessary."

"It's just to make you relaxed and calm." Sister Gudrun pulled the needle out and put the cotton wool, moistened with alcohol, on Stephania's arm. "There," she said. "We'll be going soon."

"Now I shall be quiet and relaxed," Stephania said. She smiled again, and with sudden warmth added, "Thank you very much, Sister. It was a masterpiece, that injection. I didn't feel a thing."

She lay down, her head bent sidewise, her bare arm, hanging down from the bed, limp and graceful. The others looked at her. A long while passed. Stephania swallowed a few times, then moistened her lips with her tongue.

"I'm dreadfully thirsty," she said, in a low drowsy voice, "but happy, very happy."

The telephone rang.

"It's for me," Stephania said. The orderlies came into the room. "Here we go," one of them said, lifting Stephania and letting her slowly down on the stretcher.

"Good-bye, see you later," Stephania exclaimed warmly, and waved to them in a lazy coquettish way.

"Just as if she were going to a dance," Fröken Nilsson said pensively. "To a dance," she repeated, and shook her head.

And so they took Stephania out to the operation room, smiling blissfully and suddenly very beautiful, with the blush on her cheeks, a soft luster in her eyes, and with the hunch hidden under the white blankets. After two hours the orderlies rolled the bed in. Stephania was back.

Fröken Nilsson sat up and stretched her head as far as the too narrow collar of her shirt allowed her. "What have they done to her?" she whispered. Fröken Nilsson always whispered when they brought the patients back from the operating room, as if she could never fully believe that the sleep they were plunged in was not just an ordinary sleep, that for a long time nothing could wake them up.

"God, what have they done to her?" she repeated, and her whisper became louder; now it sounded like a choked cry. For Stephania's whole body was covered with a cast — with thick layers of plaster, forming something like a huge cylinder, reaching from her waist to her head, uneven, flattened on the belly and then bulging high on the chest and in the back, and narrowing on her neck into an immense chimneylike collar that ended abruptly with a ragged edge right underneath Stephania's chin. The ends of her hair were glued with plaster. A thin streak of saliva flowed out of her mouth half open and parched with blood. Fröken Nilsson turned her head away. "Did I look like that, too?" she asked.

"When?"

"When they brought me back from the operating room. I mean, with the mouth half open like that — like, like a fish out of water."

"Yes, I guess you did."

Fröken Nilsson shuddered.

"Good Lord, who knows what that drug does to you?" I'm going for a walk, she decided suddenly. Fru Gustavsson, who was just putting a rubber sheet on Stephania's bed — you never could tell what the patient would do when she woke up — helped her into the wheel chair. "Good-bye," Fröken Nilsson waved, and she left.

"I don't think Stephania will wake up much before an hour. I'm going to have something to eat," Fru Gustavsson said to Thura, and she too left.

And so they were left alone — Stephania, motionless and panting heavily, as if the cast were too heavy for her to bear; and Thura, in spite of the fear that filled her, unable to tear her eyes away from Stephania.

Yes, Thura thought, Fröken Nilsson looked like that, and Fru Hernruth, and all of the ones she had seen brought back from the operating room . . . plunged deep into that strange sleep, heavily struggling for every breath. And they all woke up in the same way; startled, horrified and sad, as if against their will they had been forced to return from some distant and wonderful place, back into the hospital room. They moaned and cried and mumbled and were like helpless children who didn't know how to talk yet. Somehow Thura could never forget how they looked in that moment of return, and later, when they were well again, when Fröken Nilsson was loud and grumbling as before, and Fru Hernruth as quiet and energetic and efficient as ever, Thura still knew that deep inside them someone else was hidden — helpless, bewildered and childlike. Again she glanced at Stephania and — was it an illusion? — no, the body, imprisoned in the shapeless mass of plaster, moved suddenly.

Stephania was waking up. First there was darkness around her, dense, impenetrable and warm. Stephania liked the darkness; it seemed so soft and silky she wanted to touch it. Slowly in a groping, aimless gesture, she raised her arm. But the black mass around her escaped her hand moved farther and farther away. The arm, disappointed, swayed to and fro like a pendulum, and then fell back.

The darkness was now far away; instead a vague dusk surrounded her, gray, and sticky, like air saturated with dust. And suddenly a ray of light, sharp and pointed like a long thin needle, pierced the blurred twilight. Stephania did not want the light. She raised her hand to chase it away, but the light did not move. It only grew sharper and sharper, and suddenly she knew it was not light at all, but pain, pungent and insidious, hiding deep in her body, somewhere, where Stephania did not know. She wanted to place the pain, to grasp it in her hand and tear it out. Angrily she lifted her head, but the pain spread all over her body. Now it was everywhere at once, in her head, in her breast, a dumb clammy feeling, a load, increasing with every breath. Stephania sat up; she had to shake that burden now, at once, before it choked her. She wanted to move her head, but something stood in her way. She tried once more, and opened her eyes. Now the dusk was gone. Glaring light penetrated her eyes. The light and the pain became one. They were everywhere; everything, even the air she inhaled hurt. "Oh!" Stephania cried. "Oh!" The pain, as if afraid of her cry, darted back, disappeared. Now she was alone, with nothing but a complete and horrifying emptiness within and around her. She was falling into it deeper and deeper. Desperately Stephania clutched the pillow with her fingers. "Oh! Oh!" The pain returned. She was saved from the void. Stephania breathed with relief. And suddenly a great sadness seized her, a longing for the darkness, for the warmth and safety that were gone. She burst into tears, and crying desperately, felt how the fear was dissolving in her sobs, how the void was receding, until it vanished completely.

She wanted to say something, to call someone, but all the words were gone from her mind, and so she just mumbled sounds without sense and purpose, and listened to them, comforted by her own voice. A start of pain, stronger than before, shook her body. Stephania thrust her hand up, the sounds ordered themselves into a word. *"Bozhe,"* she cried, *"Bozhe."* That one word in her own language was all she could remember now.

She was not crying any longer, but the tears were on her face still. She did not wipe them off, and feeling the salty taste on her lips, sat crying, *"Bozhe, Bozhe."*

Thura lay with her eyes fixed on Stephania. "Please," she whispered, "please, Stephania, don't cry." The strange, jarring sounds of Stephania's weeping horrified her. Sometimes they furiously chased one another, and it seemed to Thura as if Stephania was struggling with someone, swearing and threatening. Or they changed into a prolonged howl, whining, complaining. *"Boozhe, Booozhe!"*

"Stephania," Thura repeated, "don't cry now. You are back. You are with us." But Stephania did not answer. She just lifted her face, red, wet with tears and saliva, and looked at Thura with blank eyes. And, swaying her body to and fro, began again: *"Bozhe, Bozhe!"*

If only Thura could know what those words meant. It must have been Polish, but what, what . . . ? Perhaps a name. . . . Fru Hernruth, when she woke up, called her husband. "Axel," she cried, "Axel, take me away from here, come here. . . ." And that was horrible enough, but then Thura at least could understand. At least she could say, Axel will come soon. Don't cry, don't. And Fröken Nilsson called "Mama, Mama," as if she were a little child again, as if her mother had not been dead for years. But Stephania's cry was different, more terrifying. "Stephania," Thura pleaded, "stop crying, everything's all right now."

If only someone would come. She had called a few times, but no one came. They all must have still been at dinner. If she only could ring the bell! She groped for the bell, but the string like a malicious live thing jumped back, slipped out from her stiff fingers, and fell upon the edge of the pillow. There it lay, just a few inches from her hand, but too far for her to reach it. And Stephania was still crying. Thura looked at her. Her face seemed redder than before . . . perhaps they had made the collar too tight. Perhaps Stephania was choking. A cold shudder passed through Thura's body. Her voice was breaking with fear. Again. She began to scream: "Fru Gustavsson, Sister Gudrun! Siste-e-er!" and then to Stephania, "Do stop crying. Please stop."

Suddenly Stephania grew silent. She moved closer to the edge of her bed, as if trying to hear Thura better. "How do you feel, Stephania?" Thura asked.

Stephania listened. The voice came to her muffled as if it had

[ 39 ]

to pass through a thick screen. First it seemed completely strange, and also the things it said were strange. But slowly she began to remember; suddenly the screen disappeared, the voice became loud and distinct.

Now she knew everything. She was in the hospital, and the voice belonged to Thura. "How do you feel?" Thura asked, because this was her "great day," because she had been brought back from the operating room. Stephania touched her body. Yes, the cast was there, wet and cold, and that was the burden that weighed upon her so heavily, and the pounding in her head, the dryness in her mouth, must have come from the anesthetics.

"I'm thirsty," Stephania said slowly. Her tongue was so heavy she could hardly move it.

"Wait, don't drink. You'll get sick." But Stephania did not listen. She grasped the glass from the table and drank greedily, holding each sip of water in her mouth, bathing the parched lips, the swollen tongue in it.

"You will get sick. Be careful," Thura warned her again.

Stephania did not answer. She lay down. And suddenly the edge of the collar began to press her neck and cut into it deeper and deeper; it choked her. She sat up again, opened her mouth to get a breath of air, and then . . .

"Oh, you shouldn't have drunk," Thura cried. "Oh, Fru Gustavsson, Siste-e-er!"

The door opened. Fru Gustavsson burst in, and after her, the orderly pushing the wheel chair with Fröken Nilsson.

"Good gracious." Fru Gustavsson wrung her hands. She pulled the rubber sheet under Stephania's chin to save the blanket at least. "Why didn't you tell her not to drink, Thura?"

"I . . . I," Thura murmured, looking at Stephania. "I forgot," she said at last. "She was crying and . . ."

Fru Gustavsson wiped Stephania's face, brought in clean linen and sat on the edge of the bed. Her big red hands slowly stroked Stephania's head. "Now," she murmured, as if she was lulling a child to sleep, "now it's fine, fine."

"Drink," Stephania whispered. "I'm thirsty."

"Oh, no. You don't want to be sick again. Just look at the nice clean sheets. But wait, we shall do something about it." Fru Gustavsson dipped a piece of cotton wool in water, and slowly moistened Stephania's lips.

[ 40 ]

Stephania sucked greedily. "Thank you," she said. "That was good."

And a moment later, without even knowing when and how, she fell asleep.

CHAPTER 5

IT ALWAYS BEGINS about dinnertime, when Fru Gustavsson brings in the silver. "There, little Thura; here's the spoon for the soup, and the fork and knife for the meat," she says every time, as if Thura didn't know what they were for herself. "Thank you very much," she says, and then when the words slowly die out in silence it starts: the dark, dull fear of something that had to come, that was coming — night.

Behind the window the sky slowly grows dark and the green of the fir tree turns deeper and deeper, until the two branches she can see from her window change into a black vague shape. The room slowly begins to fill with shadows, long gray streaks move timidly forward like the probing antennae of a huge insect. Until suddenly darkness floods the walls and the floor, and only here and there a lonely beam of light is quivering still. A small square of brightness on the wall opposite resists them longest, and Thura lies looking at it, watching the shadows creep closer and closer. Then even that last spot of light is swallowed up, and the room is covered with a gray dense dusk. Evening is here.

The others in the room are usually dozing at that hour. "Let's have a light," Thura whispers at last. Fröken Nilsson — or Fru Hernruth or whoever else it may be in the second bed — opens her eyes. "Yes, light, of course. It gets dark so early now," she says. There is the sharp snap of the switch. Light, but now the cold hostile light of evening bursts into the room. Dinner is brought in, then the water for washing. Day, so slow-moving until now, rushes as if in a hurry to come to its end. And when Sister Gudrun comes in with the medicine tray and says, "Sleep tight, little Thura," the night is there.

She may try to postpone it; she can tell Fru Gustavsson that she

[ 41 ]

forgot to say something to Sister Gudrun, "You really must call her back." It's awfully important; she may even offer Fröken Nilsson some of her cookies in the hope that instead of going to sleep she'll start talking to her. Still, whatever she does, night is here and there's nothing to be done about it. Sooner or later Fröken Nilsson yawns, looks at the clock, and says: "Let's sleep, Thura, it's getting late and tomorrow is a busy day." Again there is the sharp click of a switch, and like its echo, a sharp pang of fear in Thura. The night begins.

Feeling the fear growing stronger and stronger, Thura lies and wonders how it's possible that everything should be the same: the room, the bed, the clock, the same and yet so utterly different. The bed, so pleasant, so comfortable during the day, suddenly grows narrow, full of hostile gaps and crevices; the pillow only an hour ago smooth and cool is spongy and warm. And everything — the bed, the linen, her whole body — is filled with the faint but sickening odor of sweat, urine and rubbing alcohol.

But the strangest thing happens to the clock. It seems to tick as if it were tired. Tick — the clock says; then a long pause follows as if it had to gather strength for the next move, then tick, and again a pause, each time growing longer and longer.

The others in the room are always asleep. A little jealous, Thura listens to the sounds of their deep, quiet breathing. Fröken Nilsson snores in her own special way. The air enters her nose with a soft rustle and then, as if it met with something insurmountable, raises to an angry grunting and finally leaves her mouth with a prolonged whistle.

Often, to make the time pass faster, Thura starts imitating her. Phrr . . . she breathes in, then phuuu . . . and all the time she is trying to keep time with Fröken Nilsson. But soon that game becomes boring and Thura turns to something else . . . the light.

The blue light above the door is always the same, cold and indifferent. But the light that flows in through the narrow crevice between the window shade and the sill is like a thin golden thread embroidering all kinds of strange shapes upon the wall: lines, curves, and zigzags, quivering and brittle, and all surrounded with a faintly glowing halo.

It always seems to her that she has been looking at the light for hours, but only a few minutes have passed. The night has hardly begun.

[ 42 ]

And so Thura turns to a last remedy and tries to think about something pleasant, something wonderful that will help her forget the night and the hot bed and the stubborn crawling of the clock. She thinks of how tomorrow Fröken Nilsson will be in a good mood and how she will turn the pages of a book for her; or how it will be a warm sunny day and they will take her out on the terrace. Or she dreams that the motion picture which the hospital management has been promising for a year will finally be shown.

But since Stephania has come, Thura has forgotten the balcony, and the book, even the moving picture, and during her sleepless nights thinks only about her — how one day, and it will be very soon, too, Stephania and she will become great friends, how Stephania will tell her all her life's story, all the strange, fascinating things.

That was what Thura was thinking about that night which came after the great day. It was a particularly bad night, longer, more sticky and frightening than any other.

The sheet under her blanket had rolled down, and the bare wool lay rough and choking on her neck. Then when she tried to throw the blanket off, her hair fell on her forehead. The sweaty wisps felt like an obnoxious fly crawling to and fro. Fru Gustavsson had not cleaned Stephania's bed properly and the sour smell of stale vomit penetrated the room. Thura lay trying to count to a hundred and back.

Hundred, ninety-nine, ninety-eight . . .

A bed squeaked suddenly.

Whose bed was that . . . Stephania's . . . Fröken Nilsson's?

She lay listening.

A dark shape rose on the bed under the window. "Oh," Stephania groaned, "oh."

"What's the matter?" Thura whispered.

"I've got to call the nurse." Thura heard Stephania groping in the darkness for the bell.

"I can't find it." Stephania switched the light on. In the sudden glare the cast on her body appeared even bigger than before — a thick, gray wall that seemed to crush her.

"I can't sleep," Stephania said.

"Neither can I." Thura now felt glad she was awake.

Stephania said, "I have pains . . . many pains." Many pains — it sounded as if a whole mass of pains was hiding in the cast and attacking Stephania from all sides — cruel and stubborn like a pack of sharp-toothed animals.

"Very many pains," Stephania repeated. She had found the bell finally and had rung it. Fröken Nilsson uttered a violent whistle of protest and sat up.

"What's going on here?" she asked, rubbing her eyes. The cheek on which she had been lying was red with the pattern of the pillow engraved on it.

"That old scarecrow must be fast asleep," Stephania said.

"Oh no, she's just busy in another room, I'm sure." Thura hastened to apologize for the nurse.

"She must be drinking coffee. They're always drinking coffee and then you can ring for ages and not a soul will come," observed Fröken Nilsson.

But at that very moment the night nurse came in. "What's the matter?" she whispered in her old, tired voice. She was Sister Ingeborg, the night nurse, the oldest of the hospital personnel. Her yellowish wrinkled face seemed always to be afraid of everything; of the patients, of the doctor, of the silence in the empty halls, in which her steps resounded with a terrifying loudness.

"I've got pains," Stephania said, pointing to the cast.

"All right, all right." Sister Ingeborg turned the light off. "But you shouldn't wake up all the others. Wait, I'll bring you a pill."

"A pill?"

"Yes, a barbiturate pill. It will help."

"I don't have a toothache, or a headache, Sister. I have pains here, all over my body. I've got to have morphine."

"Let me see, although I don't think so." Sister Ingeborg turned on her flashlight and took a long slip of paper out of her pocket.

"No," she whispered, "you're not on the list; I'm sorry."

"What list?" Stephania asked impatiently.

"For morphine. Sister Gudrun wrote down the names of everybody who should get morphine. Here: Ekström, Rose, but your name's not here."

"I don't care. I'm in pain, I must have morphine."

"But dear Fröken Ackermann, how can I give you anything without Sister Gudrun's permission?" the nurse asked plaintively.

"That's ridiculous. Is any doctor here?"

"Yes, young Doctor Olson."

"Will you call him, please?" Stephania's request sounded like an order.

[ 44 ]

"How can I?" Sister Ingeborg pleaded. "He comes only in special cases."

"Exactly," Stephania said. "Mine is a special case."

"I'll go and speak to him, but . . . if Fröken were only on the list," Sister Ingeborg sighed as she went out.

"I'm waiting!" Stephania called after her warningly.

"I hope she will give you the injection," Thura said.

"She can't do anything without the doctor's orders," Fröken Nilsson murmured irritably. She felt angry. She had also had pain in her life; after all, to have your leg broken in four places was no joke, either, but she'd never made so much fuss about it. If you came to a hospital, you had to be prepared to have pain. It was a hospital, not a hotel; nobody came there for pleasure.

Stephania did not lie down. She sat motionless, her head turned toward the door. At last the door opened.

"Well, what happened?" she asked even before the nurse was over the threshold.

"Sh . . . not so loud . . . you will wake everybody up. He gave me permission, though it's strictly against the rules, he said."

"Do you want to make the injection in my arm or in my leg?" Stephania interrupted her.

"Whatever you prefer."

Stephania rolled up her sleeve and stretched out her arm. The needle glided softly into her flesh.

"Did it hurt?" the nurse whispered.

"Not at all. Thank you very much, Sister." Stephania's voice was throbbing with gratitude.

"I hope you will feel better soon. Good night." And Sister Ingeborg tiptoed out of the room.

The silence returned. But nobody was asleep. Both Fröken Nilsson and Thura lay looking at the vague outlines of the bed under the window, wondering silently if the pain had stopped and if Stephania was asleep. No, she was still awake; they could hear her sighing deeply, then murmuring something to herself.

"How do you feel, Fröken Stephania?" Thura whispered cautiously.

"Fine, Thura, very fine." Stephania's voice was deep, throaty. And Thura, though she could not see her, knew somehow that Stephania was smiling again, the same way she had smiled that morning; blissfully, very quietly.

"That's good, Fröken Stephania. It must have been terrible, all that pain."

"Pain?" Stephania repeated, as if not quite understanding. "Oh, you mean *that*," and suddenly she started laughing, softly at first, to herself only, and then aloud. "No, I wasn't in pain."

"What did you say?" Fröken Nilsson raised herself indignantly. That *was* the limit. First she waked them up in the middle of the night, moaning and groaning, and now . . . "What do you mean, Fröken Ackermann?" she asked severely.

"Just what I said," Stephania giggled. "I wasn't in pain, the cast felt a bit heavy, that was all. But you see I had it all figured out . . . after all, how can they tell if it hurts or not? And so I thought I might as well try. Against the regulations — but they gave it to me; I knew they would."

"How do you like that?" Fröken Nilsson gasped. "Don't tell me you pretended you had pains just to get morphine?"

"Sure. I wanted a *Spritze* and so . . ."

"What?"

"A *Spritze*. Oh, I mean an injection, a morphine injection. I used to get it in Germany once, so I still call it that — *Spritze*."

"*Spritze* . . ." Thura repeated. The word had a sharp hissing sound and made Thura feel the thin pointed needle drill into the flesh.

"But why on earth would you like to have it?" Fröken Nilsson decided to have all this nonsense straightened out once and for all. "It's terrible stuff — that morphine. Last time I got it, do you remember, Thura? I was dizzy, and almost got sick to my stomach. Dreadful! And next morning I said to Sister Gudrun: 'Sister . . . .'"

She stopped. Stephania was laughing again.

"Well," Fröken Nilsson muttered irritably.

"I'm sorry, Fröken Nilsson, I wasn't laughing at you. It's only the way you said it — 'terrible stuff' — but you just don't know what you're missing. Morphine is good, good," she repeated gratefully, almost tenderly, as if she were talking about someone she loved. "I feel so wonderful now, I can't even tell you how wonderful. Warm inside, and everything around me warm, and soft, too. And I'm light, oh, so light, as if I were flying. No, I don't mean that, not flying; floating. Like on a river, you know, when you're lying on your back and let the current carry you, and the sun shines right in your eyes, warm . . ." Her tongue touched the palate with a dry weary sound. "Do you see what I mean, Fröken Nilsson?"

Fröken Nilsson shook her head in bewilderment. A terrible suspicion dawned upon her suddenly. "Listen," she whispered distrustfully, "you're not one of *those,* you know what I mean, one of those addicts?"

"No, at least not yet."

"Not yet?"

"Oh, let's just skip it," Stephania murmured impatiently.

Again they were silent. Stephania sat up, groped on the table, took the glass. "It makes you thirsty, morphine," she said, "all dried out."

"Just take a sip, Fröken Stephania, and hold it in your mouth," Thura said pleadingly, "you mustn't get sick again."

"Thank you, Thura." Stephania put the glass away. "You're so nice to me, Thura; I like you, I like you very much."

The way she talks, as if she were drunk! . . . Fröken Nilsson thought angrily.

"And you too, I like you, too, Fröken Nilsson," Stephania went on hoarsely. "Yes, even you . . ." she faltered. "You're both so kind to me." Stephania went on after a while, "I'm glad, because I'm going to stay here for two years, you see, so we might as well get used to each other. Two years," she repeated, "that's terribly long, isn't it?"

"It only seems so. But really it's not so bad here, Fröken Stephania; everybody's nice . . . and . . ."

"I know exactly how you feel, Fröken Ackermann," Fröken Nilsson interrupted Thura. "It wasn't easy for me in the beginning, either. I had quite a different life back in Eskilstuna; that's my home town, Fröken Ackermann. Always seeing people, always going out, you know. . . . But you get used to everything."

Stephania did not answer.

"Everybody gets used to it," Fröken Nilsson insisted, "but . . ." She hesitated and stopped. There was something she wanted to ask Stephania, something that had puzzled her from the first. "I just wonder," she began, "what they're going to do to you, because . . . what I mean is . . . you seem fine." She faltered and stopped again. How could she say it, how could she tell Stephania that it seemed strange she came here only because she was a hunchback — a hunchback was something one just was, and otherwise there

[ 47 ]

was nothing wrong with her. "You walk fine, you don't seem to have any pain, and so . . ."

"And so . . ." Stephania drawled.

"You really seem to be all right except . . ." Fröken Nilsson felt uncomfortable.

"Except that I'm a hunchback, eh?" the hoarse voice said tauntingly. "Don't be so bashful, Fröken Nilsson. Why not call a spade a spade? It is a spade no matter what fancy name you find for it. And a hunchback, too. But . . ." Stephania's voice grew low, secret, suddenly. "But the point is I'm not a hunchback." When no one said anything she repeated very loudly into the startled silence, "I'm not, not really. Don't you see, a hunchback is someone who's always been like that, who can't remember anything else. But I was different, I was like . . . like . . ."

"Like you are in the picture . . .?" Thura helped her.

"Yes, exactly. You saw the picture, so you know. And there was never anybody crippled in my family. My parents, they were healthy, and my sister, too. Just wait till you see her."

"I didn't know you had a sister here," Fröken Nilsson said.

"Yes. She's in Göteborg now, but she'll come on Sunday, so you'll see. She's very beautiful, my sister; not dark like me, but blond and tall, very tall," Stephania repeated slowly. "So you see, I was all right like her, like everybody in the family. Then when I was fifteen something happened to my spine. It wasn't much. The doctors said it was nothing serious. I just had to take good care of myself, to sleep in a special bed, have treatments. And if it hadn't been for the war . . . Because then everything went wrong, everything . . ." She fell silent, and when she began again, her voice was high, startled. "It was really strange; yes, the strangest feeling in the world. Here something happens to your body, and you just sit back and watch and can't do a thing about it. It's as if your body were not yours at all, as if someone else was telling it what to do. I worried terribly, sometimes I thought I would go mad. Still, all the time I knew, I just felt it, that I wouldn't stay like that."

Stephania was silent for so long that they thought she had fallen asleep, when suddenly they heard her saying through her teeth, "That bastard!"

"Fröken Ackermann!" That's too much, Fröken Nilsson thought.

"Yes, that bastard," Stephania repeated stubbornly. She stopped.

[ 48 ]

The door opened and Sister Ingeborg looked in. "Why don't you sleep?"

"I will, Sister, soon. I'm fine."

"Don't disturb the other patients." The door closed noiselessly.

Stephania waited until the footsteps vanished and said, "Don't be so shocked, Fröken Nilsson. Bastard — that's exactly what he was. If it weren't for him I would have been all right now. But he refused, if you can believe it, refused to operate on me. And he was the best doctor in Germany, a spine specialist. . . ."

"Germany?" Fröken Nilsson repeated. First that talk about *Spritze,* and now the doctor. "I thought you were from Poland," she said.

"Sure I'm from Poland, but I was in Germany during the war."

"Why did you go there, Fröken Ackermann? I heard it was horrible in Germany during the war, all those bombings, and then no food. Is it true you had to eat potatoes all the time?"

Stephania did not answer, but went on: "Fisher, Erich Fisher was his name . . . the more I think about him . . . People said he could do miracles; he was the best man the Germans had. So I went to him as soon as the war was over. He just gave me one look and said, *'Mein liebes Kind, ich kann Ihnen nicht helfen.'"*

"What does that mean?" Fröken Nilsson demanded angrily.

"Oh I'm sorry, that's German; 'My dear child, I cannot help you.' He was always like that, the hypocrite, just oozing with sweetness; but of course, he wouldn't do a thing for me. Just kept refusing."

"I guess you didn't offer him enough." Fröken Nilsson nodded sympathetically. "They're all like that, the doctors; you don't give them money, you might as well be dead for all of them."

"Fröken Nilsson, how can you?" Thura exclaimed reproachfully.

"Well, here they may be a little different. But even here . . ." Fröken Nilsson stopped. She thought about the bed under the window, about Fru Hernruth. "Yes, even here they're not much better. Well," she sighed, "that's the way the world goes; without money you're a nobody."

"It wouldn't be money. I promised to give him anything he wanted. Food, clothes — those were worth more than money then. But he wouldn't even listen. I guess he was too lazy, old and fat and lazy, just wouldn't be bothered. Or perhaps he refused because I was Jewish; I just don't know. At first he would talk to me at least. But then one day I came, and he flatly refused to see me. Just like that — 'He has no time' — the nurse said. That was enough for me. And then . . ." she faltered, "yes, then I did it."

She stopped. They waited for her to go on, and when after a long while Stephania was still silent, Thura whispered: "What do you mean, what did you do, Fröken Stephania?"

"I went to them — to the Russians."

"To the Russians?" Fröken Nilsson cried.

"Yes, what of it? Everybody did it, for much lesser things. If people wanted a German apartment, or a car, they'd go straight to the Russians. So why shouldn't I? And I was all by myself then, didn't have anybody to help me, so . . ."

"That was wrong. Wasn't your sister with you?" Thura asked.

"My sister? No, of course not." Stephania's voice was hard when after a while she spoke again. "My sister wasn't with us during the war. I told you she's a blonde; she could pretend she was not Jewish, and could hide herself. But I . . . Anyhow . . . I went to them."

"I didn't mean that was wrong," Fröken Nilsson said, "but weren't you afraid? They must be terrible people, the Russians. Why, only a couple of days ago I read in the paper . . ." Fröken Nilsson tried in vain to remember what it was she had read. "Anyhow," she went on with a disappointed sigh, "they must be just dreadful."

Stephania seemed not to have heard her. "I didn't really want to do anything to him," she said, "I just wanted to scare him, so that he would agree. And it wasn't my fault the way it all turned out. Not that I'm sorry for him." Her voice grew shrill with anger suddenly. "It served him right. And anyhow, it was all his stupidity; why did he leave that picture — the imbecile!"

Fröken Nilsson could not stand it any longer. What was all that strange talk about? — Germans, Russians, the picture — one could not make head nor tail of it. "What did they do to him? What picture?" she said swallowing as if something got stuck in her throat. "I just can't understand. And what was it you wanted from him, you said?"

"I wanted him to operate on me," Stephania said. "He could do it, I knew. So I thought if I came to him with the Russians . . . to show him he could no longer do just what pleased him . . . But then when we were in the car, there were four of them, then I didn't know any longer if I really wanted it. They were all drunk, you see, the whole car just reeked of vodka. And then the house! We went to his place out at the hospital. Everything around was bombed, just stones and stones, and I hate ruins. And he lived in a wing that was left, that looked as if it was hanging in the air, with no window and the roof half burned."

"You mean he lived there?"

"Yes, he and his wife. She opened the door for us. At first I thought she was his mother, she looked so old . . . just skin and bones, and wrinkled like a dried prune. God, the way she started shaking when she saw us. She must have thought they would shoot her right away."

"Shoot her?"

"Yes, they had guns, just to scare him."

"Oh Fröken Stephania! You didn't tell them to do it?"

Stephania sat up, they could hear her panting heavily. "Come on, Thura, don't be so soft. I told you what he did to me, and that's not all either. Wait until you hear the rest. First the wife started lying: 'Herr Doctor is not at home,' she said. But the Russians just pushed her away. And sure enough he was in, sitting in his room shaking like a heap of jelly. But when I told him why we had come he grew very quiet suddenly, completely quiet. Sat down, even lit a cigarette, and then . . . But I behaved like an idiot. Instead of scaring the hell out of him I did exactly what he wanted. You see, he started explaining why he could not do it, delivered a whole lecture, and made me translate it. Just think, I stood there and repeated like a parrot all that junk . . . that I was too old, that my body was formed, that it was impossible. Until the Russians got mad . . . started shouting I had no business bringing them there, that it was all nonsense. They wanted to leave, you see, it was terribly cold there, no panes in the windows, just papers and rags. I didn't care any more either, I just wanted to get out, but then when they saw the picture . . ."

"What picture?" Fröken Nilsson almost cried.

"Oh, his son, in dress uniform, with all the medals. It was just an army uniform, but the Russians thought it was a Party one. They started yelling he was a Nazi, and then the *Kommandier*, he was the first one, hit him."

"Hit the doctor? . . . Because of the picture?"

"First him and then the others; kicking and beating him, and he started shaking all over, a huge fat man, and it looked as though

[ 51 ]

he was crying. And the wife rushed in; I guess she was too afraid to scream, just kept clucking like a hen and wringing her hands. I could hear the bones cracking, it sounded as if she were breaking to pieces . . . but they kept on beating him."

"But . . . but why didn't you tell them to stop? You could, couldn't you?"

"I tried, but they wouldn't even listen. So when they weren't looking I ran out."

"Oh, Fröken Stephania," Thura cried. "It all seems so dreadful."

"Dreadful," Stephania repeated. Her voice grew sharp, challenging. "I don't feel sorry for him. Not a bit. It served him right. It's easy for you to be softhearted, but not for me."

"But what did they do with him?"

"Don't worry, nothing happened to him. I called the hospital a couple of days later. He was back, the nurse told me."

Slowly Fröken Nilsson said, "I simply can't believe it. That they should beat an old man, just because of a picture. People don't do things like that, they just don't."

Stephania laughed sharply. She said, "You don't know what people can do; you'd be surprised if you did."

"No, no one I know would do it; certainly not here, do you think, Thura?"

"I just can't understand it. No, I can't imagine how anyone would do such a thing. No. Not here."

"Maybe not here," Stephania said indifferently, "but you never know. Still, it wasn't my fault."

"No, I don't think it was," Fröken Nilsson agreed.

"I don't either. After all you didn't want it . . . and besides, he should have agreed to operate on you. Doctor Ström agreed to, so why couldn't he?"

Stephania did not answer. Again they saw her sitting up, drinking water. Then very slowly, as if she couldn't trust her hands, she put the glass away. Fröken Nilsson glanced at the clock: it was one. Then again the sound of steps came from the hall, stopped for a moment before their room, and moved on, weary and heavy. Thura sighed softly. And at last Stephania said, her voice more hoarse than ever . . . reluctantly . . . "He did not agree, not in the beginning I mean."

"Ström refused?"

"Yes, he refused," Stephania repeated thoughtfully. "All those doctors I saw here in Sweden, each of them would look at me and refuse. 'Too old,' they said, as if twenty-three could be too old. And Ström too, kept saying no at first."

"But why?"

"Well, he said if I were younger, it would have been different. But now there's no more than one chance in twenty of succeeding."

She sat up again. The lamp above the door was shining upon her, and in the bluish light they could see her stretching her arm, opening and closing her hand. "One in twenty," she said hoarsely, and the hand opened greedily. "God, that's more — more than I ever asked for. Even one chance, one in a hundred, would be enough for me.

"Just as long as there's some hope. Even if it's only a single chance, I know I'll do it, I know I'll be all right. During the war it was the same thing. I had only one chance then, not even one in a hundred, one in a thousand at the utmost. Still, all the time I knew nothing would happen to me, I felt I'd stick it out. I told all that to Ström, but he wouldn't even listen. Cautious, so cautious," she said jarringly, and then: "So I had to force him."

"Now come on," Fröken Nilsson exclaimed incredulously. "No one has ever forced a doctor to do anything, and certainly not Ström of all people."

"But I did force him," Stephania repeated singingly, "almost."

"How, Fröken Stephania, how could you do it?" Thura asked.

"I told him I would kill myself."

"What?" they exclaimed together, and then Fröken Nilsson cried, "But he didn't believe you, he knew you didn't mean it."

"I did mean it. And I told him I had everything figured out, everything prepared. I even showed it to him — the cyanide."

"The . . . what?"

"Cyanide. That's the poison, the best one. You don't even have to swallow it. Just a tiny scratch and you touch it and it works. I heard it doesn't even hurt much. There's nothing like cyanide."

Cyanide — the word had a soft singing sound. Like the name of a flower, Thura thought. It made everything so simple, so easy. Just touch, a tiny scratch, and it works, without pain. . . .

"Poison yourself," Fröken Nilsson murmured, "no, you did not

[ 53 ]

mean it. People don't do things like that," and she did not notice
that she had used the same words once before.

Stephania said, "Some do."

"Do you still have it, that cyanide?" Thura's voice sounded as if
she were afraid to speak.

"I was afraid I might lose it or someone might take it away
from me here. So I gave it to Barbara, my sister."

"But why do you keep it still, now that Doctor Ström has agreed?"

"Just in case."

"In case of what?"

"If something goes wrong. Then I'll have to do it. Have to,"
she said, as if she did not want to, as if someone else were forcing
her.

"No," Thura cried, "you couldn't do that." There was something
Thura remembered all of a sudden, something Mother told her
once. It was when they were still living in Uppsala and in the
same house there was a girl who did something Mother said a girl
should never do — and she got into trouble. And it was just when
Mother was standing at the window that suddenly something big
and black like a huge rag, only screaming horribly, brushed the
panes and hit the ground. It was the girl. And she was stone
dead, Mother said, when they came down. "Oh, no," Thura whispered. She could see Stephania now, hurtling down past the big
window next to her bed, just where the fir tree was, only pink in
her lace-covered gown, and screaming. "You must not even think
about it," she said imploringly. "You'll be operated on soon, and
everything will be all right."

"Yes, certainly. Only . . . only Ström said he would not know
until next year if he can operate. It's all nonsense of course, still
. . . And then the operation may fail, or they might damage a nerve
or something like that. I might get paralyzed. That would be even
worse than now, to be always in bed, and not to move at all
and . . ." Her voice faltered suddenly. "I didn't mean it," she whispered, and then in the silence that grew heavy and fearful, "I'm
sorry, Thura."

"Oh, it doesn't matter, Fröken Stephania." It took Thura a long
while to say it.

"And you too, Thura; you'll get well and . . ."

"I'm thirsty," Fröken Nilsson interrupted Stephania. Her voice
too was hoarse, strained now. She turned the light on. The sharp

white glare brought back to life the yellow walls, the grass-green linoleum. They emerged from the darkness the same as ever, as if nothing had happened that night. Stephania lay in her bed, the cast bulging under the pink gown, her face flushed, her eyes staring at Thura. Fröken Nilsson drank greedily, then glanced at the clock. "Heavens!" she exclaimed, "it's almost two. Let's sleep."

"Yes," Stephania nodded. "Let's."

Fröken Nilsson was snoring already when Thura whispered, "Fröken Stephania, what did it mean, that word you were crying when you woke up from the anesthetics? Something like 'Bo . . . zhe, bozhe!'"

"Did I really say that?"

"Yes, over and over again."

"Isn't that funny?" Stephania said. "It means oh God . . . oh my God!"

CHAPTER 6

STEPHANIA slept late that morning. Dozing still, she took the thermometer from Sister Ingeborg, turned herself to the wall, and when Fru Gustavsson put the basin on her table, it was only the rattle of the breakfast dishes which at last forced her to open her eyes. She sat up. Something heavy and clammy was weighing her body down. She raised her hand and touched the wet plaster on her neck; yes, the "great day," the cast . . .

"Porridge, Fröken Ackermann?"

"No thanks, just coffee." She drank greedily, trying to chase away the stale taste filling her mouth.

"Please, do eat something, Fröken Stephania"; that was Thura. Stephania looked at her, then at Fröken Nilsson. Their eyes met hers, eager and expectant. Suddenly she remembered — the morphine, the talking, all that senseless talking last night. And now they were still staring at her, as if trying to force her to live up to some promise she had given them then. No, they were not going to get anything more out of her, not even a word. She lay down and turned back to the wall. Through the dumb pounding filling her head, she heard Fröken Nilsson's voice, inviting confidences, saying, "You must be sleepy, Fröken Stephania. We talked until two last night, you know."

"Yes, I'm sleepy," she murmured without looking at her. Of course, they wanted her to go on with the performance — she thought furiously. Performance — exactly, that was it. And she always had to do it, every time she got morphine.

Ridiculous! But last night she had surpassed herself. Wasn't it all touching? First the story of the German doctor, so helpless, so cruelly treated; then herself, penitent, conscience-stricken. It wasn't my fault — she said as if she were regretting something.

Then the second act — the story of the poor hunchback wandering from Annas to Caifas, from one doctor to another. Heartrending! How those two must have pitied her. But the climax came toward the end. She had to blurt out everything, just had to, devil only knows why. Probably she wanted to impress them, to create a sensation. "I'll kill myself," she had said and the fat one had answered: "People don't do things like that." Of course, people like Fröken Nilsson did not, why should they? When they could stay happily forever in a hospital, and listen to accordion music, and stuff themselves with cookies.

She just could see Fröken Nilsson wandering from one room to another in her wheel chair whispering to all those knitting, eating and dozing creatures, "I must tell you something — but please don't repeat it to anybody. The hunchback in my room" — the hunchback," she would say, or perhaps "the refugee," or "the girl." No, she probably would stick to the hunchback. "The hunchback," she would say, "denounced an old German doctor to the Russians, and now she regrets it horribly."

But that wouldn't be the end. For then she would bend herself over the bed and whisper: "And would you believe it? she once tried to kill herself!"

And all those heads rising from the pillows and whispering back: "Really? How do you know that?"

"She told me herself." And then to give her story the finishing touch, "She said she might do it again."

But let them talk, she didn't care!

What really bothered her was that business about the morphine. "I have no pains," she had told them last night, and she even laughed saying it. What a sensation, a drug addict in the ward! Right under the wings of Sister Gudrun. Well, now adieu morphine. She would not see as much as a single *Spritze* from now on. For they would be sure to tell the news to Fru Gustavsson, and Fru Gustavsson to Sister Gudrun, and Sister to Doctor Ström. Poor Ström — that would be the last straw for him.

She had to do something about it. But what? For instance she might say to them, I did have pains last night. But I didn't want to worry you and so . . . No, that was ridiculous, a child could see through that. The best thing was to ignore the whole issue, to behave as if nothing had happened.

But was that all? She had an uneasy feeling that there was something she had forgotten about the last night, something she had said, to whom? To Fröken Nilsson? No, to Thura. Yes — to Thura. "If I get paralyzed," she heard her own voice saying. How could she ever have done it? Certainly, it was true, every word she had said, anything was better than that life Thura had. Still, it was none of her business to open Thura's eyes; she would have them opened anyhow, and the later the better for her. But to throw it like that into the child's face. . . . Cautiously she turned and glanced at Thura. Did she remember? Thura smiled. Perhaps she had forgotten already, perhaps she never understood. Anyhow it was too late now to do anything about it. The point was to learn the lesson, never to get herself into a mess like that again. She could not help them, and all they could ever do for her was to get on her nerves. From now on she had to keep her distance — be polite and calm, but always remain aloof. That was it!

Stephania sat up and began to brush her hair. A hundred strokes, one up, one down. She let it fall in loose curls, and smiled when a few silky strands touched her forehead. Out of the drawer she took a whole collection of lipsticks and considered for a while which would go best with her blue nightgown. The deep crimson was just right. She painted two bold bows, drawing them slightly beyond the line of her lips, and then proudly and tenderly looked at the reflection of her face. Stephania was fond of her face; it had not changed, it had not betrayed her as her body did, the face at least remained faithful to her.

"Fröken Ackermann." That was Fröken Nilsson, of course.

"Yes?" Stephania turned to her icily.

"Why don't you tie your hair with a piece of tape? Everybody in here does it. Otherwise it may get under the cast. I remember Fru Hernruth, the wife of the police superintendent from Göteborg," Fröken Nilsson added, to show Stephania that although it was a public ward, still many high-class people come there; "Fru Hernruth at first tried to wear her hair the way you do. But it got under her cast, and Heavens! how it itched. And the poor soul couldn't even scratch herself. I had to scratch her with knitting needles, the longest we could find."

"Thank you," Stephania said, "But I'd rather wear it this way."

Fröken Nilsson remained silent. She felt angry. That Stephania was quite a queer bird, no doubt about it. "I like you very much, Fröken Nilsson," she had said to her last night; and today, don't-come-close-to-me. All right . . . all right. Fröken Nilsson also had her pride. She wasn't going to ask anybody for favors.

Anyhow that Stephania was nothing but an impudent show-off. The way she had fixed her face that morning — no one around used any lipstick or powder, except on rare occasions. And here Stephania was, doing it every day. As if that could help her. Fröken Nilsson felt like saying something to Stephania, something both cutting and indifferent, but at that moment Fru Gustavsson burst into the room.

"Good Lord," she gasped, "the inspection visit is almost here, and the rooms aren't cleaned yet."

"The inspection visit!" Fröken Nilsson had completely forgot it was Wednesday today. "Where are they?" she asked, opening the drawer, and taking out one of the two nightgowns she had bought especially for that occasion. "They're in with the fellows in Ward One," Fru Gustavsson answered. "And can you imagine, Sister Gudrun told me to make all the beds on her side! She must think I've got four hands instead of two. I've never had such a crazy day as this," and panting with exasperation Fru Gustavsson left the room.

Yes, it certainly was a crazy day. Immediately upon Fru Gustavsson's departure, Willy came into the room and started talking with Stephania, and in spite of Fröken Nilsson's indignant and pleading glances he did not show any intention of leaving. Then when he walked out at last, the orderly came in; Sister Gudrun had told him to sweep the floor once more. At last he too was gone. Fröken Nilsson hastily pulled her nightgown over her head.

Just then a wave of hushed whispers passed through the hall.

A moment of deadly silence followed. And then the doors were flung wide open; many feet pounded heavily on the stone floor. A slight metallic jingle came from the other side of the hall; Fru Gustavsson must have carried out a bedpan from a belated patient.

One of the student nurses tiptoed past the open door.

"Where are they?" Fröken Nilsson whispered, hurriedly fixing her hair.

"In One."

They listened. The confused noise of voices was coming closer and closer. Somebody laughed; it was Professor, of course. Fröken Nilsson emptied the remains of her eau de cologne bottle on her nightgown. And just as she was trying to cover a pimple on her face with powder, the inspection visitors came in.

Suddenly the room became white with the many hospital coats, and cold with the pungent smell of antiseptics. First Doctor Ström came in, and his eyes wandered from one bed to another; after him Professor Sjöberg, the great Professor Sjöberg himself, pot-bellied and so tall that his bald head rose above all the others, red, and shiny like a big ball. Once, when Professor Sjöberg was only Doctor Sjöberg, he had been an army physician, and as a heritage of his military career he retained his sonorous voice and even more sonorous laughter. A stranger, probably a visiting doctor, walked next to him. Behind them came the group of assistant doctors — the eager eyes of Fröken Nilsson at once discovered Doctor Liliencrona among them. Behind them came Sister Gudrun, showing by her carefully gauged distance her understanding of her position — slightly below the medical body but far above all the other nurses. She looked around, noticed a crumb on the floor, invisible to anybody but her, and picked it up, frowning angrily.

Fröken Nilsson, all tense with expectation, sat up in her bed. But Doctor Liliencrona walked by her without a word, without even a glance, and went straight to Stephania's bed, where the others were already standing. Bent over Stephania, his short strong fingers passing over the cast, Doctor Ström was explaining Stephania's case. Among all the hospital doctors Doctor Ström was the only one who on the day of the great inspection visit looked exactly as he did on every other day; his coat unbuttoned, the tails floating behind him, the bow tie perched crookedly. His voice, too, never changed in the Professor's presence. Quietly, carefully choosing each word, he was saying, "I plan to keep her in the cast

[ 59 ]

for about nine months." Then, pointing to the gnarled screws sticking out on both sides, he added something about tightening the cast from time to time and changing it when it became too big. Many incomprehensible Latin words followed, and at last, looking not at the Professor but straight into Stephania's face, he said: "It won't be till next spring that I'll know whether the operation is possible or not."

"Hmm," Professor thundered . . . and then once more "Hmm." That was all he had to say, but everybody knew that resonant mutter implied disapproval, absolute disapproval. Thura shivered and Fröken Nilsson for a moment forgot Doctor Liliencrona's betrayal. "May I see the X-rays?" Professor pointed to a huge pile of yellow envelopes resting in the arms of one of the student nurses. The little nurse blushed up to the collar of her blue dress. "Here they are," she whispered.

Professor lifted the picture to the light. The others surrounded him; standing on their toes they looked at the black plate in his hand.

"So that's how it looks." Professor shrugged.

He stepped back, for a while stared at Stephania and then at the table, until at last he picked up one of the photographs — the one in which the girl in the evening dress was smiling.

"Is that Fröken Ackermann?" he asked Ström.

"Certainly it's me," Stephania said.

"Retouched of course, don't you see it, Ström?"

"It is not. How can you say anything like that?" It was Stephania, who against all the rules of hospital discipline dared to raise her voice in the presence of Professor.

Everybody looked at her. "I know it was not," Stephania repeated. She was completely unperturbed. Anyhow, something almost equally unexpected happened. Instead of showing Stephania her proper place, Doctor Ström said quietly, "I don't think it was retouched."

Professor shrugged again.

"Perhaps. But tell me, how long ago was it taken."

Stephania hesitated. "Let me see," she said after a while. Her lips moved; she was counting silently. "Nine years ago," she said in a low voice, "in nineteen-thirty-eight."

"It's a long time, nine years, a very long time." Professor looked at Stephania, then at Doctor Ström. He bent himself over the bed, knocked on the cast, as if it were a closed door, and said: "It's still wet, but when it's dry, you may let her get up a little, Sister."

"Yes, Professor." Sister Gudrun nodded.

"And otherwise everything is all right?" As everyone knew, that question was merely a sign that the interview was over. They all started walking over to another bed, when suddenly Stephania said: "No, not everything, Professor."

"What?" The Professor turned back to her.

"I had some difficulty getting morphine last night," Stephania answered, looking brazenly at Fröken Nilsson. "I had pains, but the nurse wouldn't give it to me."

"Good for her. Hmm," Professor muttered.

"But I'm telling you I was in pain, a great deal of pain. It's completely illogical . . ."

"When the nurse says no morphine, it means no morphine"; and with those words Professor and all the others turned to Thura's bed. Only Doctor Liliencrona stayed for a moment with Stephania. He took her picture in his hand, looked at it, and then — Fröken Nilsson saw it clearly, as clearly as the day — he smiled at Stephania, the same way he used to smile at her, only at her.

The visit to Thura was brief. Thura, blushing with embarrassment over so much attention paid to her, said she felt fine; yes, she could lift her hand three inches, the iron medicine did not taste bad at all, yes, she was sure it would do her a lot of good. Professor, to indicate his satisfaction, patted Thura's shoulder with his enormous hand and said, "Now let's see if Fröken Nilsson is behaving herself."

In an attitude both of deference and dignity Fröken Nilsson was sitting up in her bed. Doctor Liliencrona was now standing next to her but happily she was able to control the trembling of her voice and even managed to glance at him indifferently.

"Fröken Nilsson has a complicated fracture of the left leg," Professor explained to his guest, and took from the nurse the envelope with the X-ray pictures. Fröken Nilsson blushed with satisfaction. At last they would know, both of them, Doctor Liliencrona and Stephania, that she was not here just for pleasure, that she too had her problems, although, of course, she knew her place and would never complain, or wake up others in the middle of the night.

"It certainly does look complicated," the guest said. "How did it ever happen?"

"She fell downstairs."

The guest doctor shook his head in amazement. Under the thick layer of powder Fröken Nilsson's face grew very pale. Now it was coming, he would not let her get away with it, no, not he. Oh, why had Anna told him everything! She could never hold her tongue.

For when Anna, Fröken Nilsson's sister, brought her to the hospital, she rushed to tell the whole story to no one else but Professor himself. She told him everything — how Fröken Nilsson was staying in her home, how there had been no light on the staircase leading to the pantry, and how Fröken Nilsson, who knew all that very well, started to climb the stairs in the middle of the night, and why — just in order to get a couple of macaroons.

That story so imprudently revealed to Professor was soon known to the whole hospital. For Professor and Doctor Ström, and even Sister Gudrun, used it as a weapon against Fröken Nilsson; they did it for her own good, of course, to show her the sad results of her excessive fondness for macaroons and other cookies.

Good God, if he'd only keep quiet now, when Doctor Liliencrona was standing next her bed, and Stephania was watching her from the other side. But the Professor cleared his throat, and then the sonorous voice said: "Yes, she fell downstairs. She tried to climb them in the middle of the night, and there was no light on them. Isn't that true, Fröken Nilsson?"

"Yes."

"Fröken Nilsson went to get some macaroons."

"What?"

"As I said, macaroons, isn't that so, Fröken Nilsson?"

Again the visiting doctor shook his head. One of the student nurses started giggling, and stopped immediately under the severe glance of Sister Gudrun.

"So now you had better remember your diet." Professor threatened Fröken Nilsson with his bony finger, and again white coats floated past, feet shuffled, voices murmured. The inspection visit was over.

Fröken Nilsson was crushed. How could he do it to her? And it wasn't the first time either. Sometimes, in moments like this, Fröken Nilsson envied Thura who had come to the hospital with polio and had nothing to be ashamed of. Among all those victims of epidemics and accidents, of great and tragic catastrophes, Fröken Nilsson, the victim of an innocent passion for macaroons, felt like a parvenu among aristocrats.

She looked at Stephania. Was she laughing at her? No, Stephania was lying quiet, her eyes fixed upon the window. Of course, she was too smart to show anything, to laugh openly. But inside . . .

Fröken Nilsson tightened her lips. She took off her nightgown. There was a big spot in the front she had not noticed before. Fröken Nilsson sighed deeply.

CHAPTER 7

SUNDAYS, TUESDAYS AND THURSDAYS are the visiting days in the hospital. The big red bus, usually almost empty, comes on those days crowded with passengers, filled to the brim with packages, bouquets of flowers. And suddenly, the moment it stops, when its door opens, everything around changes: the drive, so wide when empty, seems to narrow with all those rushing and bustling people; the revolving door, hardly ever opened, turns ceaselessly; and Willy, who most of the time dozes quietly in front of his stand, can now hardly handle all the magazines and chocolate boxes demanded by the hurried guests.

Then the elevator starts running — the visitors stream into the wards; those who have come for the first time tiptoeing timidly, the others stamping and talking very loud, too loud, as if to show that for them all the fear and strangeness is over. And now the hospital building itself changes into an unknown place. The halls and rooms are filled with figures in a variety of colorful clothes; strange faces appear, unfamiliar footsteps resound everywhere.

Visiting time begins at three, but the preparations for it start long before. Already at lunchtime Sister Gudrun distributes the food hastily. "We have to rush," she says, "today is visiting day," and in all the rooms nurses and orderlies repeat those words. Then as soon as lunch is over, the rooms are carefully put in order, flowers are rearranged, empty vases put exactly in the center of the tables, the bed covers are smoothed out, and the spots on the sheets discreetly hidden. As the final touch Fru Gustavsson combs the hair and washes the faces of all who cannot do it for themselves.

Not all the patients have visitors. But even those who don't expect anyone await the visiting hours eagerly. For even if the guests pass them with no more than a casual "Good afternoon," their very presence is like a greeting from that distant forgotten world. One of the visitors comes in a fur coat, and that means that the sun, although still gilding the treetops behind the window, is no longer warm, that fall is here; another wears a long, strangely cut dress and that is a sign that the dress that was quite new when you came to the hospital is already out of style, that things have been changing outside. And suddenly the months or years spent in the yellow room, up to now no more than sheets torn out of a calendar, grow, acquire weight and meaning. That is horrifying. But the fear lasts only for a moment. You listen to the visitors talking, watch the way they laugh, reach for a cigarette, and then put it away with an apologetic uneasy gesture. It is a strange and fascinating time, visiting hour; you don't want to miss any of it, and when at four Fru Gustavsson rolls in the coffee table, you feel the way you do in the movies when the word "End" appears on the screen too soon.

Thura and Fröken Nilsson never have any visitors. Thura's parents live very far away in the North, and as for Fröken Nilsson, her family, as she states bitterly, is no good, and her friends for some mysterious reason can never come. As long as Fru Hernruth was with them there always was a crowd of guests in the room. But on Sunday and Tuesday nobody came to see Stephania. The hour from three to four dragged endlessly, it seemed to be made longer by the silence in the room and by the cheerful noise of voices coming from outside.

On Thursday morning — just a day after the great inspection visit, and two after the "great day" — Sister Gudrun came into the room, saying: "You had a visitor, Fröken Ackermann, a lady." Stephania put her book away.

"Where is she now? Why doesn't she come in?"

"She has left. She'll come back at three. It is not visiting time now."

"You mean you told her to leave."

"Of course I did."

"But Sister," Stephania was almost screaming, "how could you do anything like that? It was my sister. She has been in Göteborg, and I have not seen her for this whole week."

"Little Thura has not seen her mother for eight months, since last Christmas."

"Thura's mother isn't here, and my sister was." Stephania was quiet now, but her face grew very pale.

"We have our regulations, dear Fröken Ackermann. We can't have people walk in and out any time of the day. The ward would look like a railway station before long."

"If you once let one person in, it would not look like a railway station," Stephania said. For a while she remained silent, and then looking straight into Sister Gudrun's face said, not loudly but very distinctly: "It's ridiculous, everything here is ridiculous."

Sister Gudrun was too flabbergasted to say anything. She left silently.

"They should have let her in," Thura said.

"They can't make exceptions," Fröken Nilsson commented dryly. Fröken Nilsson still had not got over Stephania's indifference. On the contrary, her indignation had been growing steadily. The way that Stephania talked to her on Tuesday morning, without even looking at her! It was only when she was drunk, for that's what she was after that morphine — just drunk — that she deigned to stoop and to talk to them. "Of course Sister Gudrun was right," Fröken Nilsson repeated.

With a dancing gait Fru Gustavsson came into the room. "I have news for someone," she announced.

"For me?" Stephania raised her head.

"No, not for Fröken Ackermann."

"For me?" Thura exclaimed.

"No, not for little Thura."

Fröken Nilsson moved to the edge of her bed. "You mean for *me?*"

"Exactly. A gentleman has called just now."

"Who could it be?" Fröken Nilsson thought feverishly. "The boss, or . . ."

"His name is Herr Eriksson."

"Herr Eriksson?" Fröken Nilsson moved back to the middle of her bed. She looked disappointed.

"He sounded awfully nice. He said he could not wait for Fröken on the phone, but he would come to see you in the afternoon."

"Thank you," Fröken Nilsson said. She should have known at once that it was Hasse, her brother-in-law. Every September he went to Stockholm to get some merchandise for his store.

"He said he had come yesterday from Eskilstuna. Is he a good friend of Fröken Nilsson?"

"Yes," Fröken Nilsson nodded, and before she even knew why, she added, "a very good friend, I've known him for years. You know what I mean. But I . . . I was so choosy then . . . no one could be good enough for me. And so I hardly wanted to look at him."

"And still he's coming to see Fröken Nilsson. Isn't that something?"

Fröken Nilsson took a deep breath. "Well, he's married now . . . to someone he had met through me. Actually I persuaded him he had no chances with me . . . the other was such a fine girl . . . and now they are very happy together."

"But still he came all the way from Eskilstuna to see Fröken Nilsson." Fru Gustavsson smiled conspiratorially, showing she knew very well that there was much more behind the story. She whispered: "When Sister Gudrun goes away for lunch I'll bring clean linen for your bed, so that everything will look nice and tidy when *he* comes."

"Thank you ever so much, dear."

Fru Gustavsson smiled once more and left.

"I'm so glad for you," Thura said.

"Oh, well." Fröken Nilsson shrugged nonchalantly as if male visitors from Eskilstuna were nothing unusual in her life.

"Is he handsome?"

"Oh, yes . . . well . . . he's grown sort of fattish lately. But you should have seen him before he got married."

"Have you ever told me about him?"

"I . . . I don't think so. After all he was not so terribly important. I told you before, I even did not want to look at him. I had someone else then."

Thura wondered who that someone else could be . . . the blond Anders or the navy lieutenant? But she did not want to be indiscreet and so she fell silent.

Fröken Nilsson felt a little uneasy. What came over her not to tell them Hasse was her brother-in-law, Anna's husband? Actually it was Fru Gustavsson who started it: "He is your good friend?"

[ 66 ]

she asked, and Fröken Nilsson answered "Yes" without even knowing when and how. And then it seemed impossible to explain everything. But as a matter of fact there was nothing wrong with what she told them. Anna had met Hasse through her, hadn't she? And hadn't Hasse brought her home a couple of times, before he and Anna got married? And he always talked to her for hours, and kept asking how she was and what was she doing. Often, very often she had wondered what would have happened if Anna had not been around all the time; if she herself had not been so shy, so very proper.

Yes, Fröken Nilsson thought now, it certainly was not very far from the truth, what she had told Fru Gustavsson. And aloud she said, "It will be nice to see Hasse again. Poor fellow, coming all the way from Eskilstuna . . . and especially to see me."

"Yes, isn't that wonderful of him?" Thura said.

They were late, Barbara and Thadeus; not much, only a few minutes, still it was enough to fill Stephania with sudden anxiety — like fear almost. Had they forgotten, she thought, listening impatiently to the footsteps in the hall; had anything happened? But suddenly the door opened and there they were, smiling and waving to her, and so unexpectedly beautiful — tall and shapely Barbara's blond hair shining in the afternoon sun, Thadeus gaunt and eager as he stood there, curiously glancing around. "Oh, Stephania, we couldn't find your room; they gave us the wrong room number," Barbara exclaimed rushing across the room. Stephania sat up, saw Barbara stop — but only for a moment — and already she was at the bed. "We've been so worried about you." Barbara bent to embrace her. Again Stephania saw how suddenly her fingers shrank from the unfamiliar hardness of the plaster, groped in the air, helpless, uncertain; then Barbara moved closer and kissing her repeated, "You just can't imagine how worried we were."

Stephania smiled and said: "Everything is all right, really." And when both Barbara and Thadeus were silent, just stood looking at her, she added, smiling still, but with an effort this time, "How do I look, in my . . . my new armor? You seem rather startled."

"Startled? Oh no, not at all. You look . . ." Barbara glanced at Thadeus.

"You look fine, Stephania," Thadeus said smiling broadly, "the cast is a bit big of course, but otherwise . . ."

"Otherwise you do look fine, not changed much at all," Barbara said.

They sat down, close to each other, Thadeus' arm resting over the back of Barbara's chair. How had everything been, they wanted to know, and how was it in here; not too bad, was it? And was the cast very heavy . . . ?

No, Stephania answered, it wasn't too bad in here at all, and the cast — yes, it was a bit heavy, but still she was already getting used to it. The Polish words felt strange in her lips, like food familiar but not tasted for a long time. And they too, Thadeus and Barbara, seemed a little strange, with their sun-tanned faces, their easily moving bodies and loud voices; out of place somehow in the drowsy stillness of that room.

"Yes, I guess I'll get used to being here," she said, and for a while they sat unspeaking, looking at each other.

"And what does Ström say?" Barbara asked.

"Ström says exactly what he's been saying all the time: that he promises no miracles, that he's only trying . . ."

"Tell your Ström it is all nonsense." Thadeus gracefully and impatiently tossed the dark lock of his hair that stubbornly kept falling on his forehead. "Plain nonsense. They all are like that, those Swedes, cautious, always cautious. He should have seen what I saw in the army. Some fellows were just shattered into pieces; still our doctors fixed them so that one could hardly see a thing. But here they . . . Anyhow you have nothing to worry about, dear. Just don't listen to his nonsense."

"Sh . . . dear, don't talk so loud," Barbara whispered smilingly. And it seemed to Stephania she said it only in order to put her hand over Thadeus', in order to stroke it furtively. Then she sat silent, her hands folded now over her already rounded belly, her face, soft-featured, very girlish still, and quiet, the eyes looking somewhere far above Stephania's head.

She's in the seventh month already, Stephania thought. Yes, in the seventh month, and still she found it hard to believe that Barbara was going to have a baby. We're going to wait until we really can afford it, she remembered Thadeus repeating, and now . . . had they changed their minds, or was it by chance? It seemed strange that it could happen like that, just by chance, that new life slowly growing within Barbara, that it could catch them unawares, not even wanting it perhaps. And when Barbara started saying how sorry she was they had had to go off to Göteborg and leave her to go alone to the hospital she only nodded silently, still thinking about the baby. How was it to carry it within your body, hidden from anyone else, known and felt by you only in moments like this, when Barbara sat very quiet, patiently listening to something within herself? She might ask Barbara about that — when she came alone.

"I really didn't mind coming alone. It was better that way," she said at last.

"Better? Why?"

"Oh, it just was. But tell me: what does the doctor say about you?"

"Everything is all right, she's the healthiest expectant mother one can imagine," Thadeus answered instead. "And the baby should come at the beginning of November, around the fifth, the doctor says."

"So soon?" Stephania said.

"Terribly soon, isn't it?" Barbara repeated. There was something like fear in her voice. "Thank God the hospital is not going to cost much, but later there'll be so many things to get. I really don't know how we'll ever manage," she added, her face tired and rigid, a deep furrow cutting across her forehead.

"Come on, Barbara," Thadeus said a little impatiently. "We certainly will. I'll take care of everything, you don't have to worry." Thadeus moved closer to Barbara and stroked her hair. "Cheer up, darling," he said, "you know everything will be all right, don't you?"

"Yes, I know. I'm sorry." Barbara's voice was warm again, the furrow on her forehead disappeared, the lips parted in a smile.

"I wish you could be with us when we baptize the baby." Thadeus turned to Stephania. "Perhaps we could arrange something. It would be really a shame for the kid to have someone else and not you for a godmother."

"Well," Stephania faltered, "I could hardly show myself among people in this." She pointed to the cast. "Besides, they would never let me out of here."

Barbara shook her head, and said: "Come on, what is it — baptizing the baby, just a few moments, that's all. But later . . . that's what counts. You will be with us, with the baby all the time. You know Thadeus talks so much about you that yesterday

[ 69 ]

Gross said, 'You have two wives, Thadeus, not one: both the Ackermann sisters.' " She smiled. "So my husband is your husband, and my child is going to be your child. You must help me bring him up. He will need an energetic hand. Otherwise Thadeus and I will spoil him hopelessly."

Stephania looked at them. She wanted to say something, to thank them, but somehow she did not know how. And so she only murmured indistinctly, "Yes, of course," and added hastily, "Who is Gross? I don't think I've ever met him."

Thadeus got up abruptly. "Oh yes, Gross. We've forgotten to tell you the most important news. He is a wonderful fellow. We ran into him in Göteborg, but he lives here in Stockholm. He's working in the Polish Legation as a doorman, but guess how much he gets?" Thadeus stopped and looked at Stephania. "No, you'll never guess — five hundred crowns a month. It's fabulous!"

"Yes, it is fabulous," Barbara echoed.

"He promised to find something for me there," Thadeus went on, gesticulating eagerly with his slender brown hands. "Any kind of work will do as long as they pay. Not that I want to stay there forever, you know I don't agree with the regime, but just a couple of months will do, so that we'll have a breathing space." His hands moved in a spacious gesture; "Yes, that's what we need; a breathing space." Thadeus sat down as if tired suddenly, and said, "Because it can't go on forever as it is now, it simply cannot. The work in the factory is too ridiculous for words, Stephania. You should have seen the fuss they raised a couple of days ago. I was late, just a few minutes, that was all. I kept the whole gang waiting, the foreman said. Well, so what if I did? It really is too much to take, to be ordered around by a fellow like that. He's illiterate, absolutely illiterate. . . . I know more about the works than he; our factory in Poland was bigger than anything he'll ever see in his life. Anyhow . . . it's not worth talking about. I'm going to quit. Gross will find me something and then . . ." He fell silent and sat shaking his head as if going on talking to himself.

Stephania said: "So you really think he'll do something, that . . . Gross?"

"Why do you always have to be so sceptical?" Barbara said. "If anyone should get work in the Legation, it's Thadeus. He's been for five years in the army, through the whole war, was a lieutenant . . ."

"Oh, I'm positive he'll find me something," Thadeus exclaimed, and he went on talking about Gross and then about other people they had met recently, and then again about the trip to Göteborg. At last he fell silent; Stephania too said nothing, and only after a long while did Barbara ask: "Well, anything else new, Stephania?"

Stephania hesitated; there were things she had thought she would tell them — about Thura and Fröken Nilsson, about the arguments she had had on the first day with Sister Gudrun. . . . But somehow it all seemed unimportant now. "No, there's nothing new," she said. "I guess nothing much ever happens here."

Thadeus glanced at his watch. "Gross may be calling us soon," he said. "It would be a pity if he missed us."

"If he missed you he'd call again, wouldn't he?" Stephania said.

Again they were silent. Then Barbara looked around and said the room was very nice indeed, not like a hospital room at all, and the people too seemed nice; there was nothing really wrong with them, was there?

Stephania glanced at Thura, and without knowing why, she said, "The little girl is paralyzed."

"Paralyzed? You mean she can't walk at all?"

"She can do nothing."

"Oh," Barbara said, her mouth remained half open, startled. "Oh, that's too bad. And no one comes to visit her?"

"No. Her parents live some place in the North."

"Do you think I could give her something, some cookies, fruit? We've brought you a lot . . . "

"Yes, why don't you?" Thadeus said very loud.

Barbara glanced at Stephania. "What should I say to her?"

"Anything you want. She's just like anybody else, even if she's paralyzed."

She watched Barbara filling the plate, walking awkwardly somehow to Thura's bed, heard her saying something in her broken Swedish. She came back hastily and said chokedly; "Oh, Stephania, that's so terrible, I didn't know, I gave her an apple, and she . . . she could not even take it . . . "

"I told you she's paralyzed, didn't I?"

"I know, but . . . Oh, Stephania, it must be hard on you to be here with people like that," Barbara whispered, slowly raising her hand. And Stephania waited for that hand to take hers, to feel it warm and understanding so that at last she could tell Barbara how

[ 71 ]

hard it really was to be here among these people, frightening in their complacent helplessness, and those others, frightening too in their cold forbidding efficiency. She waited. Barbara's hand moved gropingly and rested safely and gratefully in Thadeus' hand.

Stephania moistened her lips and said: "It's not so bad as you think, Barbara. No. You really must not worry about me. One gets adjusted."

"I guess one does," Barbara nodded. She glanced at Thura — a fearful and evasive glance that Stephania knew so well. "Don't stare at her," she said sharply.

The rattle of the coffee table came from the hall. In the next room the voice of Fru Gustavsson exclaimed: "Visiting time is over."

"I guess we'll have to leave now," Thadeus said.

"What shall we bring you next time?" Barbara asked.

"I don't need anything, I think. Just some books . . ." Stephania hesitated. There was something she still had to ask them. No, she thought . . . they would have told me if it had come. Still she said, "Was there any mail for me?" And it startled her that it was Thadeus, not Barbara, who answered, uneasily as if he knew why she had asked, "No, Stephania, there's been nothing for you. I'm sorry."

"Oh, it doesn't matter." She smiled crookedly. "I really haven't been expecting anything, I just asked . . ."

They did not answer, but got up slowly. The door opened and Fru Gustavsson came in saying: "The visiting time is over," and stood staring at them curiously. "Good-bye, dear, we'll be seeing you soon." Barbara bent over the bed and kissed her. Thadeus smiled and said: "Just don't worry too much, Stephania — you and your sister have real talent for worrying." Once more they waved at her from the door, and now they were gone.

Stephania leaned toward the window and looked out. They were walking arm in arm, Barbara's face lifted toward Thadeus'. She wished they would turn and look at the window. But they did not. Of course, how could they know she was sitting there?

"They're wonderful, your sister and your brother-in-law," Thura said.

"Yes," Fru Gustavsson agreed, "they really look nice. And did you have a good time, Fröken Nilsson? I looked for your guest when I came in. He must have left earlier."

[ 72 ]

Fröken Nilsson hurled the lumps of sugar into her coffee. "I did not have any guest," she said. "And will you open the window, please . . . I've a headache from all that noise."

CHAPTER 8

NO ONE KNEW exactly how it had happened. Fru Gustavsson, who although not an eyewitness seemed to have the most reliable information, maintained that Fröken Nilsson should not have lost her self-control, but — she admitted — Stephania had provoked her beyond human endurance. "I agree," Fru Gustavsson repeated to her audience, "it was a horrible, just a horrible thing to say. Yet," and here she would pause as if gathering courage for what she could not help but say, "yet, let's face it, there is a grain of truth in it."

More than a grain, her listeners agreed, and after Fru Gustavsson left they would whisper for long hours how sad it all was, and how the poor Fröken Nilsson did not deserve it; how she looked like a shadow, really like a shadow lately.

As to Sister Gudrun, she did her best to retain her usual objectivity. But even she, after having stated that there was no, absolutely no justification for quarrels, not as long as she was in that ward at least, had to admit that Fröken Ackermann was an extremely difficult person to live with. "Well," she would sigh, so deeply that the starched cap on the peak of her head would tremble precariously, "we cannot refuse anybody who needs help."

"Of course not." The patients in Three, Four and Five showed their sympathy by even deeper sighs. "Still, it's so hard on the poor Fröken Nilsson. And the little Thura . . . such a sweet child she is." And the conversation generally ended in a common disconsolate nodding of heads.

Thura, the sole witness of the incident which kept the whole ward busy for weeks, had the least to say about it of anybody. "It was horrifying, just horrifying," she would whisper to patients who, whenever Stephania was taken down to the X-ray room or to see

[ 73 ]

Professor, would sneak into the room. And then reluctantly, her whisper growing lower and lower, she would admit that it was Fröken Nilsson who had started it, but she had not meant anything, really not a thing, just a slip of the tongue, that was all. Then Thura would look at her visitors with wide-open eyes and say: "I think you'd better go, Fröken Ackermann will be in soon!" And as they were leaving she would add hastily and imploringly, "But it wasn't Fröken Ackermann's fault either — really not." The visitors of course knew better than to believe that.

It all started on that visiting day — when those two, the handsome Thadeus and the beautiful blond Barbara, came to visit Stephania, and when Herr Eriksson, the guest of Fröken Nilsson, had never showed up. Fröken Nilsson could not forget that day. Never in her whole life had anybody treated her that way. Here they came, talking a language no Christian soul could understand, laden with packages as if people were starving, and then they did not even look at her. Stephania had introduced them to Thura — the sister at least — but not to her, oh no. Fröken Nilsson did not care. She was much above things like that. Still, Fru Hernruth's husband, although a police superintendent, had not considered himself too good to talk to her. He never would pass her bed without saying hello to her and asking her how she was. But those two, those nobodies from nowhere, wouldn't lower themselves to that. All right, she would remember it.

That was one thing which bothered Fröken Nilsson, but serious as it was, it was nothing compared to the other disappointment, to the fact that Hasse had not come. He had not even called her. Had he done that at least, she could have said to Thura (only, of course, so that the other would hear her): He was *so* sorry that he couldn't come, but he had a sudden business appointment, or, He got a telegram calling him back home. That or something like that; there were a number of things which could have prevented Hasse from coming. And then she could add: Poor fellow; still, I think it's better for him not to see me, if you know what I mean. She had it all figured out, and the whole visiting day and the day after, she had waited for his call; then for a letter at least. But nothing happened. No call came; no letter. After a week had passed Fröken Nilsson lost all hope; she knew Hasse had got all the brushes he needed and gone back to Eskilstuna. He probably had remembered he should buy her flowers if he came and so he quickly changed his mind. He had always been like that, as greedy as a jay, would sell his own soul for ten öre. He wasn't worth as much as her little finger; but it was not of him but of the people in the ward she was thinking. Of course, that gossip bag Gustavsson couldn't hold her tongue and she told everybody around Fröken Nilsson was expecting a male visitor, an old beau. What did they all think about her now? Fröken Nilsson could not get rid of the feeling that they were laughing behind her back.

This feeling, as far as the other patients went, was only a faint suspicion. But with Stephania that suspicion changed into a horrible certainty. It was enough just to look at her, to hear her voice — the very sound of it, sharp and commanding, made Fröken Nilsson shudder. "Would you please close the door, would you turn the radio a little lower." As if to a servant or worse, even; and the eyes looking somewhere above you; you might as well be dirt, nothing. Yes, Fröken Nilsson was convinced, more than convinced, that Stephania was laughing at her, despised her. Each gesture, each movement of the red-painted lips seemed to say, I knew you were lying, I know why he did not come. Wistful and unhappy, Fröken Nilsson would sit down in her wheel chair and leave the room thinking: I'm not going to take it forever, I'm much too smart for that. Just wait and see, the time will come.

And it came, much sooner than Fröken Nilsson expected. It caught her unprepared, off her guard. It was a week after the visiting day. Fröken Nilsson went off in her wheel chair partly because the silence in the room got on her nerves, partly because she hoped to meet Doctor Liliencrona outside. But with her usual bad luck she missed him; all she could see was his white coat disappearing in the elevator. Bitter and disappointed, she was coming back to her room, when suddenly just in front of the door she heard a loud laugh. She stopped, put her hands on the wheels so they would not make any noise. Bent out of her chair, breathless, her mouth half open, Fröken Nilsson listened. Yes, it was she, Stephania, who was laughing. "I've never heard anything as funny as that," she said. And now Thura burst into laughter and said, "Oh God, how could she ever do it? Isn't that a scream?" And again they both almost choked with laughter.

She . . . do it . . . They were talking of her, of whom else if not of her? Fröken Nilsson pulled her gown tighter over her body and pushed the door open with her good foot. Bang — it knocked on the wall. Preceded by that resonant noise Fröken Nilsson entered the room. They were still laughing. She stopped in the middle, and looked first at Stephania, then at Thura, then again at Stephania. She even smiled, a reluctant smile that hardly opened her lips, and without a word, just looking at them in mute accusation, Fröken Nilsson clambered into her bed.

Lunch was brought in. Slowly Fröken Nilsson sipped her milk. It was neither cold nor warm and it left a wooden, stale taste in her mouth. And the meat balls were burnt, too. Fröken Nilsson pushed the plate away indignantly. Lunch was over, the shades were pulled down. Fröken Nilsson lay almost completely hidden under her blanket; that made it easier for her to go on with her observations. But nothing happened; they were too clever to say anything, of course. Stephania seemed asleep, Thura looking at the ceiling. Time passed until at last Fröken Nilsson could not stand it any longer, and without any help she hoisted herself into her wheel chair and rolled toward Thura's bed. She moved the wheels carefully so as not to wake Stephania and her face had the conspiratorial and solemn expression of one who tries to tiptoe noiselessly.

"Thura," she whispered.

Thura slowly detached her eyes from the ceiling. Two flies were dancing there and she watched fascinated at how they circled around the lamp, buzzing loudly.

"Thura," Fröken Nilsson repeated.

"Yes, Fröken Nilsson?" One fly settled itself in the middle of the lamp. It looked very funny as it crawled clumsily upon the big bowl.

"Come on." The whisper gave Fröken Nilsson's voice a menacing quality. "Don't look somewhere into the blue when I'm talking to you. Or perhaps you too are much too good to talk to me."

"I'm sorry, Fröken Nilsson. I'm listening of course. Did you want to tell me something? Did you meet him?"

"I want to ask you something. What were you laughing at, you and Stephania?"

"When?"

"Oh, so you don't even remember? Today before lunch, when I came into the room. Now you remember?"

Thura blushed. Perhaps because she always blushed easily, perhaps because there was something strange about Fröken Nilsson's voice.

"We laughed . . . yes . . . we were laughing at nothing special, really."

"At nothing? You were simply bursting with laughter."

"Well," Thura said slowly, "it was at a book. Stephania's book. She laughed and so I asked why, and she told me."

"And . . ."

"That was all."

"What was so terribly funny about it?"

"Oh, I can't quite explain it. It wasn't so much the words, but the way Stephania explained it."

Fröken Nilsson said nothing. She only shrugged.

"Oh, Fröken Nilsson, what else could it have been? What are you thinking of?"

"That's my business," Fröken Nilsson said. She smiled a cold and painful smile of wistful superiority and wheeled away.

What should she do now? Go back to her bed? No, she couldn't — she couldn't stand being in the same room with those two. She opened the door, pushed the chair into the hall, and moved through it first slowly, then faster and faster until she wandered into the distant and forbidden regions where Sister Gudrun's room was, and the private wards, then back, and again to and fro, to and fro. That Thura! That ungrateful brat; after all she had done for her, read aloud to her, written letters . . . always in her service, ringing the bell in the middle of the night. . . . And now . . . Her hand grew tired of moving the wheels. She had to go back. She *would* go back. After all it was her room too, in fact she had been there before anyone else.

Fröken Nilsson opened the door and came in. As she was passing the closet the wheel of the chair got caught into something. She stopped. It was the blue silk of Stephania's gown. Her hands trembling with sudden impatience Fröken Nilsson began to untangle it. The silk felt soft in her hands — it rustled. She looked at her own gown. The sleeves were frayed, the lapels covered with spots. Angrily she hurled the blue silk away and it caught the late sunshine and shimmered warmly. Pure silk — she thought — pure silk.

"So!" she said suddenly. "So!" she repeated, and for a moment listened to her own voice. And then she, or rather something in

her, said in a whisper, slow, loud, distinct: "Those foreigners . . ."
Fröken Nilsson stopped horrified, but she had to go on. She moistened her lips. "Those foreigners," she repeated, rolling the sounds
slowly spitting them out, "they come here" (the words came faster
and faster now), "sponge on our Swedish money, and have everything, everything we don't even dream of." She stopped. Did she
hear something?

No, the room was silent, very silent.

"Everything," she repeated in a stubborn whisper.

"Fröken Nilsson!" Thura gasped voicelessly.

The bed under the window creaked. Fröken Nilsson moved
herself deeper into the chair. She waited. She wasn't afraid, not
at all.

But the silence was still there. Fröken Nilsson wanted to move
her head, to look at the bed opposite, but somehow she could not.
And she could only hear how Stephania was sitting up slowly, very
slowly.

"Fröken Nilsson!" Stephania said.

No one answered.

"Fröken Nilsson." The sharp voice grew louder.

"Yes?" Fröken Nilsson began to roll under the frayed edge of
her sleeve.

"What did you say?" Stephania's voice was quiet, friendly almost.

"I . . ." Fröken Nilsson said absently. Why was the sleeve so
ragged? It wasn't so terribly old, the gown, or perhaps . . . I
thought you were asleep, she wanted to say. But no, she wasn't
going to apologize. What for? Yes, what for?

She raised her head. Stephania sat upright, her fingers clutching
the edge of the bed. "You heard what I said, didn't you?"

"I did. But would you repeat it, please."

Sure she would. Why not? She wasn't scared. Her feet were
cold but that was from the floor . . . "You," she began, and her
eyes closed as if she were going to recite something, "you foreigners come here and sponge on our money. Sponge," she re-
pated, "that's all you can do." So, now she had said it.

"Fröken Nilsson." Stephania propped herself on her elbows.
"Come here, closer."

The wheel chair did not move.

"Come closer, I said, I'm not going to shout."

[ 78 ]

Fröken Nilsson pushed the wheels. They began to roll; the chair was slowly approaching Stephania's bed.

Stephania sat looking at her. She had felt quiet, very quiet, until that penetrating whisper woke her up from a half-dream. All this seemed only half real; she felt as if she were watching something in which she herself had no part. But now when she saw the wheel chair and the huge woman moving toward her, the whole room seemed to move with them, and she felt that something was suddenly happening to her. Impatiently she beckoned with her hand. Faster. Her hand trembled. And now here they were, right in front of her, the wheel chair, the woman.

Stephania looked. She looked at the fat neck bulging out from the too tight collar of the shirt, at the reddish pimples on the sallow face — right underneath the nose was one, big, swollen, the white point of pus in the middle; at the lusterless strings of hair hanging around the spongy face. "You . . ." she said. "You." Yes, she had to say something, something right now, but a lump blocked her throat.

Gray mist appeared before her eyes, swallowed the room, the beds and the woman opposite her. "You," she repeated, "you liar; not one word of truth passed through your mouth." The mist grew denser; now it was almost black. She stared at it. Something emerged out of it; that was the head of Fröken Nilsson. She could not see the features, just a space, very white, and the mist dark around it. Quiet, she thought, quiet; she lifted herself higher, squinted her eyes and bent her head sidewise. Everything was strung tense in her. Now; careful. "Not a word, never in your whole life." The space quivered, but here it was back again right before her eyes. Once more; now. And with her voice sharp, clear, almost singing, almost joyful, she said: "You old heap of fat, you old ugly heap of fat."

The pale space jumped, whirled through the darkness, vanished. She breathed deeply. Now she had done it.

"Fröken Nilsson, Stephania, stop! Please stop!" That was Thura crying.

And then nothing . . . silence.

Fröken Nilson did not move. Her head fell on her breast. The ragged edges on her sleeve — why were they showing again? What did she say — fat, heap of fat?

She raised her head, but she couldn't look at her, no, she could not. Her hands of themselves began to move the wheels. Faster, faster; she had to get out of here, the bed; no, she did not want to go to bed. Here was the door, and now the hall. It was empty, thank God it was empty.

She rushed through the hall, bumped into Fru Gustavsson and passed her without a word. A door, now another door, now the left, there she was.

The bathroom was empty. She dashed to the mirror, turned, and locked the door, as if afraid someone might spy on her. And then back to the mirror. She hesitated, raised her eyes. Old ugly heap of fat. For a moment she saw nothing, just a blurred shapeless patchwork of colors. Then slowly the maze began to shape into something that was herself. She stared as if she was seeing herself for the first time in her life. Her eyes spied all over her face and neck, discovered every wrinkle, the furrows on her forehead, the two deep lines around her mouth, the double chin propped upon another layer of fat that was her neck. Old and ugly, old and ugly. Slowly she rolled up the sleeve, looked at the arm, at the flabby, thin blue veins in the hanging flesh. And suddenly with one desperate gesture she lifted herself halfway out of the chair, pulled the gown down, then the shirt. The mirror was filled with a pale shapeless mass.

Steps came from the hall. She looked once more, put the shirt on, unlocked the door, and came back to the mirror. No, she thought, it could not be like that, it was impossible. Until at last she began to cry.

And so Fru Gustavsson found her, in front of the mirror, her face hidden in her hands, her whole body shaking with sobs.

And all that time Stephania lay quietly with a book in her hand. But not a page turned; her eyes looked again and again at the same sentence: "He came out of the house and waited on the corner, his shadow long and thin in the sun. He came out of the house . . ." She knew those words by heart now; still she kept repeating them time after time just in order not to think, not to remember what had happened. Nothing had happened, nothing at all; she would not even think about that. "He came out of the house . . ." Still she could hear that voice, that whisper — "You foreigner, you have everything" — and the woman in the wheel chair seemed to be still sitting next to her bed. Until suddenly the anger returned — the throbbing, the lump blocking her throat.

She closed her eyes and pressed the lids with her fingers until it hurt. And out of the complete darkness that surrounded her, words came, words she had long ago forgotten, or perhaps never known before — filthy and hateful. She mumbled them voicelessly, grinding the syllables between her teeth — witch, old witch, slut, and then in Polish — *kurwa, stara kurwa*. She opened her eyes. Now it was better.

It was no use going on like that. She had to think it over; not what the other had said, that did not matter, but what she should do now. Quietly, logically she had to think it over. To talk to Ström? Ask him to transfer her to another room? What for, they were all the same, all those Johnsons and Svensons, the same story would repeat itself everywhere. Get a single room? That was a good idea, very fine indeed, but where could she get the money? She had just enough money to pay for one week, seven times fifteen, that made a hundred, a hundred and five, a couple of crowns less than she had. To leave altogether? That was exactly what all of them, from Professor to the maids, wanted her to do. But she wasn't going to give them that satisfaction. Yes, she was going to stay here right in this room.

She had to stay here whether she wanted to or not. She was tied to the room, to the bed by the cast, by what was hidden underneath the cast. It was she herself, her own body, that imprisoned her here, that forced her to stay with those people. There was nothing she could do about it, except just ignore the others, live as if she were completely alone. And now not a thought more about that, not a word more.

She picked up the book and struggled through the next sentence. But a feeling of unrest seized her, like that of hunger not fully satisfied, like the memory of things left undone.

From above her book she saw how Fröken Nilsson returned, sitting limply in the wheel chair pushed by Fru Gustavsson. Then the afternoon temperature was taken. In the hall someone was learning how to walk. "My legs are so stiff," the plaintive voice kept repeating, "not like my own at all." And the crutches knocked on the stone floor in an uneven clumsy rhythm. Then everything was quiet except for a radio playing far away. The clock struck six. Dinnertime.

Dusk was falling outside but nobody switched on the light. The twilight grew heavy with the smell of food. Fru Gustavsson put the plates on her table. She forced a few spoonfuls down her throat but her body revolted against the food.

"Fröken isn't hungry?"

"No." She turned to the window.

It was going to be windy tomorrow. The sky, at first pale, almost white, grew violet, pink, and then red in the distance. And the ivy was red, and the leaves of the chestnuts. From afar came the sound of sirens. Fire engines? Police? Then a dog barked, a puppy in an eager, jerky voice. She listened to those voices, but through them, as through a thin net, penetrated the heavy smacking of Fröken Nilsson's lips. And looking at the window and the tree she still could see her; how she swallowed the food in huge gulps, wiped the gravy with a crust of bread from the plate, and nibbled on the dessert as if she could not wait to get to it.

The dinner was over. Stephania asked Fru Gustavsson for cold water, yes, ice cold, and rinsed her face over and over, holding handfuls of water against her lips, her eyes, trying to obliterate the greasy smell of food, the sounds, the very presence of the other from her body. Now she felt better, only her eyes burned.

"Shall I turn on the light over your bed?"

"No," she answered, and lay in a secluded circle of darkness waiting for the day to come to an end. Ström came in, medicine was distributed, and at last the night was here.

She closed her eyes but still she could not fall asleep. Something forced her to turn to stare at Fröken Nilsson's bed. In the darkness she could not see more than the outline of the bed and the handle which Fröken Nilsson used to lift herself that loomed like two thin arms clasped together. But she could hear her breath, heavy, uneven, passing into snoring, lapsing into a whistle. And the smell was there too, the cheap oversweet perfume, the heavy odor of sweat. She turned back to the window. But everything around her, the room, the darkness, the very air, seemed to be filled with Fröken Nilsson. The jellylike flesh expanded and penetrated everywhere. She could feel it clinging to her, moist, cold, clammy. It did not help to hide under the blanket; the flesh forced itself to her mouth under her fingers. She could kill her, slowly plunging her fingers into the flesh until the whole body would shrink, quiver for the last time and come to a standstill, like a fish taken out of water gasping for air and then growing motionless, stiff. Once she saw a fish killed like that; its eyes had looked at her. Like a fish. . . . Would she look at her too?

And suddenly she saw Fröken Nilsson's eyes, or were they the eyes of the fish, round, colorless, staring at her. She did not want to look at them, she wanted to run away, but her feet seemed glued to something, to a gray dense mass that was everywhere. "Out," she cried, "I must get out." But someone was pushing her, who she could not see, still she could feel it; the dark huge shape — a man — a woman — she did not know. A voice cried something, she could not hear, the words were swallowed by the darkness, by her fear. She struggled to free herself from the gray mass, but could not. And suddenly it happened; everything around her was whirling and she too was whirling, rising higher and higher until no air was left to breathe with. Out, she thought again. I must get out. She pushed the something around her with her head, her whole body. It broke noiselessly and now she was falling down headlong, down and down, rolling faster and faster, as if on the slope of a hill, groping with her arms and legs, longing to fall, afraid to fall. At last she stopped, and felt surprised because it did not hurt at all.

The darkness grew suffused with light, greenish-pale and dusky. It was stairs she was on now, wooden stairs, narrow and winding, with the banister on one side only gaping like a toothless mouth with holes of missing banister posts. The green light was coming from a small and dirty petroleum lamp that hung on the dirty green wall. It was cold here, no roof above, the stairs were suspended in a void like those of a bombed house. And suddenly in the green light she saw a spot: spittle frozen shiny and greenish too. She could not look at it, she wanted to run away, but suddenly she remembered why she had come here. She had to hide right under the stair with the spittle. For they were coming, she could hear their steps. Now they were almost here but she stood paralyzed, her eyes upon the green spot. And here they came, their shadows first, their helmets like immense circles, their arms moving like pendulums. And now they were here, green too like everything around. No! she wanted to cry, I know it's not true, it's over now, over! But she could not utter a sound. Until suddenly the stairs began to crumble under her feet, the green figures next to her . . .

When she opened her eyes Sister Ingeborg was standing at Fröken Nilsson's bed. She whispered, "Penicillin, Fröken Nilsson." Stephania looked at her, stretched out her hand and groped for the reassuring smoothness of the blankets and pillows. She touched her face. It was wet with sweat. Sister Ingeborg left. Stephania lay forcing her eyes to stay open. She was afraid to fall asleep.

Her head ached. Vaguely she remembered that something had happened before the dream, something she did not want to think of. But the memories came — Fröken Nilsson, the words she had said, "You foreigners . . ." and then the dream. It seemed to her she had dreamed it once before. The stairs, the green light . . . Somtimes dreams return. . . .

She sat up, lit the night light and lifted the blanket until it formed a small curve. She hid the lamp in there. Now it was light underneath the covers. The light was good, and she sat looking at the yellow circle, until at last the day began.

It began like every other day. First Fru Gustavsson came in. She did not know anything yet. Sobs — that was all she could get out of Fröken Nilsson the day before. "Good morning," she said now. "A little chilly today, but lovely." A faint answer from Thura's bed only. The news about the weather was received with complete indifference. Fru Gustavsson crossed her bare arms over her breast, and looked inquisitively from one bed to another. "Anything wrong? The nasty leg is bothering you, Fröken Nilsson?"

"No, nothing is bothering me."

"Fine. Nothing. That's how it should be." Fru Gustavsson smiled, but the smile in spite of all the dimples it brought into her face found no response; it was swallowed by the silence, by the gray dusk that still was filling the room. "Come on, children, cheer up," Fru Gustavsson said, and pulled up the shades, but the room seemed to remain gray and cold in spite of all the light. Fru Gustavsson shrugged and began to make the beds. But her movements were slow and she shook the blankets with much less gusto than usual, as if the silence in the room made everything she touched heavier.

After the doctor's visit Fröken Nilsson left. She closed the door after her with an exaggerated caution which seemed to make the hardly audible creak louder than the most violent bang.

Fru Gustavsson came in once more, mopped the floor, and opened the window. It was cold outside. Stephania lay wrapped in the blankets breathing the sharp September air. From the tree behind the window, a chestnut, the green cover half open and showing the brown inside, detached itself from among the leaves and slowly fell down. There must have been many of them lying in the drive, shiny as if polished and warm with sunshine. Stephania wished she could be in the park now, to pick up and feel their smoothness in her hand. If she just could get up and leave that room, for a moment at least. The unrest she felt yesterday, the awareness of something left undone, returned. Something had changed, something was hidden in the room — in the shadows on the wall, in the rustle of the curtains. It must be the dream she had had last night that made everything strange, unfamiliar.

Dreams were curious things, she thought. Sometimes nights would pass and you would not dream at all. There would be nothing but darkness around you, soft, black and safe, and in the morning you would feel rested, but still it would seem as though the night had never been, that the morning came right after the evening. But then nights like the last one came, and the day before would seem far away as if years had passed, as if you had come to a new unknown place.

Once, it was long ago when she was a child, she had felt very much afraid of night. It was after her father had taught her the morning prayer. How did it go? She couldn't remember it, she never prayed now. Something about the tents of Jacob and how good they were. But it didn't begin with that; it began with those words she still could remember — "Blessed be Thou, O Lord, who hast returned my soul to me in the immensity of Thy mercy." It was those words which horrified her. "Why does He have to *return* the soul?" — she had asked Father and he had said, "Because He takes it away for the night."

That made the prayer even more horrifying. It suddenly reminded her of Grandmother, how she took her false teeth out for the night, and there were the teeth soaking in a glass of water on the table, the teeth looking very white on the pink shiny gums; and Grandmother lay in her bed, her jaws suddenly stiff and sunken, her lips tightly clasped together as if they would never open again. Was that how God took the soul away, how they, how she, looked without it, altogether changed, severe and empty? "And what happens when God forgets to return the soul?" she asked.

[ 85 ]

"God never forgets anything," Father told her. But she was not satisfied. She wanted to know what happened if He did not want to return the soul. "Then people die." Die, she thought. She did not understand quite what it meant then, but she knew that people wore black when someone had died in the family; black clothes and stockings and veils; the streets, the park were full of these black women, and she was afraid of them. No, she didn't want to die. And for a long time she awaited the night with fear, and when the light went out she lay trying to keep her eyes open to watch Him, not to let Him take her soul away. And she repeated the morning prayer in the evening, to remind Him to have the immensity of His mercy, to be sure to return her her soul. Still she felt a pang of horror when she knew she was falling asleep, and every morning she woke up with a feeling of unspeakable relief. He had not forgotten; she was still here, unchanged, exactly as she had been the night before.

Stephania smiled. It was funny to remember things like that. She never thought about them, and now the memories were coming, why and whence she could not tell.

She did not get over that fear for a long time, not until she became very sick. She didn't remember what it was, but she knew her room had been filled with soft red light, for Mother had covered the lamp so that the glare would not hurt her eyes. And she just slept and slept for days, and when she got up she had forgotten all about the prayer, the soul and the women in black.

Stephania smiled again. It was good to remember those things: the red light, Mother always present at her bed, and the tart taste of cold tea that Mother gave her whenever she woke up — it made her feel warm inside and safe and rested when she thought of them. How old could she have been then — no more than seven or eight probably, for it was before they had installed the electric light on their street. The gas lanterns were still there and every evening a short man, or perhaps he only seemed so short because of the long rod he held in his hands, came. He touched the lanterns with the rod and one after another they flowered with a green light that flickered for a while and then shone through the dusty glass with an even blue-green flame surrounded by a dawn of yellow halo. . . . He walked out of the light behind him into the dusk ahead of him, and she always felt scared that something would happen, that just where their house was, the lamps would remain blind, the street dark, all night long. But soon the lamp in front of their house was lit and the man and his rod disappeared in the park at the end of the street.

It was not a park, really, just wide alleys, and Mother told her that long ago walls had been there — huge thick walls surrounding the whole city so that the enemy would not burst inside. "Burst inside," that was how Mother said it, and she could visualize swarms of red-faced men storming the walls, banging on the gates with clenched fists. Perhaps that was what made the alleys somehow frightening to her. For now nothing was left to defend the city; the walls were gone, and in their stead the trees were there, and the ponds with ducks and swans, and the flower bed — an eagle formed of white flowers on a very red background. The eagle was Poland, Mother explained to her, and the red was the blood shed when Poland had to fight for her freedom. That was frightening too and she never liked to sit next to the flower bed.

But the girl did sit next to it, right on the bench that was facing the huge beak and the crown on the eagle's head. Why did she start thinking about the girl now? Perhaps it was the day, so much like the day when she had met her — cool yet full of sunshine, the air transparent, the green of the trees ready any moment to turn into yellow. She remembered that other day so exactly because it had been the first time after her sickness that she came out into the alleys. She had left them in early summer, and now the fall, the chilly air, the chestnuts falling on the grass with a soft sound like stones plunging into water, surprised and startled her.

The alleys were empty. All the children she knew were in school. She sat on the bench and looked at the ducks, their feathers, green yellow and purple on their necks, glittering in the sun. She fed them biscuits and they fought for them, greedily chasing the crumbs in the shadowy green water. But the swans, long-necked and aloof, did not even look at the crumbs. Their absolute indifference made her sad, and she sat back on her bench and waited.

And suddenly from the bench next to the flower bed with the eagle a girl got up and began to run toward her. She had noticed that girl before, for her hair was light, lighter even than Barbara's, shiny like gold, the two thick braids stuck stiff and bright on both sides of her round face. She ran very fast, the tanned legs shone in the sun, the pink starched dress rustled. Panting, the girl stopped in front of her bench. She curtseyed, and nodded her head; the red ribbons threw a purple shade on her face, and there was a golden cross and a medallion suspended on a thin chain around her neck.

"Do you want to play with me?" the girl asked.

She jumped down from her bench. "Yes, I'd love to."

"Hopscotch?"

"Sure, hopscotch."

"What is your name?"

"Stephania, Stephania Ackermann."

On the bench next to the eagle a woman got up. She beckoned. "Wait a minute, my mother is calling me." The girl hurried away raising a shower of yellow sand as she ran.

She picked up a stick and began to draw the squares for hopscotch in the sand. They were very even; she felt proud of herself. The girl came back. For a while she silently looked at her. "My mother asks if you are Jewish," the girl said at last.

She raised her head, looked. . . .

And suddenly Mother got up; she stood between her and the girl. She was very pale and her voice sounded strange when she said, "Yes, she's Jewish, so what?"

"I'm sorry," the girl said, fingering the chain on her neck, "but my mother said I shouldn't play with Jewish children." Once more she looked at them, and then ran back to her bench. And she did not curtsey this time.

Did she understand then what had happened? Probably not. And she didn't ask anything. She felt ashamed and knew Mother was ashamed too. For a while she jumped alone in the squares and then, earlier than usual, they went home.

No, she never had asked, but somehow she must have understood, for from that time on she took care not to play with children who had blond hair and wore chains with crosses and medallions around their necks. And later they moved into another house, and she always had to run upstairs very fast, for on the second floor where Judge Rozanski lived the door would open as she was passing by, and a voice of Rozanski's son or daughter would sing:

*Jewess, Jewess with a long nose,*
*Jewess, Jewess put Jesus Christ on the Cross.*

[ 88 ]

She sang those words to herself now, softly and with a quick malicious smile on her lips. Round and round it goes, she thought, and hummed the words again. There are things one should not think about. There were things one should know without thinking about them. Still, she wondered whether Fröken Nilsson wore a cross. Probably not, all the Swedes were Protestants; or perhaps a cross but no medallion.

Sister Gudrun came in with a pile of mail in her hands. Stephania eagerly watched her sorting the letters. "Here, this is for Fröken, and that too." She looked at the envelopes. An advertisement, the prospectus of a book club. Without opening them she crumpled the letters in her hand, and put them on the edge of the table. They fell on the floor, but she didn't bother to pick them up. Sister Gudrun did it, and on her face disapproval was struggling with pained reproach. "The floor is not a wastebasket," she said.

Stephania did not answer.

Sister Gudrun looked at her watch. "My, it's late," she exclaimed. She stopped before the mirror, fixed the coquettish gray curl sticking from underneath her cap, and left.

Yes, it was late. Almost lunchtime. Stephania opened her book. Where was she? Oh, here: "He stood on the corner, his shadow tall and slender in the sun."

CHAPTER 9

SILENCES ARE DIFFERENT. Some are only a pause, an expectation of sound, framed in voices like those smooth-surfaced mirrors reflecting an old-fashioned frame, clasped fast in it.

And there is also another silence, not waiting for a voice, not following the voice; silence not limited by any sound, so that it becomes a presence, a sound in itself.

That was the silence that now filled Room Number Five. It was as if insurmountable spaces and not just a few feet of grass-green linoleum separated the three beds; not a word, not even a glance bridged them. The three women went through their days each on her own, each completely alone. The silence stood between them, heavy, dense, almost tangible. Like dust it hovered in the air and covered everything around. It even managed to undermine the unshakable pattern of hospital life. For even if the others, Doctor Ström, Sister Gudrun and Fru Gustavsson, came in at the same time as ever, with the same questions as ever, all the answer they got was yes or no, indifferent, elusive words that were a confirmation of silence. And so the traditional practices, the washing, the making of beds, daily visits of the doctor, became reduced to meaningless gestures. They were like those scenes in movies when something goes wrong with the sound machine and nothing is left but shadows desperately twitching on the screen, their movements futile, no sound coming out of their lips.

The people from outside, doctors, nurses and attendants, knew it; they felt uncomfortable in Room Number Five, and they left as soon as possible; and again silence would prevail.

Time moved more slowly than ever now; there was nothing to separate it, to cut it into easily distinguishable segments. Hours, days and weeks all merged together—a silent yesterday, a silent today, a silent tomorrow.

Stephania accepted the silence triumphantly. That was exactly what she wanted: now to be really alone. Still the desired loneliness did not come. All the time she was aware of Fröken Nilsson's presence; heard the bed squeaking, the wheel chair moving, shoes hurled noisily onto the floor. That woman, invisible and remote, was a part of the silence.

Slowly Stephania trained herself not to pay any attention to her. She closed herself in her own world filled with anticipation of Barbara's visits, thoughts and memories, and above all books. Books were helpful; they forced a shape, a sense upon the languid time. But after many hours of reading she felt that they also, the people living and speaking on the printed pages, became only shadows in silence; their words sounded muffled as if coming from far away. Stephania knew that was a sign she was tired, and she would put the book away and lie quietly. For by that time she had learned the art of filling her days in many and different ways, with things that at first had seemed insignificant but now acquired meaning and importance.

—First of all there was the window, with the chestnut tree behind it all yellow now, and the sky always changing, every day a new sky to look at. Sometimes it was clear, no clouds on it, only white streaks interwoven with the blue like veins in marble. Then again just one cloud would be there, only one, but very gray and solid, the edges sharp, and the blue seemed only a thin layer now torn off to expose the dark massive flesh underneath. Or there would be many clouds, light gray and transparent, like the gauze of old evening dresses taken out from drawers and spread on blue carpets.

Then later in September rain came, the sky turned a uniform gray; nothing was left to look at there. But now the pavement of the drive was dark and shiny, the lights of the cars were mirrored in it like feelers of huge insects, penetrating through the pavement, groping their way.

The drive was another thing she would often look at. She knew the people coming there — the nurses and the attendants rushing out of the bus at seven-thirty in the morning; doctors with graceful skill parking their cars; delivery boys on their bicycles. Then later the old postman came, the bulky bag jumping on his paunch, the glasses sliding to the tip of his nose. And in the afternoon the man who visited someone in the private ward came, a tall man in gray tweeds, and a setter with sad eyes waited for him in the car with longing patience, his nose glued to the window.

In the evening, there were the lights of the city far away, and above, in the dark mass of the night sky, the red lights of airplanes, and below, red lights of cigarettes on the dark mass of the pavement. Lights above and lights below; yellow, red, blue, and all of them moving . . . moving. . . .

Sounds too were coming through the window — sirens, the rolling of trains, the whistle of a locomotive, the stamping of feet. Later she learned to disentangle from the maze of sounds the church bell that struck the time: hours in a deep bass, quarters in a thin falsetto. Stephania grew fond of the bells, and whenever she failed to hear them she felt disappointed, as if she had missed something important.

Three times a week the silence was broken by the visits of Barbara and, on Sundays, of Thadeus also. Barbara was becoming more and more stately. Her face grew somehow watchful and solemn. Thadeus was still waiting for the job at the Polish Legation. There were some difficulties, but just those difficulties themselves proved that they treated his application seriously, that he had excellent chances. Stephania always agreed with them; she was not used to much talking now, and their voices and laughter made her a little tired. Neither Thadeus nor Barbara had noticed that something had changed in her room. Thadeus had much too much news to tell her, and as to Barbara, she never had been too good at noticing things. Stephania never mentioned what had happened between her and Fröken Nilsson. Somehow she preferred not to.

And it was the monotony of the endless days which at last forced Stephania to speak to someone; not to her roommates, nor to any of the hospital personnel, but to Willy, the newspaper salesman who each morning wobbled behind his stand into the room, exclaiming: "Good morning, ladies, at your service, what is it you want today?" And even if the patients wanted nothing, Willy would limp from one bed to the other, assuring them his apples were the sweetest one could get in the whole Scandinavian peninsula, his bananas the yellowest and ripest in the whole Kingdom of Sweden. He would talk and talk, and fill the room with his loud laughter until at last, before they knew how and why, the patients had an apple or a banana in their hands, a magazine on their tables.

For a long time Stephania answered Willy's persuasion with a brief No, thank you. But one morning when it was raining and the room looked gloomy and gray, she said, just in order to fill in a few empty minutes: "Give me a magazine, Willy, and a chocolate bar — milk. Do you have any milk chocolate?"

"I have everything," Willy answered jubilantly. "The largest department store in Stockholm doesn't have what I have. Abracadabra." He moved his short arms in a circle. "Here's your chocolate bar, Fröken Ackermann."

Stephania unwrapped the silver and bit into the bar. She grimaced. "It's not milk chocolate, Willy," she said.

"What?" Willy's ruddy thick-nosed face was horrified. "A mistake!" he exclaimed. "I should never have made a mistake like that." He walked to his stand, picked up another bar, and held it up to the light. "Milk this time. It's milk chocolate, I'll guarantee," he said. "Here, and a thousand apologies."

"Thanks," and Stephania handed him another coin. But Willy raised his hands in a defensive gesture. "God forbid, I made a mistake, I must pay. No money, dear Fröken, no money this time."

"It's all right," Stephania said, "take it."

"No, never. That's a present, a present from Willy."

"Another time; here, take the money."

"But my dear Fröken, you just can't do that to me. Refuse a present!"

Stephania smiled. He looked so funny, the wisp of hair standing upright on the top of his head like a feather on a hat, the small eyes in the furrowed face staring at her imploringly.

"All right," she said, "it's a present." But she took another bar and paid for it.

Willy seemed not to feel like leaving. He stood at the bed, his hands upon the railing, and whistled softly, "Fröken is a lady, a real lady."

"Oh really."

"A lady, I've known it all the time. The moment I saw Fröken walking through the hall in that beautiful long robe, I said to Fru Gustavsson: 'Maria, here's a real lady, you will see.' And sure I was right. I can smell a lady." He sniffed violently with his clumsy nose. "Just like that."

"Thank you, Willy," Stephania said.

Willy stepped closer, bent his head over his shoulder and stared at Stephania with half-open eyes. "Fröken's so pretty, so beautiful."

"What?"

"Beautiful, beau-ti-ful, *schön*," he added triumphantly. From one of the patients Willy had once picked up a few German phrases and he used them on every possible occasion.

Stephania said nothing. She only frowned.

"I mean it. And Willy knows what's beautiful." He shook his big head in startled admiration. "All the women here, blond, blond like yellow chickens. Fröken is different — such black eyes, and the hair black, black and pretty. *Schön, sehr schön.*"

Stephania shrugged, and her hand involuntarily touched the cast.

"That?" Willy again shook his head, indignantly this time. He lowered his voice, as if confiding to Stephania a great secret. "It's the face that matters, the face only. Anyhow Fröken is going to take it off soon."

"Soon? After two years."

Willy's indignation turned into uttermost contempt. "Two years, so what? Fröken is young, young and pretty, so what's two

[ 93 ]

years? Just like two days. And then Fröken gets up and looks pretty, just right in every place."

"Let's hope so, Willy," Stephania said.

"Let's hope? What kind of talk is that again?" Willy moved still closer, looked at the plaster with eyes of a connoisseur, knocked on it with a bent finger. "Fine plaster, beautiful plaster. A little heavy, I should say, but the heavier it is the better." He lifted his hands, spread them out, and began to move them toward each other until they almost touched. "The heavier the better," he repeated. "It squeezes and squeezes, and puts everything in its place." The hands clasped noisily, "Just like that. One day you wake up and everything's gone. Nothing left."

"Sure." Stephania nodded and without even knowing why she added, "Tell it to the doctor, Willy."

"The doctor!" Willy curled his lips in scornful depreciation. "Doctors know nothing."

"Still, they take care of everything, don't they?" Stephania smiled.

Willy wrinkled his forehead into innumerable folds.

"They do," he hesitated, "in a way; but in a way they don't. Listen, Fröken Ackermann, I know this place. I was here when all those doctors didn't know how to cut their fingernails. So let Willy tell you, he may be just selling newspapers, still, he knows ... With doctors, is like with money. . . . You have no money, it's very bad, isn't it?"

"Yes, it is."

"But when you have money, even lots of it, and you don't know how to use it, it's even worse. You get nothing out of it. Right?"

"Right."

"So now, if you don't have a doctor, it's no good, you'll never get well. But if you've the greatest doctor in the whole world, and you don't know what to do with him, you'd better go home. No use staying here."

Stephania laughed. "But it's the doctor who tells you what to do, isn't it?"

"That's what *you* think. And it's wrong, all wrong. You," he poked his finger at Stephania, "better believe me," and he turned the finger at himself.

He stepped back a little, cleared his throat like an actor before a performance and began to walk across the room, first slowly, then faster and faster. Suddenly he stumbled. "That doesn't count," he said.

"What?"

"That I stumbled. Everybody can stumble sometimes. It happens. You just look at me." He made a few steps more. "You see how I walk?"

"Fine, really fine."

Willy came back to the bed, pulled up his trouser legs. "Now look," he said solemnly.

Stephania looked. From underneath the red and green checked socks the wooden legs emerged, painted shiny yellow, the knees gaping with metal screws.

"See?" Willy slapped a leg. "Wood, real wood," and he looked around challengingly as if only waiting for someone to deny it was real wood. "My best friends," he said; "wouldn't change them for anything in the world. One day Professor came to me — he likes me plenty, you know — 'Willy,' says he, 'we'll give you a new pair of legs, light aluminum.' 'Doctor,' say I — I always call him Doctor, I knew him when he was just beginning here, you see — 'Doctor,' say I, 'what shall I do with that shiny stuff, hang it on the Christmas tree? Wood for me, nothing but wood.'"

Stephania felt at a loss. One trouser leg was pulled up still, and the screws terrified her. "You certainly walk well on them," she said at last.

"Sure I do. And do you know what the doctor said when I first came here? He said, 'No walking for you, Willy,' and they wanted to give me a wheel chair, as a present, all gratis, mind you, and send me home. And I said to them, 'Thanks a lot, just find me a nice pretty nurse to wheel me around and do a couple of other things for me, then I'll go.'" Willy swung to and fro and laughed. "They couldn't find one. You see, I wanted her gratis, too. So I said, 'You got to make me walk, Doctor.' And they did. But sure, it took time. Everything takes time." He stopped and looked to see if Stephania was listening. "You see, my legs, what was left of them, I mean, not terribly much either, wouldn't fit into my new legs. So they trimmed them. Cut a piece here, a piece there, until they got the right shape. Then they started giving me legs, all kinds of them, with straps, with girdles — no good. The whole closet was full of them, so I said, 'You better take them and make a fire of them.' Until they figured out a pair that was just right.

And now I'm walking like anything. You see, that's how it is with doctors. You tell them what to do and they do it. Did you tell yours what to do?"

"I did," Stephania said. She stopped. "I guess so."

"Good girl." Willy slapped her on the plaster. "So what is there to worry about? Nothing at all." He looked at her again. "You're pretty, you know. Did I tell you that?"

"Yes, you did. Thanks anyway, Willy."

Fru Gustavsson came in, a bedpan in her hand. It was Fröken Nilsson who had rung for it. "Now, you'd better go your way, Willy," she said. "They've been asking for you in Three and Four. What kind of a businessman are you, keeping all your customers waiting?"

"Everybody's always in a hurry in that place. What's the matter? An appointment with the king? The river's burning?" Willy limped away reluctantly.

"Oh, Fröken Nilsson," he remembered, "a magazine for you, a nice little candy box?"

"No, nothing for me."

"Who wants nothing, gets nothing," Willy said sententiously. He opened the door and pushed the stand out. "Good-bye, Fröken Stephania. Good-bye." He hesitated, smiled, and said, "Yes, *auf Wiedersehen.*"

From that day on Willy stopped each morning at Stephania's bed for a chat. Smiling all over his face, clumsy, unfinished somehow, he would tell her of the time when he first came to the hospital — fifteen years ago: "Can you believe it?" he would say shaking his head. "The old Professor was still here; and what a man he was, what a man. . . . He knew more than all those new ones taken together." And then Willy would go on talking about the generations of nurses and patients he had seen in the hospital; he would show her the latest magazines and report about the dress Princess Sybilla had worn at the last court reception and what the old king had to say. . . . Stephania listened, nodding and smiling. Somehow it felt good to hear Willy's voice, very deep, then becoming higher and higher as his stories grew more exciting; it felt good to laugh again, not to look at the clock for a while. But as soon as Willy would leave, the silence would return, and she would reluctantly take a book or a paper and read, conscious all the time of the hostile glances, of the reproachful faces around her.

[ 96 ]

And so the days passed. September was over, October began, rainy and so cold that the windows were hardly ever open and the steam heat had to be turned on.

All that time, when Stephania was living between the window, the drive and her books, when summer had slowly turned into fall, and fall was turning into winter, Fröken Nilsson was persistently and stubbornly building a life of her own, a life completely independent from Room Number Five. Her day was now subjected to a rigid schedule. She was hardly ever in the room now. As soon as the doctor's visit was over she set out on her daily pilgrimages from one room in the ward to another. A proud and determined expatriate she sat in her wheel chair, the red gown pulled tightly over her body, a magazine on one side and the knitting bag on the other. The reasons for that voluntary exile were known to all. "Poor Fröken Nilsson," the patients nodded sympathetically, and invited her to stay with them a little longer. "Why should you hurry?" they pleaded, and discreetly gave her to understand that although they were much too tactful to ask any questions, still, confessions were more than welcome. But no confessions ever took place; as for Stephania, so also for Fröken Nilsson the whole affair was forgotten, for ever after.

These wanderings from room to room were not the only change in Fröken Nilsson's life. There was still another, a revolutionary change, far more important, one might say, a change about which Doctor Ström remarked that "he could hardly trust his eyes," and the Professor, that "in his old age he was starting to believe in miracles." For, after two years of resistance, at the moment when everybody had given up all hope, Fröken Nilsson, of her own will, went on a diet. And what a diet! "No, thanks, no bread for me, no cereal, of course not," she would say to Fru Gustavsson now, and to the patients who generously opened their cookie boxes for her, "Thanks, I don't want any; no, not an apple either. I never eat between meals."

At lunches, at dinners — she ate mostly in the living room now — Fröken Nilsson would push away the potatoes, offer her dessert to her neighbor, and scrape all the gravy from the meat. Her table companions were horrified. "You will starve yourself to death; nobody can live on a diet like that," they remonstrated. But Fröken Nilsson would only lift her scant eyebrows as if saying, Oh, that's what *you* think, and she would explain modestly, "I'm not hungry, I've never eaten much." And she would blush with pleasure under their admiring glances.

The climax came when Fröken Nilsson refused to take sugar in her coffee — cream had been banned long before. From now on she sipped it black, bitter. The coffee tasted terrible and Fröken Nilsson hated it. Still she would never pass up an opportunity of having a cup or two. The bitterness gave her an exciting and warm feeling of sacrifice.

The sacrifice was rewarded every week on Mondays, when Fru Gustavsson took Fröken Nilsson to weigh her. The scale was especially contrived so that the patient would not have to stand and Fröken Nilsson with the help of Fru Gustavsson and the attendant was put on it. A moment of suspense — Fröken Nilsson sat, blushing and breathless, until at last with feigned indifference she would ask, "So . . . how much is it this week?" Fru Gustavsson would look once more at the scale, bending her head backward, and count in a whisper: "A hundred and eighty-four, minus seven for the plaster, that makes a hundred and seventy-seven; last week it was a hundred and eighty-one. Four pounds less," she would say triumphantly. "Four pounds!" and clapping her hands: "That's magnificent, that's incredible." But Fröken Nilsson only shrugged, as if saying: Four pounds, that's nothing, a trifle. And there was in her face all the pride, all the humility of a victorious martyr.

And on Monday evenings when she was back in her room, she would ask once more how much it was that week and repeat the question twice just to be sure that the others had heard the news. For even if Stephania and that ungrateful brat Thura did not exist for her — she did not mind their knowing. After all, why not?

Together with the diet a series of other events took place. One day, a towel, bobby pins and shampoo bottle in her hands, Fröken Nilsson set out to the bathroom, and there all by herself, sitting in her wheel chair ("It takes an acrobat to do it!" Fru Gustavsson commented), she washed her hair, and set it carefully. No more pieces of stringy white tape for Fröken Nilsson, but bobby-pin curls every night, shampooing every week. . . . Her hair looked soft and light now. Doctor Liliencrona noticed it at once and said, "Your new hairdo is exceedingly becoming, Fröken Nilsson."

A day or two after that remark Fröken Nilsson stopped Fru

Gustavsson in the hall and asked her in a whisper to buy her two jars of face cream, one for the day and one for the night.

"The least expensive I can get?" Fru Gustavsson asked. She always said "the least expensive," it sounded so much nicer than "cheapest."

"No, the best you can get, the very best," Fröken Nilsson answered.

Cold cream in the evening, vanishing cream in the morning, new lipstick, matching fingernail polish — the battery of bottles and boxes on Fröken Nilsson's table increased steadily. And each morning she looked in the mirror. The wrinkles were disappearing; yes, she was sure of it, they had never been there. She just had been tired, that was all. She was not old yet; not she.

Busy as she was with her diet, her visits, and her pursuit of Doctor Liliencrona, Fröken Nilsson was hardly aware of what was happening in her room. Only in the evening when she came back the silence would burst into her face like a gust of cold air through the suddenly opened door, and she would feel strange and go to sleep very fast.

Between those two, Stephania busy with her books, always turned to the window, and Fröken Nilsson coming to the room as one does to an indifferent hotel suite, Thura lived lonely and bewildered, suspended in a precarious neutrality. She could not get used to the silence; she still heard in it the words that had fallen on that dreadful day, words she could not understand which kept forcing themselves upon her. Was Fröken Nilsson really old and ugly? She had not noticed it before. And even if she was, it wasn't her fault, after all. Why should Stephania say anything like that, then? And whose money was Fröken Nilsson talking of? "Ours," she said; did she mean hers too? But she did not have any money — perhaps in Eskilstuna, but that had been so long ago.

Still, Thura would never condemn Fröken Nilsson or Stephania. Thura knew it had all been her fault. Had she not blushed so stupidly, had she explained everything to Fröken Nilsson, nothing would have happened. Even later when it all started she could have said something. But she of course had lost her head. Anyway it was too late.

For what could she do now? Stephania seemed to be miles away; Thura could never bring herself to say a word to her. And how could she ever say a word to Fröken Nilsson without making Stephania think at once that she was on Fröken Nilsson's side? One thing seemed more difficult than another.

And the silence was growing more and more unbearable. Nothing to wait for, no hope that Fröken Nilsson would tell her about the Eskilstuna days, about her meeting with Doctor Lilencrona. The books on her table were never opened now, there was no one to turn the pages for her. And sometimes when the day dragged endlessly, when there was no hope that Fru Gustavsson — the only one to whom she could talk now — would come in soon, Thura would think longingly of the days when Fru Hernruth had still been with them. They used to sing every evening then, about Varmland, the beautiful land, about the Swedish flag, yellow and blue. And unexpected things happened every day, every moment almost. Fru Hernruth would read them her letters, about Karin, her daughter, who knew how to make fudge although she was not more than seven, and little Lasse, and how he refused to go to the dentist. And she would show them their pictures and the pictures of the home she lived in in Göteborg. They drank coffee almost every evening then, and they always took double servings of dessert and later smuggled it to Fröken Nilsson. Yes, those were good days, and sometimes Thura wished that someone else, even though she were less strange and fascinating than Stephania, had taken Fru Hernruth's place, someone like Fröken Brickman from Three, perhaps, who solved cross-word puzzles and knew everything about the family of the old king.

But whenever Thura caught herself with a thought like that, she would blush and glance terrified at Stephania's bed. For to think like that was treason, and Thura felt Stephania knew it, and that, perhaps, was why she never would speak to her. The more Thura thought about it the more guilty she felt, and the stronger was her decision to do something. She just had to explain to Stephania that Fröken Nilsson really did not mean anything, that she simply was nervous because her leg would not heal and she had to stay in the hospital so long. But how could she begin; how could she say it? Something had to happen to help her. Thura waited for it — for a miracle.

Once, she remembered — it was right after her operation, Fru Hernruth was very sick, and Axel, her husband, sat next to her bed holding her hand, and repeated, "Just tell me what you want,

Ingrid, and I'll do anything for you, anything. . . ." Perhaps if she got very sick, too, they all, Fru Gustavsson and Sister Gudrun, would come to her and promise her to do whatever she wanted. "Please tell Fröken Nilsson and Stephania to forget everything, to speak to each other again," she would ask them. And they wouldn't refuse her, not when she was so sick.

But she felt fine and the physiotherapist was saying she was very satisfied with her.

Then with October a new and strong hope came to Thura. For on October twenty-second was her birthday. Last year she had not told anybody about it, but Fru Hernruth had found out. And in the morning she was waked up by singing, by the light of candles. The candles burned on a huge birthday cake that Sister Gudrun was holding and they all stood around her bed; even Willy was there, and sang. Then Sister Gudrun kissed her, and Fru Hernruth handed her a little package, with a verse written on the wrapping, and a beautiful scarf inside. Later they all drank coffee and even Doctor Ström had a cup with them and ate two whole slices of cake.

Thura knew that a day like that could not be forgotten. Someone would remember it. Then when they all would stand around her bed, and the lights — sixteen this time — would flicker on the birthday cake, she would ask Stephania and Fröken Nilsson to listen to her and would explain everything to them. She had the whole speech carefully prepared and on the eve of her birthday could not close her eyes from excitement. Early in the morning she woke up and lay listening for the sound of many feet coming into the hall, for the door to open. Six — the clock struck. The hall was still quiet, empty. But of course, they would not make any noise. It had to be a surprise. At last the door opened. She closed her eyes, pretending to be asleep, so they would not guess she expected anything. But the room was very quiet still. "Thermometer, Thura." She opened her eyes. Sister Ingeborg, pale, the cap sliding to one side of her head, stood at her bed. "Yes," she said, put the thermometer under her arm, and closed her eyes again. Perhaps they were late — perhaps they would come still. But the day moved on like every other day. Nothing was said. They had forgotten. Only at noon Fru Gustavsson came with a big package. It was from home.

"How heavy," Fru Gustavsson said. "What's the occasion?"

"Nothing. Just . . . you know."

Fru Gustavsson opened the package. A pink bed jacket was inside and lots of cookies. Thura hesitated, looked around trying not to stare at anybody in particular, but at the whole room at once, and said, "Would you please . . ." She hesitated; what should be the order, Stephania first, or Fröken Nilsson . . .? "Would you please ask everyone to take some, take a lot. They are good, homemade."

Fru Gustavsson offered the cookies. "No," Fröken Nilsson said, "I don't eat any sweets."

"Thanks," Stephania said, "I'm not hungry."

Fru Gustavsson returned. "But they are homemade," Thura repeated. She looked at the untouched box. "Please, take them all, Fru Gustavsson," she said, "I don't want any, I . . ."

Fru Gustavsson took the box and left shaking her head silently.

And Thura read the letter from home, propped upon a book before her: "Dear Thura, Happy birthday to you. Here is a little gift for you and some cookies Mother baked so that you could invite your roommates for a little party. We hope . . ."

Oh, she thought — what can I do now, what can I do?

CHAPTER 10

WHEN THEY ROLLED the stretcher in she lifted her hand to her eyes and blinked. For the room was all white, the walls, the table, and even the floor covered with white paper, heaps of plaster scattered all over. It looked like a milk-bar that was next to her boardinghouse, just as shiny, with white varnished tables, and the white counter under which lay the big hearts of cream cheese. And even the nurse reminded her of the waitress there; white, full-breasted and rosy-cheeked.

"Put the stretcher here, right next to the table," the nurse said to the attendant. He pushed the stretcher and left. "The doctor will be here in a few minutes," the nurse said, and she left too; Stephania was left alone amid all that whiteness. She was used

[ 102 ]

to it now. She lay with her arms under her head and looked around.

It was the same room in which she had got her cast. She recognized the table and the lamp, just a huge bluish plate of notched glass fastened directly to the ceiling. But the rest of the room was unfamiliar. In the daze of morphine she must have not even noticed it. She looked now at the row of plaster forms under the window — molds of legs were there, some long and shapely, some thin set and clumsy; torsos of women with heavy balls of protruding breasts, and of men, some with tired bent lines of the back, some straight and square-shouldered. A part of those for whom the casts had been made seemed to have been left here in the white plaster, in the unique shapes of their bodies. A ray of sun, red, filtered through the thick ivy around the window, fell upon them, for a moment gave them a semblance of life, and then wandered farther to the big glass closets and lit a sharp glitter in the steel instruments.

So that was the room. She lay quietly listening to the silence. It was a different silence from that in her room, not filled with watching eyes, with listening ears. It was good and peaceful, and being alone was good too, really alone after two months.

Two months already — it was hard to believe it. Only that morning when Sister Gudrun said, "Fröken Ackermann needs a new chart," she had suddenly realized how long she had been here. And this time Sister Gudrun did not have to ask any questions; she filled the chart silently — name, age, place of birth. Stephania felt solemn when she watched her covering the chart with the big printed letters; it was like coming for the second time to the hospital, but now with two months behind you. Two months — it was a round, a tangible unit; you could divide the year and say one-sixth of the time had passed before the operation, or, only ten months are left. It was a measure, a standard, it made the time seem to pass faster. She felt strangely happy that morning.

Later when Ström came, she silently pointed to the new chart. He did not know what she meant. "After two months," she reminded him, "you promised to tighten the cast. Do you remember?"

Yes, he remembered and told Sister Gudrun to send her downstairs after his visit was over.

"Admiring our studio?" That was Ström. He came toward her stumbling over his rubber apron that was much too long for him. "So we're going to tighten it."

"Yes, the historic moment, Doctor."

He took off his glasses, and his eyes, vague and absent without them, made his face blurred and elusive.

The nurse came and lifted Stephania from the stretcher, set her on the floor, and stood supporting her with her arms.

Ström knelt down, looked for a while, then his hands began to move, turning the two protruding screws.

— And suddenly she felt two walls pushing at her, pressing, thick, massive walls that crushed her whole body.

"Hurts?" Ström asked.

"No, not at all. " The walls were coming closer and closer. They were rough, warped, not walls but rocks, sharp, boring into the flesh. Now, she thought, the pain growing but immediately transformed into joy, now he was doing it, now he was squeezing it, forcing it inside deeper and deeper. She felt the protruding bones receding in panic, seeking refuge some place inside, flattened, crushed. Like a bug under a shoe, like a bug.

"Are you sure it doesn't hurt?"

She clenched her teeth. "Yes," she said, "quite sure." The more it hurt the better, the faster it would go. What had Willy said — they will squeeze it, and squeeze it. Yes, now it came.

"Doctor, she's as white as chalk." That was the nurse.

They lifted her back onto the stretcher. She lay breathing slowly, cautiously, sneaking each breath out of the mass that was towering upon her. The attendant began to roll the stretcher. As they passed the door she raised her head and said, "Thank you very much, Doctor."

The rest of the day passed in a dreamy daze. The pressure was still there, like the cylinders of a steam roller; it rolled to and fro upon her body. From time to time it receded for a moment and then she would try to think, to call someone, to tell Ström. No, then he wouldn't do it again. This was the way it had to be, it was right. And again she would imagine her body flattened, remolded, forced back into its true shape.

The night came. Rooms, halls, the whole building was dark, silent.

[ 104 ]

— Pain is like a voice. During the day it is swallowed by other voices, it dissolves in the sound of steps, its sharpness merges with the insistent ringing of bells. But in the night all other voices disappear, only the pain remains, grows louder and louder within you.

Tossing from side to side, she tried to escape it, to force it to silence. But the pain was stronger than she, and at last she gave in, and lay motionless waiting for sleep.

Something was pounding in her head; no, it was high above her and then came lower and lower. "They're coming," someone cried next to her, or was it she perhaps? She stood on a street that was all empty, only a shadow was there, the shadow of an immense wall, oblique, sharp-edged, slowly coming closer and closer to her. And then, just when it was next to her, she saw it was not a shadow, it was the wall, ready to tumble down on her — the wall, the house, the whole block of buildings; stones, bricks, huge lumps. . . . It was coming, she felt it . . . right here. . . .

She was lying on the edge of her bed, her hand almost touching the floor, the blankets and pillow sliding down. What time was it? Not even twelve. Wait until the morning? No, she could not. It probably had to hurt like that. Ström would understand. Perhaps he even had told the nurse that she might have pains. Still she hesitated. But the cylinders were implacable rolling to and fro; no, she could not wait. Her hand reached for the bell.

Sister Ingeborg came in.

"My cast was tightened today, Sister. It hurts . . . horribly. I need a *Spritze,* an injection."

This time Sister Ingeborg did not protest. Stephania heard her plush slippers moving swiftly through the hall, like feet through snow.

So Ström told her. Of course he had. He was a decent fellow after all. The anticipation of morphine made her forget the pain.

"Shall I do it in the arm?" Sister Ingeborg was standing at the bed.

"Yes."

The syringe, cold, smooth, touched her arm, the needle gliding softly into the flesh.

"Did it hurt?"

"No." She wanted to be left alone.

"Good night. I hope Fröken feels better soon."

"Thanks."

It had not hurt, not when she made the injection. But now, all of a sudden she felt it, not the pricking of the needle, but something else, a center of dumb pain swelling slowly in her arm. It must be the morphine; strange . . . it seemed like a lump, hard and heavy. After a while the lump began to dissolve; in thin streams it penetrated her body, but still separate, still reluctant to join with the blood. And the pressure, that other pain which she had forgotten for a while, did not disappear; it was stronger than ever, it was increased by the pain brought by the injection. With impatience that soon changed into anguished unrest she waited for the familiar warmth, for the lightness. But her head was heavy, her feet cold. She closed her eyes trying to recall before them the picture of Sister Ingeborg, of the syringe in her hand. Was it full? Yes, she was sure it was, and the fluid in it looked quite like morphine, colorless, transparent.

Still she felt nothing, nothing but pain.

A feeling of being deceived, robbed of something, overwhelmed her. The old scarecrow, she must have mixed it up, given her some other stuff.

She rang, but no one came in. Once more. And now she lay back, her finger pressing the button, and waited.

At last Sister Ingeborg popped into the room.

"Sister, I don't feel anything." Stephania did not even bother to whisper.

"No pains?" the nurse said. "That's fine, my dear."

"Don't 'my dear' me," she said furiously. "I mean I don't feel the morphine. I do feel the pain, don't worry about that."

The head in the door disappeared almost. "Do you want a pill?"

"How can a pill be any good if the morphine was not? Come closer, Sister. I don't want to wake up everybody."

Slowly the nurse crossed the room. "Yes?"

"Are you sure you gave me morphine?"

"What else then?"

"How can I tell? You must have mixed something up. Didn't you give me penicillin instead?"

"I never mix up anything." Sister Ingeborg's whisper grew shrill with hurt pride. "I gave you exactly what the doctor told me to. Good night."

The nurse left. For many hours Stephania lay awake, until at last, tired with pain, she fell into uneasy half-sleep.

"Did you get anything last night, Fröken Ackermann?" Sister Gudrun asked in the morning. She was marking the medicines on the charts.

"Yes, something. God only knows what it was."

"What do you mean, my dear?" Sister Gudrun was in a good mood that day. The caressing words didn't suit her thin, pale lips. To Stephania it sounded like the grating of metal on glass.

"I mean the injection. It helped like holy water on a corpse. The nurse must have been half asleep when she gave it to me."

"Nobody is half asleep when she is on duty here." Sister Gudrun was back in her proper role, the rigidity of her lips reinforced by the severe sound of her words.

"I guess so." Stephania was too tired to argue. Lazily she watched the red pencil moving upon the chart. A-Q? A-Q-U-A D-I-S-T-I-L-L-A-T-A? *Aqua distillata* — so that was what they gave her. "Sister." But Sister Gudrun was at the door already.

*Aqua distillata.* Pure water; so that was what they were giving her. Anger made her forget her pain. *Aqua distillata,* she repeated, as if afraid to forget those words. All right, now she knew it all.

And at last Ström was here . . . with that punctiliously friendly smile on his face. "Good morning."

She did not answer, her eyes fixed upon the chart to assure herself that the words were still there. Patiently she waited until he finished talking to Fröken Nilsson, to Thura. Now he was coming to her bed.

"Fröken Ackermann feeling fine?"

"No, I'm not feeling fine."

"What's the matter?"

"I had pain all night." She turned to Sister Gudrun. "Did I tell you so, Sister?"

"You did."

"Before you had put *that* on the chart?"

"I . . . I guess so."

"Now." Stephania sat up. She began to speak slowly, carefully. "Let's get it all cleared up, Doctor, once and for all. You're not going to treat me like a half-wit, I'm not one. You should know that at least by now. I called the nurse last night and asked for an injection. She was too nice about it; I smelled something was wrong underneath. Sure enough, she came running with the syringe, but what was in it . . .?" She raised her hand and pointed to the red words on the chart. "Can you read it, Doctor? I hope you understand Latin, as much as your patients at least."

Ström remained silent. He looked at the chart, then at her, then at the chart again.

"Well?"

No answer. She felt like getting up, like shaking him with both hands until that indifferent politeness would vanish from his face.

"It's not an amusement park," she said in a choked voice. "I didn't come here to be amused or to amuse anybody else."

"After my visit's over bring Fröken Ackermann down to the plaster room." That was all Ström said and he left.

And so she was back in the white room with the shapes of the bodies in a long line under the window. But this time she did not have to wait; Ström himself opened the door. He must have been expecting her.

He was without his coat, just the white shirt and the linen pants. That informality made her feel suddenly lost, helpless. "Well, it's your turn to talk, Doctor," she said at last.

"Do you have pain still?"

She nodded. The nurse came in. Again she stood on the floor, again Ström knelt down and manipulated the iron screws sticking out of the cast. With unspeakable relief she felt the walls receding slowly; now there was space around her, now she could breathe again. But what was happening to her body now? Was it all coming back, emerging from where it had been forced to hide yesterday? She was afraid to ask.

"Better?"

"Yes."

"I asked you yesterday if it hurt. You should have told me."

"I . . . I thought it should be that way."

"Should . . . but not so much."

She felt tired, she longed to be back in her bed. Still, she could not give in so easily. "And what about that *aqua distillata*, Doctor? Are you short of morphine? Trying to save money on me?"

"Listen, Stephania, I told her to do it because I had to."

"You mean you really told her to give me water?"

"I had to; you know why."

"I know nothing."

"Did you really have pain the first time you asked for morphine then, after you had got the cast?"

"No," she said slowly, "I didn't. But who told you? That woman . . . that Nilsson of course."

"No one had to tell me. I knew it all the time. You couldn't have been in pain. You wanted morphine, that's all. And we cannot let you become a drug addict."

"So," she said slowly. "Now I see it . . . you were trying me out, is that it? Doctor Coué's method, autosuggestion? You gave me water, and I think it's morphine and then you can prove to me that it was all hysteria with me, what?"

"I had to do it, Stephania. It's better for you that way. I didn't think you'd really have pain."

Stephania. Only now she noticed that he had been calling her by her first name. There was something in his voice that made her feel warm and tired and very weak. Something was happening to her, melting inside; a grip had been loosened and now they were coming, all those words that had been stored in a heavy load within her. "Doctor," she said.

"Yes, Stephania."

"Do understand, Doctor. Don't refuse me morphine. I don't mean to have it every day, not every week even. Just once in a while, just when you tighten the cast, when it really hurts. I'm not going to become a drug addict. They gave it to me in Germany after an operation . . . once a week. And I didn't get used to it. I never get used to anything I don't want to. I know myself, Doctor. But give it to me sometimes. If you see I'm getting used to it, you can take it away. I give you the right to take it away. But . . ." She stopped, hesitated. "I," she said, and she was surprised at her own words, "I must have something to wait for. One must have something to wait for."

"I guess I do understand," Ström said slowly. "Everybody must have that, Stephania. But morphine — morphine is nothing to wait for."

"Why not, Doctor? At least when I get it, I stop thinking for a few hours. And I won't become a drug addict, you know that, never."

"I know, Stephania, but that is not the point. You stop thinking for a few hours, you said — a few hours and then what? Don't you see, it doesn't help? — morphine — it solves nothing. That's why I cannot give it to you, I mustn't let you wait for things that are not worth it. That, too, can become a habit, don't you see what I mean? You must find something else to wait for."

"Something else? Here?" She smiled.

"Yes . . ." He hesitated, said, "Do you have any visitors?"

"No. Why should I?"

"I hope you don't mind my talking about it. Sister Gudrun mentioned to me that you refused to see some friends of yours. Why, Stephania? Because it seems to me that . . ."

"That's something worth waiting for," she finished for him. "No, it is not, Doctor." Something in his face made her feel sorry for her sharpness. More softly she added, "I can't stand seeing those people, Doctor, I really cannot."

"I see. Well, let us wait until you start getting up, and then together we'll think of something."

"So you'll never give me morphine?" she said faintly.

"I'll give it to you if you *need* it, if we do something new, something that makes it necessary. Otherwise not."

She did not answer. Ström too was silent. She wondered why he did not call the attendant to take her back to the room. She felt numb with weariness.

"Stephania," he said at last, "I had to loosen the cast."

"I know. You must have tightened it a great deal yesterday."

"No." He looked her straight in the face. "Only a little, hardly anything."

"What?" she said. It was like the dream, like all those dreams she had had lately. She wanted to run away and could not; something horrible was happening and she stood and waited, her stomach suddenly huge and hollow, her feet cold, and she was sinking faster and faster. . . .

"We tightened it much less than we hoped to."

"But why?"

Ström only opened his arms.

"No," she said, "it's impossible. It was just the first time, it means nothing. Next time it will be different, you'll see."

"Let's hope," he said, and walked to the door.

The attendant came in. The stretcher began to roll. Halls, halls; she looked at them without recognizing anything. Now the elevator — why did they have to wait so long? — at last; and again halls; green, white, silent.

They were almost in the room when somebody cried, "Fröken Stephania, wait." She raised her head. Willy, what did he want now? The attendant stopped. Willy limped to them, his face beaming all over. "Coming back from a date with the doctor?"

She only nodded.

"Everything fine, of course?"

"No," she said sharply, "nothing is fine."

"What's wrong?"

"Everything. Things just aren't going right, that's all."

The attendant started to move.

"Wait, brother." Willy grasped him by the lapel of his coat. "I got to talk to Fröken Stephania. Things don't go right. They go slowly, you mean. And now you worry about that, what? So you think a man is like an alarm clock, you set it to wake you up at six, so sure enough, it rings at six. No, my dear. With man it is quite a different story. You say two months and it takes a year, you say a year and it may take two months. You can never tell with man. Man is not a clock. He's different."

"Perhaps, Willy."

"Not perhaps, sure. Wait, attendant. What's the rush? Got a date? She can wait. Listen, with man it's like with business, you can never tell what's going to happen. Look at me. Here I buy ten pounds of apples, red, sweet like honey, think I'll sell them, make lots of money, go to movies Sunday. So one customer gets an upset stomach, and another goes home, and the third says they're not good enough for him, and so I'm stuck with the apples; no money, no movies. So what do you think I do? I close my business? I give up? No, I forget the apples, try again. Buy bananas the next time . . . it goes fine. . . . So what's the hurry, brother?"

"We've got to move." The attendant pushed the stretcher so fast that Willy was soon left behind. "So good-bye, Fröken, and no worrying from now on."

Perhaps he was right, Willy . . . perhaps it just had to take time. . . . Who could tell? She was so tired that she hardly felt it when they lifted her from the stretcher and put her back to bed. Now she wanted to sleep, nothing but sleep.

[ 111 ]

CHAPTER II

IT SEEMED AS IF it had become the role of Room Number Five to be consistently in the limelight. For hardly had the whispers about the incident between Stephania and Fröken Nilsson ceased when something new happened, something that according to many was even more exciting. Because now not only patients but also the hospital staff were involved. And again no one knew exactly who was the culprit. Fru Gustavsson, upon whom the greatest suspicion fell, swore to the patients, to Doctor Ström, even to Professor himself, that she couldn't for her life understand how a thing like that could have happened on her side, to her patient, to one of whom she had been taking care for two years and although she admitted that it was a scandal and beyond belief, still she firmly maintained that it wasn't her fault. Sister Gudrun, whose prestige was indirectly involved, refrained from any statements; however, she told Doctor Ström vaguely, so vaguely that he could not understand what was on her mind, that things like that were bound to happen when there was no discipline, no distance between maids and nurses — a situation which certainly was no fault of hers. As to Thura, the heroine of the sad event which had thrown such a bad light on Ward Two — "a pigsty, not a hospital ward," Professor was reported to have murmured, she only said that it just happened, and that it wasn't anybody's fault, of course.

It began, as so many things in the hospital begin, in the night. Thura could not fall asleep. It happened often; Thura was already used to it. But that night seemed different from all other sleepless nights. It was not the darkness, not the blanket or the pillow which bothered her, it was her own body. A strange pain penetrated the back of her body, something sharp was boring a hole in the flesh slowly, persistently. It couldn't be anything much — Thura decided — she was just tired from lying in the same place. But in the morning the pain was still there and she had to ask Fru Gustavsson to prop her a little higher, to put the pillow deeper under her head. For a moment she felt better, but then the boring returned, and the point where her body leaned upon the mattress burned and throbbed. The next night she did not close her eyes, and so at last Thura decided to ask Fru Gustavsson what it could be. But the next day was Thursday, Fru Gustavsson's day off, and Thura could not bring herself to talk to Sister Gudrun. Then Friday came, the operation day; beds and stretchers rolled through the hall to and fro, like trains at a railway station. Thura felt she could not possibly bother Fru Gustavsson on a day like that. The week-end came, and most of the personnel was free but Fru Gustavsson hardly had time to come into the room. Finally on Monday morning when Fru Gustavsson was washing her, Thura said. "I feel so funny, somewhere in my back, Fru Gustavsson."

"In your back, little Thura?"

"Down below." Thura blushed. "It sort of burns."

"It cannot be anything too serious. Don't worry. We're changing the bed linen tomorrow so I'll turn you and have a look. All right?"

"All right." Thura agreed.

And suddenly a strange thing happend, so strange that for weeks after, Fru Gustavsson kept repeating: "I'm telling you she's not like everybody else. How could she know that? She's weird, weird is the only word for it."

For Stephania, yes, no one else but Stephania, sat up and said, "I don't think you should wait until tomorrow."

"What?" Even Fröken Nilsson forgot herself so much that she looked at Stephania.

"I don't think you should wait," Stephania repeated quietly. "She has a bedsore. Anybody can see that."

"A bedsore?" Fru Gustavsson dropped Thura's hand into the basin and water splashed all around noisily. "No one gets bedsores here. Not on my side at least."

"Perhaps." Stephania shrugged and she began to paint her lips.

Fru Gustavsson went on washing Thura. But she seemed absentminded and her eyes looked again and again at Stephania. "Does it still hurt?" she asked Thura at last.

"Sort of."

The washing was over. According to the usual schedule Fru Gustavsson had to start making beds now. But instead she walked out, and after a while returned with the attendant. "We shall turn little Thura," she said.

[ 113 ]

The attendant grabbed Thura under the arms, Fru Gustavsson lifted the legs. "One . . . two . . . here we go!" — and now Thura was lying on her stomach.

Fru Gustavsson bent over the bed, lifted Thura's shirt, and bent a little lower still. Suddenly she stepped back, her hand hit the basin on the table. A stream of water splashed down. She raised her hand, passed it over her eyes. "I . . . " she murmured, "I just can't understand it . . . how . . . in the world?"

"Anything wrong, Fru Gustavsson?"

"Nothing, dear, nothing. Don't worry. We shall wash it and put some ointment on it. It's a bedsore, a small one only." And suddenly she turned and looked at Stephania.

Stephania slowly put away the mirror and the lipstick. "You'd better show it to the doctor," she said.

"Yes," Fru Gustavsson said obediently and it sounded as if she were talking not to Stephania but to Sister Gudrun or to Doctor Ström himself.

And just at that moment Sister Gudrun, of all people, had to walk in. "So how are . . . " she began, and stopped, looking at the blankets spread on the chair, at the pool of water on the floor, at Thura lying on her stomach. "What's going on here?" she asked and without waiting for an answer crossed the room.

Fru Gustavsson moved back to make place for her. Thura, unable to see anything but a small square of the floor and the feet on it, felt something dreadful coming. "Nothing," she murmured, but the pillow choked the sound of her words.

No one heard her. The room was silent. Only the water kept dropping from the table on the floor. . . .

As if from afar Thura heard Fru Gustavsson saying at last: "I don't know myself how it could have happened." Then the coat of Sister Gudrun rustled. Hard cold fingers touched her body. She waited for Sister Gudrun to say something. But no sound came.

For all of them, Sister Gudrun and Fru Gustavsson, Stephania and Fröken Nilsson from their beds, were looking at Thura. Her body, so thin that the ribs cut into the brownish skin, looked very small in the much too large bed. And right above the muscleless buttocks the skin was reddened and peeled off until naked flesh rose in sharp protruding edges and in a warped wall surrounded a large circle covered with a thick film of green and yellow pus.

"So," Thura heard Sister Gudrun saying at last. "How do you like *that?*" and then, "Thura!"

"Yes, Sister Gudrun," she whispered, her eyes fixed desperately upon the cords of thick veins protruding underneath white stockings on Sister Gudrun's legs. She wished she could see her face now. Was it pale, almost blue, as it always was when she was angry?

"Did Fru Gustavsson change your bed last Tuesday?"

Thura hesitated. Last Tuesday? . . . Tuesday was the day when in the morning Fru Gustavsson came in with a pile of linen in her hands, and she only straightened the blankets so that Sister Gudrun would not get mad. And later during the day she and the attendant would turn her, and Fru Gustavsson would wash her whole body, powder it and change the linen. It was a great day, Tuesday, it was so good to feel all clean and fragrant with talc, and the new sheets were smooth and cold.

But last Tuesday, Thura remembered, was one of those days on which everything goes wrong. There were three newly operated patients — three "backs," of course, for backs, which gave the greatest trouble, were always sent to Fru Gustavsson's side. And just when Fru Gustavsson wanted to go out for the sheets she had forgotten to bring before, one of the "backs" rang and she had to rush there. Later another "back" spilled a whole basin of water into her bed, and then it was lunchtime. After that Thura decided it would not be right to remind Fru Gustavsson about the bed; she could skip that Tuesday.

"Did she change your bed and turn you?"

"Of course I did," Fru Gustavsson said.

"I'm asking Thura."

"She did" — it was horrible to lie, Thura knew it, but what else could she do?

"Did you make yourself wet?"

Again she did not answer. There were those two nights in the beginning of last week when Sister Ingeborg was off and another nurse came instead. Something went wrong with the bedpan then and she did not want to ring. The nurse was so clumsy and it hurt when she lifted her.

"Did you?"

"I don't remember . . . I guess not."

"Miracles," Sister Gudrun said. "Plain miracles. Everything is in best order, and here she is lying with a bedsore to the bone. But," the pause made Thura shiver, "but that was only to be expected. That's what happens when maids" — maids, she said; did she mean Fru Gustavsson? — "do too much talking and no work. Yes, it's easy to be well liked, my dear Fru Gustavsson, when you just smuggle coffee to the patients. But sometimes one has to take care of them too."

And again a pause.

"But now it's going to change." The voice was so hard, it hurt to listen to it. If she could only see Fru Gustavsson's face, red, crimson almost, and the neck above the white coat was red too. And again it was her fault. Thura said faintly, "It doesn't hurt much, Sister Gudrun, it really doesn't."

But Sister Gudrun said only: "Cover her up. You don't want her to catch pneumonia on top of everything."

At last Sister Gudrun walked out, but she left the door open as if to show that from now on she was going to keep her eye on everything. After a while she came back with a clean shirt in her hand. A clean shirt before Tuesday was given only to patients on the "great day." Thura felt proud and a little scared of that distinction. Sister Gudrun herself took the dirty shirt off. There was a big spot on its bottom — green and sticky. "What's that, Sister?" she asked.

"Pus."

Pus! Only those who had an infection after an operation had pus. "Oh," she gasped, "I see."

"Don't worry, I'll take care of it. You'll be all right." There was something very reassuring about Sister Gudrun's voice. For the first time Thura felt grateful to her.

It was an unusual day, that Monday, the first Monday in November. It looked as if a new patient had come to Room Two, or as if a "great day" were taking place. For after breakfast Sister Gudrun came in with the dressing table and put some ointment on the wound; it was penicillin, she said — and she even stroked Thura's hair. Then Doctor Ström came right to her bed, nodded angrily and sent Sister Gudrun for stretchers and for a water pillow. "You have to lie on something soft," he explained and watched while they put Thura on the stretcher, checking to see if the pillow was of the right size and thick enough.

"Is there anything you want, Thura?" he asked before he left.

No, Thura wanted to answer, but suddenly something occurred to her. The stretcher was standing next to the window, next to

[ 116 ]

Stephania's bed. "Could I stay here for a little while?" she asked. "I want to look through the window."

"Sure, little Thura," and he himself pushed the stretcher next to Stephania's bed. He was already at the door when suddenly he stopped. "Would you like to lie next to the window?" he asked.

"Well . . ." Thura said, and looked uncertainly at Stephania.

"Fröken Lungron from Four is leaving. There is going to be a free bed, right under the window."

A bed under the window, and Room Four, the room where Fröken Sunquist who solved crossword puzzles was. . . . Thura looked at Stephania, then at Fröken Nilsson. "Thank you, Doctor," she said, "I guess I'd rather stay here."

"All right," Doctor Ström said, and he left.

But hardly had the door closed after him than patients from other rooms came in. The news about the sensation in Room Two had spread immediately all over the ward. Now one after another they came in, many Thura had never seen before, asked her cautious, roundabout questions, and unable to learn anything left, saying "Don't worry dear, it will soon be all right!" Those who could not come sent her fruit and cookies through Fru Gustavsson. Even Willy dropped in, slapped Thura on the buttocks, and just to shock Sister Gudrun said, "A trifle, a bedsore, nothing but a trifle. You'll not feel it on your wedding night, Willy promises you that."

At last all the visitors left and now everything was quiet. Thura was tired, and worried about Fru Gustavsson, but somehow in a strange way she felt happy. It was funny to lie on your stomach; the whole room seemed different suddenly. New, unknown vistas had opened before her — the floor, the legs of beds and chairs looking now very big and thick, and the brass coverings on them that threw red quivering reflections upon the shiny linoleum. And the whole day was so different; yes, it was almost like the "great day," without morphine, of course, without waiting for the phone bell to ring outside, but still the clean shirt was here, and the stretcher, too.

Fröken Nilsson, who because of all the excitement had stayed longer in her bed than usual, left at last. And now they were alone, she and Stephania face to face with each other. Now the moment had come, now she could talk to her, ask her. Yes, ask her; but how? She looked: Stephania was reading the paper, her face hidden behind it. Would she get angry if she interrupted her? And how should she begin? — Excuse me, Fröken Ackermann, or Stephania, perhaps Ackermann would be better. I just wanted . . . wanted . . . She had been thinking of those words for months and now they had escaped her, hidden themselves somewhere. What if she got stuck in the middle?

The long white hand with the very red fingernails was slowly turning the pages of the paper. Thura looked at the clock. It was almost twelve. In one hour they would come with lunch. She had only one hour. Now.

She cleared her throat, but her voice remained hoarse. "Fröken Ackermann . . ."

The paper rustled. "Yes?"

No, she could not say it. "I wanted to thank you for telling Fru Gustavsson."

"It's all right." The pale red-lipped face disappeared behind the paper.

"And Fröken . . . Fröken Stephania . . ."

"Yes, Thura."

"I," she said desperately, "I hope you'll not be angry, but really I have to. You see it's about Fröken Nilsson . . ."

"What about her?"

"I mean, when she said that dreadful thing" — the words came easier now — "she didn't mean it really. I know it. She's just nervous you see . . . her leg doesn't heal, you see?"

Stephania said nothing.

"Oh, if you just could forget it, say something to her . . ."

Stephania pushed the paper away. "I'm not interested in Fröken Nilsson," she said. No, she thought, she did not feel like being dragged into that whole mess again. But it served her right. That came from putting your nose into other people's business. One day wouldn't have made a bit of difference. She didn't have to say anything to Fru Gustavsson. "Absolutely not interested," she repeated, and picked up her paper.

Thura did not answer. There was nothing more to be said. It was all wrong; she should have first spoken to Fröken Nilsson. Or perhaps she should have started differently. Thura sighed. She never had been good at talking.

Still she did not take her eyes off Stephania. For there was still something she wanted to ask Stephania, something she had been

[ 118 ]

thinking of from the time of Stephania's "great day." Should she try now? Stephania put away her paper. Thura looked at her. There were spots of gravy and juice on her sheets, on her gown, exactly like those on her own bed. That somehow made everything easier suddenly, "Fröken Ackermann!"

"If it's about Fröken Nilsson I don't want to hear."

"No, it's about me, me and the night . . . when, you remember . . ."

"What night?"

"After the 'great day,' when you had pains, many pains . . . when you got morphine." Those words brought back the blue light, Sister Ingeborg, the sleepy soft voice, saying "It's like flying . . ."

"You remember you said then, it was almost at the end, 'If the operation fails, if I stay as I am now, or paralyzed'; 'paralyzed,' you said, 'then I'll have to do it . . .' to kill yourself, that was what you said. Do you remember?"

"Yes . . . I do . . ."

"You see . . . I don't know quite how to explain it, but I thought like that — if you wouldn't want to live paralyzed, and now I'm paralyzed, so perhaps . . . do you see what I mean?"

"No."

"Perhaps I shouldn't either, you see."

"Where did you get that idea from? I was talking about myself, don't you understand? about myself and no one else."

"I do. But that's just it. If you were like me, if you were me . . . if you couldn't move yourself at all as I can't, then perhaps . . ."

Stephania listened. But it was not what she was saying that forced her to look into Thura's face, that small pointed face with much too large eyes, it was only that 'you' and 'me' coming slowly, separately from Thura's lips. Those words called for the emphasizing gesture of a hand, 'you,' and the hand pointing at her; 'me,' turning back to Thura. But the hands, limp and motionless, were lying on the stretcher. She felt them struggling, trying desperately and always in vain to overcome their helplessness; thin, withered hands. And only silence was left, as if something remained unsaid.

"Do you understand?" Thura said.

"No, not quite, would you repeat it?"

[ 119 ]

Thura did.

Stephania listened. Now she understood. That was ridiculous. Here that kid was repeating like a parrot things that had nothing to do with her, and trying to make them mean something they did not mean, trying to force her to say something she did not want to say. "Listen here. You are you and I am I," and now at last the gesture of her own hands, spacious, liberating. "We're different. What's right for me doesn't have to be right for you."

"Different?" Thura repeated. "Why?" A desperate courage seized her; she had to find out now; perhaps never again could she do it. "You said if you were paralyzed . . . and I'm paralyzed, so . . . ?"

"I don't mean that." Stephania moved closer to the stretcher; what did she want from her today? First she tried to reconcile her with that Nilsson woman. And now that story. She had to make an end of it, and fast, too. "Listen, Thura," she said severely, "what are you driving at? I said I wouldn't live paralyzed. That's right. But I was talking about myself; how many times do I have to tell you that? And you . . . you were perfectly satisfied before you heard me saying that, weren't you?" she said almost maliciously. "I heard you always saying to . . . to that Nilsson what a good time you had when Fru Hernruth was here, talking and singing and God knows what else. You never thought of a thing like that, so why start now all of a sudden, just because I said something?"

"It wasn't all of a sudden. I thought of that, not quite in the same way, but still . . . I remember one day a girl from my class in high school came to see me, and she was so terribly grown-up, with high heels and lipstick. . . . And she talked about boys I didn't know and how she wanted to get engaged soon. Then when she had left I sort of wondered how it would be when I come back to Oestrsund — that's the town I'm from, you see — and everybody's different, and I don't know anyone. . . . Later Father got sick and again I started thinking what would happen when they die, both he and Mother, and I would be all alone, you know. . . ." Thura stopped. She seemed to be listening to something. "Sometimes I'm scared, very scared," she said at last.

"You mean," Stephania said, and there was a startled horror in her voice, "you mean you've been thinking about that all the time?"

"Not always. But again and again, in the night when I can't sleep . . . or it just comes of itself. And then you said it, and I thought, Perhaps Fröken Ackermann is right. That's why I wanted to ask you what you really think about all that."

Here it was again, what she thought. . . . No, it was all nonsense. "Come on," Stephania said, "you perhaps felt like that sometimes when you were tired, in a bad mood, but never really. Just try not to think about it."

Not to think . . . she tried, but it always would come back. She had to figure it all out somehow. And here Stephania wouldn't tell her. And she knew, she had it all figured out. Thura lifted her head from the pillow. She hesitated. "Sometimes," she said at last, "I feel like that. You said that your sister would give it to you in case . . . with . . . I forgot how you called it . . ."

"Cyanide?"

"Yes. So, I thought, if I were as I am now, paralyzed I mean, and you were my sister, would you give it to me?"

If she, Thura, were paralyzed and she herself were her sister, like Barbara, would she do it? She sat staring blankly at the naked wall. And suddenly she, Barbara, walking in, her bag, that one of brown alligator Thadeus had given her, in her hand. She saw her walking toward Thura's bed, opening the bag, the small white package . . .

Would she do it? Barbara disappeared; there was only Thura on her bed, and then the fat attendant dragging her by her legs — no, what nonsense, they did not drag you out like that, not *here,* they brought in the stretcher . . .

"No," she said, "I wouldn't do it."

"But if I couldn't move, not at all . . ."

It wasn't whether she could or not, it was that bed, empty, and the attendant dragging her on the floor, or on the stretcher or whatever it was.

And here was Thura's voice again. "You see, you said I was satisfied. Sometimes . . . perhaps. . . . But when I think that I might always be in bed, or even in a wheel chair, and that I could never do any of those things other people do . . . then I think . . ."

No, it was impossible to explain it. Thura was right, and it was wrong to live like that, always in bed, fed and washed like an animal or worse; like a thing, an object. And that was one part of it; but here was Thura right before her, and she knew she did not want to see her taken away with her eyes closed and her hands, those thin limp hands, dangling like all those other hands she had seen before. Lying in bed always was one thing; and Thura, her eyes, her hands, another. She could not understand it herself. I don't know what you want from . . . she almost cried. "I wouldn't do it, that's all."

She was angry — Stephania — Thura knew it, but something forced her to go on. "But you, if you were like me, would you tell your sister to do it?"

If she were like Thura . . . if . . . Again she stared at the wall. Again Barbara was here, the brown bag, the little package. And then the empty bed, her own bed this time and nothing else, nothing more, not darkness even, not even knowing that the bed was empty.

"Perhaps you wouldn't want her to do it?"

"What did you say? Of course I would." She looked at Thura. The big eyes were still looking at her, the pupils almost immobile and very dark. "Come on, Thura," she said ingratiatingly, "be reasonable. First of all you don't have to stay as you are. There's always hope. They may find a new medicine, a different kind of treatment. And even if they don't you must remember that there are always things one can do, and then you have your home, all your friends . . ."

"Everybody says that to me," Thura said, her voice tired and sad. "But they don't really believe it, and you don't believe it either."

Stephania raised her hand, began to wrap a curl of her dark hair around her fingers. "I don't know," she said at last, "I really don't. But look, you must somehow feel it. For instance when . . . if your hands were all right now, and the doctor came and told you, You're going home tomorrow, wouldn't you be glad about that? Wouldn't you think what you would do when you were back there?"

"I would be glad, of course. And I often think what I'd do there; you see we have a small house over there in Dalarna and I have my own room. And then I think: When I can move my hands I'll read a lot — I like to read you see — and even do some knitting and needlework. Doctor Ström told me that he knew a woman who did all her cooking sitting in her wheel chair. So perhaps I could help Mother with that. And on Sundays we could all go to the movies. Father would push my wheel chair, you see. And then there is the garden around the house; it's small but very nice, and I always liked to sit there. And you know one day I remembered that there are a whole lot of stairs from the house to the garden, and that I could never get there by myself, but would have to wait until Father comes back from work. I told him that, when he came to see me on Christmas, and later he wrote me that he had figured out something about that — he would put a board from the house to the garden, and I could get up and down all by myself."

"That sounds like a good idea," Stephania said.

"Yes . . . and you know, sometimes . . . sometimes when I'm not scared I think that many things are like that board and the garden. You just have to figure out a different way of getting around, you see? But now I don't know any more."

"But that's just it, Thura." Stephania bent over toward the stretcher. "That's just what I meant. You'll have to find a different way, but you can't come and ask me what I think. That doesn't work. People are not the same, and you have to figure it out by yourself. But about that other thing — you shouldn't even think about it."

"You mean it?"

"Now I mean it."

"I . . . Don't worry about me . . . I'm going to get well." Stephania wondered if it would ever occur to Thadeus to make a board like that for her. Nonsense, what did that matter?

"Of course you'll get well, and Fröken Nilsson too, everybody does . . ."

And then all of a sudden, Stephania, as she had once before, said: "I'm sorry, Thura," and the long white hand with the very red fingernails rested for a while on that other hand — brown, thin and limp.

CHAPTER 12

THURA'S BEDSORE was healing fine. The penicillin, Sister Gudrun remarked, as usual did wonders. The redness disappeared, the circle covered by green pus grew smaller and smaller. Thura could sleep now, and her body imbedded in the soft, resilient water pillow felt fresh and rested. The guilty, abashed look had vanished from Fru Gustavsson's face; patients from other rooms stopped coming to find out how she felt. Were it not for the dressing table Sister Gudrun rolled into the room every morning, no one would have thought anything had ever happened in Room Number Five.

That hour when they two, Thura and Stephania, were alone, face to face with each other, seemed never to have taken place, and those words that had fallen then seemed never to have been spoken. The room was silent again. Only each morning, after Fröken Nilsson had left, Thura would ask — "How are you to-day, Fröken Ackermann?"

"Fine," Stephania would answer, "and you, did you sleep well last night?"

"Yes, fine, thank you."

That was all. But sometimes during the day they would suddenly raise their eyes, look at each other, and Thura would smile shyly, pleadingly, and Stephania would answer with a smile that was also groping, uncertain.

Stephania rarely thought of that scene between Thura and herself. The child was high-strung, bored by the monotony of life here, she decided, and besides there was nothing she could do about it. She had enough of her own problems and did not know what to do about them either.

For that single moment when, in the white plaster room, Ström had said, "We've tightened it much less than we hoped to," had overturned everything in Stephania's life. The order of the day was gone, the room seemed changed again. The bed opposite her, the inescapable presence of the woman in it, had suddenly disappeared; it gave way to another point — to the door, which twice a day opened to let Doctor Ström in. And the day was focused around those two moments; it was nothing but waiting for the quick steps, for the short figure in the too long white coat. For each time when she saw him walking toward her bed she waited for him to say, We've made a mistake, I didn't realize how much we've tightened the cast — or, I spoke to Professor, there's a new method, we're going to try it on you. Words like that — words which would deny what he had said before, or would promise that something would be done, that something was going to

[ 124 ]

happen at last. But nothing ever happened. Ström looked at her for a while, then at the chart. "Everything fine?" he would say, and then the door closed again and nothing was left but waiting for the next time.

The charts above the other beds gradually were covered with red and blue patterns: temperature readings and penicillin on Fröken Nilsson's, massage and iron medicine on Thura's. But nothing except for the dates appeared on hers. October twenty-sixth, twenty-seventh, twenty-eighth — and then a new chart replaced it at the beginning of a new month — November first, second. . . . Something had to happen. Stephania decided to talk to the Professor.

The day of the great inspection visit came, an important day because tangerines had appeared on Willy's stand then, and their tart smell made the patients think of fall coming to an end, of snow that would soon fall up in the North — the home of many of them — of the winter in the hospital, the first for some, the second or even third for others. The Professor seemed to be in a special, exuberant mood on that day, his voice sounding louder, his laughter more frequent than ever. He was satisfied with Room Two, he declared. Thura's bedsore would be healed soon, and as to Fröken Nilsson she was his pride and his joy.

No longer did Fröken Nilsson have to dread the inspection visits. Not a word was said, ever, about the macaroon cookies, about the belated escapade to the pantry. Now Fröken Nilsson's heroic dieting was the favorite theme. "What record have we beaten this week?" the Professor asked now. Fröken Nilsson, fragrant with powder and perfume, her hair newly washed, shiny and curled, smiled with modest triumph and looked far above Professor's head to Doctor Liliencrona to show him that the smile was for him, of course.

"Five pounds," Sister Gudrun announced proudly. Fröken Nilsson blushed. "Come on, don't get skinny now." Professor prodded Fröken Nilsson's bare arm, and nodded. "No danger as yet, but soon you'll be a real glamour girl, move around like a prima ballerina." Professor tucked up the skirts of his coat, and his big feet moved in something that looked like a pirouette. Everybody remained silent. Professor burst into laughter and all the doctors and the nurses followed that signal; even Sister Gudrun giggled discreetly.

"Acker-mann, Stephania Ackermann — How are we today?"

Stephania sat up. She had promised herself not to get excited but now the red shiny face exasperated her. She was the only one who had not laughed at Professor's display of choreography. Buffoon — she thought — all of them are buffoons and hypocrites.

"I'm always fine; nothing's ever done so why shouldn't I be fine?"

"Getting impatient, hmmmm?"

"Perhaps."

Professor looked at the chart.

"No use looking. It's not a chart, it's a calendar," she said bitingly. "Or maybe you want to check the date?"

"Well . . ." Doctor Ström said, "I think she could get up, Professor."

"How long is it since we gave her the cast?"

"Over two months — two and a half exactly."

"So what's she doing still in bed? Come on, lazy bum, up on your feet. Satisfied now?"

Stephania looked at the window. The trees were bare and meager, but their branches moved in the wind, and there was a white coating of frost on the withered grass. The air must be cold outside, sharp and fresh. "Could I go out into the park?"

"Into the park?" Professor looked at Doctor Ström and Doctor Ström at Sister Gudrun.

"So you feel like walking in the moonlight. No, my dear, not with that armor on you."

"She can go out into the hall, into the living room," Doctor Ström suggested.

"It's all right," Stephania said. "It doesn't matter."

"Good-bye everybody, and Ackermann, up on your feet!" Professor looked at the magazine on Fröken Nilsson's table, poked his finger at the girl on the cover. "Pretty," he said, and here they left and the room suddenly was very quiet and empty.

As soon as the inspection visit had left the ward, Sister Gudrun came in, a gray, shapeless dress hanging over her arm.

"I don't need it," Stephania said, "I have my gown."

But Sister Gudrun only put the dress on the chair, and said that Fru Gustavsson would come soon to help Fröken Stephania to get up.

To help her? What next? She did not need any help; her legs

were all right at least. She was going to get up, right now. It would do her good to get out of that room. Perhaps she could find a place where she could be alone and smoke a cigarette. Stephania looked under the bed. The slippers were still there and the blue silk of her gown shone through the half-closed door of the closet. She felt glad. She would put it on again, would feel the warm softness of the silk. Now she pushed the blanket away and put her feet on the floor. It was cold, smooth and firm. She grasped the bedpost, stood up. And suddenly she felt all her blood flowing in sharp thin streams down to her legs — thousands of needles piercing her feet.

"Fröken Ackermann, you shouldn't get up all by yourself. Wait. You could fall."

"Why should I?" But her head felt giddy, the floor lost its firmness, the room turned around, green, white, yellow, and melted into one dazzling mass. She grasped the post tighter. Now it was better.

"Please, go back to bed. You want me to call someone?"

"No. I'm all right."

The floor was stable again. Leaning on the wall she walked to the closet. The cast weighed heavily upon her shoulder. She never thought it would be so hard. Now, here was the closet. She opened it, took the gown out, put one arm in it. Something must have gotten twisted, the other sleeve slipped out from her hand. And now a button fell off. The dizziness returned. She stopped and took a deep breath. Now, at last. She pulled at the gown, and tried to button it. But something must have gone wrong again; the gown gaped wide open and when she pulled, the seams strained and seemed to burst. What could have happened? It was too tight, but why? Was it because of the cast? No it couldn't be that; she had bought it two sizes larger, especially for the cast. And the nightgowns, they were all right. Yes, but they were all open in the back.

She staggered to the mirror, and stood opposite it clinging to the wall, unable to raise her eyes. Her whole body shivered with cold; the cast grew heavier and heavier. And at last she looked.

Framed in the shiny blue silk her body stuck out, convex, a globe almost, two huge protuberances piled one upon another, the dirty white of the plaster showing through the transparent fabric . . . plaster sticking out of the lace-adorned sleeves. Out of the neckline, also covered with lace, wrinkled and withered, the plaster collar emerged; big, round, like a chimney; fringes of cotton wool, glued with gravy, gray and dirty around it. And the arms and the legs were short and ridiculously thin; the head above the immense torso and the wisps of cotton wool, preposterously small. And then the face, that face with carefully painted lips, powdered, and the curls falling coquettishly upon the forehead.

No, she did not want to see it, she wanted to run back to her bed, but she could not. She had to look. And now once more, the cast, the collar, a piece of lace torn off, the face, the crumbs of plaster in her hair.

So that was how she looked. And every morning. . . . Not that nightgown, please, the other lipstick, Fru Gustavsson . . . and all of that body, like a spider, nothing except the huge gray torso and the thin arms and legs. And to Barbara she had said, Bring me a new box of powder, and some eau de cologne . . .

But why didn't they tell her? Not those here, they didn't give a damn, but she, Barbara. You look fine she said, lovely, as usual. Not changed at all, she said. And she must have seen it, of course she did. But she wouldn't tell, why should she? She had always lied, always. You look as usual; God . . .

Suddenly the floor became round again, and within her everything grew hollow, cold. As usual — perhaps she wasn't lying. Perhaps that was how she had always looked, always, even before the cast, and they all knew it, all but herself. . . . No, she would have noticed. But the cast . . . she touched it on the collar and the edges that touched her belly; no, the cast wasn't thick, just an inch or two. And it was tight. Ström said it was very tight. . . . Suddenly she knew . . . the hollow within her grew, now it was all void, within, around her. . . . She had not been like that before but they had done something to her, that time when she was asleep, something they should not have done. Ström was afraid to tell her. That was why it had hurt when he tightened the cast, that was why he couldn't tighten it more. Something . . . what could it be . . .? And once more her eyes upon the mirror . . .

"Fröken Ackermann, go to bed. You're terribly pale."

To bed . . . yes, she wanted to go to bed. But it was so far away, the bed. And the cast was so heavy, no — not the cast — it was that under the cast. . . . She began to walk; step, then another step, she leaned on the wall, on Thura's bed, on the chair. . . . And here was the bed. Without taking off her gown she lay down, her eyes closed, her fingers feeling anxiously, imploringly the edge of the cast. No it was not thick, just an inch or two, just an inch. Suddenly she sat up, took a tissue, wiped the lipstick and powder off her face. And then she lay again without a thought, without feeling, except for something in her that kept repeating: What shall I do now, what shall I do?

"Fröken Ackermann?" Fru Gustavsson came in, looked at her and whispered to Thura, "Is she asleep?"

"I'm not asleep."

"Fine, so you're going to get up now." And Fru Gustavsson took the hospital dress off the chair.

"I'm not going to get up."

"But Sister Gudrun said Doctor Ström had said . . ."

"I said I'm not going to get up."

"Well, I won't force anyone." Fru Gustavsson put the dress away, looked at Thura questioningly, and walked to the door.

"Fru Gustavsson," Stephania called.

She stopped.

"I want to ask you something."

Fru Gustavsson looked at her. She certainly did not care for Stephania; she had been the first one to know what was inside her; she was the only one who would not be fooled by her outlandish manners, by all her finery. But now something in Stephania's voice, in her face, bare and pale with the lipstick off, made her voice soft when she asked: "What's the matter, Fröken Ackermann?"

Stephania raised her hand. "Oh . . . I don't know myself." The hand passed over the cast, over the plaster collar.

"What's wrong? Does it hurt again?"

"No . . . but . . . but the gown didn't fit, I just couldn't get into it . . . and it's too large, two sizes too large."

Fru Gustavsson did not quite understand it. But she understood enough to smile and to say, "Sure you couldn't. A cast is a cast, it makes you twice as big as you are."

"You mean each cast, on everybody?"

"Sure. What did you think?"

"But you can't know really. You've never had anyone like me, a . . . hunchback."

"But I've had spines, thousands of them, ask Thura. Ask her

[ 129 ]

how Fru Hernruth looked." Fru Gustavsson began to laugh, the arms, the big breasts, all her round body was shaking with laughter. "Excuse my saying so — but she, Fru Hernruth, looked like in the ninth month, with the baby right under her chin."

With sudden warmth, with a gratitude so great that it was almost unbearable, Stephania looked at that laughing, dimply plumpness that was Fru Gustavsson. "You really mean it?" she said.

"Sure I do. And the others, you just should have seen them. Wait, I'll show you something."

With incomprehensible speed Fru Gustavsson dived under Fröken Nilsson's bed and pulled out a shoe. It looked like a small canoe; wide, big, shapeless. "You see, that's what you've got to wear when you have a plaster on your leg."

Fru Gustavsson began to laugh again and Stephania felt like laughing too. "So we're going to get up now." It was the first time Fru Gustavsson said "we" to Stephania, exactly as she did to her other patients.

Stephania stopped laughing. Her lips grew tight again. "No," she said, "I don't want to."

"All right. We can wait. Fröken should rest a little bit."

Fru Gustavsson was already at the threshold when Fröken Nilsson lifted her eyebrows, and said, "May I have my shoe back, *please?*"

"How was the walk yesterday?" Doctor Ström asked the next morning.

"I didn't get up," Stephania answered.

"You didn't? Why not, if I may ask?"

She smiled and made a gesture as if to toss her hair back. But now it was pulled back and tied with a piece of tape, so she only let the smile deepen the two sharp furrows around her lips. "Too many mirrors here. Hospitals shouldn't have mirrors, Doctor."

"What does she mean, Sister Gudrun? Professor said she should get up, didn't he?"

"She refused. And I don't have time to drag patients out of bed."

Stephania looked at them. The blurred light of a cloudy November morning tinted their coats gray, made their faces stony, impenetrable.

"Doctor," she said, "the cast seems so big. Have you done anything to me, something I don't know about?"

"What? The cast is big? What new idea is that? Sure it's big, do you want it to look like a bathing suit? You're going to get up and walk."

"No."

'You are or you go home. The cast cannot work if you stay in bed."

"You mean, one has something to do with the other?"

"Of course it does. So are you going to get up?"

"Yes, I'll get up."

"Right after I leave?"

"Yes."

And so Fru Gustavsson came again. This time she did not ask anything, only put the slippers on Stephania's feet and helped her to get the dress on. It was much too long and the hem trailed on the floor. "We'll fix it in a jiffy." Fru Gustavsson took thread and needle out of her pocket, knelt on the floor and with a few stitches rolled the hem. "It doesn't look very smart," she said, "but nobody cares here. And now good-bye, little Thura, we're going for a walk."

Fru Gustavsson's arm was strong and warm. It smelled of soap, of cleanliness. Once at home they had a laundry woman who smelled like that. All day long she stood bent over the washtub, her big buttocks and broad shoulders moving rhythmically, and she sang all the time . . . something about a maple tree, a squire's daughter, and a hangman.

"So how's it coming, Fröken Stephania?' '

"Fine, I can walk alone now."

"All right, I better go to my 'back' " . . . She rang again. "Wants a bedpan, I can swear. She wants the bedpan every two minutes. Have a nice walk, Fröken Stephania."

Fru Gustavsson was disappearing in the door, when Stephania called, "Thanks a lot."

And now she walked alone through the hall, which seemed very long and wide. The lamps were lit, and she could see her shadow reflected on the shining floor. She did not want to look at it, and moved stiffly like a tightrope walker, her eyes fixed on the door at the end of the hall. Where did it lead? Yes, to the living room.

She opened it and for a while stood motionless, bewildered by the many strange faces around her. Women, all in the gray hospital dresses, sat on the sofas or in their wheel chairs pushed close to the open fire. All eyes were raised to her. The murmur grew lower, then it stopped completely. Only the clicking of knitting needles was heard, and in the corner a voice obstinately went on talking. She looked there. It was Fröken Nilsson. For a moment she hesitated, wanted to turn back, and at last slowly, maneuvering among all the wheels, crutches and sticks, she crossed the room and opened another door. From behind she could hear the murmur of voices, first subdued and then high, relieved.

She passed through another hall, exactly like the one in her ward only filled with the smell of tobacco and resounding with deep male voices coming through the half-open doors of the rooms. At the end of the hall was a telephone booth. She hesitated; should she call Barbara? No — what for? The smell of tobacco filled her with sudden longing. A cigarette, that was what she wanted.

Hastily she passed through the living room, through the hall and back to her room. The pack she had brought when she came was still in the drawer. The cigarettes must be stale by now, but it didn't matter. Here, to the left, was the bathroom. She walked in, locked the door, sat down. Now matches. Her hand trembled, the match went out. God, what was the matter with her?

The cigarette was lit at last. She looked at it for a moment, then inhaled deeply, once, and once more. But the cigarette was soft, shreds of tobacco stuck to her tongue and left a bitter taste in her mouth. She tried once more, shuddered, and flushed the cigarette down the toilet bowl. The bitter taste in her mouth merged with the heavy, tired feeling of disappointment. It was enough for today, she thought, and walked back to her room.

"Fröken better take a little rest," Fru Gustavsson welcomed her, "the visit time will start soon."

Yes, the visiting hour. She had completely forgotten about it.

"Will Fröken get up then?"

"No, I feel rather tired."

"Shall I reach Fröken a clean gown, the mirror?"

"No, thank you, I don't need anything."

The door opened, there was the sound of voices in the hall, the elevator rattling went up and down. Three o'clock. Barbara would be here any minute. Stephania without looking into the mirror passed the comb through her hair and adjusted the piece of tape in the back. Now it was five past three, then ten. The voices in the hall died out; only a belated visitor kept asking desperately for Fröken Segobörg, a new patient with a broken hip. Then even that voice disappeared and now only a subdued murmur came from the next rooms.

Stephania sat, her eyes wandering from the clock to the window and then back to the clock again. Barbara was always on time. . . . She promised she would come, she even said that she would postpone her appointment with her doctor so she could make it. Quarter past three. The drive was empty. Now the bus came; a few people got off but Barbara was not among them. Then a taxi. A tall man — yes, that was Doctor Liliencrona — came out, and an old woman walked out of the building. The church bell rang, one, two — three-thirty. Had anything happened?

Yes, something must be wrong, she felt it; she was certain of it. Suddenly it seemed to her she had known it for a long time: something horrible had to happen. The old familiar feeling, an anxious, almost longing expectation of an approaching disaster was with her again. She waited, passive, almost indifferent, for the hasty steps, for the door to open, for Fru Gustavsson or the attendant to come in and tell that it was here, it had come.

What was it? She did not know. Barbara — the baby perhaps — she was so absent-minded; perhaps when she was crossing the street — or with that mania for cleanliness of hers, she could have started washing the windows and fallen down. Or maybe it was not Barbara. It could be Thadeus; he might have gotten into trouble, into a fight in the factory. The job in the Polish Legation. . . .

Somebody passed the hall. She waited. The steps came closer, now. . . . No, they passed her door, and she lay down relieved but with the feeling that it was not over, that the inevitable was only delayed. The way she had thought of Barbara yesterday . . . And today she was right next to the telephone and did not even bother to call. But Barbara, and in the eighth month too, did not mind coming to her from the other end of the city. Perhaps it happened when she was taking the bus; the traffic was just terrible there, and no lights at all. . . .

She rang. "Will you please call my sister, and ask what has happened, why she isn't coming?"

Fru Gustavsson wrote down the number and left.

Outside in the drive a bus again, all empty this time. A woman on crutches passed by, then a nurse burdened with shopping. Why was Fru Gustavsson so long? Perhaps she was afraid to come back — and tell her . . . ?

The door opened. "The line was busy," Fru Gustavsson said, "I had to wait."

"Did you talk to her? Was my sister at home?"

"No, she wasn't."

"Who was there, then?"

"Fröken's brother-in-law. He sends his best regards . . ."

"And my sister?"

"She should be here any moment. She had left about twenty minutes ago."

"Thanks." So nothing had happened. Thadeus had stayed at home, one of his innumerable holidays probably; they were talking and Barbara must have completely forgotten it was visiting day. And she and her apocalyptic imagination. Ridiculous!

She was not looking at the clock any longer, and quietly, with neither surprise nor joy, said hello when Barbara came into the room.

Barbara rushed to her bed. "I'm so sorry, dear. I had a completely crazy day, everything was topsy-turvy and before I knew how and when, it was three, and here I wasn't even dressed."

"It's all right. We have plenty of time. Twenty whole minutes."

Barbara, still panting heavily, took her coat off and sat down. "Here are some books," she said, "and here's a cake. I made it myself. A little burnt at the bottom but one really doesn't taste much."

"But . . . but you look different today," she said suddenly.

"Why?"

"I don't know quite. Let me see. Your hair, and no lipstick. What's happened?"

"What should have happened? Just decided to let my natural beauty shine. Don't I look lovely, as usual?"

"You look fine," Barbara said. She glanced at Stephania uneasily. "But still, you shouldn't let yourself go like that. Oh, I'd

[ 134 ]

almost forgotten. Here's the powder you asked me for, and the cologne."

"Thanks. I don't need it."

"Why? What's the matter?"

"Oh well, I've found the old one. You take it back and use it. And otherwise everything is fine?"

"Yes . . . fine."

"It's really chilly today," Barbara said after a long while. She shuddered.

Stephania did not answer. She knew Barbara was waiting for her to say something, that the silence was weighing her down. Still she said nothing, only her fingers began to drum on the table.

Barbara's eyes followed the movements of her fingers. At last she put her hand on the table. "What's new?" she asked. "What does Ström say?"

"No news. You should be used to that by now. Nothing new ever happens to me."

A straight furrow cut Barbara's forehead. "What's the matter with you today? You're unlike yourself."

"As usual. The doctor says everything is going normally."

Stephania bent her head to the side. She was smiling. "And Thadeus?"

"Oh, he's fine. He'll come on Sunday."

"Working hard I guess?"

Barbara drew her chair closer. The furrow on her forehead became deeper, her face grew watchful, distrustful. "Yes, of course, why do you ask? Still in the factory. There're some difficulties with the job Gross is trying to get for him. He'll come on Sunday to see you. Asked me to send you his best regards today."

Stephania was looking with great attention at her fingernails. She began to scratch the polish off. "I know, I got them almost personally — the regards I mean."

Barbara bent forwards. "What do you mean? You've been hinting at something all the time."

"Hinting? Me? No it's just that Fru Gustavsson called to him on the phone. I was worried about what had happened to you, you see. So then Thadeus sent his regards. He probably came home early from work today."

Barbara got up and stepped closer still. She was very big now; the cautious slowness of her body gave something menacing to her movements.

[ 135 ]

"Yes," she said, "he came earlier. He wanted to talk to Gross. Perhaps you mind that?"

"Why should I mind? I just wonder . . ."

"You wonder? What?"

"Nothing, nothing in particular. Just why you always have to lie to me, that's all. He did not come home early," she said slowly, "he quit, or they've kicked him out again."

"Yes." Barbara shook her head defiantly and the yellow plait of her hair covered her cheek. "He quit. I didn't lie. I just didn't want to worry you. But he did quit. Why not? You don't expect him to slave in the factory for almost nothing, with all his abilities — his personality, his education. Or perhaps you do?"

"Do you want to hear my opinion?"

"Sure, go ahead." Barbara sat down. "Anyhow I know what you're going to say."

"Well, that's what I'm going to say. A man with a wife and a child coming doesn't leave every job after a few weeks. That's his fifth this year; quite a record, you must admit. That's one thing. And now another — He'll never get anything better; he has no experience, doesn't speak a word of Swedish, and doesn't try to do anything about it. When I knew I had to go to a Swedish hospital I sat down and learned it. But no, not Thadeus. He's a genius of course; everything will just come to him out of the blue sky. Everybody's doing something, learning a trade or a profession; working, and he . . . he drinks coffee with Gross and waits for the millions to fall into his lap. Anyhow, it's not my business, he's not my husband."

"Exact-ly," Barbara said slowly. "It's not your business, he's my husband, thank God. But," she passed her hand over her hair and eyes, "how can you say anything like that about Thadeus? After all he has done for you, coming here every week. And at home . . . I hear nothing but Stephania . . . How is she, what's she doing? And whenever he passes a store, 'Oh, if we could only buy that for Stephania,' and all that — nothing is good enough for you. And then when . . ." Barbara stopped suddenly.

"Go ahead, say it . . ."

"I've nothing to say."

"Well, now I can say it for you. I'll save you the trouble; all right? When you took and spent five hundred crowns before going to the hospital, on nothing, on nightgowns and luxuries, then

Thadeus didn't say a word. Is that what you wanted to say?"

"Yes, you've said it now."

"Sure, sure, very noble of him. But the money was mine. My share of what we got for the silver in Poland. Do you remember what you spent yours on? On your trousseau . . . yes, that was it. So I wanted to have my trousseau too."

"I did it when we still had lots left, when we hoped to get some more. And you took the last money we had and spent it on . . . on rags, on nothing!"

"So here we come. I asked you, you remember. And you said, 'Don't worry, do what you want. Thadeus will take care of everything.'"

"I couldn't tell you not to."

"No, you couldn't. You never can say no, so you say yes, and only then you take it back. That reminds me of something. Do you remember Stasia?"

"Stasia?"

"Yes, the maid we had once. Whenever you gave me something, a toy or a piece of candy, and then took it back — you always did it, give and take back, give and take back — she always said about you —

> *Who gives and takes again*
> *Will in hellfire suffer pain!*

Do you remember?" And again her fingers began to drum on the table.

"Stop it!" Barbara cried.

"I'm sorry."

"Yes," she said slowly, "I remember. But what's gotten into you, to drag it out just now?"

"Just so, just so. . . . Childhood memories, you know. And besides it just fitted into something else. Wait a moment. I don't like to misquote. 'My child is going to be your child, my husband your husband'; do you remember, not so long ago, in this very same room?" She raised her hand and touched the table with her fingers, hesitated, and put her hand back upon the blanket.

"Stephania!" Barbara stood erect now and her fingers unbuttoned the collar of the blouse as if she were choking. "That's just like you, like your old self," she said at last. "To remember everything, the toys, the candy, to remember it for years, to brood on

[ 137 ]

it like a hen on eggs. Listen, I also have a good memory. Do you remember what Mother used to say — that you are like a little thrifty housewife? You put your imaginary and real offences into cold storage and then after years you take them out . . ."

"You're lying again, you've been lying to me all the time. Besides" — Stephania lifted herself higher and looked at Barbara — "Besides, you don't know what she said later. How can you? You were not with her, with them. But *I* was, I, not like you . . . I . . ." she hesitated, stopped.

"Stephania!" Barbara lifted her hand as if to defend herself.

They said nothing now. They looked at each other with eyes wide open as if not believing what had happened.

She's pale, Stephania thought, horribly pale. Barbara, she wanted to say, I didn't mean it. I don't know what happened to me today. But she could not say a word, and only sat and looked.

"Visiting time is over," Sister Gudrun announced.

"I'd better go now," Barbara said slowly. She got up. Something fell on the floor. "Oh," she said, "I brought you some Polish sausage. I remembered you said you liked it so much, so I asked Gross to get some for me."

"The visiting time is over," Sister Gudrun repeated.

Barbara buttoned her coat and walked to the door. Stephania looked at her. No, she wanted to cry, no, Barbara! But she was silent.

And then, in the door already, Barbara cried, "Just one moment, Sister," and here she was running back. "Stephania," she cried her arms around her, "Stephania, forget it, I didn't mean it. Not one word of it; you know I'm crazy when it comes to Thadeus, and all that, the job . . . the baby coming . . . all that worries me so much. Oh, Stephania!"

Stephania felt Barbara's cheek getting wet. She was crying. It had always been easy for her to cry. No, she did not mean it, she did not know where thoughts like that came from. "It's all right, Barbara, it's all right, I have already forgotten. And you forget too. I've just been upset today. Oh, Barbara, it's not we, it's the whole lousy life we have."

"The visiting hour is over."

"Good-bye, Stephania, good-bye."

Barbara left. Stephania sat looking after her, feeling Barbara's tears slowly drying on her cheek.

CHAPTER 13

THE SNOW CAME suddenly, unlike in other years, without the usual warning of cold and cloudy days, of frost that brings in its white film the premonition of winter. Only a few days before, it had been raining; then the rain stopped, the sky looked pale but clear, and the last leaves glistened, freshly washed by the heavy drops. It was so warm that the windows stood wide open for long hours and Fru Gustavsson, shaking her head, repeated: "Real April in the middle of November. What do you say about that?" But on Tuesday morning the sky turned solid gray, the clouds hung low; their heavy, lazily moving bodies seemed to touch the window. And all of a sudden the snow fell, not the usual November snow, mixed with rain, melting immediately, but thick flakes, solid and durable.

"Just look at that snow," the patients in Ward Two said, and there was a slight note of offense in their voices. They felt deceived, deprived of something — of those long fall days, days during which, perhaps, so much could have changed, so much could have happened. They looked at the window, at the drive growing white and wintry, at the trees catching the snowflakes, storing them in heavy, fleecy piles. "Winter out of the blue sky," they said, and shook their heads.

The snow made them forget that it was Tuesday, the great inspection day. Only when the sound of many footsteps came from the hall, they hastily began to smooth their blankets, and sat up, exaggerating a little, as if trying to make up for the moment of negligence, the usual respectful expression on their faces.

Professor too seemed to be put into a special mood by the snow. "So winter is here," he said, as if he was announcing the arrival of a new patient to the hospital, as if even the new season had to be officially accepted by him. He asked Stephania whether they had snow in Poland, a question which, after the signal given by Professor himself, caused a great outburst of laughter. He pinched Thura's cheek so that it hurt, and then turned to Fröken Nilsson, saying: "You'd better hurry and get your skis ready, my dear." Fröken Nilsson, who was just wondering whether Doctor Liliencrona was going to wear his winter coat with the beaver collar (he had looked so handsome in it last year), smiled in a noncommittal way. Everybody waited now for Professor to start laughing, but instead he sat down on the edge of Fröken Nilsson's bed, and that was a sign that something important was going to happen. "Yes, Fröken Nilsson," Professor began, "it's high time for you to get up, up on your feet. You've lost so much weight, it should be easy for you now; you'll just float in the air, my dear."

"Me . . . get up?" Fröken Nilsson wrinkled her forehead as if unable to understand.

But Professor no longer paid any attention to her. "Are you still giving her penicillin?" He turned to Sister Gudrun.

"Yes, Professor didn't . . ."

"Well, it doesn't matter. You should have stopped long ago. I want her to get up and walk now. Let her use a walker for a couple of days, then crutches, then we ship her home."

"Home?" Fröken Nilsson forgot herself so much that she interrupted Professor. No, it was impossible, she didn't know quite why, but she was certain it wasn't time yet.

"Sure, aren't you happy?"

"Yes, of course, but . . ."

"So, everything is fine. She'll go home and then come back after — after let's say six weeks — and then we'll take the nail out." Professor slapped Fröken Nilsson on her shoulder and looked once more at the snow outside of the window and left.

As soon as they were out Fru Gustavsson rushed in. She knew the news, of course, she always knew it at once; one could not help thinking she stood outside eavesdropping all the time. "Isn't it wonderful?" she exclaimed. "Just think of being able to go home! I'm so glad for you, Fröken Nilsson."

"Thank you," Fröken Nilsson said. Of course it was wonderful. Still that Gustavsson didn't have to make so much noise, she had no manners at all. Fröken Nilsson lay down and turned her head to the wall. She wanted to be left alone.

Yes, she thought, it certainly would be wonderful to get out of this hopeless place. And the reason why she did not feel quite as happy as she should, the reason was . . . she sought for it, as one seeks for an object, misplaced yet certain to be somewhere, until at last she found it. It was because of Doctor Liliencrona, of course. She would have to leave him now; she would perhaps never see him again except for a few minutes when she came back for the check-up.

But didn't Professor say something about taking the nail out? She had completely forgotten it. Yes, they had put a nail into her leg, to hold the bone together, or something like that. She had always tried not to think about it; it scared her to remember that it was there, deep inside her leg, within the bone. She knew it was a special nail, but still she could not help thinking that it was just like those nails sticking out of the fence around her house in Eskilstuna: big, black, a little rusty even. But now Fröken Nilsson felt glad the nail was there. She would come back in six weeks; it wasn't a very long time either. They would have to put her under an anesthetic, of course, and again, as during the last operation, Doctor Liliencrona would give it to her. After that she would have to stay in the hospital, a week at least, maybe even more. They couldn't possibly send her home with an open wound; even Ström, heartless as he was, wouldn't do that.

Fröken Nilsson felt much quieter now, and started thinking how she should say good-bye to Doctor Liliencrona. She would buy him a present, flowers — that would be best — refined, and inexpensive too. She could see herself handing Doctor Liliencrona a huge bunch of roses — or carnations would be good too; they charged murderous prices for roses nowadays. Thank you ever so much, Doctor, for all you've done for me, she would say, or even better: I'll never forget what you've done for me. And he would answer . . .

Fröken Nilsson did not decide what Doctor Liliencrona would answer. It occurred to her suddenly that Fru Hernruth had not given her doctor the flowers herself, she'd had them sent to him. That discovery upset her a little; it would have been so nice to give him the flowers herself. But after all, Fru Hernruth knew how these things were done — wife of a police superintendent. And besides, sending them would be nice, too. He would be surprised.

Fröken Nilsson could see Doctor Liliencrona sitting in his study, at the big mahogany desk — she was sure it would be nothing but mahogany — and then suddenly the door would open and the housekeeper (not pretty; elderly, but very neat) would come and say: Flowers for you, Doctor.

Flowers? From whom could they be? And then he would look at the card and say: Can you imagine? They are from Fröken Nilsson.

Who is she? the housekeeper would ask, and Fröken Nilsson felt a sudden dislike for her.

She, she . . . he would say looking at the flowers. No, he would say nothing about her, only smile and then he would add: Take good care of them please, and remember to water them every day — Because Fröken Nilsson had decided to send a flowerpot. They would last so much longer. Cut flowers were just a waste of money.

Fröken Nilsson felt very happy suddenly. It was nice to be going home after all. She would have to write Anna and ask her to look for a room. She would not go back to the place she had lived in before, not for anything in the world. A saint could not stand living with that terrible Fru Ekelund, deaf as a stone, and turning the whole house upside down looking for her hearing aid from morning to evening. No, she'd had enough of that. Anna would have to find her a room, whether she wanted to or not. She was her sister after all, even if she would not write her a line, and her husband would never come to visit her.

There were also other things to think of. Money first of all; she couldn't have much more than two hundred crowns left, and then her clothes; the winter coat was no good at all. But there was time for all that. She was going to stay here two weeks more at least.

"Making plans for going home?" It was Fru Gustavsson again.

"Yes," Fröken Nilsson nodded. "I have to write my sister to prepare an apartment for me."

"Sure, that's a good idea. Better to start early and not have to hurry later. I think I'll bring your dress from the storage room so you can look it over and fix anything that has to be fixed."

I'm not leaving yet; there's time — Fröken Nilsson wanted to say, but then it occurred to her she might put it on when she got up, and perhaps Doctor Liliencrona would see her. . . . "All right, why don't you bring it?" she agreed.

And so the dress was there, lying on the chair, big and black, adorned with frills, with a crust of beads in the front. "What a lovely dress," Fru Gustavsson remarked. "Just look at all those beads."

"Just an old dress." Fröken Nilsson shrugged nonchalantly. "I left all the good ones at home. No reason to get all dressed up coming to a hospital." Still, she lifted the dress to the light and looked carefully to see if there were any holes in it. No, it looked really fine. Fröken Nilsson felt satisfied. It would have to be tightened a little, now that she had lost so much weight. They would make big eyes in Eskilstuna when they saw her figure now. Fröken Nilsson felt very happy suddenly. It was really wonderful she was going home. And she decided to fix the dress right now. Slowly, in order not to wrinkle it, she spread the dress over the bed, taking good care that the front covered with beads would face Stephania. And it gave her great satisfaction when she noticed that Stephania was looking at it.

Yes, Fröken Nilsson was right. Stephania was looking at the dress, noticing each bead, each frill, the sharp shine of the cheap satin. She smiled. What a horror. Exactly as she had expected. Just to think about all those beads glittering on Fröken Nilsson's protruding bosom. Well, it was her dress, her taste . . . the main thing was she would go home soon, as soon as she really wanted to go, as soon as she made the slightest effort. Professor had said it himself, hadn't he? — "Now you've lost so much weight it will be easy for you to walk." It only proved her own point. Fröken Nilsson didn't have to stay here two years, just because of a broken leg. And now at last she had found it out for herself.

Still it seemed somehow unjust that it was Fröken Nilsson who was leaving, and she herself who had to stay. It didn't probably make any difference to Fröken Nilsson where she was. She had been perfectly happy here, she would be perfectly happy at home, sporting that horror of a dress, inviting her friends, as dull and as fat as herself, for coffee, eating and talking, eating and talking. Going home seemed wasted on her.

But *she* would leave too. In six months the first operation, then after a year the other, a couple of months more, and then she would get out of here. It would be late in summer . . . she could see herself . . . in a light dress, white perhaps, standing in the door, looking at the drive shining in the sun, at the chestnuts — they would be turning yellow then. Then she would start walking down into the city, into the streets, passing one street after another, just in order to walk, to feel her legs moving, to feel the pavement under her feet, the warm air touching her face. She could not think what they would be like — the streets; all she could see were the lights, lights of all colors, red, and yellow and sharp green, like those swift flickering rays you see when you have looked for a long time at a glowing lamp, and then suddenly you close your eyes and the sparks dance in the darkness imprisoned under your eyelids. That was how it would be, light and moving forward, and the dress floating in the wind. It would come, she just had to wait, and to do everything to make that waiting as short as possible — not like that Fröken Nilsson who had stayed here two years for no reason at all. She looked at the bed opposite. It was empty. Fröken Nilsson had gone out into the living room to tell the good news to her friends.

Fröken Nilsson returned smiling and triumphant. Yes, she told Sister Gudrun in the evening, she felt very happy about going home, so happy she could hardly believe it. And still assuring herself how glad she was, Fröken Nilsson went to sleep.

But at midnight — at the time when she usually got her penicillin — Fröken Nilsson woke up. She felt she was missing something; something should have happened, and did not. What was it . . . ? Yes, the injection. She was not getting them any longer. The room, dark without the usual gleam of Sister Ingeborg's flashlight, its silence undisturbed now by her cautious steps, seemed suddenly strange and empty. So she was going home. And then she remembered — no room, and only two hundred crowns in the bank, and the coat, yes the coat. There was so much she had to think of. But not now, now it was night, now she wanted to sleep.

CHAPTER 14

BARBARA HAD PROMISED to come on Tuesday. Stephania prepared some books and linen she wanted to send home, and waited for the door to open to let Barbara in, moving dreamily and majestically, her hair wind-blown and shiny, her head very small above the swollen contours of her body. But instead Fru Gustavsson came in. She smiled for a long while, longer than ever, as if trying beforehand to quiet all the fears her words might bring. "Your brother-in-law called, Fröken Ackermann," she said. "Your sister cannot come today. She has gone to the hospital."

"Oh," Stephania said. She moistened her lips with her tongue and smiled back to let Fru Gustavsson know that she had understood her message; that she was not afraid at all. So the baby would be here any moment. That was fine, that was exactly as the doctor had said, around the fourth or fifth of November . . . it was the fifth today. Still she felt it had all come suddenly, so suddenly that she did not expect it, not yet.

Fru Gustavsson stood, still bent over her bed, looking at her, saying something about Thadeus being in a great hurry, about his being sorry that he could not have waited for Fröken Stephania to come to the phone. Of course, Stephania agreed, it was all right. She looked at the empty chair that stood opposite the bed, waiting for Barbara. It seemed to have a questioning, disappointed look. She pushed it back to one side of the bed.

It was three when Thadeus had called. She lay looking at the clock counting the minutes. It probably took about half an hour to get to the hospital. Now they must be there, they had to wait a little of course. Now the doctor has come . . . Barbara says goodbye to Thadeus: Don't worry, dear, it'll be all right. It was half past four. Thadeus should be back at home by now.

She got up, walked to the phone. Her fingers trembled as she dialed the number . . . damn it, two instead of a three; once more . . . now it was right. She stood waiting. Thadeus might be in the kitchen, or in the hall. . . . The ringing seemed to grow louder, shriller, as if impatient. While she stood listening she could see the empty room, the closets gaping wide open, things scattered in disorder, and in the kitchen a pile of unwashed dishes; crumbs and shreds of food littering the table. They must have left right after lunch, or perhaps in the middle. No one was in. She hung up and went back to her room.

Fru Gustavsson was there making the beds. "Nothing to worry about, Fröken Stephania," she said. Her face vanished for a while in a white cloud of talc and then reappeared with a small white smudge on the red cheek.

[ 145 ]

"In which hospital is she?"

"Saint Olaf's."

"That's good, couldn't be better. The best hospital in the city. My sister had her babies there, all of them, three boys. She is expecting the fourth now. I only hope it'll be a girl at last. Anyhow, she always says she wouldn't go any place else, only to Saint Olaf's; and my sister-in-law . . ."

Stephania listened patiently to the long list of members of the Gustavsson family who had been delivered of babies easily and painlessly for the last ten years at Saint Olaf's hospital. "You don't feel a thing," Fru Gustavsson was saying, shaking Thura's pillow furiously. "They give you some kind of gas, you know." Even Thura had something to add. "That's where Fru Hernruth had her baby, too," she said. She had hesitated for a moment before her lips formed the word "baby," pronouncing it cautiously as if she were lifting the small fragile body in her arms.

"I see," Stephania said. "That's fine. . . ." And somehow she felt grateful to them.

After dinner she went to the phone again. Still no one was in; Thadeus was probably too nervous to stay at home; he must have gone to one of his friends'. The best thing was to call the hospital. She looked up the number, dialed . . . "Saint Olaf's hospital," a voice said.

"Maternity ward please."

"Maternity ward," the voice repeated, then another; they handed that word to each other, echoed it in identical automaton-like voices. And at last . . . "Maternity ward — good afternoon."

Stephania hesitated, "Fru Lerner, Barbara Lerner . . ." she said haltingly. "I would like to know how she is. It's her sister speaking." "Just a moment," the voice said. There was a prolonged silence in the receiver that suddenly seemed to grow very cold in her hand. "She is fine," the voice reported at last. "She came only this afternoon."

The voice at the other end of the line let her think over the significance of that fact for a moment and then with icy politeness added that Saint Olaf's hospital suffered a great shortage of personnel and that consequently it would be greatly appreciated if no unnecessary calls were made. She would be notified as soon as the baby was delivered.

"Yes . . ." Stephania murmured. She understood. She was sorry.

Could she just leave a message for Herr Lerner to call her up immediately after . . ."

"Yes," the voice interrupted her, and the receiver was hung up.

She walked slowly back. In the room Sister Gudrun was distributing the medicine for the night. "And so tomorrow at this time you'll be an aunt, Fröken Ackermann. Isn't that nice?" she said.

"Yes, if everything goes all right."

"Sure, it'll go all right." There was not the slightest doubt in her voice. Stephania felt reassured. She fell asleep almost immediately after the lights had been turned off. In her dream she heard the phone ringing, then it stopped and it was the baby crying, she could hear the voice but the baby was hidden somewhere, until suddenly she saw it passed from hand to hand, and all the time a voice was repeating, "Maternity ward, maternity ward . . ."

She woke up. Everything was still dark and very quiet. But after a while she felt the silence around filled with a monotonous rustle as if with a distant tramping of many tired feet. It's raining, she thought, and lay listening to the drops pounding on the window, slowly, persistently, like innumerable fingers knocking patiently one after another. And the wind was blowing, she could hear it swaying the trees. Then the ringing of the bell came, muffled hardly audible — one . . . two . . . three . . . A gust of wind rose, hurled the heavy drops against the panes. She looked at the clock. It was four now. The last ring of the bell must have been swallowed by the noise outside. The window shade was not pulled down all the way and she could see the bare strip of glass, the drops on it glistening coldly in the light of the street lamp, and slowly sliding down.

Stephania got up and walked to the window to pull the shade down. It was dark: outside she could not see anything, but somehow she could feel the rain, its drops sharp and frosty, piercing the face, drenching the clothes, making them heavy, and cold. And the trees; she could sense them too, bent under the rain, dark and shiny as if covered with black polish, and farther, the road, covered with mud, that stuck to the shoes and dragged them down. With an impatient gesture she pulled the shade down. What a night . . . and only a week ago it was snowing.

Still it seemed to her that that was how it should have been; as if all the time she had known it would happen on a night just like this. Lying back in her bed, the blanket tucked tightly around her body as if the rain might penetrate even here, she thought that whenever anything happened it was at a time like that, when it was raining, and the wind too was always there . . . They always came when it rained, as if they waited for it, as if they were ashamed or afraid perhaps . . . and wanted the rain to deafen the sound of their steps. . . .

She sat up and brushed her hair off her face. It was disgusting, simply disgusting how she always had to drag one thing into another, and it had been getting worse and worse lately. Every moment was itself and something else too, something that had no connection with it, that had happened a long time ago. It was like living two lives at once. One was plenty and enough. It was high time for her to get hold of herself.

But the rustle of rain was still around her. Barbara must be hearing it too, lying alone there in the hospital room. Those nurses with the cold automatons' voices were probably no better than Sister Ingeborg here; kept sitting in the living room drinking coffee, not caring a damn what was going on.

If Barbara should start crying they perhaps would not hear her at all, or the rain might swallow her voice as before it had swallowed the ringing of the bell. Nonsense, a nurse was with her all the time, certainly; perhaps even a doctor. The best hospital in the city, Fru Gustavsson had said, and she knew what she was talking about. "The very best in all Stockholm."

. . . The best hospital. Who was it that had also been in the best hospital? It was Aunt Sarna. Yes, she remembered it exactly. The best . . . and still . . .

And she had been, was so healthy, red-cheeked, always rushing, always busy, and it was not the first child either. She had had three of them before, but wanted another one still. Stephania remembered suddenly how she had gone to visit her with Mother . . . they had had to wait then in a hall that had a floor covered with red carpet; there were mirrors all around and even palms stood in the corner. Then they had seen Aunt Sarna and the baby, lying in a small white room, all filled with flowers. Everything was fine, the doctor, small and chubby, told them, and the huge nurse assured them she was in the best hands here. But later . . . she had never been told what had happened. It must have been after-birth infection or something like that. For a few days no dinner was cooked, everybody kept whispering as if someone very tired was sleeping next door only the phone kept ringing all the time and Mother would not leave it even for a moment. Until at last she let the receiver fall from her hands; it swung to and fro like a pendulum. . . . It looked as if it would smash any moment but it did not. It's all over, Mother said, and walked out — the receiver still hanging limply in the air, and the silence ringing in it seemed to flood the room, heavy and hollow . . .

They tried to keep it secret from Grandmother but of course that could not last forever. Somehow Grandmother had found out — from the maid probably. And the next day when she came back from school she saw Grandmother sitting on a small stool, her face in her hands, swinging her body to and fro as if she were sitting in a rocking chair. She was crying in a high moaning voice that seemed to burst out of her as if she wanted to stop and could not. Stephania had never seen anyone crying like that; she wanted to run away but somehow could not, and stood staring, hidden behind the door. She looked very small, Grandmother, bent in two, her ribs protruding sharply under the thin dress, her hair falling in gray meager streaks over the yellowish neck. Until all of a sudden she tore one hand off her face — the other seemed glued to it — looked around and said in a voice that was now almost soft and very surprised: "It was the best hospital, the very best." And it was not as if she were reproaching them, the doctor, the nurse, from that red-carpeted, palm-filled house, but something or perhaps someone else who made even the best you could do of no use . . . no use at all. Stephania ran away then. The funeral was on the next day, but she did not go. Mother wouldn't let her.

So, here we are again — Stephania thought furiously — Aunt Sarna: things that had happened fifteen years ago. And if they happened, so what? Thousands of babies are born every day, Fru Gustavsson said — and everything goes all right, always . . . and the other thing had happened in Poland. With all their mirrors and palms they knew nothing about medicine. This was Sweden, here it was altogether different. . . .

She glanced at the clock. It was almost four now, thank God. Perhaps they had called from the hospital while she was still asleep, and that idiot Sister Ingeborg did not come to tell her. She got up, put on her slippers — they were cold as if damp — and walked out of the room.

[ 149 ]

Sister Ingeborg sat in the living room, the inevitable cup of coffee in her hand.

"Was there any phone call for me?"

"Phone call? Now . . . in the middle of the night?"

"I know it's night. But my sister is giving birth to her first baby. My brother-in-law was supposed to call me as soon as . . ."

"No, no one has called."

Stephania looked at her. Her skin was wrinkled as if a part of her face had been torn out suddenly, and the skin, too spacious, collapsed into innumerable folds. She must be sixty or more . . . and still working every night. Stephania suddenly felt sorry for Sister Ingeborg. She felt like staying and talking to her. Anyhow it was better than going back to the room.

"She is in Saint Olaf's. A very good hospital, supposedly," she said in a conciliatory voice.

"Fairly good." Sister took a long loud sip from her cup. Why on earth did she have to smack like that?

"I hope it'll be all right. Those things always go all right nowadays?"

"On the whole." Sister Ingeborg raised her cup solemnly. "It's all in the hands of God, of course."

"Rather, in the hands of doctors." Stephania smiled thinly. "Good night, Sister." And without waiting for an answer she walked out.

It was almost five now. Barbara had gone to the hospital at three. Fourteen hours . . . it should be over soon. Did she have pains all the time? It must be horrible, everything torn inside you, changed suddenly as if it were not your own body at all. . . . How could it be that she had never thought about that? She had never asked Barbara if she was afraid, of pain . . . or of something else. It seemed so simple all the time. She had just kept joking with Barbara about the baby, and talking about the name, about the party they would give when it was here. But she had never stopped to think what happened before it was here . . . Even last time when Barbara came on Sunday she hardly asked her how she felt, and did not even really say good-bye — just "So long — and if Junior comes in the meantime, give him my love." But . . . yes, she should have talked to her and asked about everything; and also, above all, she should have explained. . . . There were so many things between her and Barbara that had to be explained. But somehow they never really talked to each other. . . .

. . . She should have explained to her about the quarrel they had had a few weeks ago, about that and all those other things; that she did not mean them, that it just happened; something would come over her and she would say words which she did not mean — she didn't understand herself. . . .

. . . Like when she refused to kiss Barbara good-bye. "I hate emotional scenes," she had said; but it wasn't true, not a word of it. Barbara was standing opposite her, her face very pale underneath the red hat. And that time too it was raining . . . that was why Barbara had decided to leave that night. It was much safer when it was raining; the guards stood hidden in their booths, afraid to stick out their noses, and did not look too closely at who was passing the gate of the ghetto. So it was quite lucky that Barbara had just that day got her identification papers. They were made out in the name of Jadviga Wysocka, born in Warsaw, Catholic. And Mother had had to sell her wedding ring and all the jewelry she had hidden to pay the three thousand *zloty* to the man who made false papers for Jews that wanted to run away from the ghetto. It was bright yellow, that paper . . . what did they call it? A *Kennkarte* — that was it — it looked so fresh, brand-new. Too new — Mother said — one could see at once it was false. They passed the yellow hard piece of paper from hand to hand, tasted it, tried to crinkle it, and Father even sat down on it to make it look used for a long time, worn. But the *Kennkarte* refused to look worn; it remained smooth and shiny, the print black and distinct, and on the small square picture above the signature Jadviga Wysocka, Barbara looked very Aryan, smiling and blond, a big cross on her neck. And it was when she looked at that picture that both was and was not Barbara, and at the strange name underneath written with easy fantastic flourishes at the end, as if that was the name Barbara had been using all her life long, that it started. But still she said nothing. . . .

And later in the afternoon it began to rain. She never could quite understand how it could rain in the ghetto, how the drops could find any space to squeeze themselves in among all those buildings and walls that separated the ghetto from the rest of the city, among all those crowds that filled the narrow streets. . . .

Still, it did rain and Barbara, looking through the dirty panes, said: "I had better leave tonight."

"Yes . . ." Mother said, and she took Barbara's coat to sew a few bank notes under the lining. Mother could not find the eye of the needle, her hand was trembling so, and it was she herself, who had to do it for Barbara. Her hand did not tremble at all; she felt very quiet and just watched Barbara getting dressed as if for a masquerade. She had to look very Aryan, Barbara, and so she combed her hair up, the way the German women did, painted her lips bright red, and even put on high-heeled shoes and a red hat that she had not worn since the beginning of the war. She grew more and more strange, Barbara, more and more like Jadviga Wysocka smiling on the yellow *Kennkarte*.

Mother had finished sewing. Barbara put on the coat. And just as she was crossing the room to say good-bye to Father, who sat silent and motionless on the only bed, Mother cried: "Barbara, you forgot to take off the armband!" There it was: a broad strip of linen, fastened right above the elbow, white and shiny, the blue star of David big and sharply drawn in the middle. Mother started taking it off, but the armband was sewn to the sleeve, and wouldn't come off. Barbara said, "Let me do it." And she tore it off, impatiently, with anger. The white piece of linen floated for a moment and then fell on the floor. Barbara, walking toward Father, stepped on it. And then she — no, it was not she, it was something in her — said: "Barbara, don't step on it. You don't have to wear it any longer, I know; you're running away . . . but we still might . . ."

"Stephania!" She never knew who cried it out then; Barbara, Mother, Father — or all of them.

"I didn't say anything. All I meant was that not everybody is as lucky as Barbara, blond and Aryan-looking. . . . Some of us have to stay here, and can still use it — the armband I mean. As long as they let us use it, of course . . ." That was what she said then; why and what for — she did not know then, nor did she now, either.

But they were not listening. Father got up and embraced Barbara, but he was not kissing her, he only held her close to him and said nothing. Until Barbara suddenly cried: "I can't take it any longer — " and she ran to Mother, and kissed her again and again. But Mother was silent, too. "Stephania," Barbara called to her, and walked to the corner where she was standing.

[ 152 ]

. . . It was dark in the room, they had pulled the shades down so that no one would see what they were doing, and they had only one candle to light. She had noticed it, yes she knew it now — she had noticed that the big trunk with the iron-covered edges stood in Barbara's way, and that Barbara was not looking at it. But she said nothing. Barbara stumbled and fell. Father rushed to her, lifted her up. "Oh — " he cried. "You have to be more careful, dear, remember you have to be very careful," he repeated, as if something terrible had happened. It was all right, Barbara said, she had not hurt herself, it really was nothing. And, stretching out her hands Barbara said: "Stephania."

And then she had said: "Please don't, Barbara. I hate emotional scenes. You know it."

"As you wish." Barbara was very pale. She did not try to kiss her any more, only shook hands with her and left.

Then they all stood at the window and watched Barbara sneaking through the streets, almost empty now because the curfew time was near. Until at last she disappeared in the darkness, and in the rain that was growing harder and harder.

Only then Mother said: "Stephania, how could you . . . ?"

She did not answer. How could she? Yes, how could she . . . ? She did not know herself.

Did Barbara remember it? She had never mentioned it; perhaps she had forgotten it, or perhaps she did not want to remember because everything was so fine between them when Barbara had found her after the war. Yes, she was good, Barbara, good and loving — she had traveled all over Germany trying to find her. And then after she did find her at last, she took care of her, took her from one doctor to another, and spent all her time with her. . . .Only later when Thadeus came it was different. Still, she should not have done that to Barbara. "Congratulations," she said when Barbara told her she and Thadeus were getting married. "Congratulations"; that was all, and then she walked out and did not come back until late in the evening. And it was not that she was jealous. She knew Barbara would be married soon with all those men running after her; it was just that it had come so suddenly, that she hardly knew anything was going on between her and Thadeus. After that, something had changed between them. She did not quarrel with Barbara, but still it was quite different. But it was not Barbara's fault. It was her own . . . most of all.

[ 153 ]

She should have explained it all to Barbara; she would do it now, as soon as it was over, as soon as everything was all right. Those things always went all right nowadays — at least on the whole . . . on the whole.

Six o'clock. Soon the day would begin. The rain had stopped completely, but from time to time she could hear a solitary drop detaching itself from the pane and falling on the window sill with a soft splashing sound. Someone was approaching the room. She jumped out of the bed, rushed into the hall.

"Anybody called?"

"No, no one."

Stephania went back silently.

Fru Gustavsson came in at seven. "So what is it, a boy or a girl?"

"I don't know yet," Stephania said.

"Oh." It took Fru Gustavsson a little while to form her lips into a smile. "Well, of course, sometimes it takes longer. . . . Especially with the first baby. My sister . . ." And immediately Fru Gustavsson produced examples from her own family. . . . Her sister had lain seventeen hours in childbirth, and still everything went fine, and the baby was the prettiest one you could imagine, a little doll; and her cousin . . . Stephania only nodded. She lay with her eyes fixed on the door, lifting her head at the slightest sound.

Breakfast was served, then Willy came, then the physiotherapist and Doctor Ström. After he had left she got up and walked to and fro in the hall, looking at the telephone as if trying to force it to utter the sound she was waiting for. Until at last she gave up.

And then, when they had just finished lunch — Stephania in spite of Thura's imploring gaze did not touch anything — Fru Gustavsson burst in. "A boy," she cried, "I was sure all the time it would be a boy. Go to the telephone, your brother-in-law wants to speak to you."

She got up and slowly, feeling suddenly very tired, left the room. "Hello."

"A boy, Stephania, a boy! Five pounds five ounces, and Barbara feels fine, too."

She said nothing for a while, and at last, "Thank God . . . I . . . was so worried. So it is all right. What time did it happen?"

"This morning around six . . ."

"Around six?"

There was silence in the receiver. "I was awfully tired," Thadeus said at last. "I asked the nurse to call you and she forgot, or didn't have time, something like that. . . . I'm sorry, Stephania."

"It's quite all right," she said, thinking — at six, seven hours ago, he was tired. . . .

Thadeus went on talking. "God, it was dreadful, Stephania, all that waiting! I wouldn't like to go through it again. It was lucky Gross called me and asked me to come over to them. Alone I would have gone crazy, I'm telling you, I would much rather go through the whole business myself instead of sitting there and waiting and waiting. Well, it's good it's over now."

"Yes," Stephania said, "it's over. Congratulations, Thadeus."

"Thanks . . . Good-bye, dear, I'll see you Sunday." He hung up.

Seven hours, she thought again, walking back to the room.

"So the baby's here," Thura said when she opened the door.

"Yes," Stephania said, "it is here." And only now she understood — it was here, the baby, Barbara's baby. She could see it, funny, pink and warm. "Yes," she said once more. "The baby is here." Then she sat down on the bed smiling, feeling how it was rising in her, ripening slowly — a great soft quietness and sweetness.

CHAPTER 15

THE TIME of Fröken Nilsson's departure was coming closer and closer. The black dress, tightened and lengthened with a flounce to meet the demands of the "new look," was lying on her chair in constant readiness. Anna, Fröken Nilsson's sister, wrote from Eskilstuna that she had found a room for her, not too large and rather dark, she admitted, but cheap, and the landlady was very nice too. And in the bottom of Fröken Nilsson's drawer the card was hidden which she had bought from Willy to enclose with the flowers she intended to send Doctor Liliencrona. It took Fröken

Nilsson a long time of careful consideration to make the right choice; at last she decided upon a card on which two doves were painted, perched in opposite corners glancing at each other with longing pink eyes and desperately stretching their gilded wings.

Yes, everything was working out fine, and Fröken Nilsson would have been perfectly satisfied if it were not for her walking. According to Doctor Ström she was walking excellently, but Fröken Nilsson herself had a different opinion on that matter. It was a scandal — she thought — how they treated you here, forcing you to run around with the heavy plaster on your leg, and driving you out on the street before you even could take a step. In the beginning it had not been quite so bad. She walked with the help of a device that looked like one of those children's play-pens, only without the railing in the back. Fröken Nilsson stood inside it like some gigantic child, leaning with all her body upon the railings around her, and slowly pushing the one in the front. She was not afraid of falling down in it. But as soon as she got used to it a little, and ventured to walk out into the hall without Fru Gustavsson's help, Ström was here saying, "Enough of that easy life, Fröken Nilsson, it's time for you to start walking on crutches." The crutches were terrible, they hurt her under the arms, gliding to and fro maliciously. Fröken Nilsson, after a short attempt at taking a few steps, collapsed on her bed, and refused to get up.

But the next day, Professor himself commanded her to walk across the room right during the great inspection visit, and in the eyes of all. "You're healthy now, Fröken Nilsson," he said. "We can't keep you here forever," and they all looked indifferently when, all covered with sweat and hardly able to catch a breath, she struggled through the room that seemed to grow bigger and bigger and have no end at all. Fröken Nilsson did not answer Professor's good-bye; she lay panting heavily, and thought that even Doctor Liliencrona had not said a word to defend her. No, he stood there dumb like a mummy, and just kept staring at her, when she was almost falling down. Fröken Nilsson felt disappointed. She even wondered whether she should send him the flowers after all.

On the next day, Professor came again, to show the ward to some foreign doctors. He spent a long time at Stephania's bed, then at Thura's. Fröken Nilsson sat all prepared, waiting for the usual procedure, for the pile of her X-rays to be shown, for Professor to say: "And here's a very complicated case." But he did not even stop at her bed. "This patient is going to be discharged soon"; that was all, as if once you were going to be discharged you were not worth as much as a look, a single word.

In the afternoon Fru Gustavsson came in. Fröken Nilsson had to go out into the living room; yes, on crutches; and all by herself. That was what Doctor Ström had said. The walk through the long hall was even worse than she had expected. The cast on her leg seemed to grow tighter and tighter; her foot burned and throbbed, and she had to stop again and again. On the way back Fru Gustavsson had to help her, although it was distinctly against Doctor Ström's orders.

Fröken Nilsson had never had any trouble falling asleep. But this time she lay awake deep into the night. Something was pulsing and pounding in her leg; a heavy warm fluid seemed to gather within it, struggling to burst out. She tossed from one side to another, put a pillow under her leg, and at last fell asleep. But she felt something strange and hostile was happening to her.

. . .Her leg grew, now: bigger and bigger, it looked like a white pole now, it sprawled itself over the whole bed and threatened to throw her out. Then something black, like a bedbug only much bigger, appeared on the cast and crept inside, the fat body wriggling to and fro, and then it crawled on her leg, sticky, warm, and terrible. She did not know what it was, but she knew it would bite her, tear out a hole in her flesh, creep into her body. No, she cried, no! And that was how she woke up.

It was Stephania who first heard the cry. The persistent wailing penetrated into her sleep, insisted upon her waking up. Reluctantly she opened her eyes. Who was crying? Everything was silent now. She must have dreamt it. But then the cry returned — first a piteous wailing only, that stopped as if gathering strength, and then burst into a moan — loud, piercing, disconsolate. Who was it, "Thura . . ." she whispered.

No answer came.

"Thura," she repeated, "what's the matter, what has happened?"

A pause again. And at last a voice, hoarse and interrupted by sobs, said, "It isn't Thura. It's me."

It was Fröken Nilsson then. What could be wrong with *her?* Nothing much, certainly. Stephania pulled her blanket higher. She felt angry at being waked up. Going home in a couple of days, and now raising such a row in the middle of the night. It was just like her.

And here it was again, the all pervading sound, sharper than before, as if coming through tightened lips, struggling to force the cry inside. But at last they seemed to have to give in and the cry burst out, almost triumphant in its unrestrained complaint.

"What is it?" This time it was Thura's voice. "Fröken Stephania?"

"It's not me."

A hesitant pause again, and then Thura's voice: "Fröken Nilsson, what's happened? Why are you crying?" But instead of an answer, a new sound came — a strange scraping, as if a hand was desperately groping in the darkness. Something clinked — a glass pushed aside, something heavily fell on the floor.

"Do you want me to call someone?" Thura asked.

A sob and then Fröken Nilsson said: "Yes, I can't find the bell."

The thought of Thura's weak voice, straining, calling desperately into the darkness, was unbearable. Stephania pressed the button. "I've rung already," she said, trying to make her voice as indifferent as possible. Then she sat up, looked. . . . A white shape was raising itself above Fröken Nilsson's bed, thick and huge like a monstrous finger pointing to something high above. It was her leg, perched perpendicularly almost above the bed. What was the matter with her? Still she did not ask.

They waited. Fröken Nilsson cried softly, repeating one and the same thing again and again, in a voice so hoarse and tired that the words were incomprehensible. Only after a long while the refrain-like repetition became clear to Stephania: "Oh, my God," she was saying, "Oh, God," and the rest was drowned in sobs. Then again there was the searching sound, fingernails scratching the blanket, the railing of the bed.

"What is it that you want, Fröken Nilsson?" Thura pleaded. "Please tell me."

"Light," Fröken Nilsson answered, and the word sounded very loud in the silence. "I must see it. I . . . "

Stephania jumped out of the bed. Why wouldn't she tell them what was the matter with her? Why wasn't the nurse coming? One could go mad here. She walked to Fröken Nilsson's bed and turned the light on. For an instant Stephania's eyes rested on her face — it was red, swollen with tears, and feverish. The blanket

[ 158 ]

had slipped down from the bed, the immense body in the wrinkled shirt lay uncovered. She bent, picked the blanket up and laid it over her. "Thanks," Fröken Nilsson murmured. She was not looking at Stephania; her eyes were fixed on her leg. And suddenly she lifted her arms, propped herself up, in an effort to raise herself. The leg swayed. "I can't get up," Fröken Nilsson groaned. "I can't see it."

Stephania stepped closer. "What do you want to see?" Only now Fröken Nilsson seemed to recognize that it was Stephania who was standing before her . . . She hesitated. "I don't know myself. I . . . It seems to me I have worms crawling over my leg," she whispered at last.

"What? Worms?"

"Crawling all over. I can feel them, wet, sticky. And then it hurts horribly . . ." Her voice rose to a cry again.

"You want me to look?"

Fröken Nilsson nodded silently.

Stephania bent over the bed. There were no worms, of course, there was nothing but the cast grayish and heavy, except, yes . . . except that its edge cut deep into the flesh, so deep that there was a thick red line around it, and above it the skin was bluish as if the blood could not reach there. And there, right above the foot, there was a small yellow spot — she touched it; it was wet, as if the plaster was melting. "I think it's pus," Stephania said slowly.

"Pus, why, where from?" Fröken Nilsson murmured. Her reddened eyes blinked as if she were suddenly torn out of sleep.

"I wish I knew where that nurse is hiding herself," Stephania said instead of answering. She was bewildered; something had happened, something was happening now, what — she could not understand. All she knew was that she wanted to get away from here, away from Fröken Nilsson, from her cries, from the white shape perched menacingly above the disheveled bed.

"I'm going to look for her," she said, and left.

The living room was empty. She walked back through the hall opening the doors of one room after another. Blue light streamed from them, the heavy air of night, quiet breath of human bodies plunged in sleep. Someone woke up — "Who's there!" a voice murmured. Someone sighed heavily. Where was she, damn it?

Sister Ingeborg was in Room Six, the last in the hall, lifting a newly operated patient.

"Sister?"

"What is it?" she asked without turning herself.

"We've been ringing for the last hour . . . at least. Something is wrong with Fröken Nilsson."

"Just a moment. I have to give a bedpan here, first."

"She is screaming — "

"All right, all right, I'll come as soon as I can." Then as if suddenly remembering something, Sister Ingeborg turned to Stephania. "Did you say Fröken Nilsson?"

"Yes."

"But she's all right, she's going home soon."

"Something happened to her leg."

Sister Ingeborg put the bedpan on the floor and rushed out of the room. Stephania followed her.

When they came in Fröken Nilsson had managed to raise herself, and sat looking at her leg. She pointed to the yellow spot. "Do you see, Sister?"

Sister Ingeborg looked, moved closer, looked once more, and then walked out. After a while she returned with the young intern who was on duty that night with her. He looked somehow embarrassed, murmured something about the pain, and they left. Sister Ingeborg was back, the syringe in her hand.

"Penicillin?" Fröken Nilsson asked.

"No, morphine, so you can sleep."

Morphine, all of a sudden; not after the "great day," but just because of a small yellow spot. Thura looked at Stephania, but Stephania shrugged as if to say she herself did not understand it. Fröken Nilsson wanted to protest, to ask something, but before she had opened her mouth the needle was in her arm. "So, now you'll feel better." Sister Ingeborg turned the light off.

Fröken Nilsson's moaning grew lower and lower until she was silent. Her leg was resting on the bed now. "I . . . I don't understand why she gave it to me . . ." she murmured drowsily and at last she fell asleep.

Thura whispered: "Fröken Stephania?"

"Yes?"

"Something must be wrong with her, very wrong, don't you think so?"

"I don't know, I'm not a doctor," Stephania said. She didn't feel like talking.

Room Five was the first Sister Gudrun visited that morning. Fröken Nilsson, still drowsy after the large dose of morphine, answered her questions in reluctant monosyllables. . . . Yes, it hurt, and then that awful creepy feeling . . . like worms, but she said it was not worms, of course. . . .

"She? Whom do you mean?"

"Fröken Ackermann." And only then Fröken Nilsson realized that it was Stephania who last night had turned the light on for her, who had gone to call Sister Ingeborg. It was strange, very strange, but Fröken Nilsson was too tired to think about that. Later, she thought; later — and soon she was dozing again.

After Sister Gudrun had left, Doctor Ström came in. He did not wake Fröken Nilsson; he just lifted the blanket and looked at the yellow spot, at the swollen flesh pouring out of the cast as if frantically trying to free itself. "God, what a mess," he murmured, and that was pretty strong, even for him.

And a few minutes later Anders came in, the plump and pinkish attendant from the operating room, who was called to the ward only on one occasion — when an especially complicated cast had to be taken off. He walked toward Fröken Nilsson's bed and said, "Good morning, Fröken Nilsson, good morning." Fröken Nilsson did not move. Anders touched her arm.

"At least you could let people sleep when they're tired," she murmured angrily.

"You'll sleep later, but now we're going to give your leg some fresh air." And out of his pocket Anders produced a pair of scissors — big, jagged and shiny.

Fröken Nilsson shuddered. The scissors opened and closed like the jaws of a menacing animal.

"What do you mean?"

"I'm going to take your cast off." The scissors clanged greedily, maliciously, and slid underneath the cast.

Fröken Nilsson covered her eyes with her hand. Stephania and Thura shivered. They all knew Anders was a true master at opening the casts; they knew that during the twenty-five years of his career he had never so much as scratched a patient; still . . . when the scissors started gnawing on the plaster they could not help fearing that any moment the sharp teeth would bite into the flesh, hungrily tear a piece out of it.

"Sto-op!" Fröken Nilsson cried.

"Oh, Lord!" Thura whispered. Stephania closed her eyes. The scissors reappeared, glittered in the sun. No, there was no blood on them.

"Your leg is a little swollen, my dear, that's what makes it hurt," Anders said good-humoredly, and as if that explanation had removed all pain he forced the scissors under the cast again. Until suddenly Fröken Nilsson raised herself and pushed him away with all her strength so that he staggered. "Stop. It hurts!"

"All right, all right"; Anders was not offended at all. He produced out of his pocket another pair of scissors, smaller but sharper, looking more vicious somehow. "This will be much nicer," he said obligingly, and began to jump busily from one side to another, like a skillful barber performing a complicated operation on a fastidious client. Fröken Nilsson winced and groaned; small pieces of plaster flew out on all sides, the scissors clanged snappily. Suddenly she moaned louder than ever; Anders made the final and highest jump, and tore the cast apart. Then with one swift gesture he pulled it out from underneath Fröken Nilsson's leg and hurled it on the floor. And there it lay, that cast that only a few moments ago seemed to have been a part of Fröken Nilsson, incorporate with her — now just a heap of rubbish in the grayish heap of plaster dust. Layers of dry skin, hairs, crumbs, littered it, and down where the foot began the lining was yellow and sticky.

And the leg, so suddenly deprived of it, seemed very naked and defenseless. Fröken Nilsson did not want to see it; it seemed so strange, formless; the skin brown and peeling in large sheets; to look at it was like looking at a face once familiar and now, after years, withered and changed; it was not a part of her, it was just an object which she could not even lift, over which she had no power at all, something fearful in its strangeness. Still she could not tear her eyes away. Above the foot a tiny hole was gaping like an open mouth, yellow bubbles leaking out of it and spreading all over in thin streaks. And the nails were greenish and hard, and here and there a thick wiry hair stuck fantastically above the dry skin. They said hair and nails kept growing after you were dead; that was how it must look. Fröken Nilsson closed her eyes. She lay down, and said nothing when Anders proudly declared, "So, there, now it's done, you see, it wasn't bad at all." He picked up his scissors and left.

Although it was not the day of the great inspection visit, al-

[ 162 ]

though no foreign guests were here to be shown around, Professor himself came to Room Number Five. He told Sister Gudrun to start the penicillin injection again, yes, right now at once, and to send Fröken Nilsson to the X-ray room.

They took her there immediately after he had left, not in the wheel chair but on the stretcher, as they usually did only with the newly operated patients.

The next morning, before the room had even been cleaned, and crumbs and smudges of talc covered the floor, Professor came in again. He was accompanied by a small man of indefinite age who looked as if he had been patched together from many triangles — one for the nose, one even sharper for the chin, and still another — shiny black — was formed by his hair falling on his forehead. "Professor Ekström from the Karolinska Institute wants to have a look at your leg," Professor said, and turning to the stranger, "This is our Fröken Nilsson."

"Very glad to meet you," Fröken Nilsson said with dignity. She remembered the day when he hadn't even introduced her to that foreign doctor — and now, he brought a professor from the Karolinska especially for her. Fröken Nilsson felt an injustice was being mended.

Professor stepped back and the little man came closer to the bed, looked at her leg, smacked his lips. "X-rays," he ordered briefly.

"Here they are."

He passed them before his eyes one after another, shook his head and murmured as if angry at something. "So you've tried the bone transplantation too?"

"Yes, twice; it wouldn't do. We had to try the nail."

"I don't believe in the nail. One of those German inventions, gets you into trouble always. But of course, there was nothing else you could do. . . ."

"Yes, we've tried everything."

"Well . . . I told you before, I don't see any other way out . . ." And the guest shrugged his shoulders in a nervous, slightly contemptuous gesture. Then, all of a sudden he began to walk toward the door, his short legs taking enormous steps. Professor dashed after him. In the door they stopped and the guest started explaining something, his fiercely gesticulating hands swaying like the arms of a windmill.

Another X-ray; then the head of the children's ward came to see

Fröken Nilsson and then the week-end was here; quiet, too quiet somehow, after all those hectic days, but still different from all other week-ends — suspended in the heavy air of anxious expectations. But nothing happened — only on Saturday Fru Gustavsson took Fröken Nilsson's dress back to the storage room. "It will get dusty here," she said. "Take it, I don't need it now," Fröken Nilsson said, and that was all.

Professor came again on Monday, all alone this time. Without the customary retinue of doctors and nurses, he seemed smaller, his gestures had lost something of their expansiveness and his voice sounded with unusual softness. "Good morning," he said, and smiled at nobody in particular. Then he sat down on Fröken Nilsson's bed, and cleared his throat. "Well," he murmured, and he looked as if waiting for Fröken Nilsson to say something. "Well."

But Fröken Nilsson remained silent. A great indignant impatience was rising in her. Well — he says — and sits here and just stares at her as if he was seeing her for the first time in his life. What did he want from her? What was all that business about — coming here every day, he and other doctors and X-rays taken again and again . . . ? Playing hide and seek with her — that was what it looked like. Something was going on and she wished he would come out with it. "Well . . . nothing," Fröken Nilsson said furiously.

"Well," Professor repeated. "Professor Ekström from the Karolinska said . . ." and as if mentioning his august colleague's name had strengthened him, Professor began to walk to and fro in his usual manner, indicating that the moment of weakness was over. "As I said, Professor Ekström completely agreed with me . . ." He hesitated again. "We discussed your case, dear Fröken Nilsson, and you must realize" — there was a slight note of reproach in his voice, as if he knew Fröken Nilsson was unwilling to realize. "Yes, as you know, we've tried practically everything. But now this infection — and besides we've found some splinters — the bone's disintegrating, you see. So you must see there's nothing else we can do . . ."

"Nothing else? Don't tell me you're going to send me home like that?" And Fröken Nilsson pointed to the immobile strange object that was her leg.

"Of course not."

"I wish you would tell me in plain words what you're going to do with me." That was insolent, that was more than insolent, and Fröken Nilsson was fully aware of it. But after all, he could make a saint jump out of his skin, and besides didn't Stephania always talk to them like that? And right she was. They wouldn't listen to you otherwise.

"Of course, of course. . . . The point is — this is the only way. And besides it'll not be too bad either. With the artificial limbs they're making today . . . And you'll keep your own knee."

"My own knee? What do you mean now?"

"Well, when we amputate the leg it'll be below the knee, you see?"

"Amputate my leg? Cut it off, you mean?" Fröken Nilsson cried. Professor nodded silently.

"No!" She bent, grasped her leg with both her hands. "No, you cannot do it, you can't. Nothing's really wrong with it, nothing . . ." And then she fell silent, still bent over her leg, as if defending it with her whole body. "No!" she shrieked suddenly. "No-o-o!"

"Just be sensible, Fröken Nilsson, just try to understand. With an artificial limb, you'll walk excellently, splendidly."

Fröken Nilsson did not answer. She wasn't listening to him. "Good-bye," Professor said, and then already in the door, added, "We'll take you on Friday, Friday at nine."

For a long time Fröken Nilsson did not move. Then her fingers as if of themselves began to pass over her leg, feeling each pore, each muscle, the outlines of the bone, to and fro, to and fro, like patient feet wandering for the last time through a familiar place. Then they stopped upon a protruding convexity — the place where the bone had been broken, circled around the wound covered now with a piece of gauze, once, then again and again. . . . And suddenly tears, silent and big, began to fall from her eyes, rolled down her cheeks, and one after another dropped heavily on the warm flesh of her bare leg.

Thura and Stephania were silent. They only looked, marked each movement of her hand, saw the tears. And it seemed to them that in the great stillness they could hear them, as one hears drops of rain falling, and that second seemed more unbearable than the loudest, most piercing cry. Had she only said something — Thura thought — so that she could tell her everything would be all right, so that she could remind her how well Willy was walking on his

[ 165 ]

wooden legs. . . . But the silence lasted, and there was nothing she could do — just look at Fröken Nilsson, and then at Stephania hoping that Stephania perhaps would know the right word to say, the right thing to do. But Stephania's face was cold, remote, as if she were noticing nothing.

And at last Thura whispered, "Fröken Nilsson, please don't, don't cry." Fröken Nilsson did not answer.

"Please, don't, please do stop. It can't help anyhow, you just tire yourself out."

No answer.

And Thura, knowing Fröken Nilsson was not listening, knowing her words meant nothing to her, but just to stop those ceaselessly falling tears, kept repeating, "Please don't cry, please." Stephania sat up impatiently. Why couldn't Thura keep quiet now? Stop crying; of course she had to cry. Who wouldn't? Two years in the hospital, and now back where you started, lying here and waiting for that butcher to cut your leg off. Don't cry. . . . And Professor too had made it sound so easy: "You'll keep your knee — " How nice of him. Longingly she looked at the door. If she only could get out of here. But something kept her in that room, as if she felt it would be wrong to leave, knew she had to stay to watch Fröken Nilsson crying, to listen to Thura repeating: "Please don't cry, please . . ."

And again as so often before Stephania felt it was not what Thura was saying, that was unbearable, but her voice — pleading, calling for a gesture; for the movement of a hand — quieting and tender. It was as if each time Thura repeated her pleading words, she was looking at her, waiting for her to get up, to complete by a gesture what she was saying.

Stephania got up. There was no use in her staying here. She walked to the door. But before she opened it she turned back, to Fröken Nilsson's bed, straightened the blanket, and then slowly took the pillow, shook it, smoothed it and carefully put it back in its place. "There," she murmured — "so, there," and then without looking at Fröken Nilsson walked out.

The living room was empty. It was almost lunchtime and the people who usually sat there must have gone back to their rooms. Only someone's knitting, a purple half-finished mitten, lay on the sofa, and a pair of crutches stood in the corner. Stephania looking at them remembered how Professor had forced Fröken Nilsson to walk, how she moved, saying "I can't," her face crimson, her lips open struggling for breath. It must have been hurting her already. Why did all that happen? She had done everything, let herself be cut again and again, starved herself for months. And still it helped her not at all. Was it possible that sometimes, with all the penicillin, streptomycin, all the new techniques, they could do nothing? Or was it somebody's fault — Fröken Nilsson's, Ström's, Professor's? Yes, there must have been a mistake someplace. She had always been so quiet, Fröken Nilsson, so passive; never asked any questions, never paid any attention to what they did with her. Yes, you had to watch them constantly, check everything they did. There must be ways of doing it. She herself would find them out, she had to. What happened to Fröken Nilsson was an exception, an accident — but no accident would ever happen to her, she would make sure.

A few women, all in the identical gray hospital clothes, came in. They looked at her curiously. Probably the news about Fröken Nilsson had spread all over by now, and they wanted to find out all the gossip from her. A new sensation, that was what it was for them. Stephania got up hastily and walked out.

In the hall she met Fru Gustavsson pushing Fröken Nilsson's wheel chair before her. "Poor soul, she'll not need it for quite a while now," Fru Gustavsson said. "God, I'm so sorry for her, so sorry."

"Yes," Stephania said. "It's a great pity, isn't it?"

Fru Gustavsson nodded, and started pushing the wheel chair.

Yes — Stephania thought — she too felt sorry for her. But thinking it over, quietly in cold blood, what was there to get so excited about? You've seen much worse things happen, haven't you? she thought angrily. It wasn't such a terrible tragedy to walk with a wooden leg, and besides, why should she be sorry for her, for Fröken Nilsson of all people? Would Fröken Nilsson be sorry for her, if it were the other way around, if it was her leg they were to cut off? Certainly not. She wouldn't waste her pity on a foreigner, she just would start counting how much good Swedish money, her money, it cost. But of course, you had to feel sorry for her. It was typical — the good old Jewish quality — they spit in your face and you say it's raining, they would love to drown you in a spoonful of water, and you walk around feeling sorry for them. Sorry, after all that Nilsson had said to her. She tried to

[ 167 ]

remember that moment, the sallow face, the sharp voice saying, "You foreigners have everything . . . for our money." Yes, that was exactly what she had said. But still, all that did not matter now; somehow it seemed to her that the Fröken Nilsson she was trying to remember now had vanished together with the wheel chair rolled out by Fru Gustavsson, that there was no connection between the fat woman with the hateful face and the motionless figure, crying silently. She felt sorry for Fröken Nilsson whether it was right or not. Was she getting sentimental? She shook her head, and stealthily, as afraid of something, opened the door.

Fröken Nilsson was lying quietly now. Was she asleep? Stephania glanced at her. No, her eyes were wide open; they looked steadily at one point visible only to Fröken Nilsson, suspended somewhere high above her head. Stephania tiptoed by her, and trying to make as little noise as possible, slipped into her bed.

The rest of the day passed in complete silence. No one turned the lights on and they lay, with the darkness around them growing more and more dense, until Sister Gudrun and Fru Gustavsson came in with dinner. Fröken Nilsson seemed not to have noticed them at all. Sister Gudrun dealt out the food, first for Stephania, then for Thura.

"And for Fröken Nilsson?" Fru Gustavsson asked.

"I've something else for her," Sister Gudrun answered, and put on Fröken Nilsson's table a shiny metal bowl. "That's for you," she said.

Fröken Nilsson raised her eyes. Was it possible? Yes, the bowl was from the private ward! Fröken Nilsson had often watched them, silvery and shiny, carried on the huge trays into the wood-paneled hall. What was inside them she knew only from the whispers of the kitchen maids; the private patients got chicken, they said, and strawberries in the middle of the winter. No one, as far as she could remember, not even Fru Hernruth, had been treated to a meal like that.

Fröken Nilsson sat up. "You mean that's for me?"

"Yes, for you." Sister Gudrun lifted the cover. A golden-brown chicken was lying there, surrounded with asparagus. "And that too." It was a cream puff all covered with chocolate cream.

"But my diet," Fröken Nilsson stammered.

"We can break the diet for a day or two." Sister Gudrun put

her hand on Fröken Nilsson's head. The sudden caress, so unusual for Sister Gudrun, startled her. "Thank you," she said in a strange choked voice, and began to eat. The tender chicken melted slowly in her mouth, the cream puff was fragrant and sweet. Then in quiet, deliberate gulps she drank the milk Sister Gudrun had in the meantime brought for her. It was hot, it spread throughout her body, filled it with warmth so great, so good, that she had to stop and to take a deep breath from time to time. And suddenly all that had happened today, all that had happened during the last weeks seemed to disappear — Professor saying, "There's nothing else we can do"; the gnawing feeling of hunger that had not left her for even a minute during the last months, the fear of crutches, of the dark room waiting for her in Eskilstuna. . . . Nothing mattered any longer; it all seemed to have dissolved in the warmth of the white hot milk filling her now, and in that other warmth — of Sister Gudrun's hand resting upon her head.

"Tastes good?" Sister Gudrun asked.

"Very good," she said, and then, "I feel tired, Sister, awfully tired."

And it was very early still, long before the lights were turned off, when she fell asleep.

And in the morning Doctor Liliencrona came. He came very early. Fröken Nilsson was drowsing still, when suddenly a voice, his voice (she recognized it immediately), said, "Good morning, everybody; good morning, Fröken Nilsson." Fröken Nilsson raised herself abruptly, remembering instantly that her hair was not combed, that she had no lipstick on. But she had no time to do anything about that, for here he was coming already, and she could see now that he was in a gray suit, without his white coat on yet. That gave his visit a new significance: he seemed not to have come on duty at all, but privately, like the guests coming during the Sunday visit time.

"Sit down, please," Fröken Nilsson murmured, passing her hand through her hair.

"Thank you very much." Doctor Liliencrona moved himself a chair, and Fröken Nilsson watched how, gracefully sitting down, he adjusted the knees of his trousers.

"I came to tell you how deeply I feel for you," Doctor Liliencrona began.

"Thank you, Doctor," Fröken Nilsson said, although bewildered and hazy as she was she did not know quite to what feeling he referred.

"As Professor told you, we've tried everything. . . ."

So, that was what he meant. Suddenly, as if until now she had forgotten what had happened yesterday, it all came back to her now — amputate your leg, you'll keep your knee. Doctor Liliencrona's figure disappeared, and the fear was back so great that she wanted to scream, to run away from his words, from that room, from all they wanted to do to her.

But here was Doctor Liliencrona's voice again, soft and so friendly, saying, "I know you understand it, my dear Fröken, you're so brave, so — how should I say it? broad-minded. I've always had the greatest admiration for you. You never complain, you always keep your spirits. . . ."

The greatest admiration . . . Fröken Nilsson looked at him again and even brought herself to say, "I thank you very much, Doctor."

"And believe me," Doctor Liliencrona went on, moving closer to her bed, so that she could smell the sharp fragrance of his shaving lotion, "believe me it really will not be so terrible as it seems to you now."

"I believe you," Fröken Nilsson agreed. She would believe anything he said. . . . The way he talked, smiled. . . . Fröken Nilsson sighed.

"That's good." Doctor Liliencrona's white teeth gleamed under his black mustache. "You see, I know something about those things, not only from my hospital practice, but also privately, so to speak. A very good friend of mine had lost her leg in an automobile accident. And now she dances, she swims; she's the most charming woman you can imagine!"

The most charming woman — Fröken Nilsson smiled, a little forcedly this time. She felt a sharp pang of envy.

"I wish you could see her. She married last year, one of my friends. That's how I met her."

"I see," Fröken Nilsson smiled broadly.

And suddenly something new occurred to Fröken Nilsson. Married, he said, and she looked inquiringly at Doctor Liliencrona. Yes, she understood it . . . It was not by an accident at all that he had brought that friend of his into the conversation. Lost her leg . . . most charming woman . . . married, and here he was coming to see her, first thing in the morning. "I see," Fröken Nilsson repeated, and her smile was even broader than before.

"I knew as soon as I heard the sad news that you would take it like that . . . courageously." Doctor Liliencrona bent himself, and his hand resting on the blanket, moved a little higher and covered her hand. "So just keep your spirit, and everything will be all right. You'll see."

"Of course, Doctor."

The hand moved. Doctor Liliencrona got up. "Good-bye everybody; see you soon, Fröken Nilsson." And he smiled once more, a smile that Fröken Nilsson knew was secretly meaningful, directed especially at her. And when the door closed she still lay, smiling, oblivious of everything. Then she sat up and took out the mirror. Her hair was disheveled, but otherwise she did not look too bad, not too bad at all.

The day moved on so fast, so full of events that Fröken Nilsson, still filled with memories of Doctor Liliencrona's visit, did not even have time to stop and think about anything. Although it was not the visiting hour she had a guest right after breakfast, Herr Berg from the private ward, who spent the whole morning with her. Herr Berg himself had an artificial limb and he treated Fröken Nilsson with the hearty and confident affection with which one treats a prospective new family member. He told Fröken Nilsson all about the accident in which he had lost his leg, about the summer house he had in Skåne, and even promised to take her for a ride in his brand-new car. After he had left, Sister Gudrun came in with a present from him, a plate filled with choice fruit — pears, bananas, and grapes as big as cherries. A calling card was stuck in it saying — "With best wishes, Siegfried Berg, PH.D." Fröken Nilsson put the card in the most prominent place and asked Sister Gudrun to pass the fruit around. Not only Thura but also Stephania took some, and Fröken Nilsson felt strangely satisfied when she heard Stephania's "Thank you," and saw her biting into the juicy pear.

In the afternoon all Fröken Nilsson's friends with whom she used to sit in the living room came. In respectful whispers they expressed their sympathy as well as their admiration for her equanimity, gave her flowers, and asked whether it was true that Herr Berg himself, the one from the private ward, had paid her a visit. Fröken Nilsson nodded, passed the plate with the fruit and the calling card around, and looked at her bedside table, usually so empty, now crowded with flowers.

On Wednesday more flowers came, red peonies from Fröken Nilsson's sister and brother-in-law, and carnations from her boss and the personnel of the Eskilstuna Delicatessen Store where she had worked. And on Thursday the mail brought letters from them. Fröken Nilsson's sister — whom Fru Gustavsson had called the day before — wrote what a terrible shock the news was for her and Hasse, but still they hoped everything would turn out all right in the end. Fröken Nilsson felt sorry for Anna, for herself who was the cause of the shock, but deep in her heart she felt a certain satisfaction. It wouldn't do Anna any harm to think about someone else instead of herself for a change, and also it was high time for her to remember that she had a sister. The other letter, written by the boss's secretary and signed by all the rest of personnel was very nice too. It said that in those moments so difficult for her their thoughts were with her, and also how happy they would be, after that trial — the last one — was over, to welcome her back to Eskilstuna. Fröken Nilsson read parts of the letter to Fru Gustavsson. She knew the whole ward would be familiar with its contents by tomorrow, but she did not mind at all. After all why shouldn't people know that someone did care for her, that she was not all alone in the world?

She was not supposed to eat anything tomorrow, and so without any pangs of conscience she ate a double serving of each dish for dinner. Then Sister Gudrun came and gave her a glass of hot milk and a sleeping pill.

"Sleep quietly, Fröken Nilsson," she said. "Just try not to think about anything."

And so the day was over — the night was here, the night before Fröken Nilsson's "great day."

— But somehow the pill did not seem to work. It was cold in the room, and the biting chill crept under the blanket, sucked the warmth with which the hot milk had filled her body. Fröken Nilsson shuddered and hid herself under the blanket. Then the clock struck nine. And suddenly it flashed through her mind that in twelve hours only . . . that tomorrow morning at the same time they would take her down to the operating room, and then in the evening she would be back here but already without . . . No, she didn't want to think about that. There was no use, and besides it would not be too bad at all. Herr Berg had told her that, and Doctor Liliencrona too. She tried to think about Doctor Liliencrona, about the ride Herr Berg had promised her. But all the time other thoughts were forcing themselves upon her; other pictures ousted the smiling face of Doctor Liliencrona, the shiny brand-new car. Until all she could see was the operating room, the big glaring lamp and scissors, sharp and jagged, like those with which Anders had cut her cast. Would they do it with scissors, or with a saw perhaps? And what about the blood, how could they ever stop it? No, however they did it, they would do it right, and Doctor Liliencrona would be with her all the time; there was nothing to worry about. That Friday would pass as every other day had passed. Friday — and at once it dawned upon her that it was Friday tomorrow, Friday the thirteenth. Yes, she was sure about that, because on Wednesday she had got a new chart, and she noticed the date Sister Gudrun put on it — November eleventh; twelfth today, and tomorrow it was the thirteenth, and Friday too.

Fröken Nilsson shook her head impatiently. No, for goodness sake, she knew better than that, she certainly was not superstitious. Didn't she always laugh at Fru Morston from Four, when she told her she had broken her hip after a black cat had run across her path? But a black cat was nothing. There were plenty of cats of all colors everywhere, and it was just a sheer accident when one happened to pass your way. But the thirteenth, and Friday, that was more than an accident. Of course, something like that could happen to no one else but her. No, she shouldn't really worry about it; one day was exactly like another, and it didn't make the least bit of difference what date it was. Still, she wished she could ask someone about it. She wanted someone to tell her that there were no bad omens, that it was all just childish nonsense, silly superstitions. Should she ask Thura, or Stephania perhaps? Yes, Stephania seemed to be just the right person, she would know.

And only now it occurred to Fröken Nilsson that Stephania had started talking to her lately. Not much, just good morning, or good night, or sometimes she would pick up a paper for her or hand her a glass of water. Why did she do it? Fröken Nilsson wondered. Yes, she most certainly regretted what had happened between them. She must have heard Doctor Liliencrona calling her brave and admirable, she must have seen Herr Berg spending the whole morning with her, and all the flowers and letters she had got. Yes, now at last Stephania realized with whom she was dealing; she saw how terribly mistaken she had been, and now she felt badly about it. And suddenly Fröken Nilsson felt sorry for Stephania, lying there all alone, with no visitors coming to her, and watching her, Fröken Nilsson, surrounded by all those wonderful people, and thinking all the time how unjust she had been, how she had misunderstood and injured her. Yes, it must have been hard on her, so hard — Fröken Nilsson thought — that Stephania had been punished for whatever she had done, that now she herself would not mind, no, would not mind at all forgiving her. After all, it was Stephania who had made the first step, and showed she knew that the fault was hers. And she herself . . . Fröken Nilsson went as far as to confess to herself that she too was not completely right either. About that money for instance — they did not seem to have so much of it after all, the sister looked quite shabby, always in the same dress, and of the cheapest kind too. Yes, she must admit she had let herself be carried away a little; but then she had always had such a hasty temper. Of, course, it was nothing compared to what Stephania said and did to her; still . . . And now Stephania wanted to be forgiven. She should forgive her, then, right now, before tomorrow. . . .

Fröken Nilsson uttered a sigh, very loud, slightly hissing — a signal that she was not asleep, that she was waiting, willing to listen to anyone. . . . But no one answered. Fröken Nilsson sighed louder, a little angrily this time. They should not be able to sleep so quietly, not on a night like that. She faltered, clanged with her glass. Someone moved.

"Do you need anything, Fröken Nilsson?" Thura asked.

"No, only . . . it's just that pill, it doesn't do me any good tonight. I try and try and just can't fall asleep."

"I'm not sleepy either. Do you want to talk for a while?" Thura knew it: for all waiting for their "great day," the sleeping pill didn't work; no one, even those who had been quiet and cheerful during the day, could fall asleep; they all felt like talking for a while, now when the night was here, and the room stood silent and dark.

"Yes, why don't we talk a little?" Fröken Nilsson hesitated and added, "But what about Fröken Ackermann? Won't we wake her up?"

Thura, hoping Stephania would hear her, whispered: "I don't think she's asleep, it's very early still."

"I'm not asleep," Stephania said. "I don't mind you talking at all." She had heard each word they said.

Because all that time Stephania had been lying awake, feeling that Fröken Nilsson was not asleep either, that she was now waiting for the morning to come knowing that it must come, knowing that after that morning nothing would ever be the same — the days, the nights — and she herself. Again and again she glanced at Fröken Nilsson's bed, imagining each question she could be asking herself now, the fear she must feel. . . . It was an immense relief to her when the silence had been broken at last by Fröken Nilsson's voice. "No," Stephania added now hastily, as if afraid Fröken Nilsson would fall silent again, "I really don't mind. I am not sleepy at all. And besides, it's kind of cold in here."

"Yes," Fröken Nilsson said noncommittally. "I feel it too." She fell silent. Should she tell it to Stephania now? Should she say that she had forgiven her, that she shouldn't worry any longer? But somehow she could not. And so she only added, "I don't think they heat it enough here. Trying to save money on us."

And Stephania again — "Perhaps the window isn't closed. Let me see." She got out of her bed, opened the window and closed it again. Fröken Nilsson thought about that night when she turned the light on for her, when she went to look for Sister Ingeborg . . . and now jumping out of bed right on that ice-cold floor. . . . Yes, it was the very same thing. Stephania was trying to show how badly she felt about all she had done to her.

"Fröken Ackermann," Fröken Nilsson said.

"Yes, anything else I could do for you?"

"Well, it isn't that. All I mean is . . . you see . . . tomorrow . . . I just want you to know I don't mind any longer what you said, what passed between us." Fröken Nilsson stopped. It was so hard to say it, much harder than she thought it would be. She only hoped it did not sound as if it was she who was asking to be forgiven. Still she had put it rather well — what passed between us — that sounded rather well, didn't it?

There was a long moment of silence. Thura lay holding her breath, as if afraid the least noise might destroy what was now at last coming, might make Stephania say the wrong word, or even say nothing at all.

But Stephania did say it. "Yes," her voice came distinct and very quiet, "let's forget it."

Thura breathed deeply. Now at last — she thought.

"Yes," Fröken Nilsson muttered. There was an angry note in her voice. Fröken Nilsson felt disappointed. That was not what she had thought Stephania's answer would be like. Not a word that she was sorry, that she saw her mistake, just simply, offhand, "Let's forget it" — as if it was she, Stephania, who had something to forget. But still, didn't she say let *us* forget? That meant Stephania wanted her to forget, that meant she knew it was she herself who had to be forgiven. Yes, Fröken Nilsson decided she would forget. After all she wasn't petty. No one had ever said *that* about her.

"Yes," she repeated. "Let us forget," and nothing more was said, only Thura felt a sudden joy rising in her so great that she felt it flowing out of her like a warm stream into the chilly dark room.

Fröken Nilsson cleared her throat. She remarked that it seemed warmer now after Stephania had closed the window, and then quietly, nonchalantly almost, asked: "Do you know what the date will be tomorrow, Fröken Ackermann?"

"Let me see." Stephania began to count. "Tuesday was the tenth . . . thirteenth . . . yes, Friday the thirteenth."

"Thirteenth!" Thura almost cried.

"So what?" Fröken Nilsson said. "I'm not superstitious. Thirteenth or fourteenth, one day's just like another. Don't you think so, Fröken Ackermann?"

"Yes, of course."

Fröken Nilsson was not quite satisfied yet. "I'm sure if we tried to remember we could find that lots of good things have happened to us on a thirteenth. Isn't that so, Fröken Ackermann?"

"I guess so. Let me think. . . . Yes, certainly; I found my sister on the thirteenth, thirteenth of July. I remember it exactly because it was two days before her birthday."

"Was it Friday?" Fröken Nilsson could not help asking.

"I don't quite remember. No, it was Monday, I guess."

"But Fru Hernruth was operated on a Friday. And everything went well then. You really don't have to be afraid, Fröken Nilsson," Thura said.

"Of course, I'm not afraid. What do you think?" Fröken Nilsson answered: "I only asked out of curiosity; people talk so much about all those silly superstitions." She felt completely reassured now.

And again the silence returned. All three of them lay thinking about something to say, something that would help them stop thinking about tomorrow, that would push that Friday morning far away from them.

Thura was first to find it. "Do you know, I just can't forget how wonderful Doctor Liliencrona has been to you."

"Well, he has been quite nice," Fröken Nilsson answered, and her voice implied clearly that there was more, much more than met the eye in that fact.

"He has always shown so much interest in you," Thura went on. She remembered all those long stories which Fröken Nilsson, before Stephania came, used to tell her about Doctor Liliencrona, about, her meetings, her talks with him. Now, her cautious remark was to suggest that she would love to hear them again, and also, that there was someone else now, who had not heard them at all.

Fröken Nilsson hardly needed any encouragement. "Yes," she said thoughtfully. "He really has been kind to me, from the very beginning. I remember the first week I was here, he came into the room and asked me all kinds of questions, where I was from, and how had I broken my leg. And he was on the children's ward then, and had nothing to do with me."

"And, then, do you remember how he met you in the elevator and said . . ."

"It was on the balcony, not in the elevator," Fröken Nilsson corrected her severely. "He recognized me at once then. 'Hello,' he said — 'How are you on this lovely day, Fröken Nilsson?' and he even remembered that it was my leg I had trouble with." Fröken Nilsson stopped. Her words reminded her of something she did not want to think of.

"And then, when we had the birthday party for Fru Hernruth he sat next to you . . ."

"Yes, and he kept pouring me coffee, and brought me the plate with the cookies. After that Fru Hernruth said to me, 'He does like you a lot, Fröken Nilsson.' But I didn't think much of that then. I'm not one of those who make an elephant out of a fly. And besides someone else was on my mind then. But that is another story . . ." Fröken Nilsson sighed. Stephania was silent, and she began to wonder if she was listening at all. "Do you think he's nice, Fröken Ackermann?" she asked tentatively.

"Very nice," Stephania assured her.

She was listening. Fröken Nilsson decided she could go on.

"You should have seen him that day when I was operated on the last time, he was so nice . . . so nice. Here I was lying in the small room, they always make you wait there before they take you into the operating room, and suddenly he comes in. I wasn't surprised even, I just had a feeling he would come — a foreboding you might call it. 'So, Fröken Nilsson,' says he, 'now they are going to meddle with your leg again.'

" 'Yes, and not the first time either, Doctor,' say I.

" 'Just don't be afraid,' he said, and I again, 'I am not, not when I'm with you' (I had got my morphine injection already, so I was a little bit daring, you see). And then," Fröken Nilsson's voice grew now mellow and dreamy, "Then when I was falling asleep he took my hand in his."

"He took your hand? . . ." Thura repeated.

"Oh yes, he did."

"I think he must be terribly fond of you," Thura decided.

Stephania felt she too was expected to say something. "Yes, he has been very . . . very considerate of you," she remarked falteringly.

But Fröken Nilsson was hardly listening. Her voice grew sad and nostalgic when she said, "It's a pity he had to meet me here. Had I known him there in Eskilstuna . . . I looked a little different then, I should say."

"Yes, in Eskilstuna," Thura echoed eagerly and joyfully, in the way in which one repeats the name of an old friend not heard of for a long time. Once, before Stephania was here, Fröken Nilsson used to tell her about Eskilstuna, about the strange and exciting life she had there. "Yes," she said now. "It would have been wonderful if you had met him then."

"Quite different . . ." Fröken Nilsson repeated as if to herself. "From the way I look now, you wouldn't even guess what I used to be like, Fröken Ackermann, I know that. But ask anybody in Eskilstuna about Maria Nilsson; they'll know. The best-dressed woman in town, they used to call me. And my figure . . . I've gained a lot of weight since that time, you must know. . . . But then . . . and my legs . . . The man in the store where I used to buy my shoes always said, 'It's a pleasure to fit the shoes for you, Fröken Nilsson, you have the most perfect legs I've seen.' Well, it's all over now, so I might as well tell you . . . it isn't bragging now."

"Sure it isn't." Thura agreed promptly, and Stephania, trying as hard as she could to imagine that Fröken Nilsson from Eskilstuna, slender, with the perfect legs, also murmured her assent.

"It was easy for me to be well dressed," Fröken Nilsson went on, "to spend a hundred crowns meant nothing to me then, with that job I had working for Eskilstuna Delicatessen Store, the biggest one in the whole town, and they gave me raise after raise, and heavens, all those bonuses for Christmas, for vacations! My employer, the same one I had the letter from the other day, couldn't do without me. 'You . . . You're my right hand, Fröken Nilsson,' he always said to me. So, on Friday I would go to the bank, take out thirty crowns, fifty, as much as I wanted, and then Saturday morning I'd go shopping — and to the best stores only. Nothing was good enough for me, then. I was spoiled, I must say. You know . . . a suit had to be English, no matter how much it cost, and I wouldn't even look at a dress if it weren't pure silk. None of that cheap American stuff for me. And the perfumes, Fröken Ackermann, the perfumes. I used to spend a fortune on them . . . Chanel, Soir de Paris . . ."

"Chanel, Soir de Paris . . ." Thura repeated her voice full of awe. Out of the darkness they loomed upon her, the graceful, slender bottles and vials, filled as with honey, with the heavy golden fluid; fragrant, delicate. She would have liked to hear more about them, to learn more of those singing, exotic names, but Fröken Nilsson was already going on with her story. "I wish I could show you my taffeta dress," she said. "Silver gray, and I used to wear a blue gauze scarf with it. . . . That really was something. I bought it especially for a big party. The fellow I was going out with then took me there."

"Was it Axel?" Thura asked, to show how exactly she remembered everything Fröken Nilsson used to tell her.

"Heavens, no." Fröken Nilsson's voice clearly indicated that Axel was not worthy of the silver-gray taffeta dress. "It was the lieutenant."

"The lieutenant, oh, certainly, I know who you mean . . ." Thura hastened to make up for her mistake. Of course she remembered him — the lieutenant, the most gorgeous fellow you can imagine — Fröken Nilsson used to describe him to her; tall and always sun-tanned, and the hair so dark. . . .

" 'Maria,' he — the lieutenant I mean — said to me then," Fröken Nilsson went on, 'I've never seen a woman with better taste.' Yes . . ." She pondered for a while that remark, and then, as if satisfied with the result of her consideration, added, "He was a nice fellow" (madly in love with me, she wanted to add, but the phrase did not seem refined enough to her). "He was keenly interested in me," she concluded. "But I . . . well . . . he wouldn't do for me. Yes, I was too choosy then . . ."

"Is he in Eskilstuna still?" Thura wanted to know.

"No, he left . . . it was just too hard on him. All those memories, you know, and then I started to go around with another fellow. It was too much, he just couldn't take it."

"Oh," Thura whispered. She felt very sorry for the gorgeous and unfortunate lieutenant.

Fröken Nilsson stifled a yawn. "What's the use of talking now," she said drowsily. "What's gone is gone — as the saying is." She yawned again. The pill must have begun to work at last. "Sometimes," she sighed, "sometimes it seems to me I had it too good, and what comes now is a punishment . . . in a way."

"Oh, please don't say things like that," Thura pleaded.

"Yes, I had it too good," Fröken Nilsson repeated in a voice excluding any opposition. Her eyelids grew heavy; they were slowly falling over her eyes. If she could only fall asleep right now, at once, without thinking about anything. She felt very tired, maybe she could . . .

"Do you want to try to sleep now?" Thura asked.

"I may try . . . I do feel kind of drowsy . . ."

"Fine. Good night, Fröken Nilsson."

"Good night, Thura. Good night, Fröken Ackermann."

"Sleep well, Fröken Nilsson," Stephania said.

Fröken Nilsson laid her head on the pillow. She felt glad she had told Stephania a little about herself. Now she would know with whom she was dealing. She knew it now. Fröken Nilsson could hear it from the way in which she had wished her good night. She wasn't so bad, Stephania; really not, Fröken Nilsson thought, and she closed her eyes.

Morning came. The room, cold and gray, Sister Ingeborg's shuffling, tired steps and the icy touch of her hand filled Fröken Nilsson with fear. But later Fru Gustavsson came in, said good morning with her usual dimply smile, and the windows after the shades had been pulled up let in the sharp November sun and made the carnations on her table shine as if they had been freshly oiled and polished. It was a day just like every other day — Fröken Nilsson felt very quiet suddenly. She was talkative, cheerful even, reminded Fru Gustavsson to cut the stalks of her flowers a little so they could stay fresh longer, and even asked Thura and Stephania how they had slept. "Fine," they answered briefly, and their voices sounded strained, as if the air in the room were very hot and dry, and made it hard for them to breathe.

They felt as though Fröken Nilsson's fear had passed into them now; they were bewildered and lost, like people forced suddenly to participate in a strange celebration at which they don't know quite how to act. . . . For it was the "great day" again, but still so much unlike all the "great days" Thura and Stephania had seen; no nurses, no patients came in from other rooms to tell Fröken Nilsson how easy it was to correct a club-foot or to set a broken leg. Not a word was spoken about what was going to happen today. Sister Gudrun and Fru Gustavsson hardly looked at Fröken Nilsson; they seemed to be ashamed of something. Everything was done fast, almost stealthily. Fröken Nilsson was to be operated on first, at nine, and this time there was no listening for the phone or for the beds rolling slowly through the hall. Early, when they were washing still, Sister Gudrun brought the clean shirt for Fröken Nilsson and Fru Gustavsson helped her to put it on and combed her hair. And soon Sister Gudrun was back to give her the morphine injection.

And it was only then when she saw the syringe, slender, filled with the transparent liquid, that the fear reappeared — jumped upon her, as if until now she had not quite believed it would happen, as if deep in her heart she had hoped something would change at the last moment. But the needle was in her arm already, and now she knew it must come, and she lay silenced, looking at Sister Gudrun with questioning, wide-opened eyes. But Sister Gudrun said nothing, only stroked her hair and left.

Fru Gustavsson had just brought the breakfast in when the orderlies came to take Fröken Nilsson down to the operating room.

[ 181 ]

Stephania and Thura felt as if something improper was happening; it seemed wrong that they should take Fröken Nilsson without any preparations, just now when everything was so much as usual, smelling of coffee and porridge. They put their spoons away. Thura wanted to say something to Fröken Nilsson. "Come back healthy as a fish"; that was what they always used to say, but it somehow seemed out of place now. And Fröken Nilsson's bed was already in the doorway, when Thura cried in a voice that was high and quivering: "God bless you, Fröken Nilsson, God bless you." It sounded strange — so solemn and grave. Fröken Nilsson swallowed the lump that suddenly blocked her throat, waved with her hand and said: "See you soon."

"Yes, we'll see you soon," Stephania answered, and she waved back. The orderly pushed the bed out of the room.

First, when the bed began to roll through the hall, it seemed to her that it hardly moved, and she wanted the orderlies to hurry so that whatever had to come might come, so that she wouldn't have to wait any longer. But then when from afar she saw the elevator door, she felt they were rushing with a horrifying speed, and she wanted them to slow down, she was not ready yet . . . not yet. Room Three, Room Four, Room Five — doors ajar, faces flickering before her eyes, smiling vaguely, staring at her — someone exclaimed something . . . what, she could not understand. And now they were in the elevator, slowly sinking down, and inside her something was sinking too — she clutched at her bed, and breathed deeply. The elevator stopped; another hall, shorter this time, a door opened — the bed was pushed inside.

She was in the small room, in which the patients were shut for a while so they would not have to look at the big lamp, at the instruments, and at the preparations going on in the operating room. She lay looking at the white walls, at the couch covered with black oilcloth. Soon Doctor Liliencrona would come, as he had come last time. She could almost hear his steps and his voice saying: "Hello, Fröken Nilsson, here I am." She raised her head listening, but everything around was quiet. At last there were steps in the hall. She smoothed her blanket and passed her hand through her hair. The door opened. "Good morning," a voice said — a woman's voice — she looked up. It was the nurse. She felt disappointed, but only for an instant. He must be waiting for

her in the operating room — yes, certainly he was there, he
must . . .

"So, here we go," the nurse said and pushed the bed back into
the hall, then into the door way of the operating room, wide open,
waiting for her.

"The patient from Ward Two is here," the nurse announced. As
if he didn't know from which ward she was, Fröken Nilsson
thought angrily. Where was he? Washing his hands, probably.
She waited.

"Fine," a voice said at last. Fröken Nilsson lifted her head,
looked around. Because the voice was not his — it was strange,
a voice she had never heard before. . . . An orderly perhaps — an
intern that came to watch the operation. . . .

But now a face bent itself over her, an unfamiliar face, ruddy
and square, the eyes hidden under thick glasses. "Good morning,
Fröken Nilsgren . . ."

"Nilsson," she said furiously — he could at least know her
name.

"Fröken Nilsson," he repeated casually, as if there was no difference at all whether she was Nilsson or Nilsgren. "I'm Doctor
Sjögren."

So he *was* a doctor. . . . What was he doing here? Where was
Doctor Liliencrona? she wanted to ask, but she was afraid . . . she
was afraid they would tell her he was not here, he would not come
at all. She lay listening, hoping every moment the door would
open, and he would come and push aside that stranger, who had
no business here, who should not be here at all.

"So now, we'll put you to sleep, Fröken Nilsgren," the rough
voice said. She felt a cold numbness clasping her whole body,
trying her throat.

"No," she murmured, "No . . . where is he? Where's Doctor
Liliencrona?"

"Doctor Liliencrona? Oh, he's on the day clinic, replacing
Doctor Eriksson, who is sick."

Her head fell back on the pillow. So he was not coming. Friday the thirteenth she thought; yes, everything has to go wrong,
everything. But she didn't care, it was all the same now. She hardly
felt it when they lifted her up from the stretcher, and laid her on
the hard table. Only after the sharp light of the huge lamp hit
her eyes she raised her hand, as if to defend herself. The stranger

[ 183 ]

tied the rubber tube around her arm and tightened it so that it hurt. But she said nothing. It didn't matter now.

And then the stranger's voice, that voice she couldn't stand, said: "God, what kind of veins has she got? I just can't find them."

"Yes, we always have trouble with her veins," the nurse said.

"No!" She wanted to scream, to tell them Doctor Liliencrona always said she had good veins, he said it was a trifle to put her to sleep. But here something pierced her arm, sharp and cold, a needle piercing, not into the vein, but right into the flesh of her arm, blindly, like the stings of some insect treacherously falling from somewhere high above her.

The doctor pulled the rubber tube tighter still. She could hear him whistling through his teeth; the hissing sound made her shudder.

"Now I think I've got it." And again the piercing pain, and again his voice saying, "Damn! I've never seen veins like that. I just can't get it." The voice seemed to come from afar now. She raised her head. They were standing back now — white, motionless; they seemed not to be human figures at all, just objects like the table, the blazing lamp, and the queer long-necked machine next to her. And suddenly it seemed to her she was alone here, all alone in that enormous white room, with the hollow silence ringing in it. She did not want to be alone — she was afraid to be. No, they were here; the doctor, the nurse; right here with her. She lifted herself; she wanted to see their faces, so that she would really know they were here, so that she could speak to them, tell them she was scared. But now a heavy mist like a wall of opaque glass stood between her and them. No, she could not see their faces; they had no faces at all, just blurred shapeless spots. And now she knew she was alone here — she and that needle, the sting of the insect lurking in wait for her, somewhere in the glaring light and threatening any moment to change into the scissors . . . or into the saw perhaps. . . . She closed her eyes.

And here it was again, the pain, sharper than before, tearing her arm apart. Stop! she wanted to cry, but her throat was dry, and her tongue was too heavy to move. And so she only lifted her arm and shook it, trying to drive it away, that something which kept hurting her, slyly, maliciously.

"Stop moving your arm. I'm having enough trouble finding your vein."

[ 184 ]

She managed to tear her tongue away from her palate. "No," she said, "I don't want you . . . to do . . . it. Call him, call Doctor Liliencrona." She thought she was screaming but only a hoarse whisper came out of her lips.

"I told you he's busy."

"You must call him, you must. You can't make me go through this alone."

"Alone? But I'm here, aren't I?"

No, she wanted to tell him. You don't count, you don't have — what was it he didn't have? — a face, yes, a face. . . . But after all one couldn't say things like that. And so she only mumbled. "He must come, he must. . ."

Vaguely she could see the white figure step back approaching the other one until they both merged into a big white lump.

"I'll try to get him," the voice of the nurse said. "He may not be very busy right now . . ." The door squeaked. Did the nurse really go, or were they making it all up so that they could get her quiet, and then the needle again? . . . Someone was coming — the nurse — was she alone? No, another white figure followed her, taller, yes, very tall. . . . And now a voice, his voice this time: "So, here I am, Fröken Nilsson." And the relief so great that it choked her, so that she could not say a word.

She could see him coming closer to her, now he was right here; but now she did not look up, because perhaps he, too, would be changed, hidden in the dense mist; he too would have no face. And at last she opened her eyes. Yes, here it was right above her, his face, his eyes, his black mustache.

"Oh, Doctor," she whispered, "I was so afraid, I was so afraid you wouldn't come."

"I'm sorry, they kept me in the day clinic. But now I'm here, now everything will be all right. Let's put you to sleep."

The needle glided into her arm, right into the vein, carefully, friendly almost. She felt him take off the rubber tube and her arm began to swell. And suddenly the room, the table, she herself, began to whirl around — and Doctor Liliencrona seemed to move away farther and farther away until she couldn't see him at all.

"Doctor," she said, "come closer, closer."

"Here I am, right next to you."

But that was not enough, she couldn't see him. "Take my hand please," she murmured. . . . She could feel it resting upon hers, the only stable point in the turning room; warm, quiet, good.

[ 185 ]

"She's falling asleep," someone said. "We'll start soon."

No, she wanted to cry. Wait, not yet. But her lips refused to move and she only dug her fingers deeper into Doctor Liliencrona's hand. And suddenly she began to fall, and now even the hand was gone; she groped for it but could not find it. She was alone again. The scissors, she thought the scissors . . .

. . . Something heavy falling upon her eyes . . . And again she was falling into darkness, and then into nothing, into nothing at all. . . .

The room was silent when they took Fröken Nilsson out; it was still silent when the orderlies brought her back two hours later. And this time it was Stephania who got up and looked at the flushed face, at the thin streak of saliva leaking out of the open, parched mouth. "Does everybody look like that?" she asked. Thura knew what she meant, what they all meant. "Yes," she said, "everybody," and again they were silent.

Fröken Nilsson did not wake up until late in the afternoon. She let Fru Gustavsson wash her mouth with a piece of cotton wool, sighed heavily, and fell asleep again. Sister Gudrun came in from time to time, lifted the blanket, looked underneath it, and gave her a penicillin injection. Then there was morphine again; Fröken Nilsson did not wake up at all, and the day passed into night.

All the next day she lay plunged into uneasy half-sleep. Only once she roused, again late in the afternoon. She woke up. The sun was setting then; it filled the room with red glare, painted purple shadows on the walls, on the white linen. And suddenly Fröken Nilsson raised herself, hastily, anxiously as if she remembered something. She lifted her hand, all tinged red by the sun, the fingers wide spread trying to catch something. For a while she held it stiffly in the air, then slowly let it fall on the blanket, and moved it, groping, searching, farther and farther down toward the foot of the bed. But her body remained motionless and her face too, as if she were still asleep. At last her hand found the place where the blanket rose over the thick lump of bandages, and then slid down abruptly, because there was nothing underneath it. Here she stopped, and sat looking at that hollow spot. Until suddenly she raised her hand and covered her eyes, as if the eyelids were not enough. And so she sat for a long while. Then she sank back on her bed, and soon slept again.

[ 186 ]

It was Sunday night when Fröken Nilsson woke up. For a while she lay looking around, trying to gather her thoughts. Yes, it must be night now, late in the night, she thought, and wondered why should she be so thirsty, so horribly thirsty that her tongue and her lips were sore. And then she knew everything: something had happened to her, to her leg. Was it today? No, it must have been a long time ago. But somehow it did not matter now; she was too tired to think, to remember. All she wanted was to drink something cold — ice cold and sour. She reached out her hand, found the glass, and greedily lifted it to her mouth. But the water in it was lukewarm and stale; Fröken Nilsson put the glass away and shook her head, not angrily but simply sadly, and then she began to cry.

It was a low cry, very soft, like a child that knows he is alone, that there is no one to hear him. She did not quite know why she was crying; it was not because of what had happened to her, it was just that she had nothing cold to drink, and the pillow was soggy and moist with sweat, and she had no one to whom she could tell all that. She sobbed and sobbed, feeling pity for herself rising in her, very great and sad. But it was not painful, that sadness and crying; it only made her weak and tired, as if she were sitting in the bath, the water warm and friendly around her, soothing, loosening up everything inside her, and making her feel more and more sorry for herself.

She did not want anybody to hear her, and was startled when Thura's voice asked. "What is it, Fröken Nilsson, does it hurt?"

Hurt . . . ? "No," she murmured, "it does not."

"But why're you crying?"

"I don't know . . . I just am." She felt almost offended now; she did not want to be disturbed. And then the pity returned, swept her in warm rocking waves. "It's just because everything goes wrong, always . . . always."

"Oh, dear Fröken Nilsson . . . don't say that. It's only now that it seems so hard — but it'll be all right, you'll see."

Fröken Nilsson's sobs grew louder.

"Just wait, and then you'll see how things will work out." Thura hesitated. "You'll go back to Eskilstuna to your friends. You remember the letter you got from the boss? They're all waiting for you."

Fröken Nilsson did not answer. What did that Thura want

[ 187 ]

from her? Why couldn't she leave her alone? She did not want to be consoled, she wanted to cry, to feel the tears flowing in warm streaks down her cheeks; she wanted to forget everything: Eskilstuna, and the people there, and all she had ever done and said — everything except feeling sorry for herself, terribly sorry. . . . "No," she cried, "no!"

"It's just that you're tired now, depressed. But you'll see. You'll go back and everything will be just like it was before and you'll go to all those parties in your lovely taffeta dress. . . ."

" — Like before," but that was just why she was crying, just that. Fröken Nilsson felt how thoughts and words were suddenly crowding in on her, forcing themselves upon her lips, unrestrained, irresistible like the tears. She had to say them, she wanted to. . . . And before she had time to stop and think, here they were, already spoken, already heard: "I won't go to parties, I have never been to any. And . . . and the taffeta dress wasn't mine at all." And now she sobbed aloud with almost joyful relief.

"What?" Thura whispered. She didn't understand it. . . . No, Fröken Nilsson must have fever . . . she didn't know what she was saying.

"It wasn't mine," Fröken Nilsson repeated. "It was my boss's wife's. Later she gave it to me, when she didn't care for it any longer. But I couldn't wear it anyhow . . . it was much too tight."

"Fröken Nilsson, please, you mustn't say things like that. Just try to remember all you told us that night, that night before Friday. . . . All about the beautiful things you used to have, the English suits, and perfumes, don't you remember? And the dress . . . you wore it with a blue gauze scarf. . . ."

"No," Fröken Nilsson said obstinately. Suddenly she felt angry. Why didn't Thura believe her? She wanted her to know everything, to know how it really had been, to understand why she was crying, why it was so good to cry. "I didn't have any English suits," she said doggedly, "and no perfumes either."

"But," Thura whispered, "but . . ." And then as if looking for help, "Are you asleep, Fröken Stephania?"

Stephania had just waked up. She heard the sobbing, the confused whispers — "taffeta dress" . . . "perfumes" . . . and the loud hissing "No!" She couldn't understand what had happened. "What's the matter, Thura?"

"I don't know. . . . It's Fröken Nilsson; she is talking so

strangely." Thura felt glad Stephania was awake. It made things easier suddenly.

Fröken Nilsson stopped sobbing. She listened. She knew she had said something she should never have said, something horrible, and she knew Stephania had heard it. But still she did not regret it. She felt so tired now, so heavy, and it seemed to her that if she would tell them everything — all she had never told anybody before — the heaviness would be lifted from her, and everything would become simple and easy, and light, yes . . . light. But wouldn't they laugh at her, say she had lied? No, they must understand she had not lied, not at all, she just had told them how it should have been, and it wasn't her fault that things went wrong with her. She waited until they fell silent and then said: "It didn't matter how I dressed, and what I had; nobody would have looked at me anyhow. . . ."

"Nobody," Thura repeated, the word seemed to grow into a huge shape; it swallowed Axel and the lieutenant and all the others Fröken Nilsson had told her about.

"Nobody," Fröken Nilsson said, and then as if apologizing for something: "It wasn't my fault. It was all because I was so fat."

"Always?" Stephania asked, and now her voice too, like Thura's was startled.

"Always. It just runs in our family. All the Larsons — my mother was a Larson, you see — are fat. Mother was over a hundred and eighty, and she was much shorter than me. Only my sister is skinny. But she took after Father, after the Nilssons."

For a while no one said anything, and then Thura in a loud, strenuous voice said, "It isn't true, Fröken Nilsson." How could it be? Hadn't Fröken Nilsson herself told her, not once but many times, about all the parties and dances she had gone to, about Midsummer Night when she waltzed with the lieutenant, so light, so beautiful in a white organdy dress? And all those walks at the seashore, and rides in cars, and good-night kisses? No, it couldn't be true. "You're very upset, Fröken Nilsson, that's all," she said. "Isn't that so, Fröken Stephania?"

Stephania said slowly. "I don't know, Thura."

There was something quiet and expectant about her voice. Fröken Nilsson heard it, and she knew now that Stephania would not mind, that she would understand.

"When a girl is fat, no one takes her out," she said, "so there's no use for fancy clothes." The words came slowly, as if she had to tear them out of a secret place where they had been hidden.

"But . . . the lieutenant . . . Do you mean, you've never known him, that he wasn't a real person at all?"

"Sure he was . . . he used to call to see his sister that lived right opposite me."

"So you did know him, then."

"Just saw him. That's all. I never spoke to him though, do you understand?"

"Yes, I see," Stephania said. It was strange, very strange but somehow she did not feel surprised, as if all the time she had known those words would come. Of course, Fröken Nilsson was a liar, she had felt it from the very beginning. But such a liar . . . ? She must think it over, but not now; now she had to listen.

"Do you mean there was nobody, nobody at all?"

"Nobody, I told you. It just happened like that. Only . . ." She stopped. Should she tell them that too? No, she couldn't . . . But . . . but after all, Stephania had told them worse things — beating an old man for nothing, what could be more dreadful than that? "Yes, there was someone," she said slowly.

"Which one was that?" Thura cried almost. "The engineer who wanted to take you to America?"

"No," Fröken Nilsson said wearily; that Thura . . . she simply refused to understand. "He was Italian."

"How wonderful." Yes, that was even better than the engineer. They were so handsome, the Italians, so gallant. . . . She could see him, stalking into the room, graceful, black eyes shining in the olive face, and the hair very dark and shiny too. "What was his name?" Thura asked. They had such beautiful names, the Italians — Giuseppe, Giovanni, Petruccio . . .

"He had some outlandish name, but he never told me what it was. Here everybody called him Kale."

"Oh," Thura said. And then, "But was he very handsome?"

"Handsome?" Fröken Nilsson's voice sounded as if she were shrugging her shoulders. "God, no. He was so short, half my size, and bald, as bald as your knee."

Thura said nothing, and it was Stephania who asked, "How did you meet him?"

"He used to bring us seltzer."

"What?"

"Seltzer. It was after my mother got sick . . . paralyzed. She had a stroke; something happened to the blood vessels in her brain. That's what the doctor told me. But who can tell? You can never trust those doctors. Perhaps it happened because she was so fat."

"You mean she was paralyzed just like me?"

"Yes, worse even . . . just like a clod of wood. Couldn't talk either . . . just sort of mumbled. I never knew what she wanted, and then she would get angry with me. And she was always thirsty. Seltzer; that was the only thing she wanted to drink. So when I saw him — Kale, I mean — bring seltzer to people next door, I thought I might as well tell him to bring some for us too. He didn't charge more than they did in the store, or perhaps a little more — just an öre or two."

"Is that all?" Thura asked pleadingly.

"No, that's not all." She stopped — should she tell them even that . . . ? No, she could not, not that.

But it was so dark around her, and it seemed easy to speak in darkness. It was like being all alone with nothing but voices in the room, voices that seemed to say they would understand, that it was all right whatever she had done. And besides, Stephania was not a saint either; she could smell that.

"He came every week, each Wednesday, you see," Fröken Nilsson said at last. "And every time he would tell me how much he liked me, how beautiful I was. Yes . . . really. He liked women to be fat, fat and blond. They don't have many blonds in his country, in Italy, you know; they're all dark — just like you, Fröken Ackermann. So when he said to me we should go out together, I said yes. But I was ashamed to show myself on the street with him. He was so terribly short; I was afraid the boss might see me, or someone else from the store, and they would laugh. They always laughed at me. So we went out when it was dark. We went to the movies, the cheapest ones, of course. You don't make much money when you carry seltzer upstairs."

"And . . ." Stephania insisted.

"And . . . and he asked me to his room." Fröken Nilsson's voice was hardly audible.

"Where?" Thura asked.

"To his room." God, was she a child, that Thura? And here she was sixteen almost!

[ 191 ]

Stephania said: "Did you go?"

"Yes, I went to him," Fröken Nilsson said. That was all. But her words suddenly made the room darker; they filled it with something oppressive and secret.

"So," Stephania said slowly, "you slept with him."

"I did. But don't think I'm that kind, Fröken Ackermann. I had never done it before, and things like that never happened in my family, either. But he kept asking me and so I went."

"But you did like him?" Thura asked.

"No, not much. I told you the way he looked . . . short and bald; I don't understand any longer why I did it. I just wanted to find out what it all was like, I guess."

"And are you glad you went?"

Fröken Nilsson did not answer at once. "It was terrible, Fröken Ackermann," she said at last. "Just terrible," and somehow she seemed to be reproaching, accusing them of something.

"But why?"

"Oh, how can I say it? Everything was wrong. First the cats . . . he lived in some very old house . . .and there were cats on the staircase. I had never seen so many of them, a couple on each floor. And I just can't stand cats . . . And then the stairs . . . he lived in the garret, you see. I thought the stairs would never end . . . I was completely out of breath when we at last came up."

"Do you regret it?"

"Now? No. What's the use of crying over spilled milk? But wait, Fröken Ackermann, that's not all. It was the room, his room, his room that was worst of all. When he turned on the light, there were cockroaches, creeping out of the woodwork. Now if there's anything I hate it's cockroaches. I'm terribly strict when it comes to cleanliness, you see. When I saw them I just wanted to run away."

"But you didn't, did you?"

"No," Fröken Nilsson said, "I did not. I stayed."

"And . . . ?"

"I told you. It was dreadful later too," she said emphatically.

"Did you ever see him again?"

"Just a couple of times. There wasn't much money in that seltzer business, so he went someplace else to look for a better job. I was glad when he left." Fröken Nilsson stopped; she seemed to be considering something. "I just can't understand why people

[ 192 ]

make so much fuss about those things; you know what I mean. It's just awful, you can believe me."

"No," Stephania said, and her voice was now hoarse and throaty as if she too had gotten morphine. "I know it is not."

"Oh, you know, so you too did it?"

"No, it is not that."

"How can you tell then?"

"I just know. It can't be awful. It is being together, completely together, don't you see? I can't quite explain it, but don't you understand?"

"No, I don't," Fröken Nilsson said angrily.

And suddenly Thura said, "It . . . it seems to me that I do, yes, I do understand."

"You?" Fröken Nilsson asked incredulously. "What can you know about them, about *men?*" Men, she said, and now that word resounded in silence. And there they were, broad-shouldered, and strong, and smelling of tobacco.

"Do you ever think about them?"

"Sometimes . . ." Thura said. Yes, she thought about them as you think of distant places that you will never see, but which you know exist — strange and far away. "Yes," she repeated, "sometimes I do think about them."

"I guess everybody does," Fröken Nilsson said indifferently. "But they're not worth it, believe me — I know what I'm talking about." The last words she murmured in slow blurred voice. She felt tired, all empty inside. Everything was said now. . . . Should she have done it? She didn't know, she didn't care now. "Not worth it, never," she said once more, and then fell silent.

Thura waited until her breath became quiet and even. "Fröken Nilsson?" she said, and when no answer came, "Fröken Stephania, what d'you think about that? Is it true, all she told us tonight?"

"I guess so."

"But . . . the other things she told us on Friday. . . . D'you mean she was lying then, lying all the time?"

"I can't say, Thura. I don't know myself what it is. She wasn't lying, she was just making it up. Making it up, not lying, d'you see?"

"Yes," Thura answered. "But still it's dreadfully sad, isn't it?"

"Yes, it is sad."

There was nothing else to say. They lay silently. Outside a car passed. Two long streaks of light stroked the wall, the beds, crept for a while on the floor and then sunk somewhere underneath it.

And now everything was dark again.

CHAPTER 16

"HAVE A WONDERFUL TIME, Fröken Stephania," Willy said, and he stuck into the pocket of her coat a pack of cigarettes. "Take it, you can smoke as much as you want to out there." He smiled, and motioned his hand in a vast generous gesture. "Just teach her to smoke," Sister Gudrun grumbled, and Willy limped away, partly because it was almost nine o'clock and in the ward everybody was waiting for him, and partly because he was a little afraid of Sister Gudrun.

"Be careful, Fröken Stephania, don't catch cold." Sister Gudrun checked to see if Stephania's coat was buttoned. "The cab will be here soon," she added. "See you Wednesday," and she walked back to the elevator.

Stephania stepped to the door, opened it, and stood in the entrance, looking at the drive, wide and empty, slowly getting used to the sharp cool air. It still seemed incredible that here she was, all alone, without the cast, waiting for the cab to take her home. It had all happened so suddenly. After the great inspection visit Ström had come to her and said they had decided to try a new cast, one that would work better.

"Do you mean this one hasn't worked well enough?" she asked him then.

"All I mean is that the new one will be better," he answered with his usual evasiveness, and then asked her how she would like to visit her sister since they wanted her to go without the cast for a day or two. How would she like . . . that certainly was a good question. She could hardly listen to him, and as soon as he had left she rushed to the phone to tell Barbara the news. Stephania smiled now, remembering Barbara shouting so loud that the re-

[ 194 ]

ceiver seemed to burst with her voice. "It's magnificent, simply magnificent!" But it was good she had not told Barbara about the cast. What eyes she would make now when she saw her coming without it, and looking so much better than before.

Because it was better . . . there was no doubt about it. They had immediately noticed it . . . both Fröken Nilsson and Thura. Only Ström said nothing, although he too must have seen how much she had improved. But he was always so cautious, always scared to commit himself. The cab was not here yet. She stepped forward into the drive, feeling the pavement firm and friendly under her feet. A gust of wind blew into her face and brought the strong fragrance of frozen earth, of withered leaves, the pungent smell of locomotive smoke, of gasoline and dust — the smell of the city that in a large languid mass spread itself on the other side of the drive. She breathed deeply and stepped forward exposing her face to the wind so that it pinched her cheeks, and tossed her hair upon her forehead. Her feet were growing cold, but the chill made her blood tingle; she felt it vibrating, as if her whole body, freed from the drowsy warmth of the hospital room, was waking up now. She took a few steps, cautious and tentative at first, then more and more secure. The cab should come any moment now, but she felt like walking. Stephania glanced at the glass door. The vestibule was empty — good, no one would see her. She smiled, hastened her steps and turned into the park.

The earth was half frozen and furrowed, covered here and there with scant tufts of faded lifeless grass. But the trees that out of her window looked monotonous and gray in their uniform and shabby bareness seemed now strangely full of color — each trunk was of different shade, with a different pattern carved upon it. And the thin branches of a few birches lay upon the cloudy sky like an intricate lace adorning faded gray silk. Once she stopped, not because she felt tired, but just in order to touch the bark with her gloveless hand. Slowly she moved her fingers over it, feeling every fold, every crevice, glazed with frost — rough and cold.

The park ended and she turned into the street. It was early still, and most of the stores were closed, except for a baker's shop on the corner that stood wide open, and the smell of bread, sweet and so strong that it was almost palpable, burst out of it and mixed with the frosty air. It was a warm, soothing smell — a good smell to breathe in. Two boys all covered with flour were loading shiny,

[ 195 ]

chestnut-brown loaves on a truck. She stopped and looked at them, and then walked on slowly, surprised that the crowds were so large, so full of color — girls in red, green and blue coats, their lunch bags in their hands; children blinking with eyes still full of sleep, their woolen caps with fantastic tassels shining on their heads; and workers in dirty overalls, their faces ruddy and strong, the cigarettes they had not time to finish at home gleaming between their lips. She tried to keep pace with them, as if she too were in a great hurry, coming out of her own home, hastening to a familiar place, where like the rest of them she went day after day. But after a while she grew tired and stopped, breathing heavily and called a cab.

In front of the door to Barbara's apartment, Stephania hesitated a minute to prepare herself before she finally rang. . . . No one answered. She rang once more. "Just a moment," Barbara cried in her broken Swedish. "Who is it?"

"Guess," Stephania laughed.

"Good gracious, Stephania, so early. . . . Wait, I'm coming, I'm just feeding the baby." A thin, sharp voice cried . . . the baby. There was the shuffling of feet, something fell on the floor, and here Barbara stood in the doorway, her blouse still half open, her hair falling on her face. "Stephania . . . how wonderful you look. What's happened, where's the cast?"

"They're giving me a new one, so they took the old cast off. How d'you think I look? Any better?"

"Better? What a question! A hundred, a thousand times better. . . ."

The cry of the baby interrupted them, plaintive and demanding.

"Come on in. You must see him." Barbara pulled her inside. In the kitchen she stopped and turned to Stephania, smiled, and said very slowly, "He's so cute, so cute, you just can't imagine." And she opened the door.

A small bed stood opposite the window. Stephania stopped, then stepped forward. And here it was, the baby — Barbara's baby — a tiny shape, the face red and wrinkled, the open mouth showing the toothless, old gums. The baby, she repeated to herself, but still she could feel nothing; it seemed so strange, so unreal somehow, just an object, an indifferent superfluous accessory to that bed filled with blue flounces and frills.

"So . . . how do you like him?"

[ 196 ]

"Wonderful!" Stephania said, knowing that her voice was too loud and jarring. But then the baby lifted its hand, tiny but marvelously finished, a real human hand, the transparent cuticles marked sharply on the pink nails, the soft inside of the palm covered with hair-thin but distinct lines. She could see that hand grow, she could feel it resting in her own hand, trustful and firm. "Oh, it's incredible," she said softly. "I just can't tell you . . . may I kiss him?"

"Sure, only not on the mouth."

She bent reverently, and touched his head, covered with dark down, warm, a little moist. "I still have to feed him," Barbara said. "You see, I don't have enough milk to nurse him. So he gets both breast and the formula."

"I see," Stephania nodded. It was strange, strange and wonderful how fast Barbara had learned all that, how easily she had grown into motherhood, as if she had known those things always, and now she only had to remember them. "Let me hold him," she said, and reached out her arms.

"Here," Barbara lifted the child, "go to your aunt." And she went out to fill the bottle.

Stephania sat holding him closely, feeling the warmth of the little body, its fists tiny and round against her breast. But suddenly the baby was crying again, bitterly, accusingly, and his face looked angry, hateful almost.

Barbara rushed in. "What has happened? For heaven's sake, how are you holding him?" She snatched the child out of Stephania's arms, rocked it to and fro. "Now it's all right. Don't cry. She doesn't know how to hold you, what?"

"I'm sorry," Stephania said. Her arms were still outstretched and she let them fall limply.

The baby was fed and put back to sleep. It was almost eleven now. Barbara had to hurry; there was so much to do — washing and cleaning and shopping. She began to sweep, and from time to time raised her head, asking Stephania about the hospital, the new cast, about all that Ström had to say. She was in a really great rush, and so sometimes Stephania's answer would escape her, and after a while she would ask the very same question again. Stephania sat on the sofa watching the cloud of dust catching the rays of sun. She did not mind Barbara being a little absent-minded; she had always been like that, and besides they would talk later. There were many things she wanted to talk to Barbara about — About Fröken Nilsson and her Italian, for instance. Fröken Nilsson had never mentioned that again; she must have felt ashamed of what had happened that night, but Stephania kept thinking about it. What would Barbara say to all that? And then, there was still another thing: the letters from Switzerland, for which she had been waiting in vain for months.

It seemed so difficult to talk now, when the water was running with loud splashing, and Barbara kept running from the sink to the stove, scrubbing pots and mixing the formula for the baby. She was just putting the plates away when the phone rang. "It must be Mr. Gross," Barbara said. "He always calls around this time."

"Hallo." Barbara blushed a little. "Good morning, Mr. Gross, thank you, fine." She blushed a little deeper, and said laughing, "No, come on, Mr. Gross, where do you learn jokes like that?" She stopped, listening. "Yes, exactly, they don't befit your gray hair. What's new? My sister's here, yes. . . . We're having a big party tomorrow night. Of course you're invited, you and Luba. Yes, just a moment, here she is." And handing Stephania the receiver Barbara said: "Mr. Gross wants to speak to you."

"Hallo," a voice said, soft and very melodious — too melodious perhaps. "Good morning, Miss Stephania. I'm so glad to have the opportunity of meeting you at last. . . . At last," he repeated, as if he had been awaiting the event impatiently for long time. Stephania murmured something. "See you tomorrow," Mr. Gross said, this time with easy familiarity, as if they were great friends already. He hung up.

"Isn't he charming?" Barbara said.

"How can I tell? I don't know him."

"Wait until you meet him," Barbara said. "We're having a bit of a party tomorrow night, in your honor. Gross is coming, and Genia, Warszawska — the whole bunch."

"A party?" Stephania repeated hesitantly.

"You don't feel like it?" There was a slight note of reproach in Barbara's voice.

"No, it's not that, only . . . " Stephania faltered again. "I thought we would talk a little, the two, the three of us," she corrected herself hastily. "And besides, you know I feel strange about meeting people now, and . . . "

"Come on," Barbara interrupted her, "that certainly is nonsense.

[ 198 ]

Why should you feel strange? Especially now without the cast . . . you really look fine."

"I guess you're right."

"We'll have a great time, you'll see. They're all such nice people and they've been simply dying to meet you." Barbara smiled at Stephania, looked at the clock and exclaimed that if they wanted to have dinner, she had to rush and shop right now. She was also worried about the baby; it had been sneezing that morning, she was not sure whether it was not too cold for him outside.

"Why don't you go and leave him with me?" Stephania suggested.

"With you?" Barbara hesitated. "Thanks. . . . But you see, you're not quite used to him yet, and he may start crying . . . one never can tell. I'd better leave him downstairs with Fru Anderson, the janitor's wife. Are you coming down with me?"

"I think I'd rather stay here." Stephania felt tired suddenly. "I might take a nap."

"Fine. I'll try to hurry."

And now she was alone, sitting on the sofa and looking at the empty bed. Barbara was right, of course. She didn't know anything about babies. But suddenly she remembered his face, as he started crying in her arms, angry and malicious. . . . She turned her eyes away from the bed and looked around at the room filled with shabby furniture, the covers on the chairs faded and dirty, a big hole right in the middle of the carpet. The dust had gathered in it, forming fleecy gray tufts. We'll have to clean the room for the party, she thought. Yes, the party . . . she shouldn't have objected to it; Barbara seemed hurt. After all, it might be good to dress up again, to be among people. . . . And it was they who wanted to meet her, wanted it even though they knew all about her. No, there was no reason to be afraid of the party; it was actually a good idea, very good indeed.

The clock struck one. In the hospital it was lunchtime. Fru Gustavsson was dealing out the food with the big, shiny spoon. "One or two potatoes for you, Thura? Wait, I'll come and help you." It was nice the way she always said that, and not "I'll feed you." She was nice, Fru Gustavsson. And Sister Gudrun was nice too — the way she behaved when Fröken Nilsson was about to be operated on was really decent. And now she wondered whether they had changed Fröken Nilsson's dressing today. They were supposed to. It must have hurt terribly when they did it last time. But she said nothing, Fröken Nilsson, not even a word. She too was nice, Fröken Nilsson, in her own way.

A heavy truck rolled through the street and the windowpanes trembled. Behind the wall, a querulous voice was saying: "I told you not to run, I told you you would fall down." She listened. The words merged into a monotonous murmur. When Barbara came back, she was still asleep.

Around six, Thadeus returned from work. He seemed tired and gloomy; and the overall with its too short sleeves made him look meager and lanky.

"Hello, Stephania, good to see you." He kissed her, and then glancing at his dusty shoes, at his dirty hands: "Excuse me, I must civilize myself," he murmured, and disappeared into the bathroom. After half an hour he emerged from there, clean shaved and smelling of eau de cologne.

"Hungry?" Barbara asked.

"No; who could eat after a beastly day like that?"

They sat down to dinner, crowded at the very small table. Thadeus ate listlessly, grumbled that the soup was watery, and at last pushed the plate away.

"What's the matter?"

"Nothing." He shrugged, got up and began to walk to and fro in the narrow kitchen. "God, if I only could get those twelve hundred crowns."

"What for?" Stephania asked.

Thadeus started explaining. There was a fabulous business, one of those affairs that you just have to put in a small sum, ridiculously small, and money would start rolling into your lap. It was export to Argentina — a gold mine. And all he needed was that lousy twelve hundred. But Michaelson refused to lend it to him.

"Who's Michaelson?"

Thadeus snapped his fingers disdainfully. "A nouveau-riche. Son of a peddler, or something like that. But he simply sits on money. Still wouldn't lend me any — wants a guarantee. I told him my name should be guarantee enough for him . . . but . . . ."

Stephania felt bewildered. She did not understand why the business with Argentina was so fabulous, nor why Michaelson should have lent money to Thadeus. She asked a few questions, but Thadeus murmured reluctantly that it was a long story, and that

[ 200 ]

Stephania would not understand it. "But Barbara knows I'm right."

"Of course you are, darling," Barbara assured him, and they got up from the table.

Thadeus felt very tired and they decided to go to bed early. There was no bed for Stephania; Thadeus had to borrow one from Fru Anderson. "Sorry we have to put you in the kitchen," he apologized. "That's what comes of having a factory worker for brother-in-law."

"I really don't mind," Stephania assured him. She felt so tired that it didn't seem to make any difference where or how she slept.

Barbara brought in the linen and made the bed. "Good night, dear, sleep well." They both kissed Stephania with sudden warmth as if again apologizing for something.

Stephania undressed and lay down. The bed was hard and so narrow that the pillow kept sliding down onto the floor. An annoying noise disturbed the silence — it was water falling drop after drop into the sink. Stephania got up. She looked for the switch, could not find it, and groping among the unfamiliar objects standing in her way, she walked over to the sink and turned the tap off. Something must have been wrong with it, for the water kept trickling. She stood for a while listening to the even drizzling sound and at last went back to bed. In the next room the baby cried out suddenly, as if horrified by something. "Sleep, darling, sleep," Barbara murmured drowsily. The crying stopped — the voice died out slowly. The air was sticky and smelled of food, of soap and dampness. And through the crack in the door a different warmth was flowing, the quiet warmth of human bodies lying in secure closeness to each other, plunged into restful sleep.

The party was scheduled for seven. Thadeus came home early from work to help with the preparations. "I told the foreman I had to see a doctor," he announced, very pleased with himself. For more than an hour he occupied the bathroom, and after he reappeared at last, he began to hurry Barbara and Stephania, complaining that women could never be ready on time, and that Mr. Gross would find them in their slippers still and in those horrible house coats.

But they were ready ahead of time; Barbara looked very lovely in her best dress of blue silk, and Stephania too felt rather satisfied with herself. It was much better, she could see it now in that plain black dress, and when she sat with her back leaning on the arm of the sofa, one could not notice much, not terribly much really. She let Barbara put some lipstick on her mouth, and even agreed to wear a pair of earrings. "Just choose the smallest ones," she objected, "after all . . ."

"No after all," Barbara cut her short. "You look lovely, that's all there is to it."

Stephania nodded absently and sat looking at the freshly polished furniture and the piece of colorful cloth Barbara had stuck under the hole in the carpet. She felt afraid suddenly — why she did not know.

The bell rang and Thadeus rushed to the door. There was the loud noise of welcoming; someone laughed, someone said, "Thadeus, don't kiss strange women, not when your wife is with you!" Again laughter, this time Barbara's, and the guests came into the room. "Mrs. Warszawska," Thadeus introduced the woman hanging on his arm, tiny and delicate, with a pale face, very red lips, and a huge mass of reddish hair falling in artful disorder upon her cheeks. "And I'm Genia," the other, evidently more at home, introduced herself. She had a sharp thin voice which did not fit with her ample body and with her face, which large as it was seemed too small for the enormous fleshy nose. They both sat down next to Stephania. Genia asked her how long she was going to stay, Mrs. Warszawska complimented Barbara on her dress, and then they fell silent.

"Is Mr. Gross coming?" Mrs. Warszawska asked.

"Yes," Barbara said. "He should be here any minute."

"Have you met him?" Genia whispered reverently to Stephania.

"No, not yet."

"Oh, he is just wonderful, you'll see."

"Extremely interesting," Mrs. Warszawska agreed, and turning to Barbara added, "Is he bringing Luba?" And when Barbara said yes, of course Luba was coming, Mrs. Warszawska, lowering her voice discreetly, began to explain to Stephania. "She used to be Gross's secretary, that Luba, once, when he had a small import-export office or something like that. And now . . ." Mrs. Warszawska smiled confidently, "oh, you know what I mean."

"Is he going to marry her?" Genia's whisper was breathless with excitement.

"*Quelle* nonsense. Of course not. Strictly *entre nous,* she is an absolute peasant, good for one thing only. . . . But to marry her!

[ 202 ]

She is Russian," Mrs. Warszawska said after a while as if that explained and summed up everything.

The bell rang. "Perhaps that's Gross." Thadeus hurried into the hall. But the new guest could not possibly be the handsome Mr. Gross. He was short and awkward as if his meager misshapen body felt embarrassed by the magnificence of his head with the sharp features of an Assyrian knight. "That is our intellectual." Mrs. Warszawska performed the ceremony of introduction. "Studies painting in the Art Institute."

The intellectual silently bent his too magnificent head, poured himself a glass and withdrew into the corner.

While Thadeus was serving the drinks another guest arrived, the engineer, who in spite of the loud and hearty welcome given him by Genia seemed shy and worried, somehow, at a loss what to do with his long limbs that hung loosely as if ready any moment to detach themselves from his body. He too asked Stephania how long she was staying, and the intellectual joined them inquiring how she liked Sweden.

The bell rang twice impatiently. "That must be Gross," Thadeus explained. Genia looked into the mirror, and Mrs. Warszawska put another layer of rouge on her already crimson lips. Even the student straightened his shabby jacket and passed his hand through his bushy hair.

In the hall Thadeus was saying with gentle reproach: "Where have you people been so long?" And then the melodious voice: "Oh, you know how it is in the Legation, they are never through on time there."

The door opened. "Here they are at last," Thadeus announced triumphantly.

"Yes, here we are, and a thousand apologies for keeping the company waiting," and Mr. Gross began to shake hands on all sides.

Stephania looked at him. Yes, Barbara was right; he was handsome, a little overrefined perhaps; still . . . She felt herself blushing when she saw him walking straight to her; he was not too tall but shapely, his dark hair gray on the temples brushed carefully, the very red lips smiling under the gray mustache. Mr. Gross put the two bottles he was holding by the necks on the floor and took her hand in his. "I am so glad to meet you at last." He bent over and Stephania felt his lips, his mustache touching her hand.

"So, let's have something to drink!" Mr. Gross turned to Thadeus. "None of that Swedish stuff, it tastes like distilled water. Here's vodka, honest-to-goodness Polish vodka, ladies and gentlemen."

He poured a glass for Stephania, another for himself, and sat down next to her. "So you are Miss Stephania," he repeated slowly. He seemed to taste her name, to turn it in his lips as he was turning the glass of vodka in his hands.

Stephania smiled with embarrassment. But Mr. Gross was perfectly at ease. He went on asking her all the usual questions, but pronounced in his carefully modulated voice they seemed to achieve a new, special significance.

The rest of the company gathered round them. Mr. Gross scrutinized them one after another, with his eyes resting upon the art student. "And how is our future Rembrandt?" he asked. "Everyday I'm waiting for the announcement of your exhibition." Everybody burst into laughter; the student too grinned vaguely as if not knowing what to do with so much attention. But Mr. Gross had already forgotten him. "Mrs. Warszawska, you look charming as usual. Luba, you should have a dress like that."

"Yes, Richard," Luba said obediently, turning toward him her broad docile face, her large eyes searching his face as though she could not quite understand him.

Mrs. Warszawska smiled. "Come on, flatterer, instead of compliments give us some new gossip from the Legation."

"It wasn't a compliment, it was the most solemn truth. . . . And as to gossip, my dear, what can I, a mere doorman, know?"

Everybody laughed in a way that implied that they all knew well that Mr. Gross's position, in spite of appearances, was quite different from that of a doorman.

"You certainly know enough, Mr. Gross." Mrs. Warszawska shook her reddish hair.

"Well, wait . . . now I remember something, something capital, more than capital, believe me!" He made the gesture of a conductor giving the sign for the last chord of the finale. Everybody fell silent. Mr. Gross plunged into a long story about a medal with which the consul was supposed to decorate a Swedish dignitary, and which, of course, he gave to the wrong person: a scoundrel, a son of a bitch (if the ladies would please forgive him that unparliamentary expression), and . . ."

"And . . ." Genia and Mrs. Warszawska echoed.

"And, believe it or not, he had to go there, and say in his French, in his French, you understand, that he had made a mistake, and that if His Excellency did not mind, he would like to have it back. His Excellency was furious: the other Excellency, even more so. . . . He came back to the Legation looking like . . . like . . ." Mr. Gross could not decide what the unfortunate consul looked like. He burst into hilarious laughter and everyone followed suit. For a while they were silent. Then Genia came forward; she wanted to know how Stephania could stand living with those Swedes; they were just like fish, so cold, without any feeling.

"It's not too bad," Stephania said, listening with pleasure to her own voice, so quiet and self-assured. "I just shock them once in a while, but it's good for them."

Everybody laughed again, and she too was laughing, sipping the strong liquor, smoking one cigarette after another. In the mirror opposite, she could see her face with the hair surrounding it in soft waves, the lips shapely and very red, the earrings tinkling with each movement of her head. Yes, she thought, Barbara was right, they were all such nice people, and the party too was wonderful.

"I'm convinced you'd be a success anywhere." Gross looked at her affectionately.

"You really think so?" Stephania shook her head, and the earrings tinkled louder, challengingly.

Mrs. Warszawska glanced to another side of the room, where the engineer stood discussing something violently with the painter. "I'd better circulate a little," she said, and walked off swinging her body gracefully.

"We must talk more later on," Genia said to Stephania, and she followed Mrs. Warszawska.

Stephania was left alone with Mr. Gross. "Isn't this a wonderful party?" she said promptly. Her throat felt very dry suddenly.

"Yes, certainly. Do you want another drink?"

"Yes, I don't mind getting a little tight tonight."

Mr. Gross took her glass. "I'll be back soon," he said, giving her a long conspiratorial glance as if a secret understanding existed between them. Stephania sat waiting. And when a long while passed and he still had not come back, she stood up and looked around.

In the opposite corner Mr. Gross was sitting next to Mrs.

Warszawska, his arm around her, laughing loudly. So he had forgotten he was supposed to come right back — it did not matter, nothing mattered much now. She emptied her glass, filled it again, and sat alone, staring at the transparent liquid in the glass, at the red point of the cigarette gleaming in her hand.

More glasses were filled, and the voices sounded louder now; a bluish cloud of cigarette smoke spread over the room, slowly grew denser and denser. . . . No, nothing mattered . . . Stephania repeated to herself.

"Come and join us," someone said. It was Barbara. She took Stephania's hand and led her over to the group surrounding the art student. He was arguing about something, gesticulating with his glass, and shaking his black mane violently. The engineer, at whom this harangue evidently was directed, stood hidden safely behind the ample shape of Genia, and kept exclaiming, "I disagree, I absolutely disagree."

"There's nothing to disagree about." The student emptied his glass and handed it to Barbara, motioning silently toward the bottle. "Nothing at all. You're impressed by the philistine way of life of that *petit bourgeois* paradise. At least admit it, be honest about it, be honest. But," he looked around accusingly, "but is that right? Is that what we're supposed to be doing? Are we going to sit here, working for a few crowns in the factories? We," he took an enormous gulp, "we survivors have a message, a message. . . . . And I . . . I know I don't fulfill it, painting pictures. Who needs pictures? But I'm going to quit, I'm going to Israel. That's what everyone should do . . . you too, engineer, you too."

"You've been quitting for the last two years, my dear sir," Mr. Gross shouted from his corner.

"Bravo, Mr. Gross!" Genia applauded. They all laughed. Stephania too tried to say something, but no one was listening. Somehow they all disappeared suddenly, until only the student was left, sitting with his head on Luba's lap.

Stephania walked back to the sofa. From afar she heard Mrs. Warszawska saying, "I wish you could understand me, Mr. Gross: I am flippant, I'm sophisticated, but . . ." The rest was lost in a whisper. Then Mr. Gross's voice said, "I understand much more than you think, much more."

So he was still with her, Stephania thought. "I wanted so much to meet you," he had said! Well, he certainly had satisfied his desire fast, he and all of them. "They're dying to meet you," Barbara had said yesterday, and now . . . But she didn't care, no, not a bit. Again she lifted the glass; it was empty. Slowly she managed to get up and started walking toward the table. Suddenly she stumbled on someone. It was Luba, sitting on the floor with the student. "They can laugh at me, but . . . I . . . believe the message," the student murmured. "Yes, of course," Luba agreed, her eyes glancing desperately at Mr. Gross who was again filling his glass. "Richard," she exclaimed plaintively, "remember your liver." Mr. Gross shrugged indifferently, and so Luba began to stroke the hair of the student.

Stephania struggled by, passed Barbara and Thadeus smiling, happy as if only now they had discovered each other. Here was the table, at last. "I want more," she said reaching out her glass. But no one heard her. "More," she repeated. The room started to whirl suddenly, something happened to her hand, the glass fell on the floor and broke with a shrill sound. "I broke it," she said, looking around challengingly. But again no one answered. She turned around. Next to her Genia and the engineer were kissing. "I broke it," Stephania cried. The engineer freed himself from the embrace. Stephania began to laugh. God, it was funny, screamingly funny.

"Please don't let me disturb you," she said in a high breaking voice. "I too used to do things like that . . . once upon a time, as the saying goes, once upon a time."

She kept laughing, but they did not look at her, simply walked out and disappeared in the kitchen.

"Well, let them go." She tried to walk back to the table but could not. "Where'd the bottle go? Who's hiding the bottle from me? I can have that at least, can't I?"

"You want a drink? Let me bring you one." It was Mr. Gross.

"Oh, Mr. Gross, welcome back. So you want to give me a drink. But please don't forget to come back. You've been so-o . . . so absent-minded." She was laughing so hard that tears began to roll down her cheeks.

"I never forget anything," Mr. Gross said gravely. And here he was back already, took her hand in his, stuck the glass into it. "Here, hold it fast, Stephania."

"So, you remembered this time," she murmured, looking at him; but his face seemed blurred, everything was blurred around her.

Mrs. Warszawska came toward them swaying her hips like a cabaret dancer, or perhaps it only seemed so to Stephania because everything was swaying and whirling. "Enjoying the party?" she asked.

Redhead . . . Stephania thought . . . I hate redheads. "No," she said . . . "I . . . I am" . . . bored she wanted to say, but here she was laughing again. It was all so funny, so terribly funny.

Mr. Gross laughed too. "You're perfectly charming," he said. She looked at him; now she could see him again . . . very distinctly . . . the sharp crease of his pants even, the white handkerchief in his pocket, and that . . . what was it? Yes, a pin, a pin with a pearl in his tie. She hated him suddenly, without any reason, just because he was the way he was, so polite, so nonchalant. She wanted to say something horrid to him, something cruel, so that he would stop smiling, would stop looking so dignified, so impenetrable. . . .

"Cigarette," she said commandingly. He took one he had just lit out of his lips and put it into her mouth. For a moment his hand rested upon her hair. She shuddered. "How noble of you, Mr. Gross . . . your last cigarette; how touching. Like giving a beggar your last shirt; isn't it so?"

"It's nothing but a pleasure," Mr. Gross hiccoughed, but even that little mishap could not destroy the gallantry of his answer.

"Noble," Stephania said through her teeth, looking straight into his face. "But, believe me, philanthropy doesn't pay. Please don't sacrifice yourself."

"Sacrifice myself? I told you it was a pleasure."

"No, I know what I'm saying. Don't waste your precious time on me. Go where you came from, where you've been all this time. Just say you'll be back soon, that'll be enough."

"But, I . . ."

"What's the matter, Mr. Gross?" Barbara came up to them. Stephania staggered to her feet. "Hello, Barbara, hello, beautiful blonde. Are you happy tonight? I'm fabulously happy, indescribably; anybody know any more superlatives?" she cried.

The room grew silent. They were looking at her now, at least. "God," the student sighed. "She's high, I should say."

"High?" she repeated, turning to him. "I'm drunk, blind drunk, my dear. What did Mr. Gross call you — my dear Rembrandt. Do you mind?" She looked around. "Does anyone mind? Everybody has to have some pleasure. Genia and the engineer know that, don't you? So I drink. Barbara, dear, you don't mind, do you?"

"Stop," Barbara said; she took Mr. Gross's arm as if to take him away.

"Just a moment." Stephania grabbed her hand. "Just a little moment. You can spare that for me, can't you? I . . . I . . ." She took someone's glass from the table and drank it down. "I . . . I want to deliver a message; yes, I too have a message . . . dear Rembrandt, I too. Don't be noble, Mr. Gross, handsome Mr. Gross, don't stay with me. Go with her." She grasped his arm, laid it around Barbara. "Go to her, go to the blonde, to the healthy one, that's my message. I said, to the blonde, to the healthy one. Well, what are you doing still here? Go!" she cried.

"Stephania," Barbara said.

"Go, you too, both of you!"

"I want to stay with *you*." Mr. Gross took her hand and made her sit on the sofa. "You all leave us now," he commanded, and filled a glass, put it to her lips.

"No, I've had enough, more than enough."

"Come on, drink; now, that's a good girl," and he put his arm around her.

"Go away, go. I don't want it."

"Why?"

"Why?" she said slowly. "Don't you know why? Haven't you noticed? You have to wait, Mr. Gross, not long, just two years . . . wait . . . until I'm mended . . . yes, mended; that's good, isn't it?" She wanted to laugh and was surprised when she felt herself crying.

"I don't want to wait." Mr. Gross plunged his hand into her hair. He emptied his glass. "Do you know why I drink, Stephania?" he whispered.

"No."

"Because I'm like you . . . proud, too proud to let myself be seen. But when I'm drunk I take off my mask. You too, Stephania, you're proud, you wear a mask too; don't deny it. And please, forgive me for calling you Stephania, but I can't be formal with you. We have too much in common, don't you see?"

"Enjoying yourself?" Mrs. Warszawska stood before them, the student next to her.

[ 209 ]

"Excellently, and you?"

"Superbly. D'you know what he has been telling me? He's going to Israel, right now, tomorrow. He says — Why should the milkman die for me?"

The student stepped forward, shakily but bravely. "Exactly, why should he?"

"Right you are. Although the opposite is equally true, why should you die for the milkman?" Mr. Gross answered.

The student staggered closer to them. Mr. Gross brushed him off with a gentle gesture. "Will you excuse us, please. Stephania and I are having a private conversation."

"Sorry, awfully sorry," Mrs. Warszawska lisped, and they disappeared.

"They," Mr. Gross waved his hand disdainfully, "they don't understand anything. Herd — that's what they are — part of the herd. But I understand you, Stephania, better than you think." His voice assumed deeper and deeper tones. "You must trust me."

"Having a good time?" This time it was Genia.

"Wonderful." Mr. Gross turned his back on her. "They won't leave us in peace, Stephania; let's go out."

"Let's." His arm still around her, she got up and let herself be led out into the hall.

It was dark here, dark and warm with all the coats and scarfs scattered around. Mr. Gross seated her on the only chair and settled himself on the floor at her feet. The door to the room was closed and the noise faded; it seemed to come from very far away. She felt almost sober, suddenly quiet and solemn. Something was going to happen, something very important. . . . She looked at the figure at her feet. His face was invisible in the darkness; only the cigarette gleamed. Then that too disappeared; he must have put it out; she felt his hand touching her face, taking her cigarette out of her lips. And now he was kissing her. She was not surprised, she knew it was going to happen . . . it had to happen.

"You're a strange girl," Mr. Gross said at last.

In the room Mrs. Warszawska began to sing — *"Ich bin von Kopf bis Fuss auf, Liebe eingestellt . . ."*

"Strange . . . why? There's nothing strange about me . . . just . . ."

"Just what, Stephania? Tell me . . . tell me everything. I want to know everything." He hiccupped again.

A sudden distrust rose in her. Why did he want to know? What was there to know? He just had to use his eyes, to look.

"You really want to know?" She smiled maliciously into the darkness. "Wait." And now she grasped his hand and bore it high up to her shoulders, where the big protruding lump was — the hunch. "Here, do you feel, do you know now?" she said in a hissing whisper. "That's what's strange; that's all there's to know."

"I understand, Stephania. But you're mistaken about everything, yes, about everything. All right, let's say your body's a little different. . . ."

"Deformed, terribly deformed."

"Well, deformed. But what does it mean, the body? It's the soul, the soul that matters. Look at Luba, she's beautiful, she's healthy and so what? Is she happy? Can she make me happy?" Mr. Gross sighed. "Look what's inside, Stephania, inside."

She felt him moving closer, smelling of cigarettes, eau de cologne and liquor.

"The soul? What do you know about my soul . . . what do I know about it . . . ?" she wanted to ask, but said nothing and let him stroke her hair. "I'll help you, Stephania," he said. "Just let me do it."

Help — how could he help her? Suddenly she felt like getting up, like running away. She tried, staggered, fell back on the chair. "Help . . . why not?" she said at last, "yes, why not?"

"We must have a talk together, a long talk. . . . Let's have lunch, just the two of us."

"When?"

"I'll call you. I'll call you tomorrow. You wait for me."

"Fine." She felt like smiling again. "I like waiting. I like to have something to look forward to."

"And after that . . ." Mr. Gross wanted to say something, but suddenly the door opened, the noise burst in, the light . . .

"So here's where they're hiding!" the voice of Mrs. Warszawska exclaimed.

"Richard," Luba said, looking at the glass in his hand, "don't drink any more; think of your liver."

Mr. Gross struggled to his feet. "You see, Stephania?" he said bitterly, "That's what I meant." He walked back into the room. Stephania, leaning on Barbara, followed him.

And again she sat in the sofa, the student next to her saying

[ 211 ]

something about life and art, reality and illusion. She didn't listen. From afar she heard Mr. Gross's voice and then Mrs. Warszawska exclaimed laughing: "Please stop, Mr. Gross, stop telling jokes like that. You're making even me blush, yes . . . even me."

The next morning was rainy and dark. Thadeus had overslept. He scolded Barbara for forgetting to set the alarm clock, and rushed out banging the door. Barbara had a headache and she was worried about the baby; Fru Anderson with whom he had been left last night had forgotten to keep him dry and now he was sneezing again. She walked around depressed and silent, looking desperately at the wild disorder — cigarette ashes, broken glass littering the floor, pieces of clothing scattered everywhere, and a big pile of dirty dishes in the kitchen.

Stephania was glad to be left alone. She sat, her head heavy, a dry, bitter taste in her mouth, trying to remember everything that had happened. It had happened only a few hours ago, in the very same room, but now she could not understand it any longer.

Barbara began to sweep. "It's like a pigsty," she murmured. The broom fell out of her hands, and she sat down hiding her face in her palms. "If I don't get out of here soon, something will happen to me." She got up, her face looking worn out and old.

"Can I help you?" Stephania asked. "Let me put the things away."

"No, you don't know where anything goes. I'd rather do it myself than explain."

Still Stephania got up, took a dust rag and began to wipe off the crumbs from the table. Something fell to the floor suddenly; a heavy white cloud rose into the air and covered the carpet.

"What have you done now?" Barbara cried.

"Nothing . . . it's just a compact. . . ."

"I told you not to touch anything. There's not enough space here for two to move around."

"I'm sorry." She walked into the kitchen, poured herself a cup of coffee. It was left over from yesterday, bitter and stale, and there were sticky traces of lipstick on the cup.

"If you'd come back into the room, I could start sweeping the kitchen."

"All right," Stephania said, "I'm coming."

She looked at the clock. It was ten now. Mr. Gross had called around twelve last time. But if he wanted to see her for lunch he would have to call earlier. "We'll have a long talk," he had said. "I'll help you. . . ." He probably had not meant a word of it. Or even if he had, he must have forgotten it by now; he had been completely drunk, . . . and she had, too. How could she ever have talked to him like that? It was shameful, like being naked in front of a stranger. Still he had promised her; he ought to remember.

Barbara came in and started making the beds. Stephania hesitated. "I think he's rather interesting, Mr. Gross," she said at last.

"Yes," Barbara murmured. The baby sneezed. "God, if I could get my hands on that Anderson I'd show her . . ."

And suddenly the phone rang. "Let me take it," Stephania exclaimed.

It was Genia. She wanted to know the address of the engineer.

"Tell her I don't know," Barbara said, "and that I don't have time to talk to her now."

Stephania repeated the message and sat looking at the street, at the uneven cobblestones, at the black pond in which the drops of rain drew large trembling ripples. If he didn't call by twelve she would leave. She should try to be back for Ström's afternoon visit. The phone rang again. "Let me get it," she cried, but Barbara was already holding the receiver.

"Hello. Yes, good morning. Fine, Mr. Gross."

Stephania stood next to her, waiting.

"Yes, just a moment."

She reached out her hand for the receiver. "He wants to talk to me?"

Barbara looked at her with surprise. "No. He just wants to know if he left a tie pin here, a pearl tie pin."

"Let me look," Stephania said slowly. There was nothing in the room. And suddenly she remembered last night in the hall, when he kissed her, she had heard something falling down. She went into the hall and pushed the chair aside. Yes, here it was. "I've found it," she called.

When she came back Barbara had already hung up. "Did he . . . did he say anything?" Stephania asked.

"No, why? Just told me to give the pin to Thadeus. They're meeting for lunch tomorrow."

"I see," Stephania said. "That's nice for Thadeus." She put the pin on the table. "I think I should go now, Barbara."

[ 213 ]

"Don't you want to wait for Thadeus?"

"I'd love to, but I really should be back early." Yes, she wanted to be back, to lie down in her own bed, to ask Fru Gustavsson for some hot tea, fresh, served in a clean cup. She walked to the phone and called a taxi.

Barbara walked with her to the head of the stairs. "Good-bye, Stephania," she said, kissing her. She stepped back, hesitated, "And . . . forgive me if everything wasn't quite as it should have been."

"Everything was all right, really, it . . . it couldn't have been nicer," Stephania finished hastily, and started downstairs.

They were just serving lunch when she came back to the hospital.

"Welcome back!" Fru Gustavsson said, waving to her with the big serving spoon.

"Thank you," Stephania said, walking over to her bed. Yes, they had changed the sheets. Everything was white and fresh, and the blanket was turned down, friendly and inviting.

CHAPTER 17

IT WAS WILLY who brought to the hospital the news that Christmas was coming — Willy who before, with his cherries and apples and oranges, had reminded them that summer was here, and fall, and winter, as if keeping track of seasons and holidays were a part of his work. And now, a week after Stephania's visit home, when she was staying in bed waiting for her new cast to dry, he came into the rooms and announced: "Christmas cards, ladies, lovely Christmas cards!" The day was sunny and dry, Christmas seemed still far away, and in every room the patients exclaimed reproachfully: "The cards! Already, Willy?"

"First of December, ladies." Willy shrugged his shoulders helplessly to show it was not his fault that time was passing so fast. "Yes, yes; Christmas is here again," he sighed, and the cards were passed from one bed to another; criticized, compared and admired.

No one bought them yet; they just wanted to see what they were like. And from now on looking at Willy's cards became a part of the morning program.

That was how it started. Because at the sign given by Willy all the rooms of Ward Two plunged into a rush of feverish activities. An end had come to the leisurely talks, to the long naps, to the listless perusing of magazines. Instead, knitting needles clicked, crochet needles flickered in the swift hands, and the beds were covered with shreds of wool, pieces of linen and colorful threads. Fröken Haagen from occupational therapy had become the most important person in the ward; loaded with patterns and wool skeins, knitting needles sticking out of her pockets, needles and pins covering the front of her blue uniform, she hurried from room to room, giving suggestions for Christmas presents, helping out in critical moments when the thread got twisted, or a stitch dropped.

The work began immediately after breakfast, and never stopped all day long. Even during the doctor's visit a needle would clatter suddenly to the floor, or a ball of wool would roll off of a bed, and in the evening the lights were not turned off until midnight — Sister Ingeborg closed one eye and pretended to notice nothing.

Together with the fever of work, an air of conspiracy permeated all the rooms. Because presents were prepared for the whole personnel, and these had to be a complete surprise, of course. Those who sat in the living room, therefore, were always on their guard, and hurried back to their rooms as soon as any of the nurses or maids appeared. "Hide it, she's coming!" they whispered. "Quick!" And Sister Gudrun or Fru Gustavsson, who had seen so many of those Christmas preparations, would look at the flushed faces, at the hands hiding something under the blankets, and say: "What on earth is going on here? Are you angry at me?" The patients would look at each other secretly, and there was always someone who would start giggling. "Hush," the rest would whisper angrily, but also pleasantly excited. And after the danger was over, they would say, "Heavens, that was close. Do you think she noticed anything?"

It was especially difficult to hide the preparations from Sister Gudrun, who was always calmly wandering from room to room. But instead of medicine tray or a syringe she would hold in her hands piles of shiny paper, green, red and gold. "If you people want to have Christmas you have to help," she would say, and throw part of her burden on every bed. Even those who were the busiest would put away their work, and now scissors snipped and rows of golden stars, of fantastic animals and chubby angels were lined on the bedside tables. The floor was constantly littered with scraps of paper and shreds of wool. But Sister Gudrun said nothing.

But in Room Five only one person was working — Fröken Nilsson. It was impossible to speak to her now — all day long she sat, four needles in her hands, balancing innumerable balls of wool each of a different color and counting the stitches. Both Stephania and Thura respected her desire for silence; they knew Fröken Nilsson was knitting socks for Doctor Liliencrona.

Thura, of course, could do nothing. Last year Mother had sent her presents for everybody — gloves, stockings, compacts. But how could those cold, impersonal things anybody could buy in a store, compare to those handmade gifts, carefully worked on, prepared for weeks? No, she couldn't ask Mother to buy the presents again; she had to find something else. And it was Fröken Nilsson who, reluctantly tearing her eyes from her work, gave her advice: "Don't you have at home any knitting or needlework you had done before . . . before — you know what I mean?" she asked.

Thura knew what Fröken Nilsson meant. Yes, she said, she had a whole drawer full of it, she had always been so fond of needlework. Fröken Nilsson wrote a letter to Thura's mother, asking her to send some of it, and a few days later a big package came. Stephania, since Fru Gustavsson was not supposed to know anything, unpacked it. One after another she took out the delicate serviettes, pieces of filigree lace, gloves with colorful figures embroidered upon them. "Did you make all that?" she asked.

"Yes, I used to be quite good . . . I mean I always liked to do things with my hands." Stephania and Fröken Nilsson looked at those hands resting motionless now as if very tired after all the work they had done. Until Stephania said angrily, "Well, I'm not going to waste my whole day here," and she hid Thura's presents deep in the drawer.

Stephania was the only one who seemed completely unaware that Christmas was coming. "No, no cards for me," she told Willy, and to Fröken Nilsson's question as to what she was going to give her sister and the baby, she answered: "Nothing, nothing at all." And then she walked out of the room.

The Christmas preparations upset Stephania. "This place is turning into a madhouse," she told Barbara, and murmured that it was ridiculous, worse than ridiculous, hypocritical and false. All the year long they hated each other, quarreled and gossiped, kept saying that Fru Gustavsson was lazy, that Sister Gudrun was a dried-up spinster; and now all of a sudden everything was forgotten, and for three weeks they were simply oozing with Christmas love, sentimental and disgusting. Anyhow, Stephania added, it was not her holiday, and thank God she didn't have to worry about it. That settled it, and she went on reading, ignoring Fröken Haagen from occupational therapy; she even refused to help with the preparations of the Christmas-tree trimming. But one day when Fröken Nilsson raising her eyebrows asked, "What are you going to give to Sister Gudrun, Fröken Stephania?" Stephania shrugged, and went out to call Barbara.

"You'll have to get some Christmas presents for me. I don't want them to think I'm stingy . . . you see."

"What should I buy?" Barbara asked.

"Anything, just so they won't start gossiping. Stockings . . . that would be fine. The largest size . . . they both have feet like elephants. Thanks a lot. Now I hope they'll leave me in peace. . . ."

But they did not. Because a few days later when Stephania came into the room she saw Fröken Nilsson frantically hiding something under her blanket. "It's only me," Stephania said, "you don't have to be so scared." But Fröken Nilsson, her face all red, murmured she wasn't scared at all, and that Fröken Stephania was imagining something. Still, she remained motionless with her hands hidden under the blanket. After a while Stephania walked out of the room. Something occurred to her suddenly. She stopped, listened. "Good gracious," she heard Fröken Nilsson saying, "I just put it away at the last moment; do you think she saw it?"

"I am sure she didn't," Thura answered.

"I just hope she'll like it."

"Of course, they're lovely, simply lovely."

So that was it. She was preparing a present for her. And — Stephania remembered suddenly — there had been a package among the things Thura had got from home which she wouldn't let her open. "It's just paper," she said, but still she told her to put it into the drawer. They're crazy, she thought; I should have told them it was not my holiday. She shrugged, and went to the phone to call Barbara again.

"That Christmas fever is catching," she said. "I need some more presents, for Thura and Fröken Nilsson."

Barbara was in a hurry, the baby was crying. "All right, I'll get you some more stockings."

"Stockings?" Stephania repeated. That was just like Barbara . . . stockings — for Fröken Nilsson with her stump in the heavy bandages, for Thura who would never take a step. "Wait, hold on," she said furiously. "What do *they* need stockings for?"

"Well, what do you want?"

"Let me think a moment." What could Fröken Nilsson want? Books — no, she had probably never read anything in her whole life . . . and suddenly she remembered — she used to wear it with a blue gauze scarf. "Buy a gauze scarf, blue, pale blue."

"Does it have to be blue?"

"Yes."

"What else do you want?"

"Just a moment." And for Thura, for Thura who could have nothing that one had to hold in hands, who could use nothing to wear . . . and suddenly she exclaimed: "I know what, an aquarium." Yes, that was good. She had one once, when she was sick herself and could not get up. Mother had bought it for her then, and said: "All you have to do is just look at it." And she could do it too, Thura — look. "Yes, a small aquarium with goldfish."

"That must be expensive," Barbara said.

"Doesn't matter, I still have some money here."

She smiled when she returned to the room. She could see Fröken Nilsson trying on the blue scarf, and the aquarium standing next to Thura's bed. That certainly was a good idea. She felt satisfied with herself.

And Christmas Day was coming closer and closer. Each mail brought new piles of packages; they were not opened, only put away in the storage room, where they had to wait until Christmas Eve. A tall fir tree stood in the living room, and the orderlies standing on the ladder covered the walls in the rooms with colorful pictures. Fröken Brickman from Four practiced Christmas carols all day long on the organ, and Willy had to get a new supply of Christmas cards and wrapping paper, too, because the patients were hastily finishing the last presents, wrapping them

[ 218 ]

carefully and hiding them in all kinds of odd places where neither Fru Gustavsson nor Sister Gudrun could discover them.

And now Christmas Eve was here. The last packages were put away, last scraps of paper were swept off the floor. The rooms grew silent suddenly. No lights had been turned on — perhaps because Sister Gudrun and Fru Gustavsson were busy decorating the tree, or perhaps because those lying there wanted to remain in darkness so that for a while they could be left to themselves, and think, and remember. . . . And outside the windows the trees stood, covered with snow that had fallen a few days ago, white and sharply chiseled on the smooth cloudless sky.

Until suddenly Fru Gustavsson came in, exclaiming "Hurry, children, hurry! We'll be going out soon." The lights were switched on. She helped them to dress in their best nightgowns, and bedjackets, and do up their hair with colorful ribbons instead of the usual pieces of white tape. The rooms smelled of powder, of perfume; Fru Gustavsson more flushed and worried than ever rushed from bed to bed — "Who else needs help, who's ready?" and again, "Hurry, dear, hurry, we'll be starting soon."

The general excitement reached its climax in Room Two. Fröken Nilsson, who for the last few days had been walking on crutches, met Doctor Liliencrona. He not only wished her happy Christmas but also told her he would come for supper. Fröken Nilsson decided, therefore, to wear her own dress. Fru Gustavsson, at the last moment, was sent down to the storage room. But here, a button was missing right on the front of the dress! Fröken Nilsson could not find it. . . . Then something happened to the lipstick, and her powder was all gone; she had to borrow some from Stephania, but it was dark, much too dark. . . . Fröken Nilsson was desperate.

Stephania too put on her own dress, the same one she had on at Barbara's party; it was wide enough so that she could wear it over the cast. Even Thura wore a light-blue nightgown instead of the hospital shirt and, when they were about to leave she asked: "Do you think I'd look very silly if I put some lipstick on?"

"Not at all," Stephania said, and she herself put some rouge on Thura's delicate and childish lips.

The doors to the living room were wide open and lights were flowing out of it, lights of all shades and colors — the cold even glow of the big lamps, the flickering of the many candles in

[ 219 ]

wooden holders on the long tables covered with white cloth, and the red shine of the fire burning in the fireplace. One after another the patients entered the room, some in their beds, others in wheel chairs, still others walking supported by canes and crutches. "You'll sit here, Fröken Stephania," Sister Gudrun said. She looked very festive in her black uniform, and her hair, not covered by a cap this time, was curled into an incredible number of ringlets. "Here, Fru Gustavsson, let's put little Thura next to Stephania. And where's Fröken Nilsson?"

"Still dressing," Stephania answered. They had left her trying to get into her dress. The fate of the Nilsson family had reasserted itself: Fröken Nilsson had gained weight again.

The room was full now, and the excited faces, colored by the many lights, looked almost beautiful. "Let's start," Sister Gudrun said. She helped Fröken Brickman to get up, and led her to the organ. Voices passed into whispers and then died out. The organ uttered a deep sound . . . Fröken Brickman, a little too loudly, began, "Stilla natt, heliga natt." And now they were all singing, at first timidly, then loud and freely. . . .

But suddenly a strange noise disturbed the song — a heavy tramping and the sound of wood knocking on the stone floor. It came closer, grew louder and louder. Sister Gudrun was the first to turn her head, and then the others. There, at the far end of the hall, Fröken Nilsson slowly moved forward, her body big and shining in the black satin dress suspended between the crutches. Slowly she struggled ahead, the crutch first, then the leg, then another crutch. Everybody stopped singing. Only Fröken Brickman, oblivious of everything around her, went on playing. Heavy gusts of sound poured out of the organ and joined the hollow knocking of the crutches as if to accompany Fröken Nilsson's toilsome and difficult progress — a step, a wave of sound, a step again. Until at last she was in the living room, stopped, and took a deep breath. The organ uttered the last triumphant sound. Fröken Nilsson with a sigh of relief collapsed on the chair. The crutches fell on the floor.

"I'm sorry," she murmured.

"It's all right," Doctor Liliencrona sitting opposite her said. "You're doing fine, Fröken Nilsson, you're a real champion." And only then everyone burst into loud relieved laughter.

The organ started playing again. They sang one carol after

[ 220 ]

another. Only Stephania was silent. She did not know the songs, and sat looking into the fire, her face cold and indifferent as if she were bored.

The singing was over. Sister Gudrun walked to the tree under which packages were lying piled high one upon another. In complete silence, she picked them up, read the names out loud, and Fru Gustavsson took them over to their owners. The rustle of papers was mixed now with exclamations of joy, of surprise. "A present, for me ... I would never have expected it!" Sister Gudrun and Fru Gustavsson exclaimed whenever the package was addressed to them. The pile under the tree was growing smaller and smaller. The beds and the floor were scattered with boxes, books, articles of clothing.

But the space around Stephania's seat was empty still. She sat waiting. Someone's name was called — she started — no, it was not hers. There was nothing for her, of course, why should they have bothered to prepare Christmas presents for her? She must have imagined something that had never happened. And now they all were looking at her, at that bare space around her, thinking, wondering what could be the matter with her, feeling sorry for her. But it only served her right. She shouldn't have come, it was not her holiday, she should have been in her room, alone now, not here; she had no business here. She wished she could get up and leave but was afraid Fröken Nilsson and Thura would try to stop her. No, now she had to stay, perhaps later, yes later ...

"Fröken Stephania, this is for you."

"Here I am," she answered, quietly, but a feeling of relief as great as if she had escaped some great danger overwhelmed her suddenly. Slowly she unwrapped the package. It was from Thura: a dozen white handkerchiefs all covered with embroidery, edged with narrow lace.

"D'you like them?" Thura asked eagerly.

"Oh, yes. Thank you ... ever so much."

"Fröken Stephania." Fru Gustavsson handed her another package. It was from Fröken Nilsson — a pair of bed socks knitted in glaringly pink wool.

"They're lovely, Fröken Nilsson," Stephania said.

"I'm glad you like them," Fröken Nilsson answered. She wore her new blue scarf gracefully draped around her neck and nodded condescendingly when Doctor Liliencrona said: "It's remarkable how well blue goes with your complexion."

After all the presents had been distributed, the orderly came in and put a big package in front of Thura.

"What's that?" Thura looked at Stephania.

"Ask Fröken Nilsson to open it for you."

The paper fell on the floor. Thura looked wide-eyed at the glass bowl, at the green thicket of seaweeds inside, at the two goldfish, darting to and fro like flickers of light. "Is . . . is that for me?"

"For you, Thura."

"Oh Fröken Stephania, I . . ." Thura stopped. looked at her. And later when Stephania leaned over her head, Thura lifted her hand — three inches, Stephania thought — three inches, and laid it on Stephania's hand. "Thank you," she said.

Stephania was silent.

Supper was served now. They ate slowly. Fröken Nilsson remembered last year's supper and decided after a brief consideration that this time the food was much better; the ham so much more tender, and not too salty either. Then Doctor Liliencrona told them about the Christmas he had spent in Italy.

"Tell us something about Christmas in Poland." He turned to Stephania when he had finished his story.

"What shall I tell you?" She smiled, but her voice was strained and her face crimsoned.

"Oh anything, you have such interesting customs there. I hear, for instance, that trolleys and buses don't run on Christmas Day."

"They don't."

"And the food, what kind of food d'you have?"

"Pretty much the same as here," she answered curtly, and started eating again.

They did not insist any longer. Someone began to talk about Christmas in the North, up there in Lapland.

Stephania did not listen. Christmas in Poland — she thought. They wanted to know how it was there, but now they stopped asking. She knew why they stopped — they did not want to awake old memories in her — memories of the family happily gathered at supper, of the Christmas tree standing at home. How tactful it was of them! And what if she should tell them — right now, point blank — tell them that there was no Christmas supper, no tree, that she was Jewish, and it was not her holiday, and she had no business here among them . . . ?

[ 222 ]

"I hear the buses don't run there," he said. No, they didn't run, everything was silent and quiet there, she thought, and she felt surprised at how clearly she remembered it — the white empty streets, the lights, and those days before Christmas. And now it came back, that strange feeling as of hunger, the way it used to come every year, long before Christmas, as soon as it grew cold and the air smelled of chestnuts burnt on small stoves with the red lamp glowing next to the slender chimney. Yes, then it started: the waiting for the forest of fir trees to grow and suddenly in the old marketplace, for the gold stars and silvery angel hair to shine in the store windows.

There was one place she remembered now — a small shabby store in an old house with a vaulted roof. It smelled of gingerbread and honey — that was what they sold there; and all the year long, nothing but the yellow jars stood in the window. But before Christmas the jars disappeared and a manger stood there, made out of gingerbread — with real hay inside, and on it the baby pink and round and almost real too. She stood and stood there, breathing in the sharp fragrance of spices and honey, wondering why the baby was naked and lying in a manger. She asked Father, but he told her she did not have to think about that, she was Jewish and Jews had nothing to do with it. Still, whenever she passed the store she would stop and look and then walk over to the marketplace, dark green with fir trees, and the *crèches* stood in long rows, filled with clumsy wooden figures, their faces featureless and painted with bright colors.

And in the evening again she would sneak out of the house and walk through the streets, looking at the shop windows, all silver and gold and green, and listening to the carols sung by boys carrying *crèches* from house to house, their voices clear and a little sad in the frosty air. . . .

"Why don't we have Christmas?" She had asked it again and again even though she knew the answer would always be the same: "We have *Chanuka* instead, don't you know?" Yes, she knew that every night Father lit the small thin candles in the old candlestick, one on the first night, then two, then three. But how could the small quivering lights compare to the blazing Christmas trees, or the candlestick so old that the silver was almost black to the pink baby in the gingerbread manger?

No, she did not want to have *Chanuka*, she wanted to be like

[ 223 ]

other people, to have Christmas as all of them had. And every day she would sneak into the stores where they sold the trimmings for Christmas trees, and make believe she too was shopping, and touch with reverent fingers the soft web of angel hair and the smooth glass of big colorful balls until some one of the salesgirls would ask, "May I help you, young lady?" And then she would rush out breathlessly, feeling they all knew she did not have a right to be there . . . that she was just pretending.

And all the time throughout the cold December days she waited eagerly and fearfully for *that* night to come . . . for Christmas Eve. Everything grew quiet then; the trams, the cars and buses disappeared from the streets, and the whole city was not the same at all, but silent, as if it were asleep. And suddenly there would be lights in all the windows and songs sounding from everywhere, until you did not know where they were all coming from — from a house nearby, or from the next street; the whole sleeping city seemed to wake up and sing — and the bells rang. Only in their home everything was silent and mute, and in the window the solitary flame of the *Chanuka* candle quivered as if it were freezing. . . .

"Another piece of cake, Fröken Stephania?"

"No, thank you." Only now she noticed they were through with supper. They began to sing again. "Wouldn't you sing a Polish carol for us?" Fru Gustavsson asked, when all their repertoire was exhausted. And again everybody was looking at her. A carol — she thought; she knew one only that their maid had taught her once. But she would not sing it, no . . .

"Please do sing for us," Thura whispered, and suddenly she began and felt startled hearing her own voice.

> *"He lies in a manger;*
> *Who would come*
> *To sing carols*
> *To the little one . . ."*

They listened. She had a nice voice, Stephania; at first it seemed a little too sharp but slowly it grew very soft and deep.

"Thank you, Fröken Stephania, that was really beautiful," Sister Gudrun said when she had finished. Stephania nodded silently. She was glad they didn't ask her for another song. For now it was time to return to the rooms. One after another the beds were rolled out, then the wheel chairs' turn came, and at last those who could walk began to leave. Stephania got up. In the hall Fröken Nilsson stood talking to Doctor Liliencrona.

"Thank you for the beautiful socks," he was saying.

"They're a token of my gratitude," Fröken Nilsson said, stammering a little.

Stephania smiled.

In the room Thura said: "It was a lovely evening, wasn't it?"

"Yes," she said, "lovely, little one."

Stephania wondered why she had said "little one." It must have been because of the song. . . . yes, the song.

CHAPTER 18

CHRISTMAS WAS OVER. The red-nosed Santa Clauses and the golden stars disappeared from the walls, the green tissue shades were strippd off the lamps, and in the undisguised glaring light the rooms looked suddenly barren and cold. And as the old dullness returned, old bickerings started anew. Again Fru Gustavsson quarreled with Sister Gudrun, and the news of it soon spread all over the ward. For not only had Fru Gustavsson, in spite of Sister Gudrun's distinct prohibition, given clean linen to Fröken Brickman before the Sunday visit-time, but also — Fröken Nilsson heard it with her own ears — she had told Sister Gudrun she knew what she was doing, and knew it better than many head nurses who thought so much of themselves. The patients divided promptly into two factions; gossip was eagerly repeated from mouth to mouth, and eager whispering was resumed as soon as the door closed after Sister Gudrun or Fru Gustavsson.

Much good it has done them, all that Christmas good-will and sweetness, Stephania thought with a triumphant smile. But in spite of that smile there was rising in her a hollow feeling of disappointment, of bereavement almost. When after Christmas Eve she had sat next to Thura, the sound of songs still round her, saying "little one" to her, then everything had seemed easy and simple, filled with a peaceful certainty that from now on everything would change, would be like that moment — assured, free from fear and doubt.

But nothing had changed. Days passed, cold, sunless, January days. A thick layer of frost covered the windows, hid the sky and the familiar shapes of trees, made the world outside more distant, more unattainable than ever. The lamps had to be turned on all the time, and the sharp yellow light blurred all the difference between morning and evening; the hours seemed to be plodding on without direction. Stephania felt as if an impenetrable wall separated her from the days she was waiting for, from that moment in which at last she would be free of that room where nothing ever seemed to happen, and of the cast imprisoning her body.

She tried to pierce that wall through, fix dates which would break monotonously identical days. On the sixth of January it will be five months since I came here, she would think, and each morning she would glance at the chart, measure the time between now and that date, but then the sixth of January was here, dark and motionless as every other day bringing no change, no news. Ström never had anything to tell her. "Fröken Ackermann — as usual," he would say — and leave without even looking at her. She could not stand that meaningless murmur of his, and would leave the room during his visit and sit in the living room.

It was there that Sister Gudrun found her one afternoon. "Where are you hiding," she said angrily. "Don't you know the doctor comes at this hour?"

"He doesn't come to me, anyway."

"Not to you? He comes to everybody; what kind of talk is that? Hurry, he wants to see you."

"Really? He wants to see me?" Stephania repeated, breathlessly hurrying to the room. Ström was already standing in the doorway. "Tomorrow at three we'll tighten the cast." That was all he said.

"Tomorrow? But that's wonderful, Doctor," Stephania exclaimed. She wanted to ask him some questions, but Ström only nodded and left hastily.

She stayed awake until late that night. Usually Ström would tell her weeks before about tightening the cast, and the unexpectedness of his announcement this time seemed to give it a special importance. Something unusual would happen tomorrow — she knew it — something really decisive. And then she remembered —

morphine — he had said she would get it if they did something different, something unusual. Maybe she would get it tomorrow. Stephania smiled. It was clever of her not to have said anything about it to him — he would never know how much she cared for it. And tomorrow she would say, offhand, casually: "Did you give the instructions about morphine, Doctor?" Just like that, quietly, as if it meant nothing to her. Then in the evening Sister Gudrun would come, the syringe in her hand.

She closed her eyes, somehow already feeling that morphine-lightness, the slight dizziness and above all the warmth, so slowly and cautiously tiptoeing into her body. There would be no talking tomorrow night; that would spoil everything. She would just lie quietly, as if listening to it, feeling it spread all over her body, the stream of warmth growing wider and wider. And then she would think — this time something good, something she wanted very much, was waiting for her. About the . . . letter, that it came at last, that it said . . . No, that was the last thing she wanted to remember on that morphine night, that letter which she had been expecting for weeks, months now, expecting in vain. . . .

But there were other things she could think of . . . of the day when she would leave the hospital; yes, that was good, there was so much one could imagine about that day. . . . Perhaps she would meet him again then, the charming Mr. Gross who so firmly believed it was only the soul that mattered and the body not at all. And perhaps then he would have time for her, would not forget a lunch engagement. But by then she would be too busy for him; then there would be so much else to do. . . . There would be streets to walk through, and parks with benches hidden under the leafy trees, steps softly sounding in the evening silence, and the slender elongated shadows of passers-by merging out of the darkness; there would be theaters, and the concert hall so white and austere, the lonely figure of Orpheus, pensively and sternly gazing at you; and also the cocktail lounges that she used to pass, the light dim and secret there, making the faces vague, silent, and expectant. . . . Then the revolving door turning, and she walking in, but not alone — for then she would never be alone. Stephania sat up and looked into the dark room. They were asleep already, both of them, Thura and Fröken Nilsson. She smiled. Poor Fröken Nilsson, saying on that night after her "great day," "I can't understand why people make so much fuss about it." Yes, she understood nothing, nothing at all. "It's being together," she had answered her then. Only that was important, nothing else, not even the oppressive unrest that again and again would now rise in your body — like pain almost, only worse — shameful somehow. Yes, it was only that: not to be alone, that mattered.

She could see herself walking through the street next to a tall figure, leaning upon an arm warm under the rough tweed, listening to a voice, to footsteps so willingly and easily merging with the sound of her own steps.

Where're we going now? she could hear the voice say.

She hesitated and smiled. She knew the place where she would go first — the boardinghouse. I lived there for almost a year, she would say. And now she saw it, the big yellow building, the heavy gate with the shiny copper handle. Fru Olsson, the landlady, would open the door; she would be dressed in discreet gray, as always immaculate; the only wrinkles about her person splattered haphazardly, untidily somehow, over the withered face. First she would not recognize her, then — Fröken Stephania! Is that you? — you've changed, she would start saying, and then check herself. Because she was so tactful, Fru Olsson, she and all of them, oh, so tactful. And when they hurt you, they did it courteously, hiding it skillfully under the pleasant words, the gracious smiles. Still they did hurt — and how!

She saw them now, one after another: the two sisters that lived next to her, very blond and full-bodied, pretty in a heavy sluggish manner, and the medical student who lived upstairs; then the tall girl with a narrow eager face like a hound's, and the architect who drank too much.

She had avoided them, she wanted nothing from them but to leave her alone. But they would not. First there were only the tentative smiles, and casual remarks exchanged as they passed her in the hall. Then they started coming, not because they wanted to; oh, no. She could feel how they hated those perfunctory visits filled with meaningless questions, with dragging silences. Still they came; they felt it was their duty. The two sisters came first and brought her some books and magazines; then the others began to drop in, until almost every afternoon the room was filled. But then when it grew dark outside they left hastily, the women rushing back to their rooms to change, to put shoes on with even higher heels, and even more brilliant earrings. . . . Because right after dinner they would all leave for the movies, for a night club or a party, leave glancing at her uneasily, saying: Have a nice evening, Fröken Stephania — I certainly will, she could hear her own voice, sharp, and defiant. And when she was alone again in the gloomy dining room, silent except for the asthmatic rattle of the old radio, she would get up and, hidden behind the curtain, watch them crossing the street, the girls clinging to the men, the high heels clicking, the voices loud and clear in the evening air. Later when she was falling asleep she would hear them coming back, still talking and laughing.

Did you have a good time last night? she would ask them in the morning.

Oh . . . nothing special, we just took a walk.

It was always like that: Nothing special; the embarrassed smile, and the uneasy glance. And at dinner, when someone would ask, What time does the party begin? or, Where're we going tonight? there would again be a confused murmur, all eyes suddenly avoiding hers. They thought she did not know she was not good enough for them, never good enough for those evenings; as if they could hide it from her, hide the voices and the laughter, and the music coming from the living room, and the sound of dancing feet. But she did know it, and one day at last they learned it. It was late in the night — she remembered — and again there were voices and music coming from the room next to her this time. She could not force herself to go to bed, but sat in the dark room, listening. Until at last she got up and walked out. The door was open; a broad stream of light fell into the hall. Then as she was coming closer, the door slammed hurriedly. She stood and waited, and then without knocking walked in.

And now again she could see herself standing there, in her old skirt and a shabby sweater, among women in rustling taffeta and shiny satin, men skillfully balancing the tall cocktail glasses in their hands. At first they did not notice her; then one after another heads turned; they felt she was there. In the sudden silence she said, Would you mind being a little more quiet? There're some here who want to sleep even if there's a party going on.

The sisters came to apologize next morning. They were so sorry for the noise and for not having invited her, but it wasn't a party really — just a few people dropped in.

[ 229 ]

That was all right, she interrupted them curtly, only she would appreciate it if in the future . . .

Soon after that, the visits became more and more rare until at last they stopped altogether. It must have been too much for them, coming every day, pretending they enjoyed it. And besides, she was not too hospitable either.

But she would go back there, go, and not alone this time. They would all come to see her, would stand there embarrassed again, with nothing to say now that she would not need their pity any longer. And she would say, We used to have wonderful times here together, didn't we? and then take the warm strong arm, and say, Come on, dear, we've so much to do still. . . .

She smiled. Yes, that was how it would be, and she would think of it again tomorrow night, with the morphine warmth in her, the things around blurred and no longer real, and those images, the ones she waited for, suddenly distinct, tangible. . . . Tomorrow, she thought, but somehow the joy had faded and only the bitterness of the memory was left.

Still she slept quietly the rest of the night and woke up light and cheerful, remembering she had something to look forward to today. The morning moved on fast; hardly was breakfast over when Fru Jungdahl, Thura's therapist, was here. Then Sister Gudrun came in, the packet of mail in her hand.

"Anything for me?" Thura and Fröken Nilsson exclaimed at once.

Stephania said nothing. She never had any mail, what was the use of asking? Page fifty-two, yes, this was where she had stopped last time. And just when she started reading Sister Gudrun said, "Fröken Ackermann, I have a letter for you."

"For me?" . . . No, it could not be that letter, it certainly was one of those ridiculous advertisements she got from time to time, or . . .

"How strange. It must have been sent to the wrong address first, to Poland, I guess."

"To Poland?" The book fell down, she jumped to her feet, snatched the letter out of Sister Gudrun's hands. So it was from him, at last. . . . Her hands trembled when she was opening the envelope; she had to stop, and then start again, — tearing it open clumsily from all sides.

The letter was short, just one page. Stephania looked at the big

[ 230 ]

scrawling handwriting, and began to read; suddenly she lifted it closer to her eyes as if she could not quite see, and then very slowly put the letter away, sat down. . . .

"Any good news?" Fröken Nilsson asked cheerfully.

Stephania looked at her blankly. "Did you ask something?"

"Just if you got any good news?" Fröken Nilsson murmured. "In that letter, I mean."

"Oh, the letter, yes, yes, very good news." She snatched the sheet of paper, crumpled it in her hand and walked out of the room.

"What's eating her now, I wonder?" Fröken Nilsson asked angrily.

"I . . . don't know," Thura said. "Maybe it was the letter, maybe the news was not so good."

She walked down through the hall filled with people, the radio roaring at the top of its voice, and then again into another hall, empty at last — quite.

The door to the medicine room was open; no one was there. She went in and closed the door carefully, and stood staring at the long rows of bottles filled with yellow, purple and green liquid, at the instruments in the glass-closet, sharp and shiny. Something rustled in her hand . . . yes, the letter. Why had she brought it there, what was the use of reading it over again and again . . . ?

Still, something forced her to open her hand, smooth out the crumpled sheet and lift it to her eyes. And again she was reading, stopping at each word, as if trying to learn it by heart, to remember it forever. . . .

"Dear Stephania." She skipped the first few lines, awkward apologies for the long silence; yes, here it was — the reason. "I asked you, and how often you yourself know best, to let me come to Poland, to meet you there. You always refused, without ever giving me an adequate reason for it. Your explanation that it would be dangerous for me to come from Switzerland to Poland cannot certainly be considered sufficient. It was not dangerous at the time when I wanted to come, even now it still could be arranged. You obviously didn't want to see me; why, that is less clear to me. Maybe you have met someone else, maybe you felt all the time that there is no use in our meeting each other, now when so much has changed. Still, whatever the reason is . . ."

[ 231 ]

The reason . . . so that's what he wanted to know. No, he never would learn it, no matter what he was thinking, anything, everything was better than what she would tell him, than the truth. . . . Her eyes again skipped a few lines, moved down to the bottom of the page, where he was saying he had waited long enough, and now, when again he found someone he could care for . . . so he was going to be married on the twentieth of January. The twentieth — that was yesterday, the twentieth . . . perhaps it had happened at the same moment when she was talking to Ström . . . perhaps . . . Carefully she folded the letter, in two first, then in four, and got up. . . . Her whole body was stiffened, it seemed to be covered with frost; and each breath ached, as if the air around her was a sharp-edged stubborn mass with which she had to struggle. Cold, she thought, I'm cold, and walked over to the radiator and put her hands on it. She felt the frost melting, and then slowly, the palms folded as if afraid to lose any of that precious warmth, she lifted them to her face.

Now her face too grew warm, her eyes burned as though she had been crying for a long time, but inside her, everything was still, hard, frozen. And again she had to open the letter, to look at it. "Dear Stephania," only now she noticed it. "Stephania," he had said for the first time in many years. The first time after that evening together when suddenly he had said, "Stephania, that's too big, too solemn a name for you." And he called her "Steph" after that, saying it softly and secretly, that name invented by him, known only to the two of them. "Steph" — and she would look at him, at his gaunt sharp face softened suddenly, and always high above hers because he was so very tall. She could feel him, see him next to her, and not until now did she suddenly grasp that it was over: his voice, and that tall body leaning over her, and the smile . . .

She sat down, bent in two, as if hiding from a blow threatening above her, threatening to strike any moment, to hurt. But it was from within, it was deep inside her, that the pain appeared, piercing, choking. And slowly, as if she had to be very careful now that she had to carry that pain within her, Stephania got up and walked back to the room.

"That's all," Doctor Ström said. The nurse cut off the sharp edges that had left thick red marks on Stephania's body and put a piece of felt underneath.

"Now it should be better," Ström said, and without another glance at her, walked over to the corner, where the plaster casts were standing in a long row.

Stephania looked at him, hesitated, and said at last, "Doctor."

"Yes?"

"You remember last time you said that when you did something new, something different, you might give me that . . . morphine, I mean, and I thought . . ." His face, stern, reluctant, made her stop suddenly.

"It's nothing new, nothing different, what we've done today."

"But usually you tell me long before; this time it came so suddenly. . . ."

"Suddenly, because we could not decide whether to do it at all or not. So you don't need any morphine. . . . Morphine," he repeated through his teeth. "That's all you think of, what? Sometimes I wonder if you understand at all what's going on here, if you realize that it's not a child's game you're playing, not just an easy way of getting morphine, that there's something serious, yes, very serious at stake. . . . But you seem to care about nothing."

Something in his voice startled her. "I do care, Doctor, you know it. I understand it is serious. But . . . but you sounded so strange, Doctor . . . has anything changed?"

He walked back to her, looked straight into her face. "No, nothing has changed. That's it, nothing. Do you understand?"

"Nothing? What d'you mean? You . . . mean that things are not going as well as you hoped, as you expected?"

"I hoped?" he repeated, seemed to be about to say something, and checked himself at the last moment. "I didn't expect anything, you know that, you must know it," he said at last. "I refused to guarantee anything, I made no promises. And here you sound as if I had given you all kinds of hope, promised miracles . . . and . . ."

"I know, Doctor, I understand everything," she said fervently, trying to propitiate him somehow by that prompt agreement. "But tell me, aren't you satisfied? Did you expect . . . ?"

"How many times should I tell you that I've expected nothing, almost nothing. Look here, Fröken Ackermann, you're not a child any longer. You knew what you were going into, didn't you? I didn't hide anything from you. So here it is: we're not making very much progress. Very little, actually."

[ 233 ]

"But some, Doctor, some."

"Very little."

"Well," she said slowly, trying to gain time, so that she could force some order upon her thoughts, "you said yourself you didn't expect any miracles, didn't you? You said that nothing has changed. So it is still there, the chance, just as before."

"One chance, perhaps."

She did not want him to go on, she had to force him to silence, deafen the sound of his last words. "As long as there's one chance," she said hastily and waited for him to finish.

But he said nothing and so she had to say it for him. "Everything will be fine, Doctor, it'll just take time, lots of time."

"We'll see." That was all he had to say.

She stood silent, numb suddenly, unable to understand. . . . The letter, his words, his voice both tired and warning merged into one feeling, into the fear that choked her, filled her mouth with a bitter taste. "I see, Doctor," she murmured at last, "I understand, I really do, but . . . if only you could give me morphine . . . just today, you must," she cried, and then, her voice almost a whisper, "because something has happened to me today." Slowly she raised her hand and rubbed it against her cheek. "Something went wrong."

He moved closer and bent over her. And Stephania, looking at his face, softening suddenly, felt how something was surging within her — a desire to tell him everything, tell him about the months of waiting, about the letter.

No, she could not tell him that, she must not. With an effort she tore her hand away from her face, said, "If I only" . . . what was it that she wanted to say? "If I only could sleep tonight, quietly . . . for one night. . . ."

"I'm sorry, Stephania," he said slowly, "I must have been too brusque before. I didn't mean to be. But try to understand: I cannot do it, I have no right to. Whatever has happened to you today, morphine will not help. . . . I explained all that to you once before. . . ." He pulled a chair closer, said, "Sit down, you must be tired." And when she sat down he went on. "Do you remember what we talked about then, last time I tightened the cast?"

Stephania only nodded.

"Well, I've been thinking about it, and there are a few things I want to suggest to you."

Stephania shrugged. The trustful warm feeling was gone, the

[ 234 ]

anger returned. "Suggestions," she repeated. Why don't you take up knitting, that's probably what he would say, that or something like it. Fool that he was, fool and coward. He was afraid someone might find out about the morphine and that was why he refused. "Go on, Doctor," she said impatiently, "I am listening."

"I hear you have a very good voice, Stephania."

She laughed sharply. "I didn't know my fame had spread so far already."

"And so it occurred to me," he went on as if he hadn't heard her, "that you might like to spend a few hours a day in the children's ward; teaching them songs, organizing games."

She looked at him and said harshly, "No, thanks."

"Why not, Stephania?"

"I don't want to." She hesitated not knowing quite what else to tell him. "I don't like children," she said at last, "and they don't like me either. A case of mutual antipathy, Doctor."

"Well, I'm not so sure you're right," he said shaking his head. "Still, I don't want to force you into anything. But I also thought about something else. Fröken Brickman, the one who plays piano, wants to organize musical evenings for the patients. Fru Hensson from Four will play the recorder and you could sing."

"No, thanks."

"Another case of mutual antipathy?" His voice was angry now.

"Maybe. But more than that too. Don't you see," her voice rose, "it's ridiculous, it's all wrong, what you are doing here. You want to make it pleasant, the life in here, so nice, just like home, what? And at the end they find it so pleasant in here that they forget what they have come here for, they simply don't feel like leaving, do nothing about it. That's what has happened to Fröken Nilsson, that's what's happening to most of them. . . . And you instead of forcing them to remember all the time that this is a hospital, that they should get out of here as soon as possible, that it's not a place one enjoys, but . . ."

"Look, Stephania, it isn't as simple as that. They stay here for years. You can't do anything but wait year after year, you just cannot. These years in the hospital are like all other years. Something must be done with them; waiting itself is not enough."

"All right," she said wearily. "It may be so. Anyhow I don't feel like participating in Fröken Brickman's musical soirées."

"Fine, don't if you don't want to. But," he got up and said, again severe, "I can't let you go on like this, just counting the days to the moment when you leave, just figuring out what's going to happen after the two years are over. They're not over yet, and . . ."

"What is it that you want me to do, Doctor?" she interrupted him impatiently. .

"You might even help Fru Gustavsson in your room; do things like washing Thura, feeding her, and then in the other rooms. We have plenty of patients who can't do anything for themselves."

"If you want me to, I'll do it." Stephania shrugged again. "It makes no difference to me. Still, that too solves nothing, Doctor; just like morphine: nothing at all."

"I'm not pretending I'm solving anything, Stephania. Still I do think it's better than morphine."

"I doubt it." She grinned, and got up. And suddenly she was walking toward the door; Ström too got up and hastened after her, saying, "Stephania . . ." He stopped, then added haltingly, "Please do not hesitate to come to me when you have a question, a problem, any problem. Remember, any time I'll be glad . . ."

"Yes, Doctor," and she looked at him, at his face smiling in clumsy encouragement, and repeated, "Thank you very much, Doctor. Perhaps . . ."

Next morning when Fru Gustavsson came in to wash Thura, Stephania said: "Let me do it today." And that was how she started those busy days, the hours distinctly marked by washing Thura, feeding her, by running errands for Fröken Nilsson, serving coffee, by helping with making the beds, and at dinner. In the beginning she found it hard; not because she grew tired, but because somehow she felt ashamed of her own strength, ashamed that it was she who was doing everything for them, she could walk and could move her hands. And above all, it was their gratitude that was hard to understand, their constant saying — "Thanks a lot, Fröken Stephania," "You're so kind, Fröken Stephania." "Stop that nonsense," she would answer, her face cold, hostile almost. She was not kind, she was not doing it for them, but for herself, only for herself.

But soon she got used to it, and began to like those morning hours, when she would take Thura's hands in hers, wash them carefully, when she would pass the comb through Thura's brown

[ 236 ]

soft hair and then put the mirror before her and hear her ex- claiming: "My, I certainly look clean and nice now, Fröken Stephania. You wash and comb me so well, even better than Fru Gustavsson."

In the afternoon she would sit next to Thura, both of them reading, Stephania turning the pages of Thura's book. There was something peaceful about those hours that helped you forget; the silence interrupted only by the soft rustle of pages, by Thura's voice asking eagerly: "Do you like your book, Fröken Stephania? because mine is just wonderful."

And it was Thura also who initiated their singing in the evenings. "Would you sing something for us?" she asked once. "You have such a nice voice; everybody liked it so much when you sang then, on Christmas Eve."

"Nonsense," Stephania murmured in reply. Somehow she did not like to be reminded of that evening, and besides she didn't feel like singing. But both Thura and Fröken Nilsson insisted so hard, and the evenings seemed so long, sleep came so unwillingly lately, that at last Stephania agreed. From then on she sang for them almost every evening, when the preparations for the night were finished and the lights went off in the rooms, and only muffled footsteps and whispers disturbed the great silence of the hospital night. They were strange, those songs Stephania sang for them — the melody sad and slow-moving, and then suddenly ris- ing high, clamoring. And the words too, sharp and crowded some- how as if coming in an angry rush, seemed strange to Thura and Fröken Nilsson. Stephania would explain them: they spoke of a river called Niemen, red with blood, and of the day of glory, a day of freedom and blood; or of soldiers that threw their fate upon a bloody holocaust. For no matter what song it was, the word blood was there — sometimes with glory, sometimes with free- dom, or love, but always there, sounding so different than in Swedish, louder and more piercing somehow.

"Are they all so terribly sad, those Polish songs?" Fröken Nils- son wondered.

"Sad? I never thought they were."

"They certainly are. They give me goose-flesh, if you want to know the truth," Fröken Nilsson answered. And she would try to teach Stephania some of the songs she knew; cheerful songs, about the sailor, Olaf Anderson, and the girl he brought from

Cuba, about Kale and his dancing on Midsummer Night, about lights kindled at home, on winter evenings. Stephania learned them easily; still, when she sang them they seemed changed, harder, more melancholy, almost like those outlandish songs of hers.

CHAPTER 19

MANY STARTLING and unexpected things had happened in Ward Two: first there was Fröken Nilsson losing her leg almost on the eve of her going home; there was Fru Hernruth whose infection had vanished suddenly, practically overnight; and Fröken Brickman, the organ player, whose arm started healing all of itself, just when Professor wanted to operate on her again. Yes, there were many events like that, disasters striking slyly and cruelly, when least expected, and recoveries no longer hoped for, miraculous almost. Still, nothing had ever seemed more wonderful and more surprising than the news that Thura would soon begin to move her hand.

Both Ström and the Professor had told her that, and the patients all over the ward repeated it to each other. And they all added how much she deserved it, poor Thura, always so quiet and patient, and how wonderful, how unbelievable almost it was that a turn for the better had come to her at last. Not that both Ström and Professor had not been promising it to her all the time. "One day we'll play ball together, Thura, you and me. Just wait and see," Professor would say on each of his visits. But somehow the waiting for that day had grown so long that no one believed in its coming any longer. And when Professor again would make that joke of his about the ball, or about Thura playing piano better than Rubenstein, all, nurses and patients alike, would just smile — very politely but guiltily too, the way one smiles at birthdays of very old people, wishing them many happy returns and knowing all the time that there cannot be many more any longer. And here all of a sudden Doctor Ström came to Thura and said: "If you only try hard enough, you will move your hand soon, just in a week or two."

It all happened in the last week of January, on that strange Thursday when it was snowing so hard that half of the personnel had come late to work, and the whole day was topsy-turvy with things happening out of order, so that it was like in a room unexpectedly rearranged by a strange hand; you did not know where to look to find familiar objects. In the afternoon the beds were not made nor was the floor swept, and then when it was least expected, the door opened and Doctor Ström walked in with Fru Jungdahl, Thura's physiotherapist, behind him. No, one never could say about Fru Jungdahl that she was just walking; she would come in practically dancing, her toes barely touching the floor, her gaunt muscular body swaying rhythmically.

But on that day there was something unmistakably special about Fru Jungdahl's dancing entrance, and above all about the tone of her voice, when gracefully halting before Thura's bed, she said: "So, now you'll see, Doctor. Lift your arm, Thura, one . . . two . . . now!" Fru Jungdahl clapped her hands. "Now!" Slowly Thura raised her arm. "Do you see, Doctor, she can lift it almost straight up; isn't that excellent?"

"Really excellent," Doctor Ström agreed.

Fröken Nilsson and Stephania looked at each other with surprise, with disapproval even. It was no secret that Thura could lift her arm fairly high, but what good was that, when the hand was still completely lifeless, when not a single finger even stirred? Fröken Nilsson shrugged, and Stephania nodded in silent agreement.

But here was Fru Jungdahl's voice again saying: "Now try to move your hand. One, two," just like that. "Move your hand," she had said, as if it were the easiest thing in the world for Thura to do.

"What?" Thura whispered.

"Try to move your hand," Doctor Ström repeated.

"You mean me . . . my hand?" Thura said haltingly, staring bewildered from one to another.

"Yes, you. Go ahead and try," Doctor Ström answered, and both he and Fru Jungdahl began to move their hands, bend and unbend their fingers. "Just like that, you see."

[ 239 ]

"Like . . . that?" Thura murmured following each of their gestures with startled eager eyes. "But how . . . how can I?"

"Try," Fru Jungdahl commanded.

"Yes . . . yes. Just let me see." Thura wrinkled her forehead. Her face grew red, crimson almost, the teeth cut into the parted lips. They could hear her panting heavily, each breath short, jerky, as if she had to struggle for it, as if she were lifting an immense burden. But her hand remained motionless; the fingers, widely spread and crooked, hung down limply. "I'm sorry," she whispered. "I tried. . . . but I can't."

"Try!" Doctor Ström almost shouted. He stood bent over the bed, his fingers touching Thura's hand, his face watchful as if he were listening to some hardly audible whisper. "Now, once more!"

And again the heavy panting, the teeth cutting into the parted lips, and the hand motionless, not even a quiver passing through it. "Tormenting the poor girl," Fröken Nilsson muttered to Stephania.

"Hush," Doctor Ström hissed. And then aloud, triumphantly he exclaimed, "A flicker, a distinct flicker, Thura!" Thura seemed not to have heard him. "I can't try any more," she said. Her arms fell back upon the blanket.

"But the flicker, Thura, the flicker is there."

"A . . . flicker?" Thura repeated. "You mean a muscle is moving, like when I started lifting my arm?"

"Yes, exactly. You just have to work hard from now on. You must try again and again, and believe you can do it."

"I see, Doctor," Thura said. Her voice was uncertain, dazed; she still seemed to understand nothing.

They left, Doctor Ström all smiles, waving his hand at Thura, and Fru Jungdahl dancing on her toes, the gray head lifted triumphantly. In the door they stopped. "So remember, Thura, keep working."

"Yes, Doctor." And now there was a long silence. Thura lay, her arm still suspended in the air, her eyes fixed upon her hand. "Did you hear what they said?" she asked at last. "I can hardly believe it . . . I . . ." And if only now understanding what had happened she cried: "Oh, Fröken Stephania, Fröken Nilsson, that's just too wonderful!"

"It certainly is," Fröken Nilsson said. "But I've been telling you all the time you shouldn't worry."

"Yes," Thura agreed, although as far as she could remember Fröken Nilsson had never spoken to her about her hand. She turned her head and looked at Stephania.

Stephania got up, walked over to Thura's bed. Slowly, with great care, as if she were touching some very fragile and precious object, she took Thura's hand in hers. "It's wonderful, Thura," she said, "but remember what Ström told you. You must work on it."

"Yes, Fröken Stephania," Thura answered, and then with something like fear in her voice, "I'll try, I really will."

And she did work on it, Thura. All day long she lay with her arm raised, her face flushed and covered with sweat. "One . . . two . . . now!" she commanded herself, and then, "The flicker is there, the flicker! I must do it." Again and again she tried, but all in vain — the hand would not move.

Sometimes it seemed to her that something was quivering in it, that the fingers were about to stir, any minute, right now; but just when she would look at them, imploringly, hopefully, something would paralyze their movement, as if another hand, invisible and powerful, lurking somewhere around, had grabbed her own hand and forced it to a stand-still.

She tried to learn from others. With eyes eager, almost greedy, she spied upon all those hands, moving so easily, so effortlessly, as if they possessed secret knowledge, which they were jealously hiding from her, and which she had to capture from them unawares. Hands, hands — all her days were filled with nothing but hands — clasping and unclasping, with fingers spreading and bending. In the morning it was not the washing any longer that was important: now it was the careful and intense study of the way in which Stephania or Fru Gustavsson lifted the basin, or how they dipped the washcloth in it, of the incomprehensibly intricate manner in which their fingers wrung the water out.

Then breakfast, and again hands — gently putting the plates on the table, unfolding the napkins, skillfully manipulating the spoons. And in the afternoons when Stephania turned the pages of a book for her, Thura would hardly read; she would lie waiting for the moment when Stephania's slender fingers would take the page, lift it. . . . She knew each detail, the bending of every joint, the quiver of every muscle; still the very secret somehow always escaped her. Her hand refused to move, it seemed to be not a part of her own body, but an independent creature with will of its own — stubborn, spiteful, hostile. And here, as days and then weeks passed, everybody expected her to do it — impatiently, almost angrily. "You don't want Fröken Stephania to wash you today. You can do it yourself, can't you?" Fru Gustavsson joked every morning . . . "I'm sure you've good news for me today," Doctor Ström said on each of his visits.

"No, I still can't, Fru Gustavsson; no, no news, Doctor," she would answer, looking at them imploringly as if asking forgiveness for the disappointment she had given them.

After two weeks the hand quivered, but so slightly that one could hardly notice it. "You must try harder, Thura," Doctor Ström said. "You still have a long way to go." She tried as hard as she could, but again days passed and nothing had happened, only that imperceptible trembling was there; it made her feel even more guilty, that pitiful quiver; it seemed to mock the great hopes others put in her, it just showed how little she could really do.

"You must do it, Thura," Doctor Ström repeated. "Try to think how you did it before you got ill, think about something that you liked to do — knitting or embroidering — and figure out the way you used to do it: that might help," he would advise her, and Fru Jungdahl would add severely: "You must have faith that you can do it, Thura. Faith — that's the main thing."

"Yes, Doctor; of course, Fru Jungdahl," she would answer obediently.

But once during the great inspection visit, something unusual, something truly unbelievable took place. "If you were working really hard, Thura, you could do it," Professor said, while all the doctors, nurses, and therapists stood around her like a group of implacable judges. And then Thura, yes Thura, who had never before raised her voice to anyone, who hardly ever dared to say a word to a doctor, looked around and shouted — bitterly, accusingly: "I can't do it, I told you I can't, I try and try and nothing happens, nothing!" She lifted her arm and reproachfully exhibited to the silenced, bewildered crowd that yellowish withered hand of hers.

Then, looking at Professor, at his hand, red, fleshy and muscular, she said wistfully: "It's easy for *you* to do it: but how can you know what it's like for me, how can you tell me what to do?"

[ 242 ]

There was nonchalance, almost pride, in her voice, as if she were bragging about a peculiar privilege, about a terrible painful elevation that nobody but she could grasp. No one answered.

At last Professor said, "Hmm. . . . Don't get upset, Thura," and he stroked her head and left. Only then Thura understood what had happened. "How could I ever say anything like that?" she murmured. "He must be terribly angry with me."

"Angry, so what? Don't let that worry you," Fröken Nilsson said. She was in a bad mood herself; again Professor had not said when she would get her artificial limb. "It's good for them to hear a word of truth from time to time. They sure think they've swallowed all the wisdom in the world, all those doctors."

"Still, I don't think I should have said it," Thura answered, looking at Stephania.

Stephania was standing at the window, her fingers drumming upon the pane. "Thura," she said.

"Yes," Thura answered absently. She was watching Stephania's fingers. How could Stephania do it — she thought — bend all of them at once, and so fast, too.

"Thura," Stephania repeated, "you at least could listen when someone is talking to you."

"I . . . I'm sorry, Fröken Stephania . . . I was listening, really I was."

Stephania turned to her. "It was childish, childish and stupid, that performance you gave."

"A performance?"

"Yes, all that shouting at Professor, all that ridiculous talk about him not knowing what it was like for you."

"Oh," Thura gasped. "I'm so sorry, Fröken Stephania. I really don't know what happened to me. But all of them standing around me, staring, as if it were my fault, as if I did not *want* to do it."

Stephania gave her a prolonged look. "Well," she said slowly, "it is your fault, Thura. Whose if not yours?"

"Fröken Stephania," Thura cried, and then looking at Fröken Nilsson as if asking her for help, "how can you . . . you say that?"

Slowly Stephania began to walk toward Thura's bed. "You've talked yourself into believing that you can't do it. That's all."

"Why should I do that? No . . ."

"Why?" Stephania interrupted her. Her voice sounded as though she were grinning, but her face remained severe, tense, and she

[ 243 ]

sifted her words slowly, hardly opening her lips. "And why should you try to get well, why should you care, Thura dear? It's so nice here, so quiet. Everybody is so kind, bringing your food right to the bed, doing everything for you. So . . . why should you bother? Isn't that so?" She snapped the last words sharply.

"No! You don't really mean it. You can't . . . you . . ."

"I mean it, every word of it. You can do it, but you simply don't feel like it. I know it. Ström wouldn't have promised you anything unless he was dead sure of it. He certainly is cautious, Ström, and how . . !" She walked back to the window. Her fingers were drumming on the pane, slowly, jerkily now following the halting words. "There're some who would give anything to hear a word from him, just one word of promise. . . ." The hand tore itself from the window and balled into a fist in a helpless, angry gesture. "A word, even, of encouragement . . . and here you . . ." She turned back to Thura. "He told you right out, that the flicker is there, that you can do it and you, you just don't care, it all means nothing to you."

"No!" Thura cried. "You have no right to say that. You don't know how hard it is for me to do it." And again as before, scornfully and haughtily, "It's easy for you to talk, Fröken Stephania."

"Fine, fine. You can have it your way. It's not my business, believe me."

"I didn't mean it, Fröken Stephania. I just want you to understand."

"I understand everything, Thura." Stephania sat down on Thura's bed, and went on almost in a whisper. "It's just that you have to do it, Thura. You must. Perhaps . . . yes, perhaps it's not good that you're working all by yourself. Let's do it together, you and me. So I could show you how to do it, explain . . ."

"But you're already doing so much for me, Fröken Stephania. All that washing and feeding . . . I really can't take more of your time."

"My time?" Stephania smiled. "Well, Ström and Professor don't keep me too busy, as you probably have noticed. So I've plenty of time, Thura."

"If you really don't mind, then I would love it. Thanks a lot, Fröken Stephania."

"Nothing to thank me for," Stephania murmured, and she walked out of the room.

[ 244 ]

"She certainly was mad," Fröken Nilsson said. "I thought for a moment she was going to hit you, the way she looked. . . ."

Thura did not answer. Only after a long while she said, "Did you hear what she said about Ström?"

"That you can surely do it if he told you so? I guess that's right. Still, why should she get so mad?"

"I don't mean that, I mean about Ström and the others. That to others he says nothing, and they . . ."

"Yes, I remember."

"Do you think she meant herself? That he says nothing to her?"

"Herself?" Fröken Nilsson hesitated. "Well, it may be, Thura, it may be. He hardly ever looks at her when he comes in, and Professor also. . . . But that would be too bad, Thura, just too bad."

"Oh, that would be dreadful, Fröken Nilsson. But I'm sure she'll get well, that he will tell her, only later maybe. It just has to take time!"

"Sure, it takes time. And she wants everything at once, Stephania. As if the ground were burning under her feet." And Fröken Nilsson kept shaking her head long after she had finished speaking.

It was hardly nine o'clock when Stephania turned the lights off that evening. "You need lots of rest, Thura," she said. "Try to fall asleep at once."

"I think I will, Fröken Stephania. I feel rather tired."

"Just don't worry too much, Thura," Fröken Nilsson murmured drowsily. "Then you'll sleep."

Fröken Nilsson turned her pillow, sighed deeply and soon she was snoring softly. For a while Stephania tossed restlessly, then she too grew quiet. Thura lay with eyes closed, waiting. But sleep would not come. It was the same way with moving your hand, she thought. She wanted to sleep, she tried as hard as she could. Still, just when she felt most tired, when she was sure sleep was coming, something would chase it away. Like now . . . there were footsteps in the hall; someone, yes, it was Sister Ingeborg's voice, said, "She is in Three, Doctor." A door opened; footsteps again. And now although everything was silent, she couldn't fall asleep. Feeling she was breaking her promise, Thura opened her eyes, looked around. A narrow line of light sneaked in through the

[ 245 ]

crevice in the door; on the panes, down where the shades did not reach, frost glittered and sparkled in the shine of the street lamp. And next to her bed, there was the aquarium, the lamp fastened to the glass cover burning so that the water would not get cold. She liked to look at the aquarium in the night; it seemed so different than during the day, more important somehow — a solitary square of green and golden light, big and shiny in the darkness that surrounded it. The plants too seemed changed, of deeper green, entangled into a fantastic, terrifying little thicket. And the fish, one rushing to and fro, the other motionless, suspended in the clear water, only the delicate and transparent fins moving constantly showing it was awake. Fish never slept, Stephania had explained to her; and when one said a fish was asleep, it meant it was dead. Thura liked the term for that fish-death; it somehow made you feel they never died really. Now she lay looking at them; they were so cheerful, glittering like new copper coins. But sometimes when they opened their sharp mouths they suddenly seemed bigger, like some cruel and dangerous animal. Thura smiled — it was good to have the fish here, it made you feel less alone to know that they too were awake.

Wasn't it wonderful of Stephania to give her the aquarium? Stephania — she thought of her with a sudden feeling of guilt. How could she have answered her so cruelly today! And lately neither she nor Fröken Nilsson ever asked Stephania how she felt and what the doctor had told her. She had always been on her feet, Stephania, and that made them forget she was a patient just like them, waiting still for her "great day," waiting to get well. But Stephania would get well, she could do anything she wanted. In the spring they would operate on her; then another year; and then she would leave, healthy and beautiful, looking exactly like that picture she had on her table.

Yes, Stephania would go home one day, and Fröken Nilsson, too, soon, in a month or two. Suddenly she felt afraid of that day when both of them would be gone, when she would be left alone; afraid of the unfamiliar faces staring at her from their beds, of the strange voices. . . .

Or perhaps she too would leave; they might send her home before she could move her hands. Things like that had often happened, after all. Like that patient in Four; she had to leave, and could not even take a step. "They couldn't help her, so why should she have stayed and taken a place needed for others?" Fru Gustavsson had said then. Perhaps one day Doctor Ström would come to her and say: "You must go home, Thura. We can't do anything for you." And then . . . of course, she wanted to go home, Stephania was wrong about that. Only she did not want to go now, when she still could do nothing, so that it would be again like two years ago when she had been at home for a few weeks before she came to Stockholm. All the time Mother sat by her bed and kept asking — "Do you need anything, Thura? Tell me, what can I do for you?" And all her aunts and cousins had come, all wanting to do something for her, until she felt tired of all those questions, of all those eyes staring at her anxiously, of the voices, lowered and solicitous. It was not at all like being back at home; it was much more like a visiting time that lasted not one hour, but day after day, and left you worn out and sad, too, because they all tried to do so much for you and there was so little you wanted. But if she could only move her hands, then everything would be different.

It was strange to think how much you could do with your hands — sewing and knitting, and turning the pages of a book, and cooking, yes, even that. Doctor Ström had told her once about a woman who did all her cooking sitting in a wheel chair. Thura glanced at her hands; they seemed so small, so unimportant lying there quietly in the greenish light of the aquarium lamp. And yet . . .

"Try to remember how you moved them before," Doctor Ström kept telling her. To remember — but how? That too was strange, Thura thought. It was only three years since she had become sick, and yet it seemed to her that it had always been like that — nothing but the hospital and lying in bed and other people doing everything for her. Those years before, when she had been just like everybody else, when she could walk and move her hands, had shrunk, vanished almost completely. Nothing was left of them but a few memories of birthdays, of trips and holidays, but so vague and distant that she did not know whether what she remembered had ever really happened.

It was the small insignificant things that she could remember much better. Not many of them either, just a few: breakfast hastily swallowed before rushing to school — yes, that she remembered, and the sweet taste of cocoa, that was always too hot and burned her tongue; and the sharp touch of the brush with which Mother smoothed her hair every morning; then the smell of freshly cut grass; and the touch of the window sills on summer mornings, so warm with the sun that they seemed like living creatures when you passed a hand over them. But what was the use of remembering trifles like that, when the really important things, those Doctor Ström wanted her to know — the way she used to write or sew — had vanished tracelessly, and only what did not matter at all kept coming to her mind? Like the nights — that she had not forgotten — those nights when she could not fall asleep because she was so terribly afraid. When she was little it had been different, as if there were no nights at all then, only day following after day, and a few hours between them that did not even count. But when she was six, or seven perhaps, yes seven — she was in the second grade then — the nights suddenly emerged out of their hiding and were there, more important than the days, longer, and so frightening that days were nothing but anxious waiting for the nights.

— It all started after Mother had got sick, very suddenly, and in the middle of the night had to be taken to the hospital. She had not been there long, just a week or two at the most, but still everything had changed after that. Even if Mother was back, even if you sat next to her, and watched her walking around the house, still all the time you felt that she was not *really* there, that any moment she could disappear again. Those two strange men in dark uniforms could come back and carry her out on the long stretcher, and take her away not for a week this time, but for much longer, forever perhaps. Thura smiled. It had been silly of her to think like that, but then she could not help it, could not help fearing when night came that Mother would leave again without even saying good-bye to her.

But of all those hard and long nights the worst were those when Mother went out in the evening and she had to stay with Fru Andersson, always munching on something, and she talked so loud that the whole house seemed to be full of her. But then Fru Andersson stopped coming.

— That too she could remember, as clearly as if it had happened only yesterday. It had happened on a winter night, very much like this night now, the windows white with frost, and the streets outside all covered with snow. Mother had to go to visit some friends, alone; Father was in Göteborg then. She did not want Mother to go, and in the afternoon she took the keys from the closet and hid them under the mattress, so that Mother wouldn't be able to get her dress out, and would stay at home. But when Mother started looking for them all over the house, she suddenly felt afraid, and put the keys back on the table. She managed to stay very quiet when Mother was getting dressed and only when Fru Andersson came and started stamping heavily in the kitchen, fixing the coffee and nibbling on the cake, did she begin to cry, and asked Mother to come back soon. "I'll be back at twelve," Mother promised, kissing her good night. She looked so pretty then in the good black dress with red flowers at the belt, and smelled so nice, of perfume and powder. But the smell and the rustle of silk made her feel even more lonely and afraid. Mother seemed changed, strange somehow, and she closed her eyes kissing her good night, trying to see her as she always looked in the evening, the mother she knew so much better in the old faded robe and slippers shuffling softly because they too were old and much too big. "Will you come to see me when you're back?" she asked then. "Yes," Mother promised, and told her, just as Stephania had today, to fall asleep at once. But as soon as Mother had left, she jumped out of the bed and watched her walking through the street . . . until at last she disappeared behind the corner.

What happened later? Thura thought now — had she fallen asleep? Yes, she had, and perhaps she had nightmares then, and kept tossing on the bed, because when she woke up, her whole body was trembling with cold, and the blanket lay on the floor. She picked it up, looked at the clock. It was ten minutes to twelve — Mother would be back soon. She lay listening and waiting for the door to open, for Mother to come in. But not a sound disturbed the silence around. Then — how funny that even now she could remember still — she closed her eyes and began to count — to six hundred, for then the ten minutes would be over, and Mother would come in. She counted slowly, finished at last, and when still she could hear nothing, she started all over again. Until suddenly she stopped. Everything seemed so quiet around, and the clock yes, the clock was silent too. She opened her eyes looked. It still read ten to twelve; the clock had stopped. What time could it be? — twelve, or one, or much later perhaps. She jumped out of bed and rushed to the window. The bus was not running any more, the street was empty. It must be terribly late. . . . Perhaps,

[ 249 ]

she thought, Mother had come and she did not hear her, perhaps she was back in her room. . . . She rushed out of the room, crying "Mother, Mother!" but no one answered. . . . And Mother's room was empty, just as she had left it, the robe still on the bed, the slippers lying in the middle of the floor. She could just see herself, as she sat there on Mother's bed, stroking the robe, again and again, and listening. . . . Still, no sound came, not even from the kitchen, where Fru Andersson usually sat.

It was then that she suddenly felt she was alone in that soundless house. She got up and ran downstairs, to the kitchen. It was dark. "Fru Andersson!" she cried, running into the pantry, into the bathroom, and then from room to room turning the lights on, calling Mother, calling Fru Andersson, looking into every corner. But no voice answered, only the boards of the floor cracked and the doors banged loudly in the silence. She was not thinking of Mother any longer, she just wanted Fru Andersson to be there, she or anyone so Thura would not be alone in that house, which suddenly seemed so huge and unfamiliar, as if she had never seen it before.

Then, back she rushed upstairs, turned the lights on there, came back down tiptoeing so that the floor would not crack and sat down at the table. A cup with a few drops of coffee in it was standing there; it seemed to be warm still from the hands which had held it. She stared at it, feeling quieter, but only for a short while. Soon she got up, and went to the window. It was snowing again; the air was filled with dense falling flakes; she could not see the street any longer, nothing but snow whirling before her eyes. Then at last she started crying. But the sound of her own voice terrified her; she tried to stop crying and could not.

Soon she was sobbing, again, first softly and then louder, stopping from time to time, listening to her own voice.

Then . . . Yes, what had happened then . . . ? Thura hesitated for a moment; the pictures crowding before her eyes grew vague, as if someone had been showing them to her, and now suddenly had hidden the rest away from her. Later . . . she repeated to herself . . . And now she knew: she had run back to Mother's room and lain there, hidden under the blanket, her head buried in the pillow. And all those thoughts that had come to her then. . . . Something must have happened to Mother, that she was sure of — but what? Perhaps Mother had fallen down, hurt herself, and then they had taken her back to the hospital. Or, and this was even more terrible, she had fallen with no one around, and she lay there alone in the cold, crying. Or if it had happened in the middle of the street, and a bus came suddenly, before she could get . . . They had taken her to the hospital and had called Fru Andersson to her, but about Thura they had forgotten. . . .

It was when that thought about the bus and Fru Andersson going to hospital had come to her that she ran downstairs straight to the door and tried to open it. It was locked; Mother must have taken the key. But there was still the back door. She rushed there — it was locked too. Still the key had to be somewhere in the house. One after another, she opened all the drawers, and threw everything out of them upon the floor. The key was not there. But at last she remembered — in the kitchen on the top of the closet, that was where Mother always used to put it. She took a chair, climbed on it and looked. Yes, right in the middle, there it was, a big old-fashioned iron key. But she could not reach it.

Again she climbed down; pulled the chair closer, tried once more. The chair shook; the closet seemed about to tumble down on her any moment. But she stood there on her toes, stretching the arm farther and farther, until it hurt. Now, thinking of it, she could again feel the tension, in her armpits, in her fingers. . . . And she reached it at last; oh, what a relief it was to hold it in her hands, the iron so cold in her fingers, the sharp edges cutting into her palm. It was hard to open the door, but she did it at last, and in slippers with only the shirt under her coat, she rushed out into the street, right to the corner behind which Mother had vanished before. There she had to stop; where should she go now? And just as she stood there thinking, someone appeared on the other side of the street, someone tall . . . in a black coat. "Mother!" she cried, "Mother!" Yes, it was Mother. Thura smiled now, thinking how angry Mother had been finding her alone on the street, without stockings and shivering with cold. But when she told her Fru Andersson had left, Mother was not angry any longer. She took her home and put her to bed, with plenty of blankets wrapped around her so that she would not catch a cold. And after that night Fru Andersson never came again. For she had left for no reason at all, just because it was late and she felt tired.

Wasn't that funny? Thura wondered, that she could remember all that, even the way in which she had crawled under the bed looking for her slippers, and the switches clicking angrily when she had turned them on, and the key, above all the key, cold, weighing heavily in her hands. Perhaps that too was what Doctor Ström meant by remembering — no, that could not be it. Thura sighed.

She felt cold, like on that night, she thought. For now too the blanket had slipped down; only a little, but still it left her arms and chest bare. If she rang and Sister Ingeborg came in, Stephania might wake up and see she was not asleep. Perhaps . . . perhaps she could try to pull the blanket herself; it couldn't be too heavy. If she only could grasp it with her fingers. Slowly she lifted her arm, stretched it out. Now . . . the thumb first, then the big finger, first the thumb . . . one . . . two! No, it didn't work. Once more. She closed her eyes; not to look, she thought, not to look. And now she forgot which finger it should be, and how the joints should move; that night from years ago came back before her eyes, the shaky chair, the closet; stretch, she thought, more, more still, like then, like with the key . . . now, farther, farther still. Something touched her fingers, or — had her fingers touched something? something warm, fleecy. . . . She opened her eyes, yes, she could see it, she was sure, the thumb had moved, and the big finger too; only a little, still . . . "Stephania!" she cried. "Stephania!"

But now her arm, as if she had lost all her strength, fell back upon the blanket; the fingers were again limp only they quivered slightly.

She lay panting, her eyes wide open, unable to think, only afraid, terribly afraid of something.

And here was Stephania standing next to her. "What happened, Thura?"

What happened — she thought vaguely — "I'm sorry, Fröken Stephania, I woke you up, I didn't mean to."

"But what happened? Tell me."

"I don't know any more. It just seemed to me that . . ."

"That what?"

"That I moved my fingers . . . a little, but it couldn't be."

"Were you asleep? Did you dream it, you mean?"

"No, I wasn't asleep. I was thinking."

"So . . . you did it, Thura," Stephania cried. "You did it!"

"No, I don't think so, it was just for a moment, that I thought . . ."

[ 252 ]

"I'm sure you did it. You must try again. Right now."

"No," she whispered. "I can't." She glanced at her hand. "I know I can't."

Stephania moved closer to her. "You must try. You did it before, and now you are afraid again. But now you know you can, you know." She was whispering, but the sound was loud and piercing, as if she were trying to shout and could not.

"I can't," Thura whispered. "Please leave me."

"You must. Do you hear me, you must."

Thura only shook her head. She was not looking at Stephania, but at the wall where Stephania's shadow spread itself, huge, formless, swallowing the wall, the bed. She feared that shadow, feared Stephania's toneless cry, and her face — pale in the greenish light, menacing.

"Go back to bed," she whispered, "you'll wake Fröken Nilsson."

"Don't worry about Fröken Nilsson. Try!" On the wall a finger, thick like the pendulum of a giant clock, began to move to and fro, and then the whole hand was there, balling into an enormous fist as if preparing for a blow.

"What are you waiting for? Try!"

"I'll try," she murmured. Yes; she would, just to force Stephania to leave, just to get rid of that whisper, of that shadow threatening her.

"Now!" Stephania hissed.

She raised her arm. And again as before there was nothing in her, not a thought, only dense mist around her, and that whisper, "Do it the way you did before, like before . . ." Then someone, yes, Stephania of course, crying: "Thura, you did it!"

She opened her eyes. The thumb and the big finger stood close to each other, trembling, but they moved, yes, they did move. . . .

"I did it, really?"

"Yes, you did it!"

From her bed Fröken Nilsson murmured sleepily, "What's going on here?"

"She did it, Fröken Nilsson." Stephania exclaimed sitting down on Thura's bed. She too was gasping heavily.

"Oh, Fröken Stephania, I still can't understand . . ." Thura murmured.

Fröken Nilsson grabbed her crutches, limped toward them.

"Could someone please tell me what happened? Two o'clock at night, and here they sit chatting as if . . ."

"I'm sorry, Fröken Nilsson."

"Stop being sorry! She moved her fingers, she really moved them."

"What?" Fröken Nilsson stepped forward, the crutches slipped from under her arms and fell on the floor with a loud bang. At the last moment Fröken Nilsson grasped the railing and sat down on the bed. "Oh," she said. "Isn't that something — just look!"

And now they both sat silent, looking at Thura. Until at last Thura said: "Th . . . thank you, Fröken Stephania."

Fru Gustavsson was the first one to hear the news. Stephania had told it to her before Fru Gustavsson even had time to report that the day was cold but lovely, or to ask them how they had slept. "My, my, that certainly is a surprise!" she gasped, and as soon as she had finished making the beds she ran out to bring the news to her patients in other rooms. Right after that Sister Gudrun came in, followed closely by Doctor Ström and Fru Jungdahl. "So, we have done it at last, Thura," Doctor Ström said, looking around. "Now everything will be easy, you'll see."

Doctor Ström was right this time. Everything had become easy suddenly. In the beginning Thura's fingers moved slowly and uncertainly, then with greater and greater ease. After two weeks she could turn the pages of her book and even sometimes tried to eat by herself.

But it was not those few things which she could do now that were important; somehow those fingers still quivering and groping had changed everything around her. The world seemed larger, richer now. Things that she was only able to see before acquired new dimensions. They could be felt, touched, each of them in a different, peculiar way. There were friendly things that wanted to help her, and went willingly easily to her hand; others tried her strength, offered resistance; she had to find all kinds of ingenious tricks to master them. There were the rough and resistant covers of books; and apples smooth and deceitful and slippery; pages that rustled gently, ingratiatingly when she turned them and the washing sponge, soft and inviting. Every moment Thura discovered something new and when she would manage to pick up a book or open a stubborn drawer, she would lie smiling, for a long while, still startled by all the variety and richness that suddenly had entered her life.

And to Stephania, Thura was reminiscent of Barbara when she was pregnant; for she had the same smile, secret and vague, as if with great wonder she was listening to something within herself.

CHAPTER 20

IT HAD BEEN a bad afternoon — dull, moving sluggishly in the heavy, unfriendly silence. Outside it was raining again, just drizzling; the melting snow looked soiled and withered and even the sky seemed drab and untidy like a street long unswept — the gray clouds, low-hanging and tattered, chased to and fro by the wind. The rain was bad for Fröken Nilsson, her stump began to hurt again; she lay groaning and repeated again and again: "If I've rung once I've rung a hundred times. And nobody will come, of course. They're all fine if you don't need them, but the minute you want something . . ."

Stephania did not answer. Thura only murmured something about Fru Gustavsson being busy with the new patient in Four; she too felt tired and disappointed. There would be no reading this afternoon — she thought. Almost five and Stephania had said nothing about it. She had been acting strangely, Stephania, all day long, so silent — almost as if she were angry, and doing nothing: just standing at the window and staring.

Suddenly Stephania turned to her. "What's the time, Thura?" she asked.

"Ten to five," Thura said, looking at her hopefully. But Stephania went back silently to the window. So it was almost five already, she thought. Soon it would be dark and then it would be time, when the first star came. That was what Father always used to say . . . funny, he had never trusted the clocks when it came to that; it was the star that had to be the sign. But how can one see stars in weather like this? Well, around five-thirty should be right. And now she might as well get everything ready.

[ 255 ]

She opened the drawer of her bedside table, took out a small package, and slowly began to unwrap it. Fröken Nilsson and Thura watched her curiously. First came a carton, and out of it a glass, just a glass, filled with something grayish-white — like wax. Yes, it must be wax, and on top there was a wick, very thick and long. Stephania put the glass on the table.

"What is it, Fröken Stephania?" Fröken Nilsson asked.

"That," Stephania said, bending to pick up a paper from the floor, "that's a light . . . the light for the dead."

"For . . . what?"

"For the dead," Stephania repeated, and tossed the paper into the wastebasket. It sounded strange the way she had said it, so slowly, as if it was difficult for her to pronounce it.

Fröken Nilsson glanced at her uneasily. "I see," she said, "I see. Are you going to light it?"

"Yes."

"Well" — Fröken Nilsson felt nervous suddenly — "Just be careful, dear. I read in the paper once a whole house had burnt down from a candle. It was in Malmö, or someplace in Skåne, I guess. Anyhow candles are dangerous."

"Not this candle." Stephania took the glass and began to turn it in her hand.

Fröken Nilsson could not stand it. "You're going to break it," she murmured. "How long is it going to burn?"

"Twenty-four hours, until tomorrow evening."

"Well, as long as you're not going to burn all of us alive."

"Fröken Stephania will be careful," Thura said. She too was looking at the glass, at the yellow label on it covered with unfamiliar, pot-bellied letters. "What's written on it, Fröken Stephania?" she asked. "It looks kind of strange."

"That's Yiddish, and it says . . . let me see . . . It says, 'Anniversary Light for the Dead'!"

"Anniversary," Thura repeated. That was even stranger. Anniversary made you think of a wedding anniversary or something like that, and here it was of . . . "I've never seen a candle like that before," she said at last.

Stephania smiled. The way they looked at it . . . and it was nothing but a glass, an ordinary glass. . . But it was not that that had startled them, it was what she had said; as if they had not heard the word before, as if they had forgotten that there was anything like . . . like death. And perhaps that was it, the main difference between them and her. They could forget — she never. Part of my national heritage, she thought, and smiled again.

"Fröken Stephania," Thura asked, "is the light for all the dead or just for one person?"

"Just for one."

"I see, so you would remember, is that it?"

"Remember?" Stephania repeated. "I wonder . . ." Yes, that was what Father always had said. But that was not it really. "Well," she said at last, "I don't quite think so. It's rather because . . . because we are afraid of death. We — the Jews I mean." Why on earth did she start talking about that? Perhaps because she had been thinking of it so much lately.

"Everybody is afraid," Thura began.

"Yes, but we have more fear than you Gentiles. We . . . yes, we know it better than anyone else, I guess that's why."

Fröken Nilsson shook her head indignantly. "You know it better? Well, that's really something, Fröken Stephania. As if anyone could know it better than anyone else. Everybody knows it, Jews, Gentiles, all the same. I know it, don't worry about that. I was with my mother when it took her a whole week to die, so I could really see it. And then my father before . . ."

"Yes, I know. But that isn't what I meant. We know it differently. And when we are afraid it's in a different way too."

"I can't understand what you mean, Fröken Stephania," Thura said. "After all, everybody is afraid, I told you that. And it must be pretty much the same for everybody. Like Fru Hernruth when she was so very sick — after her operation she got an infection, you know. She started crying and she said, 'Sister' — Sister Gudrun was with her all the time then — 'Sister, d'you think I'll die? I'm so afraid!' So you see. Do you remember, Fröken Nilsson?"

"Sure I remember. She kept moaning like that all the day long. And there was nothing very wrong with her, just a little fever. I had to get out of the room, she made me so nervous."

"You see, and even I sometimes, when I start thinking about it, I get scared too."

"Sometimes, but for us it's all the time, you see. Once in a while I guess you may start thinking about it, but otherwise . . . otherwise you really don't believe in it. Even if you talk about it, you say, 'When I die,' or 'After my death,' or something like

[ 257 ]

that, you don't quite feel it really may happen. It's like in Poland before the war. Everybody talked about its coming, that it must come, and still no one believed it."

"Come on, Fröken Stephania, that's real nonsense, if you'll excuse me. Have you ever met anyone who didn't think he would die sooner or later?" Fröken Nilsson protested.

"Think . . . That's something else, but deep inside you, you don't feel it, you don't believe. Otherwise you never could talk about it so easily. Do you remember Fru Gustavsson the other day talking about her husband? She said, 'He lost so much weight I thought he would die'! Just like that — as if she were saying: I thought he would go to the movies. And it isn't that she doesn't care for him. She does. But she just couldn't imagine it might happen. And you too, Fröken Nilsson; you too, Thura, all of you; perhaps when you get very old you'll start believing it. But we believe it all the time and that's why we are scared even to talk about it."

Fröken Nilsson shook her head indignantly. "Now look here, it's you who started all this, after all. I certainly don't care for that kind of talk."

"Yes," Stephania said slowly, "there you're right. But it's the first time that I've talked like that. I don't know why. Something must have come over me. Usually we never talk of it. You see we know so much about it that it just gets too hard. . . . So we pretend not to know. We remember not to remember death, if you see what I mean. We don't want to talk about it, or mention the word even. Like when I was little, back at home in Poland, my aunt died and Mother, whenever she referred to it, always said: 'We had a disaster in the family' — a disaster, not death. Or when Father took out the insurance policy he said, 'In case something should happen to me.' Even the very word scares us. We think if we don't mention it, then perhaps it won't happen, or at least it will be easier to forget." She hesitated as if trying to remember something. "Yes," she said at last. "One has to forget. Unless . . . But that again is a different story."

"And the light?" Thura asked. "Don't you burn it because you believe that there is something . . . that they . . . the one for whom you light it, might somehow, know about it . . . ?"

"No, not at all. Even if we pretend that that's the reason, it's only because we are so scared. When Father lit it he always said:

[ 258 ]

'This is for Grandmother,' 'That is for Aunt Helen,' quite as if he were saying, That cup of coffee, that seat is for her. So in a way, he — all of us — can think one never really dies, that something is left, something that cares about having the lamp burning for exactly twenty-four hours, from evening to evening. And then we start thinking we too will never die completely, we too will care about it. So you see, it's not for them, the light; not for the dead . . . It's for us."

For a long while no one answered. At last Fröken Nilsson raised herself noisily in her bed, and said: "I think we have so much trouble in life that there's no use worrying about something that we can't ever change anyhow. That's just making more and more trouble." Fröken Nilsson glanced at the clock. She wished dinner would come. She felt hungry and besides, it would be good to end this silly talk. "Would you believe it, it's almost six and I still haven't had my pill? And it hurts and hurts as if someone was sticking needles into me."

"Let me try to get it for you." Stephania got up from her bed.

When she left, Thura said, "She's been terribly upset all day long. Do you think it's because of that?" She pointed to the light.

"How should I know? She never tells us anything — just a word here and a word there so you can make no sense out of it." Fröken Nilsson wanted to add something but at that point Stephania came back.

"I hope it will help," she said, handing Fröken Nilsson the pill. "And do you want anything else before I lie down?"

"No, thanks."

"And you, Thura?"

"No, thanks just the same!" But when Stephania was passing her bed Thura stopped her suddenly. "Fröken Stephania?"

"Yes?"

"Do you — do you believe that there is something after that?"

"After what?"

"After death."

Stephania looked at her silently. She shrugged; the shoulder hunched; it almost hid her face. When it emerged it was changed — the lips narrow, everything sharper, severe. It was, Thura thought, a strange face; terribly quiet, frozen and old. "After that — of course there is nothing after that," Stephania said and walked back to her bed.

"Some people believe there is," Thura said.

"I can't understand it. Perhaps they only think they do. I couldn't ever."

"But why?"

"Why?" Stephania repeated. "It just seems impossible. To believe in something like that you have first to believe that you are important — everything about you, life and death, yes, death too. It's hard to explain it. I don't mean that it's easy to die — without any pain; or that one should not be afraid. But it must be . . . it must be . . . dignified, I guess that's it. Sometimes it does happen that way . . . with a doctor trying to make one life last longer, a week, even a day; with the whole family around crying and hoping that perhaps it still won't happen: and then when it does happen, mourning a long time after and remembering. That way, with so much about it — then perhaps you may think it is impossible that something so important should end completely; that there simply *must* be something after that. But if you had seen it happening the way I saw it . . ."

"How?" Both Thura and Fröken Nilsson asked.

"Differently."

"What do you mean?"

"Just different," Stephania said and that was all.

— Like that time, Stephania thought — like the time when Mother lay in that dirty cold barracks — the typhoid hospital, on the bare bunk right under the roof that leaked. Soup was brought in, and she had to leave Mother and climbed down from the bunk to get some, and argue because they did not want to give her soup for both of them. But Mother did not need the soup. It was all over when Stephania came back, and it happened so quietly, so suddenly, that the other people in the bunk did not even notice it. And later the same man who had brought the soup came in and took the body out, just like that, dragging it by the legs on the floor, because he was not strong enough to carry it.

Then there was the huge crate next to the latrine smelling of Lysol and filled up to the top. They emptied it only once a week. It wasn't worth it to do it more often. And she did not even cry; she was much too sick and too hungry to understand anything. Yes, when you saw it happening that way, then you could not talk yourself into the idea that you were going to live forever; then you knew it did not matter at all whether you lived or not

— it all happened by chance — without any reason — no, none at all.

The door opened. "Good evening, everybody. We have liver, carrots and potatoes for dinner," Sister Gudrun announced.

Fröken Nilsson sat up. "Liver for me, and carrots, but no potatoes," she said, and her voice was loud, filled with relief.

After dinner Stephania lit the candle. The flame was small — you could hardly notice it in the brightly lit room — so that both Thura and Fröken Nilsson almost forgot about it. But when night came, when the lights were turned off, it seemed that the flame had grown suddenly, and you couldn't help seeing it — tall, sharp and quivering, as if it were choking in the glass too small for it and were trying to jump out. Yellow, trembling shadows spread all over the ceiling, the floor, the beds, and made the room look different; the night seemed different too, restless — somehow waiting for something. But all of them stayed silent, and lay watchful and tense staring at the light.

Stephania knew the others were not asleep. It was probably because of the candle, she thought. She should never have lit it; it was just a ridiculous habit with her, nothing else. Still she did it, year after year — as if she needed it, as if she had to look at it in order to remember. . . . She did remember — not once a year but always, all the time, until she was no longer aware of it. It was like a pain you have so constantly that you don't think about it any more. But still it is there, worse even, because you can have no relief.

Again and again she would see him. Sometimes a voice sounding like his would bring him back, or a figure passing her by on the street, stooped, the head bent, or a smell that was like the smell of the tobacco he had used. Yes, even that was enough, a word, a single gesture, as if he were lurking everywhere, always waiting to come back to her, bitter, accusing in his downtrodden silence.

But she could never visualise his face: his face had vanished somewhere and that made everything harder still. She felt he would have blamed her for that, too, for remembering so many other faces, strange and indifferent, and never his — perhaps only the smile sometimes, somehow vague and awkward. But everything else she could remember, she could still see it exactly; the way he had sat on the last evening, bent, his head in his hands;

and how he brought water from the well and always spilled a little on the floor and looked at her as if he were afraid: then the tone of his voice when he said, "This can't last much longer. Remember the whole civilized world is fighting for us." She would remember him not because she wanted to: it just happened all of a sudden. She would read something, or talk to someone, or wake up in the middle of the night and suddenly a word or a gesture would bring him back — force him out of somewhere within her.

In the beginning, when the war was still going on, she didn't think about him at all. Then, it seemed to make no difference whether you were still alive or not; everyone thought it was a matter of weeks, of days only. And everyone said then, "Those who have already gone"—gone, they said, not died, as if they had only left for another place—"they had better luck than we. They had not been through half as much as we, and anyhow we will go after them—the sooner the better." She too thought so then, and often it seemed to her that for once he had been wiser than she, that he had known the right thing to do and had only hidden it from her out of malice. And she would imagine him standing there at the door and looking at her for the last time, looking not reproachfully, not with envy, but with a scornful, almost triumphant smile.

But when in that small German town she had heard the cry "The war is over!" when she knew she would live, then the remembering started.

First she tried to tell herself it was better that he was dead, better than to be left with no one but her, crippled — with a hunchback. But later Barbara returned and then she began to feel him all the time — or rather not him, but the void — the void in the place where he should have been and was not, because . . . because of her. No, no — she shook her head as if trying to chase something away — no it was not *because* of her. And yet . . .

Sometimes she would think she had done the right thing, the only thing she could do — in a way that was wrong, perhaps — but even that could be understood, even that could be forgiven. Then again it would strike her with a sudden and terrible clarity that she was guilty, guilty of everything. Again and again she had to return to it, live over everything that had happened between him and her. Until at last — it was when she was in Poland

— she decided to ask others; she wanted them to judge. They all said it was her duty to save herself — that she had only performed her duty, and she was right. But she knew all that meant nothing; they were talking of themselves, not of her. For they, all of them who survived, had done what she did, in a less terrible way perhaps, but still . . . And by forgiving her they forgave themselves, too. So there was no use asking. . . . But still she wanted to ask someone. Why? she wondered, closing her eyes and covering them with her hand as if hoping, in that total darkness, and more completely alone, to be able at last to find out, to understand. . . . Now she knew that there was no excuse, no justification. But still, if she could only tell everything to someone who had never been there, who did not even know what had happened, someone who would not try to excuse himself or her either, someone who would just know that certain things were right and others wrong. Because there must be a right and wrong — a wrong, always the same, no matter if it was wartime, no matter if one was afraid.

That was what she wanted to know — the answer, once and for all, no matter how terrible the answer was. Just to know, and not to have to go back again and again and ask as she had asked a moment ago: "Was it because of me or not, or . . ." But there was no one she could ask.

Stephania sat up. The pillow had become hot and soggy; she shook it, drank some water and then turned her head. On the opposite bed Fröken Nilsson too was sitting up.

"We shouldn't sleep during the day." That was Thura. So she too was awake. "I did and now I can't sleep, either."

"Why aren't you asleep, Fröken Nilsson? Is it the light that disturbs you?" Stephania asked. "I could take it out into the living room."

"No, not at all. Please, don't bother."

And again they lay silent. Stephania knew that they were looking at her now. She heard Fröken Nilsson clearing her throat. And at last the question came: "For whom is that light, Fröken Stephania?"

"For my father. Today is the anniversary of his death." She hesitated. "Today . . . or at least I think so; I can't know for sure."

"I see," Fröken Nilsson said, "I see," but her voice showed she could see nothing.

[ 263 ]

And Stephania knew that now they were waiting, they wanted her to tell them. Of course they thought it would be something interesting that they would talk of later and wonder about — something like Fröken Nilsson's confession — No, they would have no confessions from her, not about that. . . . But — and the thought came as suddenly as if it was not hers — as if someone else had whispered it to her. Perhaps it was their right, perhaps they *should* know. Know, why? It was her business, only hers. Yes, but they liked her, they trusted her so much; came to her with everything, asked, "Should I do this, Fröken Stephania?" "Do you think that's right?" and if they knew . . . maybe they wouldn't even talk to her. Maybe . . . She could just hear Fröken Nilsson saying to Sister Gudrun: Either you take Stephania out of the room, or me. I've heard something about her . . . And then Thura — How could she have done it? And I always thought she was so wonderful. . . . But how could she tell them? How? They had not been there. They would not understand.

And then, with equal suddenness, it occurred to her that she must tell them just because of that; for perhaps it was they who could tell her, who could judge.

Stephania sat up. "I . . ." she began, and stopped feeling suddenly very weak as if she had been walking for hours so that there was no breath left in her. She moistened her lips, swallowed. "I left him," she said. "That's why I don't know."

"Left? When?"

"Then."

"You mean then, when he was dying?"

"In . . . in a way. It was before they took him . . . the Germans."

"Took him where?" Fröken Nilsson asked.

"I don't know. Somewhere . . . to kill him."

"To . . . but why, why, Fröken Stephania?" Thura whispered, and Stephania knew her face was now startled with fear as it was when she had told her about the cyanide. Perhaps she should not have started. Still they had to know, someone had to know.

"Because he was Jewish," she said.

"You don't mean it!" Fröken Nilsson exclaimed. "Just because of that?"

How little they knew, as if they had lived in a different world. But that was right; that was what she wanted . . . "Of course, Fröken Nilsson, they took all the Jews, almost all."

[ 264 ]

"But . . . it's impossible, after all, look, you . . ."

"I," Stephania said slowly, "I ran away."

"And he?" Thura asked. "He couldn't?"

"He looked very Jewish. And they always recognized a Jew, so . . . I was afraid they would take him and then us, me and Mother with him . . ."

"Just think, just think that they didn't get you," Fröken Nilsson said. "You really cannot thank God enough for your luck, Fröken Stephania."

"Luck? It wasn't luck. It was that I cared about nothing but running away, don't you see? I left him . . . all alone . . . and just ran away." And she lifted her head trying to see their faces.

"Well, what else could you have done?" Fröken Nilsson said at last. "You were young, so you did not want to get killed, so . . ."

"No," Stephania interrupted her, "no!" So here was the judgment, and again it was wrong, all wrong. She still had not told them anything. They had to know everything, from the very beginning.

"I could have done something," she said. "I could have tried, per — ," she checked herself in the middle of the word; there was no "perhaps"! She could always have tried. "I could have saved him," she said loud, very loud, "if I had only wanted to."

"Fröken Stephania!" Thura cried.

"She just figures things out so she can worry about them, don't you see, Thura?" Fröken Nilsson said. "Before, she said herself they took all the Jews, and that he looked Jewish."

"It isn't true," Stephania cried. "I know it is not," and she went on faster and faster as if afraid they would stop her. "I didn't want to, that's all. Because — I guess, I felt he was in my way, and I . . . Yes, now when I think of it, I must have hated him."

Why did they say nothing? First they wanted to know, and now they were too frightened to answer. "Why don't you say anything?" Her voice sounded as if she were smiling.

"I . . . I just can't believe it," Thura said, at last. "Unless he did something dreadful to you . . . or . . ."

"No, nothing. It was just that I felt it would be easier without him."

"No, Fröken Stephania, no!"

"You always try to make everyone into a saint, Thura. I know.

[ 265 ]

When I remember things that had happened between us, between me and him. Like . . ." She hesitated. What should she tell them? There was so much, so much . . . "Like then, the last night, before they took him . . . in the mill."

— Yes, she thought that would show them what it was like, in the mill. And now she saw — the big dark room; the people so crowded that they seemed like one huge rugged body; the hollow sound of wooden shoes stamping on the floor. It was cold in there and they all were freezing.

"You said something about a mill," Fröken Nilsson reminded her.

"The mill . . . yes. It was in a small village. We lived there then, working on an estate, German of course. And then we had to get flour, we never got money, you see; only food . . . terribly little, too."

She stopped: she was again leaving herself a little door to escape, putting in something that would excuse her. "Only food, and very little," so that they would say: Poor Stephania, so starved, no wonder that she was nervous. She said quickly: "The point is, we were to get flour, a bag for each family. So we went to the mill, Father and I. We came first, before anyone else was there, so we would be sure to get it. They never had enough and if you came later you just got nothing. So we waited, and then the others came, a hundred people or more. We were supposed to stand in line, but nobody would. They all pushed forward terribly, everybody trying to be first. But he, Father, he just would not. He had always been so terribly polite and shy too. So he only stood there, and when the rest were knocking each other down he just kept saying 'Pardon me, madam, it seems to me I came before you. Excuse me.' They wouldn't even listen, and we were pushed farther and farther down to the end. I tried to push, myself, but I couldn't do much, I was already sick then, you see. So I only kept saying to him, 'Why don't you push yourself? Why don't you do something?' But he only smiled. . . ." Stephania paused. "He had shaved his mustache to look younger," she said after a while, "and his face looked so strange — as if it were naked, and the smile too, kind of pleading. 'I can't push, I don't know how,' he said to me, and again: 'Pardon me . . .' And then we were the very last and the bag we got was smaller than the others, and the flour darker and damp too."

"But," Thura said, "you couldn't have helped getting angry, even if . . ."

"Wait, that's not the end. Then we started walking home. It was already dark. And we had to go through some woods — small woods, but still — the ground was all covered with snow, and he kept slipping and stumbling on the roots. And I just kept rushing him. 'Hurry up,' I told him, 'you don't want us to get shot, do you?'"

"Shot?"

"Yes, they often shot people walking in the darkness, even before the curfew."

"Well," Fröken Nilsson said, "no wonder you were scared."

"I was. But that wasn't why I kept nagging him, a few minutes more or less couldn't have made so much difference. It was only that I could not stand seeing him like that . . . bent, almost crawling, and the bag dangling and hitting his legs. That was why . . ."

"Oh, how can you remember how you felt, what you thought? It was years ago, after all."

"That is the kind of thing you remember, Fröken Nilsson. Just let me finish. He kept shifting the bag from one shoulder to another; he was not very strong then, you see. And when he stopped again I snatched the bag from him, simply tore it out of his hands, and started almost running with it. And he ran after me, whining, really whining, 'Give it back, Stephania, give it back, you know you should not carry things.' I told you I was already sick."

"Did you give it back?"

"No . . . and when he wanted to help me, to put his hand under the bag at least, I told him to go away. 'You only make it heavier,' I said. And that wasn't true at all. Then we came home — we lived in a peasant hut then — and Mother stood in the door. She was worried about us. And then when she saw me with the bag, she cried: 'How could you let her carry it?' And he only murmured something, but she didn't even listen."

"And you, you didn't tell her!"

"I . . . I said nothing."

"Nothing?"

"I told you, nothing at all."

"Oh . . ." Thura whispered.

"Now you see!" Stephania exclaimed. There was something like triumph in her voice. After a while she said. "Then he sat all evening alone, his head in his hands. And Mother did not talk to him, and I didn't either. And that was the evening before they took him."

"You didn't know they were going to?"

"Of course not. It came all of a sudden in the morning, when it was still dark." All of a sudden — she thought; they were still asleep. And then someone began to shriek in the hut nearby, loudly — terribly loud. And then footsteps, first only a few, then more and more, coming from everywhere. She tried to look through the window but it was too dark to see anything, and so she only stood listening to the voices that grew louder and louder. Others must have heard them too; narrow streaks of light shone through the crack, in the blackout shades. Then they woke up, Mother first and Father after her — ran to the window, started dressing, though they did not know what it all meant. Then, yes, then someone knocked on the door, so hard that it seemed it would burst open any moment — that was the butcher's wife who lived nearby. "We all have to go, the mayor said we all have to go," she cried. But Father did not believe it of course. He said she must be mistaken. "We got our flour for the whole winter and they wouldn't have given it to us, if they wanted . . ." Stephania remembered how he stood there, suddenly silenced by his own words, and then shook his head and said once more it was a mistake, it had to be. But she only kept repeating, "The mayor said it, the mayor!" and then others came in and said the same thing, so they knew it could not be a mistake.

The room was full of people then, all shouting, all asking, "What are you going to do?" "Do you know what we'll do?" But Mother only cried, "No, no, how should I know, get out of here!" She was rouging her cheeks. She always did it when they were coming, so she would look younger. But now her hand trembled, and there were just red streaks all over her face. And he stood next to her, passing his hand above his lips, as if he had forgotten the mustache was gone and kept looking for it. And again and again he said: "Don't you think it must be a mistake?" Then the mayor came. . . . Yes, that was how it began — suddenly, terribly suddenly: she thought and perhaps if it had not come so suddenly, if she had had more time to think . . . just an hour, just a few minutes, even, all that would never have happened. After all, before, in the ghetto, when the Germans came to take the men, it was she who had hidden him in the basement, it was she who had said, "There are no men in the house." But she had no right to tell those people that; suddenly or not, that was the way it had happened, and the rest did not count, could not count at all.

She said: "It was early in the morning. The mayor of the village came and said in German — he was Polish but he always tried to talk German — then, he said: *"Alle Juden 'raus!"*

"What does that mean?"

"All Jews must leave, and he also said we were allowed to take twenty-five pounds of luggage."

"Where did he want you to go?"

"Oh, you still don't understand. To the tracks, and then to the trains . . . and then . . ."

"Then where?" Fröken Nilsson insisted.

Thura said, "Don't you see? To be . . . to be . . ."

"Oh I see," Fröken Nilsson whispered. "Oh good God! Just to think about that is too much."

Stephania was not listening. "I just stood there," she said. "I couldn't understand what was going on. Only when I saw Mother packing, throwing anything she saw into the bag, then I asked, 'What are you doing?'"

"And she said: 'I'm packing.'

"And then . . . then . . . I don't know how to tell you about it. It was as if I were choked, the way I felt. Everything just rose up within me and stuck right in my throat. I couldn't breathe, nor speak."

"What happened to you?" Fröken Nilsson asked.

"Fear. I guess that was it. And suddenly it was over, only I felt cold as if I were freezing. I tore the bag out of her hands and said "We must run away. . . . We must." She stopped.

They looked at her, and she sat on her bed without moving as if she suddenly had fallen asleep.

"Fröken Stephania," Thura said.

"Yes . . . yes. I'm almost through. I put on my coat, brought Mother's coat, and said, 'Wash your face, you can't go like that!' But she still didn't understand, so I pushed her to the door, terribly hard. She almost fell down then. 'Come on!' I said, 'or it will be too late.' I felt again as though I were choking, because I thought I had heard the trucks coming. But I was wrong — they

[ 269 ]

came later, we saw them on the road. Then she understood at last what I meant. 'Run away, but what about Father?' she cried. And I . . . I had completely forgotten about him as if he hadn't been there at all. I looked at him. He was packing, folding everything very carefully, as though afraid his things would wrinkle. And then when he saw us staring at him he asked very quietly, as if he were only a little surprised, perhaps: 'Are you going to leave me here alone?' I did not answer, I pretended not to have heard."

"You really couldn't take him with you?"

"Oh I don't know, I don't know any longer. He looked so very Jewish: dark hair, and his nose, and then I was so scared. I was only sixteen then, and he should have . . . No!" she cried. "Don't listen to me! That's not true at all! I could have tried, people younger than me did it. I just didn't want to, I know it now. That's why I said nothing to him, just told Mother to put her coat on. But she didn't want to go. She said she wouldn't leave him. But I forced her, I said: 'I'm not going without you, and do you want me to get killed?'"

"You see," Thura said, "you did everything to save her."

"To save . . . Once I thought so too. But now I think it was just because I was afraid to go alone. I needed her."

"You always have to twist everything around," Fröken Nilsson said.

"Perhaps I wanted to save her; it's not important now. It's only . . . he . . . He stood at the clothes chest, things lying scattered around him. And then he said, 'Myrele' — my mother's name was Myra, you see, and that was a nickname, like for children. He hadn't called her that in years. But now he said, 'Myrele, what should I put on?'"

"Why? . . ."

"Don't, Thura. Let me finish now, let me finish. I said then, I said . . ."

"What?"

"I said . . . 'You . . . idiot, what difference does it make?'"

"You . . . what?"

"'You idiot,'" she repeated loud and clear, and then imploringly almost, "Now you've heard it, haven't you?" After a while she said, "Then I took Mother and rushed out."

"And he . . ."

"He must have gone after us, just to the door, because on the street I heard him crying: 'Stephania, aren't you going to say good-bye to me?'

"Mother wanted to go back but I wouldn't let her. 'We have no time' — I said. So I just waved my hand, but I didn't look back . . . not even that.

"And later when we turned around the corner, I saw him; he was standing in the doorway, and in his hand he still had the shirt. First it looked as if he were waving with it. But it was only the wind. He did not move. Just looked."

She fell silent. And they were silent too. A sound of steps and voices came from the hall. It was Sister Ingeborg and the night orderly. They listened, greedily almost, to those quiet voices, to the familiar footsteps.

They're going to have coffee — Fröken Nilsson thought. She wished she could get up and leave and sit in the warm well-lit room sipping hot coffee listening to Sister Ingeborg.

But there was Stephania's voice again. "So that was how it happened — Now you can see, can't you?"

"I see nothing," Fröken Nilsson cried. "Anyone would have done the same thing in your place. You were only sixteen, almost a child, like Thura. He should have taken care of you, not you of him. Perhaps you shouldn't have said — what you did at the end. That was wrong. Still you were so scared, so nervous. And besides what else could you have done? Taken him with you? No. Stayed?"

"Yes," Stephania said, "stayed. Others did. They didn't care what happened to them. They knew they had to stay."

"What good would that have done?"

"He wouldn't have been alone. No one should die alone, no one."

"Alone or not alone, what difference does it make? Like my mother . . . I was with her to the last moment, all the time, and she held my hand. But then she died anyway, didn't even know I was with her. So . . . you see, if one has to die one just dies."

"But don't you see? You were with her, you held her hand And he . . . "

"You couldn't help him. So just stop thinking of it. Listen to me, Fröken Stephania. People have done much worse things in life, and not given a damn about them, if you will pardon the expression."

"I don't know, Fröken Nilsson. It can't all be so simple." So now she too, Fröken Nilsson, thought she couldn't have helped it, she was not guilty. Still . . . perhaps, like those others in Poland, she too was trying to excuse herself; perhaps she too had done something like that or was afraid she would. . . . And also it might be the way in which she herself had told them everything. It was the truth, but still not quite. Like that, "I was only sixteen," or, "He looked so Jewish" — always saying something that would excuse her, always making them see that whatever she had done, it was not really her fault but the fault of everything around her. That was all wrong. It was only she herself who had done it. Perhaps it was easier to do it because things had become so terrible. Still, she did not have to do it. Perhaps Thura understood.

"Thura," she said, "it's not as simple as Fröken Nilsson makes it out. Don't you see that?"

"I don't know, Fröken Stephania," Thura said slowly. "How can I tell? I wasn't there, I can't judge. I . . ." No, she thought there was nothing she could say. It had happened, and no one could do anything about it. She just wanted Stephania to know that between them nothing had changed, nothing would. But how should she say it. "Fröken Stephania," she said at last, "it all happened long ago; you've changed, you wouldn't do it now, not in that way."

"Perhaps . . ." Stephania said. "Perhaps I would, perhaps I wouldn't, who can tell?"

Thura did not answer. They lay silent, looking at the light. The wax had melted, the flame had sunk deep inside the glass and filled it with a yellow glow.


CHAPTER 21


"IT SEEMS THAT we are going to lose some of our patients soon," Doctor Ström remarked during one of his visits in Room Five. Because things were really looking fine there. Thura's hand was moving better and better, and Fröken Nilsson was getting her artificial limb at last. She lived now in a constant rush and excitement, preparing shoes and stockings for the day when she got up, and going down to the workshop to try on her prosthesis, as she referred to it learnedly.

"It fits marvelously," she would say coming back from the fitting, "not an inch too wide, just perfect," and it sounded as if she had been trying on a new dress or a hat. The preparations that preceded Fröken Nilsson's visits to the workshop would make anyone think she was setting out to an elegant fashion-place: not only would she put lipstick on and clasp her hair with a shiny metal clip, but also — and this was an extravagance unheard of in the whole ward — she would adorn her hospital dress with a white piqué collar, pinned with a brooch Fru Gustavsson had bought for her.

"Just look at her, she certainly has fixed herself up." Fru Gustavsson shook her head whenever she took Fröken Nilsson down to the workshop. "Well, one has to look decent when one's going out among people," Fröken Nilsson answered. People — she said modestly and casually, but Thura and Stephania knew she was referring to all her new friends whom she had met in the workshop. First there was Herr Johansohn, the fitter, who as Fröken Nilsson had pointed out was more than interested in her, called her "dumpling" and from the way he behaved one easily could see . . . what it was that one could see so easily Fröken Nilsson had never explained, but the implications were obvious. "Of course, I don't pay much attention to him. I have my mind somewhere else now," she would say looking at the picture postcard occupying the place of honor on her bedside table. The card was from Doctor Liliencrona who was on vacation now, skiing in Norway.

Then, her thoughts wandering back to Herr Johansohn, Fröken Nilsson would add that he certainly was nice and handsome, and that after all she could not refuse to talk to him.

Herr Johansohn, however, was only one of Fröken Nilsson's new friends. There were many others, most of them living in the city and coming to the workshop for fittings of new artificial limbs. Fröken Nilsson had long and interesting chats with them and a few times she was even taken out for a ride in a car. She came back from those escapades flushed and excited, bringing into the quiet room the smell of fresh air, and echoes of the faraway fascinating life of the city. "It's so nice out there," she would say;

[ 273 ]

not on Kungsgatan or Vasa Vagen, not in the city even, but just "out there," dreamily and secretly, as if those spaces outside of the hospital were so vast, so wonderful that only those vague, distant words could describe them. And she would tell them about it — about the streets, so unlike the drive here which was still filled with ice and snow, but clean and dry, as if spring were already there; about the store windows and the lovely things she had seen in them, spring suits and coats, dark green most of them — for that, Fröken Nilsson explained, would be the color of the season; and also about a new movie — one with Gregory Peck whom she simply adored.

Thura and Stephania listened, eager but somehow bewildered also. For suddenly Fröken Nilsson seemed a little strange to them, no longer living completely with them, but also "out there," in that unknown world to which spring came so much earlier, where it mattered what the color of the season was or who was playing in the latest movie.

"Do you think you'll go out for a ride?" Thura asked reverently each time Fröken Nilsson went down to the workshop. "Maybe," the answer came with a smile secret and hopeful.

"Maybe, one can never tell what's going to happen," she said one day. But hardly an hour had passed and here Fröken Nilsson was back, not in her wheel chair, but walking, really walking, leaning on two elegant black canes. She stopped in the doorway, looking at them silently.

"Fröken Nilsson!" Thura cried. "Look at her, Fröken Stephania, she — she's walking!"

"Certainly I am," Fröken Nilsson said nonchalantly as if there were nothing unusual about it. She stepped forward and put the canes away. For a moment she swayed precariously and had to grab the arm of a chair; but no, she would not give in, and soon she stood leaning on nothing, turning around like a model displaying a new dress. "So, how do you like it?" she asked. "Can you tell which leg it is?"

They knew of course which leg it was; how could they ever forget it was the left one which they had seen first in the cast and which then had vanished with a terrifying suddenness. Still Thura said hesitatingly: "The right perhaps . . . or the left? It's impossible to tell."

"Absolutely impossible," Stephania agreed.

"The left, of course," Fröken Nilsson exclaimed. She took her canes and started walking through the room, uncertainly, as though she was not quite sure where she was going and casting her leg out stiffly, a little like a soldier marching on parade. "No more laying in bed for me," she said energetically, and after covering the bed with the polka-dot spread, she went out for a walk in the hall.

After a few minutes she was back, her face red and covered with sweat.

"Something must be wrong with that leg. It's so heavy, I can't take a step on it," she said, pulled the cover off, and without looking at Thura and Stephania, lay down. "Well, it may look exactly like a real leg, but believe me, you're better off when you have one of your own flesh and blood, and not made of wood." She sighed bitterly, and angrily pushed the prosthesis under the bed.

The next morning the same thing happened. Fröken Nilsson got up and walked around for a while, but soon she was back in bed, saying furiously that no one could be expected to walk with a monstrosity that weighs God only knows how many pounds. She had a grudge against Herr Johansohn, her new friend, against Doctor Liliencrona even. All those wonders they had been promising her — that she would walk, dance, and what not — and now look. Doctor Ström came in, and then Sister Gudrun, who told her to get up; but Fröken Nilsson shook her head, and said she had had enough for today. And were it not for Willy she might have completely given up all attempts at walking.

No one, not even Professor, knew how it ever happened that Willy became the trainer of all amputees. He himself took it as a matter of course, and whenever a patient started walking Willy would be there, marching him to and fro, drilling him mercilessly like a sergeant his recruits. Not that Willy himself walked so well; he had two artificial limbs to cope with, and most of his pupils surpassed him after a lesson or two. But no one in the whole hospital was Willy's equal at understanding the difficult art of walking on wooden legs; no one could explain as clearly as he all those ingenious and sly tricks of holding the body erect, of making the steps small and even.

The day after Fröken Nilsson's ambitious and unsuccessful attempt at getting up, Willy came in and walked straight to her bed. "So," he said, "Johansohn told me you got your leg. Where is it?"

With a dejected gesture Fröken Nilsson pointed to the corner. "There, and tell your Johansohn he can have it back."

Willy paid no attention to her. He lifted the prosthesis and looked at it with the eyes of a connoisseur. "A real beauty, I must say. So, what are you doing still in bed, Fröken Nilsson?"

"I'm tired."

"Tired? Come on, don't tell me that. Let's go for a walk."

Fröken Nilsson shook her head doggedly. But no one could get rid of Willy as easily as that. He talked and talked, until Fröken Nilsson, although groaning and complaining, had to give in. She got up and made a few steps, exaggerating her limping so that Willy would at last see how tired she was, and would let her go back to bed.

Willy watched her, his face covered with so many folds of disapproval that the eyes and the lips disappeared completely and only his clumsy nose stuck out.

"No," he exclaimed at last, "stop! Just sit down and watch me." He got up and took a few steps. "You see, that's the way one walks. And I'm doing it with two of them," and he slapped his wooden legs which answered with a dumb hollow sound. "If I had only one, like you . . . oh then . . . " He stopped shaking his head as if overwhelmed by all the wonderful vistas which that very thought opened before him. "Well, we must take the good with the bad as it comes. Isn't that so, Fröken Stephania? Here we go, Fröken Nilsson."

Fröken Nilsson murmured she felt more dead than alive, that the prosthesis was no good; Johansohn had been too busy with all his fancy patients from the private ward to pay any attention to her.

"Does it hurt?" Willy asked, and without any ceremony lifted Fröken Nilsson's skirts.

"Now, that *is* the limit!" Fröken Nilsson gasped indignantly.

"Come on, I'm just like a doctor," Willy said, adjusting the leather straps. "Now, is it better?"

"A little better," Fröken Nilsson admitted reluctantly. And although she promptly added she wished Willy would mind his own business and not plague her for no earthly reason, she agreed to walk across the room a few times, and then even walked out with him into the hall.

Willy came each afternoon from that day on and Fröken Nilsson did not mind it any longer. She was getting used to the artificial limb, and besides Doctor Liliencrona was coming back soon and Fröken Nilsson wanted to surprise him by her accomplished walking. "I just can't think what he will say seeing me walking toward him, and with only one cane," she repeated, looking longingly at the snow-covered hills on the postcard, on which she could picture to herself Doctor Liliencrona sliding down gracefully, in an elegant skiing suit; more handsome, more stunning than ever.

And also, strange as it was, Fröken Nilsson began to like Willy's visits. "Not that he's anything special," she said to her roommates, "but he's nice to talk to, so I don't mind him."

It was quite different talking to Willy than to Doctor Liliencrona or Stephania even — Fröken Nilsson thought. With them you had to watch each word, so they would not think you had no polish, no education whatever. But with Willy you could say anything that came into your mind, simply because he did not matter too much — like Thura in a way.

If only Willy would open his mouth from time to time, Fröken Nilsson thought wistfully. That certainly was a funny thing with him; as long as he was showing her how to walk, he talked and shouted, and acted as big as if he were God knows who . . . Professor himself, one would think. But as soon as they sat down for a moment he would grow mute like a fish, just sit there and stare at her as if he had never seen her before, and just twist his tie in his hands.

Only once while they were drinking coffee in his room it happened that Willy, stammering and stumbling, told her this and that about himself. A day before, Willy had not come. Fröken Nilsson sat waiting for him; the afternoon without the usual walk seemed long and dull. And when next afternoon Willy came in, she said reproachfully: "So, where were you hiding yourself yesterday? I waited for you."

"You . . . waited for me?"

"For who else then?" Fröken Nilsson snapped back angrily.

"I had some business to settle in the town," Willy murmured. He hardly paid any attention to Fröken Nilsson's walking that

[ 277 ]

afternoon, and on their way back to the room he asked halt-ingly: "I wonder, I was thinking . . ." He stopped and looked at Fröken Nilsson, and after a long while he added: "As I said, I was wondering if you would have time to come for a cup of coffee to my room. I live down on the first floor, right where the order-lies live."

"Sure, I have time," Fröken Nilsson answered.

And next afternoon after the usual walk, they both went down to Willy's room. It was so small that the few pieces of furniture left hardly any space free, but also so clean that Fröken Nilsson exclaimed with admiration. "One would never know that a man was living here all by himself. You certainly are tidy, Willy."

"Well, a fellow learns everything when he has to. Cleaning, cooking, everything. If you haven't got a woman, you got to do it by yourself." He poured the coffee and put out the cookies on the plate.

"I guess so," Fröken Nilsson murmured, still looking around. Something about that room made her feel queer. It was clean all right, and quite comfortable too, but . . . as if no one were really living in it. Not a picture on the wall, not a serviette on the table; the furniture just the same as in the hospital waiting room; even the cups were the same as those in the ward — thick and plain with the big letters saying Royal Institute for the Handicapped. As if he had nothing of his own, Fröken Nilsson thought, and munch-ing on the cookies asked: "Wouldn't it be easier for you to live with the family, and not all alone? Or haven't you got any?"

"I have brothers, two of them. Each six feet tall, and healthy . . . never in their life been to a doctor. And they're all right, too. But to live with them . . ." Willy shrugged.

"Why not?" The way that Willy talked, you had to drag each word out of him.

"Oh . . . I went home, after I got my legs. And they were nice to me, but . . . They're married, both of them. And you know how it is with married folks. . . . They sit in the evening, talk about all kinds of things you've nothing to do with, and so you just sit there and feel as necessary as the fifth wheel on a cart. And then the job . . . I used to work in the grocery store, you see. But then when I came back they wouldn't take me. 'Too hard for you, Willy,' the man said. So I packed my things and came back here."

"Here, to the hospital?"

[ 278 ]

"Where else? I didn't know a soul in Stockholm then. And just then old Magnusson, who had the stand before me, retired. So I took it over and stayed."

"But you like it here?" Fröken Nilsson asked.

Willy did not answer at once. "Like?" he said at last. "It isn't bad. When a fellow is alone, he has to like everything. One place is as good as another; makes no difference."

Fröken Nilsson nodded silently. It was strange the way Willy talked today.

"You should find yourself a woman," she said at last.

"A woman? Me? More wood in me than flesh and bones." He laughed, but somehow Fröken Nilsson did not feel like joining him. Willy stopped abruptly. "Want some more coffee?"

"Yes."

While he poured the coffee, Willy asked, "And you'll be going home soon, I guess?"

"I? Oh, it depends . . . on many things," Fröken Nilsson answered dreamily. When he comes back many things may happen — she thought, smiling through the dense coffee-steam.

Willy seemed not to have heard her. "Yes, everybody leaves," he said. "Sure, why should anyone stay here?"

And again they sipped their coffee silently. It was good coffee, hot and strong, and the cookies were good too; but still Fröken Nilsson felt secretly worried about something. No matter how hard she tried to think about Doctor Liliencrona and all that might happen after his return, her mind kept wandering back to Eskilstuna, back to the room where she used to live — dark and shabby, the narrow sofa covered with greasy spots, the rug threadbare, back to those meals that she ate there, always alone, at the table that wobbled at the slightest move.

"I better go now," she said at last.

"Thanks for coming." Willy got up. He cleared his throat as if about to add something. Still he remained silent, and without a word brought her back to the room.

Soon after that, the talks with Willy came to an end. The day of Doctor Liliencrona's arrival drew near, and Fröken Nilsson spent all her time practising her walking. Hour after hour she paraded in front of the mirror, asking anxiously if she kept herself straight enough, if the steps were not too big. And in the evening, when tired, every muscle in her body aching, she lay in bed, she would count — only four days left, only three. . . . Again and again she pictured to herself the moment of her meeting with him. It would be in the hall — she decided first. She would walk toward him, and he, plunged in thought (somehow Fröken Nilsson was convinced that Doctor Liliencrona was always plunged in thought), would notice her all of a sudden. And then . . . yes, then he would rush to her and take her hand, her both hands into his, exclaiming, Oh, Fröken Nilsson, how wonderful! I'm *so* happy for you. . . . And then . . .

Each evening Fröken Nilsson changed that picture; considered new, more alluring possibilities. Perhaps she should stay in the room instead, pretend she was in bed still, and then just when he would be about to leave she would get up and say quietly, Let me walk with you, Doctor. Or (and this sounded even better) she could wait for him at the window and rush down as soon as she saw him coming, so that she would be the first to welcome him back. We missed you, Doctor, she would say, and then he . . . Fröken Nilsson could never quite imagine what Doctor Liliencrona would say but she felt convinced it would be something important and very wonderful, something she had been waiting for a long time without daring to name it even.

At last the day of Doctor Liliencrona's arrival was here. To her own surprise Fröken Nilsson slept soundly that night in spite of all the excitement. She got up early in the morning, put on the hospital dress with the white piqué collar, decided it did not look right, and at last asked Fru Gustavsson to bring her her dress from the storeroom. But Fru Gustavsson was in a bad mood that morning. Fröken Nilsson had been here for three years almost — she murmured wistfully — so she should know patients were not allowed to parade in private dresses for no good reason. For no good reason . . . Fröken Nilsson had it on the tip of her tongue, the explanation of how perfectly good her reason was, but at the last moment she checked herself. Things like that should not be made public, not too soon at least — she decided. After long consideration she borrowed a brooch from Stephania, and cleaned the spots that yesterday's dinner left on her dress; it still did not look quite right, but after all, he wasn't the type who paid too much attention to appearances.

The final choice for the place of meeting with Doctor Liliencrona fell upon the living room, with its comfortable armchairs, so inviting to intimate conversations; Fröken Nilsson went there right after breakfast and took a seat next to the door. Her eyes upon the door, she answered absently to greetings and questions. Yes thanks, she was fine; yes, Thura and Fröken Ackermann were fine too — she muttered angrily. Why wouldn't they leave her in peace? She had more important things on her mind today. After a while she decided the living room was not the right place at all. The hall would be better. Looking around, listening, she walked to and fro, raising her head at each sound, each voice. Doctor Ström came in, and Sister Gudrun, but Doctor Liliencrona did not appear. Fröken Nilsson felt exhausted. I should not look tired when he comes, she decided, and went back to the room.

She did not want to lie down for fear her dress would get wrinkled. Instead she pulled the chair to the window and sat down waiting. Hours passed. Doctor Liliencrona was not there.

"Do you know whether Doctor Liliencrona has come back?" Fröken Nilsson asked the student nurse.

"Which one is Liliencrona?"

Not to know *him!* Fröken Nilsson thought angrily. And the way she had said it — "Liliencrona" — as if they had grazed pigs together. "The very handsome one with the black mustache, that's Doctor Liliencrona," Fröken Nilsson explained indignantly.

"Oh, I don't think he's so handsome; anyhow, I guess I saw him passing through the hall."

"When?"

"Something like an hour ago."

So he *was* back; he even passed by their room. But why didn't he come in? He must have had his reasons for it; perhaps Sister Gudrun had been with him and he did not want to have any witnesses when meeting her. Yes, it actually was a good thing that he had not come in, Fröken Nilsson decided, and again she sat waiting.

Lunch was served, then coffee, then Willy came to take her out for a walk. Fröken Nilsson sent him away angrily; she felt more and more nervous. And just when she was about to go back to the living room, the door opened and there was Doctor Liliencrona, looking just as she had pictured him to herself — sun-tanned and smiling and more dashing than ever. "Hello, everybody," he exclaimed. "Good afternoon, Fröken Nilsson, good afternoon, Thura."

Fröken Nilsson got up. Small steps — keep yourself straight —

[ 281 ]

she thought, but soon she could remember nothing, see nothing, only the face of Doctor Liliencrona was before her eyes, closer and closer. . . . Fröken Nilsson took a deep breath, stopped. "What a surprise, just look how she walks! Bravo, Fröken Nilsson, my congratulations," Doctor Liliencrona exclaimed, and just as she had hoped he took both her hands in his, and held them (a little longer than necessary, Fröken Nilsson thought.)

"You see," he said, "I told you you would walk fine, and you certainly do. As well as that friend of mine I mentioned to you, better even."

A friend, she thought. Yes, of course that was the one who got married. Of course he *had* to bring it out now. Fröken Nilsson preferred to say nothing. She only smiled and listened to Doctor Liliencrona congratulating Thura on moving her hand.

A moment of silence followed. Fröken Nilsson, her eyes beaming, looked at Doctor Liliencrona. She felt he was preparing himself to say something, something important and unusual. And now he stepped to the middle of the room and smiling more broadly than ever said, "I too deserve congratulations."

"What has happened, Doctor?" Fröken Nilsson asked breathlessly.

"Guess."

"Doctor has been nominated a docent," she ventured.

"Heavens, no. I'm glad they keep me here just as a plain doctor. Another guess?" This time no one answered. Doctor Liliencrona stepped closer to Fröken Nilsson and leaning upon the chair on which she was sitting, said, "Well, I got married." And he lifted his hand on which something glittered brightly . . . a wedding ring.

Fröken Nilsson looked at him . . . at his hand . . . at the ring. No, he was only joking, it was impossible, it could not be possible. She opened her mouth trying to say something but no sound came, only her lips remained parted as if she forgot to close them. She stared at him imploringly, but Doctor Liliencrona was silent. Fröken Nilsson could not stand it, that look on his face, that smile. . . . She let her head down. Something pricked her chin; it was the brooch she had borrowed from Stephania — it had opened. She tried to close it, but her hand trembled so hard that the pin rolled on the floor.

Doctor Liliencrona picked it up and handed it back to her. "So, why are all of you so silent? Did you think I would never marry?" he asked.

"Congratulations, Doctor," Stephania said very loudly, her eyes fixed upon Fröken Nilsson.

"It happened so suddenly . . . but of course my best congratulations," Thura said.

And at last Fröken Nilsson, without raising her head, thinking still that it could not be true, that it all was a terrible mistake, said: "Congratulations."

"Thanks," Doctor Liliencrona answered, and went on telling them that his marriage was not sudden at all, he had been engaged for two years, and that he had found the nicest little house in Sodra.

"You certainly were lucky about the house," Stephania said, again looking at Fröken Nilsson.

Fröken Nilsson felt she too should say something. But no, she could not.

Doctor Liliencrona glanced at his watch. "I had no idea; it's almost four," he exclaimed, adding that his wife was coming to pick him up in two hours, and left saying once more as he stood on the threshold, "I'm so glad that you walk so fine, Fröken Nilsson." The door closed.

Fröken Nilsson got up, walked over to her bed, and threw herself upon it. Now he's gone, she thought, now I can cry. But only a piercing emptiness was within her, as if she had not eaten for a long time; her eyes remained dry. Somehow that emptiness bothered her, she felt bewildered, deceived almost by it. I'm too crushed to cry even, she thought.

"Fröken Nilsson, I know it's terrible," she heard Thura saying, "but try not to think about it. It can't be changed, so . . ."

It was only after Thura had said it that the emptiness disappeared and Fröken Nilsson felt herself swept by sorrow, bitterness, and above all anger; anger against Doctor Liliencrona who had deserted her so shamelessly after all that had happened between them, at that silly Thura, chatting about things she could never understand. Try not to think, as if it were possible not to think about such a blow! Fröken Nilsson turned furiously to the wall, silence returned, and suddenly that silence made Fröken Nilsson realize Stephania had said nothing to her. Had she left the room?

Carefully Fröken Nilsson raised her head and glanced to the other side of the room. What she saw was so startling, so shocking, that Fröken Nilsson had to sit up. Stephania sat at the table, reading, quietly turning page after page as if nothing, nothing at all had happened. How can she? Fröken Nilsson thought. The anger in her grew stronger, anger aimed at Stephania now, at that heartless creature, reading now at a moment like this. Not a single word of sympathy did she have for her, not as much as I'm sorry, Fröken Nilsson — not a glance even. But of course, why should Stephania say anything when she was not even thinking about anyone but herself, selfish and false as she was?

False — yes, that was the only word one could find for her. Not only that she did not care, Stephania; she seemed glad, even rejoicing; even the way she had said "Congratulations, Doctor," loud, shouting almost, as if her heart was melting from joy. And it was . . . it was . . . because Stephania had been jealous of her all the time, jealous because the doctors never so much as looked at her; that was more than clear. Only she herself, of course, was too trustful, too goodhearted to pay much attention to it. Never had Stephania said a word about Doctor Liliencrona, even when she had told her how he came to her, to the operating room. "It was nice of him," she had said, as if "nice" was the word for it. And now when that woman, one of *those* (yes, Fröken Nilsson was convinced that Doctor Liliencrona's wife was one of *those*), had taken him away from her, now of course Stephania was triumphant about it. But I'm not going to worry about it, Fröken Nilsson thought; from now on Stephania is as good as dead for me. And casting a prolonged and challenging glance at Stephania, Fröken Nilsson turned back to the wall.

Dinner was served. Oddly enough Fröken Nilsson felt hungry, but she knew it was only her shattered nerves that gave her that painful feeling in her stomach. "No, nothing for me," she said when Sister Gudrun put the plate on her table; "no, not dessert either," and she glanced at Stephania who was eating quietly, practically stuffing herself. She wouldn't notice even if I starved myself to death, Fröken Nilsson thought bitterly. She had a heart of stone — Stephania.

The sharp appetizing fragrance of beef stew spread all over the room; Fröken Nilsson felt the hunger in her growing stronger and stronger. Well, even if it was only nerves she still had to eat;

now more than ever she needed strength. When Fru Gustavsson comes in to ask who wants more food, I'll ask her to bring me something, Fröken Nilsson decided. But just this evening Fru Gustavsson did not come in. Fröken Nilsson took a few stale crackers out of her drawer, slipped them stealthily into her pocket and walked out into the living room. She had just finished eating when the clock struck six. "At six my wife is coming to pick me up," he had said. Fröken Nilsson swallowed the last cracker hastily, and rushed back to the room. She had to see that woman.

She opened the window without asking as usual if anyone minded it, and stood leaning upon the sill, waiting. Stephania got up. "So we shall see Fru Liliencrona now," she said, taking a place next to Fröken Nilsson. That insolence of hers; just shameless! Fröken Nilsson thought, moving far to the corner.

She was so indignant that she almost missed the blue car, which with an elegant swing parked in front of the entrance. A woman came out of it, tall, very slender, the light hair — dyed of course — loosely falling on the brown shiny fur coat. When she turned to the door Fröken Nilsson caught a glimpse of her face — young, softly rounded, the red full lips flaming in the golden sun-tanned skin.

"Extremely pretty," Stephania's voice said quietly.

No, that was too much. . . . "Pretty?" Fröken Nilsson cried scornfully. "With pounds of make-up on the face everybody can look pretty. You've got wonderful taste."

Stephania did not answer. Fröken Nilsson felt now was the proper moment to leave the window. Still something forced her to stay there, to watch how fast and easily that woman tripped on her high heels to the door, how Doctor Liliencrona came out, and she took his arm. . . . No, she could not stand it any more. Fröken Nilsson slammed the window. "I don't feel like freezing to death," she said.

Fru Liliencrona — she thought — so that was the way she looked. Pretty — no, she was not pretty, it was just an easy life and lots of money that made people look like that. A painted doll she was, with nothing inside probably. Still Fröken Nilsson could not forget that woman — so slender, moving so lightly, the fur coat, a real beaver — shimmering so softly as she walked, walked arm in arm with him back to the car, back to their home. Some people have everything in life, she thought, and others . . .

[ 285 ]

And perhaps all of them were thinking the same thing, because suddenly Thura said softly, "I wonder what it is like to be like her . . . pretty and rich and married."

"I guess it can't be too bad, Thura dear," Stephania laughed. She was standing next to the window, black now, impenetrable; the evening darkness clinging heavily to the panes.

Everybody was talking about Doctor Liliencrona's wife. Sister Gudrun brought the news that she was from a very good family — daughter of a *Landrod* in Skåne. Fru Gustavsson said she was the most charming creature one could imagine, with a voice so sweet it was a true pleasure to listen to it. Fröken Nilsson listened, feeling how, slowly, something heavy and choking crept up her throat, higher and higher. . . . Now I can cry, she thought, and when Fru Gustavsson left she burst into sobs.

"Don't, Fröken Nilsson, please, it is so sad, but still, you mustn't cry," Thura said.

She was a good child after all, Thura; not too clever, but she at least had a heart, not like Stephania. . . . And her face buried in the pillow, her whole body shaking, Fröken Nilsson cried louder and louder.

"Fröken Nilsson!" That was Stephania. So at last she did notice her. . . . Fröken Nilsson stopped crying; still she did not answer.

'There is really no reason to cry, Fröken Nilsson."

No reason — She tore her face from the pillow. "What?"

"All right, all right. I know you kept talking about him all the time, you even might have thought of him a lot — everybody needs something to think about. But to make yourself miserable about it . . . that certainly is a nuisance."

"A nuisance you said? A nuisance to cry when I've lost *him?*"

"Oh, lost him, what do you mean by that?" Stephania's voice grew loud with impatience. "You're not a child, you must understand that there was actually nothing in that whole story, that you simply had a crush on him . . . like a teen-ager on a handsome teacher. It was all your own imagination, Fröken Nilsson; after all you hardly know him."

"How can you, how can you say anything like that, after . . . after you saw all that has happened between us, between me and him?"

Stephania stepped closer, passed her hand through her hair, and at last said very calmly, "I see . . . and could you please tell me, what actually *has* happened between you and him?"

"You have to ask that?" Fröken Nilsson snapped back. As if she had not seen anything, as if she and everybody did not know. "What has happened?" she repeated. "Well, everything . . . everything. . ." She groped for words but somehow she could not find them; the emptiness was back in her, and she felt as if she were sliding, down and down, with nothing to hold on to around her.

"Well, why don't you tell me?"

No, Stephania was not going to catch her like that. All kinds of things happened between them, so many that it was impossible to put them into words. Yes, they were much too deep for words.

"You know what has happened, you don't have to ask," she cried.

"For instance, what?"

"You've seen it yourself. He kept coming here, to me, only to me, he sent me the card. . . ."

"The card was addressed to all three of us."

"But it was to me, he mentioned you . . . yes, just through politeness, that was all. And then the talks he had with me, and then the operation, he came as soon as I called him, you can ask anyone if he didn't come. Now, you see!" she exclaimed triumphantly. All her anger against Doctor Liliencrona was gone. He was back with her now, they both stood united against the enemy defending their common past from Stephania who so slyly was trying to rob them of it. "So, now you know," Fröken Nilsson repeated.

"I'm sorry, but I still know nothing. He kept coming here, but so does Doctor Ström and others. . . ."

"Doctor Ström?" Fröken Nilsson mimicked her scornfully. "Sure he does, he's *our* doctor, he *has* to come. But Doctor Liliencrona is in the children's ward. He had no business coming here, and still . . ."

"That's the greatest nonsense I've ever heard, Fröken Nilsson. He came here because he's a bone-fracture specialist, because you were an interesting case."

"Interesting case! That's what you think. He could have just looked at the X-rays if that was all he wanted to know. But his coming to the operation and his telling me about that friend of his who got married. . . . Don't tell me there was no special meaning in that."

[ 287 ]

"None whatsoever. He told you about the friend in order to encourage you. And sure he came to the operation. Don't think it was so pleasant for him, for all of them to keep you here for two years and then . . . Fröken Nilsson," Stephania spoke now softly, persuasively, as if to a child, "I don't have to tell you all that, you know it better than I. You just refuse to see it. Why should you make a tragedy out of nothing? You spoke to him a few times and that was all that ever happened between you, so . . ."

Fröken Nilsson shrugged. "Don't think you know everything." She paused. Oh, certainly there were many things she never had revealed to anyone; all his smiles, and the tone of his voice, and the way he took her hands in his. . . .

"Yes," she said solemnly, "you don't know even the half of what has happened, not, not a quarter. I didn't tell you, why should I have . . . ?"

Stephania tried to say something but Fröken Nilsson went on breathlessly. "Let me tell you, had he never gone on vacation, had he never met that woman — and believe me, she must be quite something, I can smell that — had she not grabbed him . . ."

"He didn't meet her on vacation. They had been engaged for two years."

"No, that's not true. He just had to say that because . . . because he was ashamed. And soon he will regret it, marrying her I mean. He regrets it now, believe me."

"How did you figure that out?"

"I . . . I feel it."

"Intuition, what?"

Fröken Nilsson hesitated . . . "Yes, in . . . intu-i-tion," she said bravely.

"Look here, Fröken Nilsson, what's the use of all that, of this make-believe game? It was good once, but now . . ."

Fröken Nilsson lifted her head, looked straight at Stephania's face. And Stephania did not avert her eyes, but stared back at her steadily, coldly. Suddenly, as if in a desperate effort to escape, Fröken Nilsson turned her head away. She knew what Stephania was talking about, knew it with a clearness that was startling and terrible. Stephania remembered all she had told them, that night after the operation. She herself had hardly ever thought of that night after the "great day"; it was like those faces bending over her bed then, featureless and dimmed by the haze of morphine, of

[ 288 ]

pain; until she no longer believed that it really had happened, until she never came back to it. And now . . . no, it is not the same, she thought. Perhaps talking about Eskilstuna — then she made up a thing or two, but not too much either. After all the boss *had* sent her flowers, after all Hasse, Anna's husband, wrote to her and said he was so worried about her. Still, what she had said about Doctor Liliencrona was different, she hadn't made up anything, it all *did* happen.

"You can call it make-believe or whatever you want. Still I know what I know about him and me. Of course, I can't tell all that to you. Certain things cannot be made public, Fröken Stephania." The lucky aptness of that phrase restored Fröken Nilsson's self-confidence. She even managed to raise her eyes and look at Stephania.

"So, you," Stephania lifted her hand and pointed at Fröken Nilsson, "you really imagined that anything, anything serious might have come of it?"

She was beginning to understand, at last, Fröken Nilsson thought. "Of course, why not?"

"Why not? Don't you see it could never be possible?"

"Because of my leg, you mean? Let me tell you, there're men who don't pay any attention to things like that. Fortunately not for all men is a woman only a body, Fröken Stephania." The last words Fröken Nilsson exclaimed joyfully; and even smiled.

Stephania said: "I've heard that before, not long ago either. It's only the soul that matters; did he tell you that too?"

Fröken Nilsson hesitated. "In a way he did. Besides, he didn't have to. I know how he feels about those things."

"Perhaps he's one of those unique exceptions, one who doesn't care. But it's not the leg only; the leg is least important in a way. It is everything . . . your age, you're eight years older, and . . ."

"Seven, not eight; but so what?" Age did not matter much either, she thought. There were plenty of men who preferred more mature women to all those giggling teen-agers. There was even a king, was it in Denmark, or in England perhaps? who married a woman older than himself. Fröken Nilsson wished she remembered that incident more exactly so she could quote it to Stephania. But the details had escaped her memory, and so she said only, "Age is not everything."

"Age is not everything, nothing is. But if two people have absolutely nothing in common . . . I hate to talk like that to you, Fröken Nilsson, but I just want you to be sensible. His background is different, his education, his interests, so how could you have ever hoped that anything would happen between you two? Your thinking you could marry him is like my believing I could marry a . . ." and Stephania looked around as though searching for a suitable example.

Fröken Nilsson's eyes followed hers, stopped on the window, on the mirror which was reflecting Stephania, her dress bulging over the cast. At last they stopped upon Stephania's bedside table, upon the picture of the tall handsome man — about whom Stephania had never told them, never mentioned his name even.

"As if I believed I could marry . . ." Stephania repeated.

Fröken Nilsson hesitated. No, I should not, she thought, but already she was saying it, shouting it sharply and distinctly, "As if you believed you could marry him," and the outstretched finger, accusing, pointed straight at the picture.

"Fröken Nilsson, don't, no!" Thura cried.

Stephania said nothing. She looked at Fröken Nilsson very slowly, walked to the table, took the picture off. For a moment she looked at it, carefully as though she had never seen it before. Then hastily, almost fearfully, she tore the drawer out and threw the picture in it. The harsh, clear ringing sound of breaking glass cut the silence. The door banged, slammed furiously.

"Fröken Nilsson," Thura muttered, "how could, how could you ever do it to her?"

The living room was empty and dark. But in the fireplace embers were still glowing with soft reddish light, casting slender shadows upon the walls. Stephania sat staring at them, at the sharp tongues mounting in a last desperate effort out of the embers, glittering for a while and then collapsing with angry hisses. Around her everything was quiet, and she listened to the stillness thinking how good it was to be alone at last without the high indignant voice piercing your ears, without those eyes staring at you maliciously.

But now something interrupted the silence: the sound of breaking glass; she could hear it again, jarring, sharp, and then dying in a thin plaintive echo. For a moment she felt like rushing back to the room, like putting the picture back upon the table, so empty and deserted without it. Nonsense — she thought angrily — what did it matter whether it was there or not? And that did not matter either, those words Fröken Nilsson had tossed into her face.

Still she could not forget it, that rough spiteful voice, the finger rigid, accusing, pointing at his picture and then at her, uniting them for a moment only in order to separate them, to show the ridiculousness of her square deformed body next to his, healthy, slender, beautiful. That fool, that insufferable fool, she repeated angrily. And still, foolish as she was, she always knew how to choose the most sore spot, how to strike so that it would hurt, hurt — no, someone like that could never hurt her, she should not think about it at all, not even for a moment.

The door opened and someone whom she could not see in the darkness came into the room. "Fröken Ackermann." It was Sister Gudrun; what did she want from her?

"Yes?" she said dryly.

"You know patients should be in their rooms after eight."

"I'm sorry. I'll go back soon."

"Very soon. It's half past eight already." Sister Gudrun looked at her warningly as she walked out. That stupid old martinet, she thought, pacing to and fro angrily. "Patients should be in their rooms after eight." Important, wasn't it? That and all the insane rigamarole of rules here, all that absurd discipline. Fools, that was what all of them were.

But actually she herself was the greatest fool among the whole lot of them, getting mixed up in that ridiculous Liliencrona affair, trying to save Fröken Nilsson from that great passion. . . . And the way she had worried about it, spent hours at a stretch thinking that something should be done, that poor Fröken Nilsson should not again get involved in those imaginary affairs now that at last she was about to start a normal life, when some man could get really interested in her.

It certainly was a mystery, she thought shaking her head, how anybody as sensible as Willy could ever care for that woman. But he obviously did, talking about her, asking whether she had a friend in Eskilstuna, whether she planned to go back. . . . And the explanation he had given, when she once asked him what he saw in Fröken Nilsson . . . "She's brave," he had said then, "not like most women moaning and groaning when anything happens to them. But she knows how to take things easy." Well, perhaps she knew how to take real troubles easily, simply because she was

[ 291 ]

too stupid to understand what they meant; but this, of course, was a great tragedy — losing Doctor Liliencrona after what had happened between them. That fool.

"Fröken Ackermann, I was sure you would be in your room by now."

"Don't worry, I'm not going to stay here for the night," she murmured furiously, and got up.

Slowly, trying to postpone the moment of return to the room, she walked through the hall. It actually serves me right, she thought; one should know when to keep quiet and mind one's own business. But no, she of course had to convert Fröken Nilsson to the right path. All that strategy she had planned for that noble purpose — how she should talk to her quietly, but without any sentimentality so that Fröken Nilsson would at last see how unreasonable, how childish that infatuation for Liliencrona was; how she should make Fröken Nilsson understand that nothing ever had happened, that it all took place in her imagination only. Well, she certainly was successful. But at least she'd had a good lesson for the future. From now on she would know better than to stick her nose into other people's business.

The door from the room was open. For a moment she hesitated, and was just about to walk in when suddenly she heard her name. So they were talking about her — interesting, wasn't it?

"But I'm sure Fröken Stephania didn't want to offend you" — that was Thura of course, the eternal peacemaker; she too ought to learn how to keep quiet.

"Don't tell me that. The way she talked, 'There was nothing between you — !' I thought I would . . ."

"But there was no ill will in that; you should understand it. She just didn't know what had happened, she hasn't been here long enough and . . ."

"She didn't know? A child would know it, the way he treated me; but that I could understand. She didn't notice, didn't pay enough attention to me to see anything. But that isn't the worst part of it; it's the other thing that got me. Did you hear her, did you hear how she said in that sweetish voice of hers: 'Did you really believe that something serious could ever come out of it?' That was the limit, then I just couldn't restrain myself."

"But she said it only to show you . . ."

"To show me, you know what? To show me that I'm not good enough for him, not good enough for anybody. All that fancy talk about differences, about backgrounds meant only that. I'm smart enough to see through it. But of course, she is good enough for anyone she wants . . . a princess . . ."

"I don't understand; what do you mean, Fröken Nilsson?"

"Of course, you're a child, you don't understand it. But that picture on her table, what do you think she keeps that for? Oh, I can tell you; she's sure something serious will happen between her and that fellow, she will get him, that's what she believes. Of course, she's good enough for him even if she . . . Oh, you know what I mean. But that doesn't matter to her; she thinks she's good enough for anyone. And you know why — because she is refined, cultured, because she knows how to use fancy words. But I'm just a simple Fröken Nilsson, a nobody, so of course how could I have ever hoped . . ."

That was going too far. Furiously Stephania pushed the door, and now she was standing right before Fröken Nilsson, watching with a queer sharp joy how her face grew red, then crimson, how her hands clasped and unclasped frantically.

"Well, Fröken Nilsson?" she said at last.

No answer came.

"I heard everything," Stephania said, wondering at her own calmness. "And now let me tell you just one thing, and that is the last you're going to hear from me. I didn't think I was good enough for him. Even if I use fancy words, I knew I could never have him. So I had to give him up, just not to make a fool of myself, you understand? And just because I didn't want you to make a fool of yourself I was trying to tell you that . . ."

"Oh," Fröken Nilsson exclaimed, "you gave him up because, because . . ." She hesitated, looking with horrified eyes at Stephania.

"Because I'm a hunchback, exactly," she snapped back, and walked toward her bed.

Fröken Nilsson did not answer for a while. She only kept staring at her, shaking her head and passing her hand over her face. "Fröken Stephania," she said at last.

Stephania glanced at her silently.

"I'm sorry. I shouldn't have said it, I . . . I'm terrible sorry."

Stephania only shrugged, and began to undress.

"I really am sorry," Fröken Nilsson repeated. "I . . . I thought you yourself hoped . . . you know what I mean, and that you thought I . . ."

"What difference does it all make?"

"Don't you see I felt you meant that anybody is better than me . . ."

"I'm going to put the lights out," Stephania said. "Do you want anything, Thura?"

"No, thanks a lot," Thura said. "Only . . ."

"Only what?"

"It makes a difference, Fröken Stephania. It's like the time . . . with my hands."

"Your hands, what has that got to do with this?"

"Don't you see? When I tried to move my hands and everybody, Professor, Doctor Ström, told me it was so easy, then I . . ."

"I see nothing. Are you all right, you don't need anything, water, or another blanket?"

"No, thanks. But all I mean . . . is that it's easier to believe someone, I mean to take advice from someone who has the same trouble in a way. Just as if they too couldn't move their hands, either, and then . . ."

"I guess it's time to sleep," Stephania murmured, turning the lights off.

. . . What did she want, Thura, with all that talk? she thought lying down. Did she mean that before she took the liberty of advising Fröken Nilsson she should have confessed to her her whole life story so that Fröken Nilsson would be assured she had the same problems? Certainly there was nothing they would have enjoyed more than a dramatic statement like that . . . "I too loved a man, but I had to give him up because I am a hunchback, and therefore I'm entitled to tell you . . ." Sure, they would have simply loved it. Thank God she had enough sense left not to do anything of that sort at least. People could try to help each other, advise each other, without confessing to each other. And that business with the hand, that was quite a different story. It was clear that if you were strong and healthy you could hardly understand those that were sick, tied to their beds. Like Ström telling her in the beginning — you should be able to accept your limitations. That was something else, then, of course she had to think it was easy for him to talk when he himself . . . But what did it have to do with all that had happened now between Fröken Nilsson and herself? Nothing, nothing whatsoever.

. . . Or perhaps . . . the thought struck her so suddenly that she had to sit up, perhaps there was something to it? It was hard to

[ 294 ]

believe what others told you when you felt they were so much better off, that they could have all you never could. Not because you were jealous, but because you knew they could never understand how you felt. Nonsense, she shrugged, when you came up against something really important then perhaps it was the right thing to say: I know what I'm talking about, I've been through the same thing. But in that case, when you dealt with nothing but a stupid infatuation, then to start confessing, telling stories about yourself . . . no, that certainly was not the right way.

Stephania closed her eyes, trying to fall asleep; still she could not. Fröken Nilsson kept tossing from one side to another — still mourning for Doctor Liliencrona, Stephania thought angrily. She heard Fröken Nilsson take a glass, put it back on the table, and begin to grope for something else again.

"Fröken Stephania," she heard her voice at last. "I just want you to know that I really didn't mean . . ."

"I want to sleep, Fröken Nilsson, so if you don't mind . . ."

Fröken Nilsson sighed. "You see," she said hoarsely, "it was a blow for me, a terrible blow. Even if perhaps I didn't quite realize that he didn't care for me quite in the same way I cared for him (although he likes me, he still likes me, I know it), only in a way . . ." Fröken Nilsson sat up abruptly. Something fell on the floor.

"Now what?" Stephania turned on the light and looked. And suddenly she felt like laughing; Fröken Nilsson was still sitting in her dress, the piqué collar wrinkled, torn off, hanging limply around her neck, and was looking at her with round sorrowful eyes . . . a broken glass, with a puddle of water around it, lay on the floor.

"It was a blow," Fröken Nilsson repeated, trying desperately to stop the water, that in large drops was falling from the table onto her bed.

"Well," Stephania put her slippers on, "perhaps I underestimated it, the strength of *your* feelings, I mean."

"Yes, that's exactly what I had on my mind," Fröken Nilsson exclaimed both triumphantly and imploringly.

"I guess I'd better clean that pond up." Stephania nodded and began to dry the water from the floor.

Fröken Nilsson watched, murmuring apologies, and then she said, "It's so hard to forget him, Fröken Stephania; still, I'll try."

[ 295 ]

"You must try," Stephania said, wrung the rag out, and turned the light off again. She certainly was a funny creature, Fröken Nilsson, she thought, smiling at Fröken Nilsson and also at herself, because suddenly she felt sorry for her. After all, perhaps she should have told her about herself in the very beginning, if that could make things easier for her, then . . . Because even though Fröken Nilsson had made up that whole Liliencrona story, even though she had talked herself into that great affection for him, she believed in it now. His marriage might have been a little unpleasant for her, not a blow certainly, just a little unpleasant . . .

"Good night, Thura," Fröken Nilsson said, "good night . . . Fröken Stephania . . ."

"Good night, Fröken Nilsson." Stephania smiled. "Try to sleep; you have a hard day behind you."

"It certainly was hard, Fröken Stephania," Fröken Nilsson said gratefully. "But I'll get over it, I must."

CHAPTER 22

THE CAB WAS WAITING downstairs. The driver helped Fröken Nilsson to get in; Willy slammed the door. "Here we go," he said. Fröken Nilsson smiled at him silently. It was nice of Willy to take her out to the movies, she thought. Yes, for all his funny ways he certainly had been a great help to her — Fröken Nilsson sighed, thinking how much she had needed help in those last weeks — when everything was so hard, so difficult that she often wondered where she got the strength to stand it. First the blow — Fröken Nilsson always referred to Doctor Liliencrona's marriage as "the blow"; then all those troubles about her going home. "You're going back home right after Easter," Professor had said, just like that, offhand, without even asking her if she had a place to go back to. It certainly was a nice home she was going back to — the room Anna had found, shabby and dark and a walk-up too; third floor. Well, you couldn't afford to be choosy if you only had two hundred crowns left in the bank, and no job. Fröken

Nilsson sighed; she remembered the letter Herr Eriksson, for whom she used to work, had written. A bunch of lies — that was what the whole letter amounted to — how happy he was that she was well, and how much he regretted that unfortunately he had no vacancy, that in her present state she should look for something easier, less tiring. They all were nice, as long as you did not need anything from them — Fröken Nilsson shrugged. There was no use breaking your head about it now, she decided, and moved closer to the window.

The day was warm, the sidewalks shone in the sun, white and clean as if freshly scrubbed; the passers-by, their coats swirled by the breeze, looked light and cheerful, and traces of green, shy and pale, still showed here and there on trees and bushes. Fröken Nilsson felt very light and festive suddenly. "A lovely day, isn't it?" she said, and smiled with pleasure when the cab stopped and Willy paying said nonchalantly, "Keep the change, driver." He really knew how to behave, Willy, quite like a gentleman.

The theater was one of the best in the city, with colorful neon lights glittering above the big glass gate, with marble steps, and a doorman in crimson livery to open the swinging door for them. The vestibule — all mirrors and purple carpets — was empty; the picture had already started. "This way please," a boy also in livery, but this time deep blue, said as he led them down into the hall, where it was dark, solemn and very quiet except for the soft music coming from somewhere high above. "Here," the boy whispered, and Fröken Nilsson with a deep sigh of satisfaction sank into the plush-covered chair. It had been a long time since she had been to the movies, and now Fröken Nilsson sat looking around — first at the screen, where a tall man in uniform was saying something to a girl with a big bunch of flowers in her hand; then at the silvery shaft of light piercing the darkness and at last at the motionless figures around her. Their faces were hidden by the dusk, but still she managed to notice a most unusual hat worn by a lady next to her, the broad shoulder of the man in the next row. And there, right in front of her, a couple sat, a boy and a girl — his arm around her, her head resting on his shoulder. Fröken Nilsson forgot about the couple on the screen, the hat and the interesting man next to her, she sat looking only at those two. For now it was back, that painful and familiar feeling of envy, of curiosity and great sadness that it was never she, always others, who sat like that so close to each other and then would walk out together, their hands clasped, their faces smiling. . . . Kale used to move close to her in the movies — and how close — but it was altogether different with him; he put his arm around her, not because he cared for her but . . . He certainly was disgusting, Kale, thought Fröken Nilsson, and again she looked at the couple in front of her. Her eyes met Willy's; he too was staring at them — she knew it. For a while they watched each other, then at the same moment averted their eyes and pretended to be watching the screen.

Fröken Nilsson felt tense, expectant; she sank deep into her chair, so that her head almost touched Willy's shoulder. She waited, felt Willy move closer. And now he put his arm around her, and now exactly like the girl in front, she laid her head on his shoulder.

"Are you comfortable?" Willy whispered.

"Oh yes." And she wondered . . . and hoped that perhaps in the back row someone noticed what had happened, and was watching her enviously and sadly just as she had watched the couple in front of her before.

They sat so, close together until the picture (a very sad one; Fröken Nilsson had to dry her eyes all the time) was over, and big letters forming the word END jumped out upon the screen. Willy moved away abruptly, and when light flooded the room they sat far apart as if nothing had happened.

"Did you like the picture?" Willy asked.

"Yes." Fröken Nilsson blew her nose noisily, and suggested they should wait until people around them left the theater. They sat silently, embarrassed somehow, afraid to say anything. The hall grew empty at last. "Let's go." Fröken Nilsson got up.

But something was changed now. The floor, which before had sloped down helpfully, was now rising steeply, the carpet had grown too soft, and she felt almost as if she were walking on a sponge; the leafy pattern seemed to entangle her feet, to lurk for her fall. But Fröken Nilsson did not give in. At the start she had to lean upon the chairs a few times, but soon she had found the proper rhythm and balance, and felt with triumph she had overcome the hostile steepness of the floor, the uncertain softness of the carpet. Only slightly leaning on her cane, she moved forward, in even steps, swinging her free arm nonchalantly.

Over at the exit door people were still moving into the vestibule. But the hall was empty, and the silence around them echoed their steps, filled the huge room with a dumb hollow pounding that seemed to grow louder and louder. The people at the door heard it, one after another heads began to turn as if news of their arrival had spread from mouth to mouth. Now all of them were looking: silent, expectant eyes stared at them with hesitant curiosity, with shame, fear. At them? . . . No, they could not be staring at *her,* she was not walking so poorly as all that: slowly perhaps, but her steps were not even limping. Was it at him? At Willy?

Fröken Nilsson stopped, looked back. Far behind her, his legs widely straddled, his hands grabbing the arms of the chairs, Willy was climbing up. Now he too stopped, glanced at her, and smiled. Fröken Nilsson turned abruptly. Yes, it was at him they were staring, and if they looked at her too, it was only because of him, crawling there clumsily, wobbling in every direction. She started walking as fast as she could, her eyes fixed upon the people at the door. She tried to tell them, with her look, with her whole body, she was not like him, she had nothing in common with him, she was exactly like them, like that tall woman moving toward the door, swinging her bag in her hand; like that boy, moving forward so swiftly and easily. But they did not understand her; they kept staring. He should not have brought me here, she thought. He had no right to, when he knew how it was with him, how others would stare.

Something fell on the floor. It was her purse; her bag had opened. She stooped, picked it up, closed the bag. Just as she started walking again Willy caught up with her. "So here I am," he said panting. Certainly, here he was! He should have had more sense than to run after her, she thought, when together they approached the door. Around them voices grew lower and lower, turned to whispers. Then even the whispers stopped. People moved aside making place for them, and now they walked between two long lines, silent, the eyes of all fixed upon them. "That certainly was some climb," Willy said aloud, so loudly that everybody could hear him. Fröken Nilsson did not answer; she turned her head away. She counted every moment, every step; at last! Here was the vestibule, and now the street.

"Would you like to go for a cup of coffee?" Willy asked.

"No, I'd rather go home."

She said nothing on the way home, and when Willy asked her

to go out with him next Sunday, she only shook her head. "I can't," that was all she said.

But back in the hospital when he walked with her through the hall, watching her with sad troubled eyes, Fröken Nilsson suddenly felt sorry for him. It wasn't his fault after all, she thought. Still I just can't take it. "Thanks a lot, Willy, it was very nice," she said, "but next week I really can't, all that packing you know . . ."

"Yes, the packing, of course. . . ." Willy nodded, and he walked away.

Had Willy noticed anything on that Sunday evening? For he never repeated his invitation, and also his visits to Room Five stopped. "Lots of work before Easter," he explained; and when he came in with his stand, he would just hand them the magazines and papers, and leave. It's better this way, Fröken Nilsson decided; why should he get all upset over her, when she . . . But as days passed, and she hardly ever caught a glimpse of Willy, she began to feel disappointed. After all he could come and talk to her sometimes, she thought, or did he really feel hurt? Fröken Nilsson had to admit to herself that she had not been too nice to him that time in the movies. Perhaps she should say something to him. . . . Yes, that seemed the right thing to do. "Would you come with me to the park, Willy?" she asked at last. "I'm not used to walking outside alone yet, so if you don't mind . . ." No, Willy did not mind at all. They went for a long walk, and from that time on, he renewed his usual visits, although only a few days were left to Easter and he must have been busier than ever.

All over the ward the preparations for the holiday were in full swing. Again as before Christmas scissors clicked busily, scraps of many-colored papers covered the floor. Again the walls disappeared under big placards, on which Easter chickens, round and very yellow, walked serenely among purple and orange Easter eggs. Then Good Friday came. The room, all golden and blue with daffodils and Easter lilies, became quiet, filled with the gentle silence of April dusk. Fröken Nilsson too got flowers, a huge bouquet from Willy. She asked Stephania to put some of them on Thura's and her table, and nodded pensively when they assured her Willy was the nicest, the most considerate person they had ever met. "Yes, he can be nice," she agreed, thinking that perhaps she should have gone to the movies with him after all.

As on Christmas, so also on Easter supper was served in the living room. Again the patients appeared, dressed in their own best clothes, and again Fröken Brickman played the organ and hymns were sung, songs remembered from home. Until at last when it grew dark outside, fewer and fewer voices joined the singing, and slowly the patients began to return to their rooms.

Fröken Nilsson did not feel like going back just yet. She felt tired — somehow sad. Only a few months ago, on Christmas Eve, it was Doctor Liliencrona who, instead of that stupid nurse, sat next to her. She had given him the socks that she had knitted for him and he said, "Thank you very much, I certainly appreciate them," and the way he looked at her. . . .Yes, things looked different then; now in a few days she would be back in Eskilstuna, alone, with no job. . . . Well, worrying had certainly never helped anyone. Fröken Nilsson got up and started walking back to the room.

"Fröken Nilsson!" someone called her suddenly. It was Willy limping hastily across the room. "You aren't going yet, are you?"

"I guess so. It's getting late."

"Won't you stay for a little while?"

"I might." Fröken Nilsson sat back on the sofa. Willy, though there was still plenty of room left on it, sat down in a chair nearby. "Thanks for the flowers, Willy," Fröken Nilsson said.

"Oh, nothing to thank me for," Willy murmured, and then he sat silent, without even looking at her, as if he had completely forgotten she was there.

Fröken Nilsson glanced at him impatiently; what did he want from her, first asking her to stay and then sitting there, without saying a word, just twisting his tie in his fingers? She looked around. The window was open and a warm breeze smelling of young leaves came into the room, swayed the curtains and the delicate heads of daffodils. In the men's ward they were singing still, and the soft voices, subdued by distance, filled the room. A lovely evening, Fröken Nilsson thought. She wished someone else was sitting next to her instead of Willy, someone who would know what to say, what to do at a moment like that. He certainly did not have much sense, Willy, just sitting there, staring at the carpet as if that was the only important thing in the world. Fröken Nilsson cleared her throat angrily, Willy raised his head and looked at her, but still he said nothing, only twisted his tie faster and faster until it was twisted up into a string. Fröken Nilsson felt like snatching it out of his hands. She said: "I'm sending my things home tomorrow."

"Oh," Willy said. And after a while: "What did you say?"

That was too much. If he did not want to talk he could listen at least. "I'm sending my things home tomorrow," she said through her teeth, and got up.

"You're not leaving yet," Willy exclaimed imploringly, jumping to his feet.

With a resigned sigh Fröken Nilsson sank back on the sofa. Willy too sat down, on the sofa this time, but far in the opposite corner. Fröken Nilsson noticed it. She shrugged scornfully. "Well, what is it you want?" She yawned ostentatiously.

"I . . . nothing . . ."

"Well?"

"It's only . . ." Willy lifted his head, pointed to the window, behind which a big, brightly lit building loomed.

"That's for the hospital personnel," he explained.

"I know."

"Do you see the windows on the second floor, those with white curtains?"

"Sure I see them."

"The Sogströms live there."

"Do they?" Fröken Nilsson said bitingly.

"Yes," Willy assured her eagerly. And now he was talking so fast that she could hardly follow him. "Gustav Sogström. He works down in the X-ray room. But now he has a job in Göteborg that pays better, so he's going there."

"I see," Fröken Nilsson interrupted him, looking at her watch.

"Yes, he's leaving next month, so the apartment will be empty. It's very nice; I think so at least, I don't know what you . . . But it's nice. Two rooms, and a kitchen with an electric stove, and an icebox, everything you want, and only a hundred twenty crowns a month . . ."

"That isn't so cheap, after all."

"Oh," Willy exclaimed regretfully, "and I thought . . ."

Fröken Nilsson could not control herself any longer. "What difference does it make whether it's cheap or not — that, and all that talk about Sogström and his apartment, and God only knows what else? I'd better go now."

[ 302 ]

Willy grasped her hand. "Please, do stay. You see . . . I thought . . . I . . ." He stopped, turned his head away. "I thought that if we got married, you and me, I mean . . ."

"What?"

"Married."

"You and me?"

Willy nodded. "I knew you wouldn't agree," he said staring at the floor.

"No, it isn't that, it's only . . ." Married! — He had proposed to her . . . So it had happened to her — a proposal! — she thought, and felt both happy and a little disappointed that it had to be that way, with Sogström and the kitchen and the apartment — so different from the way she always thought it would be. Still he had proposed to her! He . . .

She looked at Willy. "I don't know," she said. "I'll have to think it over."

"Certainly," Willy murmured, and then as if only suddenly grasping the meaning of her words he exclaimed, "So you didn't say no, you really didn't?"

"I told you I must think it over. Tomorrow I'll tell you."

"Tomorrow," Willy repeated, and without another word he got up and started walking to the door. He must have forgotten altogether about his walking because he stumbled and staggered, and had to lean on the chairs again and again. In the doorway he stopped. "Good night," he said, and then he was gone.

For a long while Fröken Nilsson sat motionless, breathing heavily; then she too got up and started walking toward her room. What will they say to it? she thought. Thura, Stephania above all? She had to tell them, of course, but how . . . Fröken Nilsson stopped, thoughtfully. She could say, He proposed to me, or perhaps, He asked me to be his wife — No, that didn't sound right either. He asked for my hand. That was better, Fröken Nilsson decided. No, the best way was to tell them nothing at first, and only after they noticed, for they had to notice that something unusual had happened, only then she would tell them, and very quietly too — Willy asked for my hand. Willy, what kind of a name was that, like a ten year old boy's. He should be called William, she decided, opening the door.

"Where have you been so long?" Thura asked.

"Oh, nowhere . . ." Fröken Nilsson said with a vague gesture.

With a deep sigh she lay down and buried her face in the pillow. But no one said anything. Fröken Nilsson sighed once more, louder this time. Still neither of them paid any attention to her. Fröken Nilsson sat up, looked around.

Only then Thura asked, "What's the matter, Fröken Nilsson? Anything wrong?"

"No, nothing, only . . ." She groped for words; how was it that she decided to tell them? But everything became confused suddenly, she remembered nothing. "He wants us to get married," she blurted at last.

"Who?"

"Willy."

"Fröken Nilsson, how wonderful," Thura cried. "Did you hear, Fröken Stephania, Fröken Nilsson and Willy are getting married."

"Really?" Stephania's book noisily fell on the floor.

"I . . . I don't know yet. . ."

"Did you refuse him?" Stephania asked.

"Oh no, you did not, you could not do that," Thura whispered pleadingly. "He's so nice, he likes you so much."

"I know, still . . ."

"So you don't care for him?" Stephania asked.

"I do in a way. He's so kind, and . . . but I don't know, I cannot . . ."

"What's wrong with him?"

Fröken Nilsson did not answer at once. "I know it is not right," she said at last. "I know I should not be thinking that way. Still, it's the people . . ."

"What people?" Stephania asked.

"All of them, everybody around, not here in the hospital, but *out there*. I know it's not right of me," she repeated, "but that time when we went to the movies . . ."

"What happened then?"

"It was the way he walked, he was crawling practically, and everybody looked at him terribly, and at me, because of him, you see . . . I . . . I . . . was so ashamed that I was with him, I pretended not to know him at all. . . . If I could have, I would have run away, just left him there . . ."

"You really mean it? Left him alone there just because he couldn't walk?"

"They were staring . . . so terribly."

And then Stephania moved closer to Fröken Nilsson and said, her voice strange, strained and toneless. "You would have run away and left him, when . . . when he was crawling practically, as you said?"

"I told you, didn't I, how they looked at him, a whole crowd. And I'm not like that, I walk better, I just couldn't stand it. . . ."

"I see, I see," Stephania said.

"So you think it was just awful of me?"

"I don't know, how can *I, I* tell? " Stephania whispered back.

"But now? What should I do now?"

Again Stephania said: "Don't ask me, I can't tell you. Perhaps Thura may."

"Me?"

"Yes, you, you much sooner than me."

"Well, I don't know either. How can I? But do you think that otherwise you care for him?"

"I think so. You know, no one has ever been so kind to me, never in my whole life."

"Because only if you care, only then you might get used to it, only then if you cared enough for him you wouldn't want to leave him any more."

"I guess I do care for him, but I can't say now for sure. I feel so confused. But I'll think it over tonight. Anyhow I won't be able to close my eyes, not even for a moment."

"Yes, do think it over," Stephania said, putting the lights off.

She and Thura lay sleepless but silent, looking persistently into the darkness, as if trying to guess from the vague outlines of Fröken Nilsson's face her thoughts, her decision.

And Fröken Nilsson kept tossing from side to side, thinking — Do I care for him . . . really, or does it only seem so to me now? Yes, she cared for him, even if sometimes he got terribly on her nerves. But most of the time she liked him: he could be so nice, like taking her to the best movie in town, or sending her flowers . . . or (and this seemed somehow even more important) the way he would listen when you talked to him, never laughing at you, never getting impatient. . . . Was that what Thura meant — did she care enough for him, enough not to do it ever again? She sat up and said: "Now it seems to me that I do care for him, Thura."

Out of the darkness Thura's voice answered. "But d'you think you could go out with him again, and . . ."

[ 305 ]

"Before, I thought I never could. But now I figure it differently. All right, what does it matter if they stare? People always stare, they're just like that. If only I could always remember how nice he can be."

She fell silent. Thura did not answer. Fröken Nilsson turned herself to the wall. Even if I refuse him I'll do it gently, she thought. I'll say, I love you dearly, Willy, but like a sister only; or, I have sisterly feelings for you, Willy, or . . . But should I refuse? God, it was all hard. Fröken Nilsson felt very tired suddenly. Her thoughts kept slipping away somewhere; instead pictures, vague as if seen from afar, came before her eyes — a room with white curtains, and then a kitchen very clean and white . . . with an icebox, and an electric stove. . . . The Sogströms are leaving, someone said; then the voice changed, the kitchen vanished somewhere, and instead Doctor Liliencrona was standing before her saying, Congratulations, Fröken Nilsson, I'm so happy for you. Until he too disappeared, and instead Anna her sister was there, saying to someone to whom she could not quite see: Can you imagine! Maria got married, who would have expected it? And among all those pictures Willy popped in and out — Willy with flowers in his hands, Willy twisting his tie, Willy climbing up something that looked at one time like a ladder and at another like a mountain. Until at last she could see herself in a long white dress, and a veil saying, I have sisterly feelings for you. . . .

Fröken Nilsson slept long that morning; she did not wake up until Fru Gustavsson came into the room, exclaiming: "Eight o'clock, Fröken Nilsson, hurry up!" Slowly she opened her eyes.

"Good morning, Fröken Nilsson," Thura said, and there was something unusual in her voice. Then Stephania — "Good morning," and her voice also sounded solemn and demanding. Fröken Nilsson rubbed her eyes and suddenly she remembered — the proposal. "I'll think it over tonight," she had said, and here . . .

"So what did you decide?" Thura could not wait any longer. Stephania got up and looked at her.

"I . . . I guess I will say yes." And promptly, before they could say anything: "I thought about it, thought and thought all the night long. And now I feel it's the right thing to do."

"Well, congratulations," Stephania said.

Thura whispered: "Oh, Fröken Nilsson . . . how wonderful."

# CHAPTER 23

IT WAS WHEN the thaw started with grayish masses of snow gliding down from the roof, with the icicles dissolving sadly into heavy drops, that it began — a restlessness at first intangible like pain that had as yet no time to ripen, a premonition only. Only later when Fru Gustavsson came in, changed, somehow festive, and in a voice high and jubilant said: "It certainly smells of spring today"; when the wind, moist and warm, burst into the room, Stephania recognized it, that feeling not of restlessness any longer, but of fear — fear of that spring Fru Gustavsson had brought with her, of that air so soft and fragrant touching her cheeks, of the patches of blue shining in the gray sky. For suddenly she remembered that it was already March, that in a few weeks May would be here, and that moment when everything would have to be settled and decided would come — her "great day." She had been waiting for that spring eagerly, often with angry impatience, but now it seemed to have caught her unaware before she was prepared for it. Because even if only a few weeks remained, everything was still uncertain and vague, just as in the very beginning, just as in the fall when many long months were left; for now, as then, Ström still had nothing to say.

But then in early March, it was still easy to forget the spring and May drawing closer and closer. Soon the cold weather returned, the trees stood bare and meager, and the sky was covered with uniform dull grayness — a winter sky still. The fear disappeared — not completely though; it hid itself somewhere deep within her waiting for a better moment to come back. And it did return, stronger, undeniable this time, on that afternoon when Barbara came in with a bouquet of violets in her hand, and said: "Look, the first spring flowers, aren't they lovely?" Stephania, staring silently at the deeply colored delicate petals, at the tiny leaves, knew with a sharp almost painful clarity that now spring was here, that only a few weeks remained. From that day on, there was no escape from it: outside the trees grew covered with green, first shy and tentative but soon sturdy and bold; shafts of sun rays pierced through the panes, touched her face like friendly fingers, and the sky washed by the many rains was all blue and clear. April first, April second — the chart reminded her each morning — only four weeks left, only three. But Ström seemed not to notice it at all; a few times he had tightened her cast, had taken X-ray pictures, but he never would say anything, and also from his face, cold and stern, she could guess nothing, even if by each of her words, her gestures, she tried to force him to give her a sign at least. . . .

Today I must ask him, she decided each morning; but again, when he stood there talking to Thura only, as if not noticing her at all, the words would die on her lips and she would think, I'll wait until tomorrow when he's in a better mood, when I'll have exactly figured out all I want to tell him. But the next day she would say nothing, and then another day would come, and still . . .

"Do they tell the patients about the operation, when it's going to be, what they are going to do?" she asked Thura at last.

Thura looked at her. "Some would give anything to hear just one word from him of promise . . . of encouragement," she remembered Stephania's wistful voice saying that time many months ago just before she had started moving her hand. Slowly she said, "No, I don't think so, Fröken Stephania. I guess they think we can't do anything anyhow, so why tell us. We would only get nervous and upset, don't you think so?"

Stephania nodded silently; perhaps Thura was right after all, perhaps there was no use in Ström explaining everything to her, no use in asking him. No one ever asked any questions here; Thura didn't, nor did Fröken Nilsson. All one could do was to wait patiently and not think too much, yet not think . . . But how could she try to think, how could she forget that spring lurking for her everywhere, in the bouquets of daffodils on the tables, in the gaily colored coats of the visitors, in the constant questions — "Why don't you come to the park with us; it's so lovely there, a real spring day already?"

"No, thanks," she would answer obstinately. "I'm too tired, I'm too tired." And she stayed in the room even if Doctor Ström and Sister Gudrun kept persuading her she needed more fresh air, more exercise.

There was also another reason why she avoided the park — the people who filled it, who with the first warm day swarmed out of hiding, out of the big red-brick building with the huge inscription SCHOOL FOR CRIPPLED AND HANDICAPPED. Students, they were called, and that gay lighthearted name sounded like a mockery when applied to those figures, each of them mutilated in a different ingenious way; there were some whose bodies seemed to be composed of those un-co-ordinated limbs twitching constantly in some overpowering ecstasy of joy or grief; others dragging on stick-thin withered legs the much too heavy braces; some walked widely straddling, their torsos crouched in two; still others, as if fastened to their wheel chairs, pushed the wheels with raspy spiderlike hands, their heads too big for the childishly undeveloped bodies, shaking rhythmically; and then worst of all, the ones sitting in chairs with a statuesque repose, the hands folded on their laps, and transported like objects, by others, from place to place.

But it was not the mutilation of their bodies which horrified her most; many of the patients she had met in the ward were equally disfigured. But *they* were still in the hospital: the awkward gray dresses they wore were a badge of their rebellion; they had not yet accepted their state; they struggled, had some hope left. Those in the park had consented by now to their mutilation, and existed in comfortable agreement with their bodies, with that world of theirs stretching from the red brick building to the park, in which they diligently imitated the world outside. Carefully they adorned the deformed bodies; garish ties shone on the withered necks, trinkets dangled on the muscleless groping arms, frills and ribbons quivered on the shapeless torsos. They talked in loud robust voices, laughed joyful, exuberant laughter. There were couples among them who in a mock-imitation of those couples *out there* sat late into the night in the park, embraced smiling at each other, forgetful of the crutches they needed for each step, refusing to remember their hands trembled and shook at each caress.

It was that unawareness, that ease with which they accepted their life which forced her to shun them; but they, like that early and unwanted spring, seemed to be everywhere. They stared at her when she passed the window, waited for her in the hospital vestibule, always smiling at her a confidential, knowing smile that claimed a community she refused to accept. There seemed to be a

[ 309 ]

secret allegiance between them and the spring, and it was from both she was constantly struggling to escape.

She felt relieved and grateful, therefore, when after Easter the preparations for Fröken Nilsson's wedding began, and the days were now filled with hectic rush and confusion. Willy, or William as Fröken Nilsson called him now, decided they should spend their honeymoon in a hotel in Skåne, and Fröken Nilsson was preparing herself eagerly for that event. A trunk full of her clothes had arrived from Eskilstuna; Fröken Nilsson tried each dress on, changed a frill here, lengthened a hem there. A few times she went shopping in town, and when she came back papers rustled, boxes were opened, and the new purchases were proudly displayed to the accompaniment of enthusiastic exclamations from Thura and Fru Gustavsson.

Stephania discussed each detail with her, spent long hours on the question whether a suit or a white dress would be more appropriate for the wedding ceremony, and helped Fröken Nilsson with the sewing and ironing. Days passed faster and more easily now; the chatter of Fröken Nilsson rose above the laughter and the voices coming from the park. But often in the night she would wake up, struggling for breath as if an unbearable burden was oppressing her, and also her dreams grew strange, filled with thin greedy arms groping for her, with branches heavy with leaves stretching toward her, and sometimes Ström's severe face would appear and gaze at her silently.

The big suitcase all packed stood in the middle of the room. Fröken Nilsson looked at it, at the tag on which big letters said — *Fru William Olsgård, Hotel Corona, Skåne*; then she opened the closet and the drawers to make sure that she had not left anything. "I guess that's all," she said sighing.

"Why don't you rest a little?" Stephania asked.

"Yes, yes, I'd better." Fröken Nilsson sat down. But soon she started fidgeting in her chair, got up and began to pace to and fro across the room. "I feel so nervous, like . . . like before a 'great day,'" she said at last.

"Don't worry, everything will be fine," Thura consoled her.

"I know, it's just my nerves, and then leaving you, and the whole place," she added, looking at that room, in which everything was so familiar to her — even the few ink spots on the polka-dot cover, even the smudges left by her cane on the grass-green linoleum. "I hardly can believe that tomorrow at this time I won't be here."

"That certainly is hard to believe." Thura nodded.

"I'll write you about everything."

"Yes, don't forget to do that," Stephania said.

"And then as soon as I come back from my honeymoon, I'll come to see you every visiting time. Or even more often than that; Sister Gudrun might let me in."

"I'm convinced she will," Stephania assured her. She smiled — poor Fröken Nilsson; all day she had been like that, restless, looking at them, promising to write, to come and see them as though she felt guilty it was only she who was getting married, who was leaving. Exactly like Barbara before her wedding. Then too, on that last night, they sat silently; just a word thrown out from time to time; looking at the packed trunk, at the white dress spread over the chair. And then too there was that feeling of weariness, of sudden void, for everything was prepared and finished, and there was nothing left to do — just waiting. And Barbara, like Fröken Nilsson now, kept walking to and fro, looking once more at everything and repeating those very same things about writing, about coming back soon. . . . And she, watching Barbara, had felt that she was preparing herself to say something. She did say at last: "Why don't you write him to come?"

"So how does it look?" Stephania heard Fröken Nilsson asking. She was trying on her new suit again.

"It looks fine."

"Don't you think I would have looked better in white?"

"Definitely not," Stephania answered, wondering how many times Fröken Nilsson had asked that question before. "Very few people actually get married in white nowadays," she added reassuringly, so that she could safely return to that evening two years ago.

"You want him to come, what? So that he would see me, the way I look now? No," she cried, "how could I, ever?" And Barbara angrily — "You don't know what you are doing. You're too proud, and you'll lose him in the end."

"Well, I'm proud, there's nothing wrong with that. I'd rather lose him than let him see me, now." She did not wait for Barbara to answer; she knew what Barbara would say. But she rushed into

[ 311 ]

another room, and stayed there until Barbara came in and said, "Let's not talk about that. There's no use, anyhow. . . ."

"Don't you think I should put the flower a little higher?" Fröken Nilsson inquired anxiously.

Convincing Fröken Nilsson that the flower was just in the perfect place, Stephania wondered what would have happened if she had written to him then. No, it was impossible to think about it, impossible even to imagine that she should have seen him, spoken to him, that he should have known everything. No, it was better this way, even if Barbara was right, even if she had lost him in the end.

. . . And not only the very thought of meeting him again was strange and improbable, but everything — that she had once known him, that she had been with him — that too seemed hard to believe somehow. Not that she had forgotten him, and all that had happened between them. She still remembered everything, each word, each gesture. But it was a different remembrance — vivid yet distant, like the memory of something you had read about or heard of somewhere, but which had never happened in your own life. It was as if that Stephania, healthy, with nothing to hide, who used to sit next to Jan, her hand in his, was someone else, someone she herself had hardly known.

"I'm still worried about that trip to Skåne, I must tell you," she heard Fröken Nilsson saying. "I told William we cannot afford it. But you know William; he just said 'Leave it to me, Maria . . .'"

"I think it's very nice of him to take you there," she murmured. William? For Heaven's sake, why did she have to change his name? And why did she have to always talk about him. From morning till evening, nothing but William . . . William said this, and did that, as if they were the first couple ever to get married. It got on your nerves, that constant talk, it made you feel very much alone, incomplete somehow. . . . Or perhaps all couples were like that . . . perhaps she and Jan too . . . She and Jan — why should that sound so remote, so impossible to her? she thought bitterly. It was quite like her to remember exactly, to relive again and again everything that ever had gone wrong, each mistake and failure, all that was good — that meant something to her — that had to fade, to vanish, somehow as if it never had happened.

Stephania looked around. Fröken Nilsson was fastening the buttons on her suit-jacket; Thura seemed to be dozing. Noiselessly she opened the drawer and took out the picture. The face seemed changed, as if scarred under the broken glass. She took the splintered glass out; now it was better, now it was the same, almost the same Jan she had known, only the smile motionlessly clinging to his lips still seemed different; strange. "To Steph" — she read the words in the corner. Yes, it had happened, she thought with relief, with gratitude.

But suddenly, just when she was about to put the picture back into the drawer, she felt they were looking at her, both Thura and Fröken Nilsson — silently, inquiringly. For a moment their eyes met. Fröken Nilsson nervously bit off the thread. Thura lifted her hand, pretended to be looking at it. It was unbearable, their tactfulness, Stephania thought. She said, "I guess I was getting a little nostalgic. Everything just smells of marriage here, and so . . ." She started laughing. It sounded too loud, too startling, that laughter — she stopped abruptly. "I'm sorry," she murmured. "It just came over me, you know, a funny feeling . . ."

"I know what you mean," Thura said.

Fröken Nilsson stopped sewing, sat turning the needle in her hand — if she could only stop being so damned embarrassed. And now she got up, cleared her throat: "Do you know, a day or two ago, William said, 'When Fröken Stephania gets well, men will be just crazy about her; pretty as she is, and smart too.' Honestly, that was what he said."

Stephania felt she had to help her. "Crazy about me, that would be too much to expect. But I might get married. Most people do, after all. If . . . I mean . . ." She stopped, said much louder, stubbornly, "When I get well, why not?"

"Sure, you'll get well, and then . . . just wait and see. You'll find someone just to your liking — nice, handsome."

"Let's hope," and against her will her eyes looked at the picture she was still holding in her hand.

Fröken Nilsson could not resist the temptation. "You mean that you and he . . ." Her voice grew more and more hesitating, she stopped and only stared at Stephania, her eyes both curious and pleading.

"He and I . . . no, never. I told you it was over."

"Well, I thought things might change. Like me and William, I never thought we could ever get together, and now . . ."

"No, it isn't the same thing. You see he got married."

[ 313 ]

"Oh, I'm so sorry."

"Nothing to be sorry about, Fröken Nilsson. Things often come to an end, one way or another. Besides it's an old story; I've had lots of time to get over it. It's five years ago, as long as that, since I last saw him."

"So he is not here in Sweden?"

"Of course not. I met him in Poland . . . in the ghetto."

"Where?"

"In the ghetto. Oh, of course, you don't know what that is. It was the place where we had lived the first two years of the war." Strange, she thought, how you had to explain each word used then, as if a special language had been spoken in those days, a language understood only by those who had lived through them. "It was — how can I describe it to you? — just a few streets the Germans had cut off from the rest of the city. And walls around them, high walls so that you could not get out when you wanted to. Yes," she repeated slowly, "you could not get out when you wanted — that was it — the ghetto."

"Sounds like a prison."

"It was like a prison, except that we lived in houses, in apartments. Terribly crowded though, fifty thousand people just squeezed into those few streets. And more were coming each day, from villages and towns around. The Germans didn't let them stay there. At the end there was not an inch of space left — two or three families in each room."

"In one room?"

"Yes, just separated by closets, like by walls. It was funny, in a way, knocking on a closet and asking 'May I come in to your part?' He too came from a town nearby, Jan, I mean . . ." Jan, she said again after years, and now the very sound of that name brought back everything and made it live again.

"Was his name Jan?" asked Thura.

"Yes, Jan."

"That's a beautiful name."

"I guess so, rather." And now she could see him, no longer as in the picture, well dressed with the paper-photography smile on his face, but as she had seen him then for the first time, in that awkward coat much too large for him, in high boots all splashed with mud, standing in the dark stuffy room, saying . . . The billeting office had sent him to us, him and his sister, Rosa was her name, and the baby. The husband was gone by then, but the baby was still there. . . .

Stephania stopped — what was the use of dragging out all those old stories? Still it was good to talk about it, to remember, to speak his name aloud, the name of the place where she had met him . . . "Yes," she repeated, "the baby was still there."

"A baby, that must have been wonderful, Fröken Stephania," Thura exclaimed.

"Wonderful, you said?" Stephania laughed and again as before that laughter did not belong there; she let it die out slowly in the astonished silence.

Wonderful — Thura must have thought it was a lovely pink thing, like those babies in the advertisements. Baby — you could hardly call it that, it was just something skinny and gray-faced like a shriveled old woman. "We were told we could stay here," Rosa had said, rocking the child in her arms. And Mother stood silently, looking at that bundle of rags out of which the crying came, shrill and angry. At last she started talking. "No, it was impossible," she said; grownups she would not have minded, but a child . . . How could they stand all that crying, working as hard as they did, getting up each morning at six . . .

She would have left, Rosa, who was so shy and quiet, but then Jan stepped forward; he said nothing, but very quietly took the child out of her arms and put it on the bed.

"Of course we'll stay," he said, without even raising his voice. "Wait until you've been driven from one place to another, in the cold — like us; then you won't mind a room with ten babies in it." And he sat down and started unpacking their things. . . .

"No, it was not wonderful, Thura," Stephania said. "It was not a place for children, the ghetto. The . . . baby cried and cried, it seemed she could never stop. And when you looked at her, you just couldn't understand where she got the strength for all that crying, she was so terribly skinny, just skin and bones — wrinkled and yellow. I guess she cried because she was always hungry; you couldn't get any real milk in the ghetto, just skimmed, as thin as water, and even for that they didn't have enough money. . . . And then it was always cold in the room; we couldn't get enough wood. So no wonder that the child cried." . . . No wonder, she thought; and it seemed to her she could hear it now, that cry, not like a baby's at all but old, bitter and reproachful.

"All night she cried. Mother could not stand it. You couldn't blame her, she was working so hard, scrubbing floors twelve hours a day. I know she tried hard to say nothing, but sometimes she just could not take it, she would shout, 'Couldn't you make her stop, for a moment at least?' And Jan, he was so fond of the baby, would shout back: 'What d'you want us to do, choke her?'"

"Oh, Lord," Thura whispered.

"I'm sorry, Thura, I . . ." Stephania hesitated. "I didn't want to bring all that in. I just wanted to tell you about him, about Jan. But somehow it's all so mixed together, he, and the baby, and the ghetto."

"I don't mind, Fröken Stephania; it's just so sad that a baby . . ."

"Yes, it is. But later, you know, we got used to her. Mother gave Rosa a blanket to wrap her in, and I got some milk for her. We almost liked her, I guess. Sometimes when she was fed, she smiled, and then she looked pretty, almost like a real baby, like other babies here."

"But how did you manage to get milk for her? It must have been terribly difficult, wasn't it?"

"Sort of. I bought it in the factory; one of the workers, he was not Jewish so he did not live in the ghetto, brought it. And I smuggled it into the ghetto."

"Smuggled it in, what d'you mean?" Fröken Nilsson asked.

"I had to hide it, underneath my clothes. They — the guards at the gate — always opened our bags. Sometimes they searched you, too, took off the clothes, everything . . . and when they found something, then . . ."

"Then . . ." Fröken Nilsson repeated.

"Oh, you know what I mean," Stephania said wearily.

"But then they could have killed you too, Fröken Stephania! You should never have done that! If the baby was yours or someone's in your family, then maybe, but for a strange child . . . no, never!"

"Oh, I just . . . I don't know. I simply had to. I knew it wouldn't really help, there was never enough of the milk and besides the Germans were taking all the babies then. So I knew they would take her too, sooner or later. Still I just could not stand hearing her crying."

"I still say you should never have done it. Especially if you knew . . ." Fröken Nilsson faltered, stopped.

"I think it was wonderful of you to have done it, Fröken Stephania." Thura disagreed timidly.

"Wonderful." Stephania mimicked her angrily. "Everything is always wonderful to you, Thura. I told you I just could not stand that crying; it got on my nerves. Anyhow, very soon she stopped crying, not completely, just kept whining, very faintly so you could hardly hear it."

"Did you get enough milk for her then?"

"No, of course not. It was just that she was not strong enough to cry any longer; she started dying."

"Dying?"

"Yes. She didn't just die, the way it happens with babies sometimes, when they get high fever, or something like that. She was dying slowly, like very old people with whom there is nothing really wrong, only they grow weaker and weaker every day. One night she stopped crying completely, all of a sudden. It was so strange, like when a clock stops ticking you know. And Mother cried, 'What happened to the baby? It's so . . . so quiet.' Then Jan got up . . . looked . . ."

"And what had happened?"

"It was all over."

"You mean . . . she was dead?"

"Yes, she was . . . dead."

"Oh, Fröken Stephania!"

"I guess it was better that way. I told you it was not a place for babies, the ghetto, and then a few weeks later, they took her — Rosa." She stopped, waiting. But this time they did not ask what it meant; they knew now, they remembered still.

"They took only her? And he?" Thura raised her head, looked at Stephania.

Stephania understood. "He wasn't with her, he was working. Rosa was not. She stayed at home, and cooked for all of us. If he had been there with her he could have done something, perhaps. Yes, I don't know how but I'm sure he could. He was that kind, you know, you just looked at him and couldn't help believe he could do anything. But he was not there; and when he came back it was too late."

— Too late, she thought. And perhaps Rosa even had passed her, in one of those trucks so crowded that the covers on them bulged on all sides, and sometimes a hand hung out, a leg —

[ 317 ]

suspended in the air as if belonging to no one. And they were big, those trucks, could hardly pass through the ghetto gate.

They were coming back from work then, and stood before the gate when the guards cried, "No one is allowed in." They stopped, an endless line of people stamping impatiently because it was cold and they all were hungry and tired. First no one understood what it meant. Then a whisper came, grew into a murmur, uncertain first, groping, until someone cried, "They are taking them, taking all who stayed at home — children, old people, all of them." Still they seemed not to understand quite what it meant and stood silently, staring at the trucks passing one after another their motors rattling shrilly, then disappearing in the heavy November mist. Still a truck, then another, the rattling died out in silence. The gate opened; it was over.

"You mean," she heard Thura saying, "that they had taken her already, that she was gone when he came back?"

"Yes, that was how it happened. I met him on the street and we ran home together. When we saw the window dark, we knew; still we kept hoping somehow. Then, I remember, we stopped before the door. We couldn't make ourselves open it. He did it at last and turned the light on. But no one was in, of course. Only the pot of potatoes was still on the table, and salt, spilled all over. And one potato was lying on the floor, the knife still in it, the skin half peeled hanging down in long rings . . . and . . ."

"And?" Thura repeated.

"It's not really important. Only then he, Jan, bent, picked up the potato, peeled it to the end, very slowly, and threw it into the pot so that the water splashed all over . . . but he said nothing, nothing at all."

"Were you and he . . . friends then?"

"Friends . . . yes, but not in the sense you mean it. That came later. He stayed with us, you see. But I never thought about him in *that* way, he just lived with us, that was all. But one day," she hesitated, "it's so hard to explain because nothing really happened, only it was as if then I noticed him — suddenly, differently. He forgot to take his papers with him, *Ausweis* we called it — something like a work card. I found it, rushed after him. It was in the morning, very early, around five perhaps, everybody was asleep still . . ."

— That was how it started — she thought. First the room, dark,

[ 318 ]

the sleeping figures spread everywhere, on beds, on chairs, on the floor even, motionless and breathing heavily, frightening. And the air stale, heavy with the smell of sweat, of many unwashed bodies. Then the staircase, dark too, littered with refuse, broken glass rolling from under her feet, and smells again — from the latrine, from the garbage pails. . . .

"What happened then?" Fröken Nilsson asked.

"I told you; nothing really . . . But somehow . . . it was dark, the streets were still empty. I could see nothing, not the houses or the walls, only the snow, white and fresh under my feet. Everything seemed so . . . so spacious suddenly, not like the ghetto any longer, and the air too felt fresh, crisp and clear. It was like in the summer when you suddenly come out of the city and into the country, into woods. I can't quite explain it, but it all seemed so important then . . . I just ran and ran, not because I was in a hurry, but because it felt so good to move fast with nobody around you. . . ."

"Did you find him?"

"Yes, he was still there in front of the work office. I found him at once, he was so tall you see."

"Yes, he looks very handsome in the picture."

"Handsome, yes, I guess so, but then it was something else. You couldn't help noticing him, not because he was good-looking though. You see, all of us were somehow crouched then, like people passing through a very low door or gate, bending their heads, watching out, scared. . . . But he was different, never scared — always straight, holding his head so high. . . ."

"Yes, yes, he really looks darling in that picture," Fröken Nilsson repeated.

Stephania did not hear her. "He stood there," she said, "without a cap, though it was cold, his hair very light, and the spade on his shoulder; he was working at shoveling snow then. But the way he was holding it, not like the others — bent as if they could not lift it — but easily, almost like in the picture, the skis."

"I see what you mean," Thura said.

"Then, when I saw him, everything seemed changed suddenly; I felt so light, so safe, as if it was all over — the war, the ghetto, everything, as if I'd come not to give him the work card but just to go for a long walk with him. I guess it doesn't make much sense to you, but that was the way I felt."

[ 319 ]

"Did you talk to him?" Fröken Nilsson's voice was slightly impatient.

"Not much. I just gave him the card, and he smiled. . . . But in the evening I waited for him in front of the house."

"Was he in love with you then?" Fröken Nilsson asked.

"In love?" Stephania repeated; she smiled. It sounded so strange to hear it called love — that which was between Jan and her; the word seemed too solemn, too big for it. It was — just sitting and waiting for him, and knowing that he too was waiting for her. Love? Perhaps it was, perhaps not, still, whatever it was, it was good.

"I don't know if he was then, or ever, even. Perhaps he just got used to me, living with us, seeing me every day. But I didn't know he cared for me until a few days later, when . . . when he brought me something."

"What was it?" Thura exclaimed.

"Nothing unusual, Thura dear, don't get excited. Just a doughnut."

"A . . . doughnut?"

"Yes, I know it must strike you as ridiculous. But we had almost no food then. There was plenty of it outside, in the city, but you were not allowed to buy any. It was dangerous even to walk into the store. But he did not care, just pretended he wasn't Jewish, walked into the store, and bought it . . . for me."

"How wonderful, Fröken Stephania," Thura whispered.

"It was not the doughnut that mattered, it was the way he gave it to me, just took my hand and put it into his pocket." . . . It was in the dark hall, she remembered, filled with old junk, high quarrelsome voices coming from everywhere. . . . "But then, with the rough touch of the tweed, warm with his body, with his voice saying, 'No, I don't want any, it's all for you,' everything became quiet, safe somehow."

"Even if it was only a doughnut, it was nice of him to buy it for you," Fröken Nilsson remarked; her voice passed into secret whisper. "Tell me, was there anything, anything serious between you?"

"What d'you mean?"

"You know."

"You mean, did I sleep with him?"

Fröken Nilsson only nodded.

"No," Stephania laughed sharply. "Never. But it was not because I didn't want to, Fröken Nilsson dear; please don't overestimate me, I'm not as virtuous as that. It was only because we never could be alone. Never," she repeated, the sharpness gone suddenly from her voice. She thought of those nights when she felt him lying so close to her, could see him tossing restlessly, could hear his breath. Sometimes she felt like reaching out, taking his hand in hers; but she couldn't, the others were always there, they seemed to be watching. "We couldn't even find a place where we could be alone quietly," she added.

"I know exactly what you mean." Fröken Nilsson shook her head sympathetically. "It was the same thing in my home when my friends came. My parents were old-fashioned people and they couldn't understand that times change. I always had to go to the park or someplace like that."

"The trouble was there were no parks in the ghetto, Fröken Nilsson. Not even trees, nothing but pavements and houses and people, people everywhere.

"No," she said after a while, "there was a tree in our back yard, an acacia I guess; it was hard to tell, bare as it was with only a few leaves on it, and half withered too. We went there sometimes, but someone was always already sitting there, and other couples stood waiting around. It was ridiculous," she said indignantly, as if the shame she had felt then returned when they stood under that tree, meager and crippled like a shabby decoration of a provincial photographer with other couples around, just one of them suddenly, not unique at all, not important any longer. "We stopped trying then, and sat on the staircase in a small niche."

— Those must have been the same stairs of which she dreamed after her quarrel with Fröken Nilsson — crooked, hardly lit by an oil lamp, the smell of cheap grease and of the latrine clinging to them, and voices; the sharp angry voices of tired people, heavy stamping, banging of doors coming from everywhere. But they did not mind it; it was good to sit together in the dark secluded corner, to talk almost in a whisper, as if trying by the softness of their voices to create some pretense at least of intimacy.

"What did you talk about, Fröken Stephania, d'you remember?" Thura asked eagerly.

"Let me think. About nothing special really; mostly how it would be after the war. He used to say, 'I'll meet you in freedom.'

[ 321 ]

In freedom — queer, wasn't it? As if it were a place one lives in. Or . . . perhaps it meant for us just that; a place; streets through which you could walk alone with no guards around you; and home, not crowded with hundreds of people, but real homes where you would have your own room, which you opened with your own key. Do you see what I mean?"

"Yes," Thura whispered, "of course."

"Or sometimes we would talk about how it used to be before, before the war. You see, his parents had had an estate once, and he used to ride horses, and go fishing and do all kinds of things like that. It was hard on him to be in ghetto, harder than on me, I guess. Sometimes he would say — 'I can't take it. I must get out of here.' He could have run away, I guess, but he did not."

"Because of you?" Thura asked.

"I . . . I think so. We got used to each other. Still it was terribly hard on him . . . to stay." And again she could see him, the way he used to look on these evenings together, when he sat bent slightly, his gaunt face hidden in his hands. And again she felt that tenderness for him, that pity almost, and fear too — fear because he could not take it, because he seemed so young to her suddenly, a boy almost. "Don't hide your face," she would say to him then, or, "Don't stoop like that." But she really did not mean it, she would just say it so that she could take his hands away from his face, pass her hand over his shoulder; so that she could touch him, tell him by those gestures how she felt — for it was too hard to do it with words.

"How long had you been with him?" Fröken Nilsson asked.

"Five months."

"Five month only?"

"Yes, he moved in in the fall, and in the spring they took him."

"*They* took him?" Thura cried.

"No, it wasn't what you mean. They only took him to a camp. It wasn't far from the ghetto, just a few blocks; I passed there each day going to work, I could see the barracks, the wires, but never him. He was so close, and yet . . . He might as well have been in another country."

"And later, did you see him again?"

"No, never."

"Not after the war, either?"

"No, not then either."

[ 322 ]

Fröken Nilsson said: "D'you mean that was all that had happened between you?"

"Yes, that was all," Stephania repeated. Her voice grew surprised, then sad, empty somehow. Yes, that was all — she thought — just a few months in which nothing really had happened. "I'm sorry, Fröken Nilsson," she said. "I should have warned you it wasn't going to be a great romantic story."

But then Thura raised her head, looked at Fröken Nilsson reproachfully, and her voice high, strained, she cried. "No! No, how could you ever say anything like that, Fröken Nilsson?" And then to Stephania, urgently, imploringly: "It was beautiful, so beautiful, Fröken Stephania. Everything — the way you met him that morning, and then he bringing you the doughnut, and what he said about meeting you in freedom. So beautiful, I just can't understand how you, Fröken Nilsson, could . . ." She hesitated, "Of course I know nothing about such things," she said slowly, "still it seems to me so much, all that was between you, so much, I just can't think how there could be more."

Stephania did not answer. Beautiful — was that what Thura had said? Perhaps it was. She felt the void that Fröken Nilsson's words had hollowed in her filling again with clear good certainty; it was beautiful, it was much — all those evenings together, and hands touching, and all the words they had once said, and the sudden silences.

"But why?" she heard Thura saying, "why didn't you see him again? I'm sure . . ."

"No!" Stephania interrupted her. She knew what Thura was trying to say and she did not want her to say it. "No," she repeated and then with sudden, pleading helplessness. "Don't you understand, Thura, how could I, the way I am now? I was different then; something was wrong with me already, but no one could see it. I was pretty then, Thura, really pretty, he always said how much he liked the way I looked. So how could he later?"

"But he liked you, so perhaps . . ."

"No, he couldn't take it, nobody could."

"Still, it seems to me, you should have tried, you shouldn't have been afraid."

"Afraid?" Stephania repeated. "Did you say afraid?"

"Yes, you were afraid to meet him, weren't you?"

After a long pause Stephania said, "I don't know, I've never thought of it that way." "You are too proud," Barbara had said and she had answered: "Proud? I have the courage to risk losing him." . . . And now Thura saying she was afraid. Was she right, Thura? Could you be proud just because you were afraid? That sounded strange, still . . .

"And he never tried to see you?" Fröken Nilsson asked.

"He did, many times. But he has been in Switzerland since the end of the war and I kept giving him all kinds of excuses why I couldn't meet him: that it was dangerous for him to come to Poland, that I couldn't leave . . . I thought maybe later, when things changed with me . . ."

"But he must know you're here. You wrote him from here, didn't you?"

"Oh no, I wrote but I mailed each letter to Poland first, to some friends, and they sent it to him."

"So he doesn't even know, that . . . that you haven't been well?"

"Of course not."

"Well," Thura said, "I don't know but . . . if you had tried perhaps . . . then . . ."

"What's the use of thinking like that: what might have happened, if . . . ? It's over, once and for all."

"Well," Fröken Nilsson said, "it's a pity certainly. He sounds like a nice fellow. But don't worry, there're plenty of men in this world. You'll find another."

"I hope so, if . . ." and again as before she corrected herself, hastily and with anger. "When I'm well again."

"Of course you'll be," Thura said.

And now suddenly they both looked at Thura. How could they have talked like that when she was here? Thura who never . . . I should say something to her, Stephania thought. Still she could not, she hoped Fröken Nilsson would say it, yet felt afraid of it.

But here was Fröken Nilsson saying: "You too Thura, one day . . ." She stopped.

Thura looked at them, first at Fröken Nilsson and then at Stephania quietly, inquiringly. "No," she said, "how could I, ever? I would like to, but I know it's impossible, and so . . ." her hand moved in a gesture that was both questioning and resigned.

"Well," Fröken Nilsson said, and murmured something they could hardly understand, something about God's verdicts and about not giving up hope. No one answered. "I guess I better go now, I've got to talk to William," she added, and rushed out of the room.

She shouldn't have left me alone, Stephania thought anxiously, feeling the desire rising in her to get up, to run out. But no, she couldn't do it. And now Thura said, "Of course I would like to be like everybody else, but . . . there's nothing I can do," and again her hand moved, soothingly, very quietly this time.

"Oh, Thura, it all seems so wrong, so . . . I just don't know what to say," Stephania whispered. She fell silent and sat looking at Thura's hand thinking, It's good she has that now, yes, that at least . . .

CHAPTER 24

THE WEDDING TOOK PLACE in the living room with all the doctors, nurses and patients from Ward Two present. Everything went smoothly. Fröken Nilsson looked very nice in her new beige suit, and the cakes and cookies provided by Willy met with general approval. Fröken Nilsson, or rather Fru Olsgård now, walked from one guest to another, shaking hands and beaming. And when Doctor Liliencrona came to her saying, "You certainly couldn't have found a better man," she looked right into his face and said firmly: "I certainly think so, Doctor." After the reception was over the couple left for Skåne, watched from all windows, followed by cheerful exclamations, by reminders to write, to take good care of themselves.

On the next morning Fru Gustavsson changed the linen on Fröken Nilsson's bed; it stood now clean and inviting, waiting for a new patient. But no one came; the ward was to be closed for the summer months at the end of May and except for emergency cases no new patients were taken in. The bed remained empty and whenever Thura or Stephania looked at it, it seemed to them that any moment the door would open, that Fröken Nilsson would come in.

"I wonder what Fröken Nilsson is doing now," Thura would say, and hastily correct herself, "Fru Olsgård, I mean." But somehow they could never think of her that way, they still could not quite believe that she was Willy's wife now, that she had left for good and would come back as a guest only, exactly like other visitors, burdened with packages, and rushing once the hour was over back to her own home.

And also the cards that regularly came from her — picture cards with the sea incredibly blue and the sky cloudless and even more blue — seemed to be written not by Fröken Nilsson but by a stranger, whose name only they had heard vaguely. They all said the same thing, those cards: that the weather was fine, that both she and Willy felt well and hoped Fröken Stephania and Thura felt well too. They read the cards carefully, said how wonderful it was that Fröken Nilsson liked it up there in Skåne: but silently they thought how strange it was that Fröken Nilsson was writing them, the same Fröken Nilsson who only a short time ago had been right here in their room, spent her days with them, and who now on the shore of that too blue sea was living among strange and distant people a strange and distant life.

"I can hardly wait for her to come back," Thura would say, and Stephania would nod in agreement, astonished herself by the gap that Fröken Nilsson's departure had left in their life. The days now, after the constant rush and excitement of preparations were over, grew long and dull again. Except for the brief visits of Doctor Ström and Sister Gudrun hardly anyone ever came into the room. Fru Gustavsson was transferred to another ward for a few weeks; the old man who had for four weeks taken Willy's place would without a single word put the paper on the table and leave. "Just wait for a couple of weeks when it'll be really warm," Thura consoled Stephania. "Then we'll go out on the terrace; it's so nice there, you can see the whole city, and the drive."

But they did not have to wait as long as that even; the first day of May was sunny and so warm that Sister Gudrun told the orderlies to take all the patients out on the terrace. Each bed close to the next, they lay there with their eyes half closed, feeling the sun touching their faces unexpectedly strong and warm, murmuring lazily how hot it was, a real summer day, and how fresh the air felt, so different from that in the room.

Stephania sat next to Thura, a book in her hands. Still she could not read; the gaudy brightness of the white asphalt, of the sky above her, the sun-filled air disturbed her and forced her to look around. She stared listlessly at the trees far down below, just very big green spots splashed heavily among the hospital buildings, at the smoke crawling up in thick, gray coils, growing thinner and thinner, until at last it melted tracelessly in the clear sky.

"Fröken Ackermann."

She looked over her shoulder. Sister Gudrun was standing in the door. "Yes?"

"Your sister is here."

"My . . . sister?"

"Yes, downstairs in the hall."

"But it's Monday, not a visiting day . . ."

Sister Gudrun shrugged. "I told her, but she insisted she must see you right now. So if you could sit with her somewhere in the park, I don't mind."

Stephania was not listening. "Yes, of course," she murmured absently and already she was hurrying through the terrace, opening the door.

— What could have happened? she thought, impatiently pressing the elevator button. Yesterday, on Sunday, Barbara had not come and now . . . She had not even bothered to explain anything: "I can't make it today," that was all she said on the phone.

Where was the elevator? Angrily she pressed the button again, thinking how strange it was that she had not minded it; she was relieved, glad almost, that Barbara was not coming. There was something about Barbara's visits that tired her out and left her with a restless feeling of discomfort, of anxiety. Barbara seemed so changed lately; there was a weary note in her voice, and sometimes she would talk feverishly and then lapse into silence and sit listlessly, only her eyes wandering around, as if searching for something. Still, when she had asked her once whether anything was wrong, Barbara shook her head angrily — no, everything was in good order; she was a little tired, that was all. But yesterday on the phone she sounded queer somehow, talking too loud and then putting down the receiver hastily, as if afraid Stephania might ask her something. And now coming suddenly, on Monday, in the middle of the day.

The elevator was here at last. She got in and stood counting impatiently the floors it was passing — fifth, fourth, God, how

[ 327 ]

slowly it moved. At last the elevator stopped, she got out and ran into the hall.

At first the hall seemed empty. Only after a while she saw Barbara standing at the very end, clinging to the window — as if she were trying to hide herself, looking so small suddenly in that shiny whiteness around her. "Barbara!" she cried, "what's happened?" Slowly Barbara tore herself away from the window. "Nothing," she murmured, "really nothing." She lifted her hand wearily. Stephania stood looking, following the movement of that hand, dirty with traces of smudge on it, passing first over the hair, then over the eyes, down to the chin; there it stopped covering part of the mouth as if trying to enforce silence. And suddenly, looking at that face, the eyes half covered by the lids, the lips clasped and narrow, she knew what it was, that change in Barbara; not the voice only, not the eyes, but everything about her — Barbara looked old. That thought was so incomprehensible, so frightening in its incongruity that Stephania had to turn her eyes away. "Let's go down to the park," she said. "The park . . . fine," Barbara answered absently. She began to walk, stiffly and heavily; the torn hem of her dress hanging awkwardly around her legs. There was something about that dress, ragged and dirty in spots, something so shabby, that Stephania felt the fear growing stronger and stronger in her. She could not wait any longer . . . grasped Barbara's hand.

"Tell me what's the matter, the way you look . . ."

"I'll tell you later, I want to sit down." And again they walked silently down into the park, green and filled with sun, the shadows dark, distinct on the yellow sand.

"Here?" Stephania pointed to a bench. Barbara sat down silently; with the heel of her shoe she began drawing figures in the sand, then erased them, until a thin yellow cloud rose in the air. And only after Stephania again grasped her hand and cried — "You must tell me now, what are you waiting for?" she hid her face in her hands, and started sobbing tonelessly; only the shaking of her shoulders told Stephania she was crying.

"What is it? The baby? Is he sick?"

Barbara shook her head.

"Did anything happen to Thadeus?"

Again only a denying gesture.

"For Heaven's sake tell me, what's wrong?"

[ 328 ]

"Everything," Barbara murmured, without taking her hands off her face, "everything. Oh, Stephania, I can't take it any longer." And now she was crying aloud, her whole body shaking, pressing her hands closer and closer to her face, as if she were trying to stifle the sobs and could not.

That is the first time I've seen her crying, Stephania thought. That too, like the thought of Barbara getting old, was incongruous, terrifying. She didn't care any more what had happened, she just wanted Barbara to stop crying. "Barbara, don't," she whispered, moving closer, putting her arm around her, stroking her hair. Until at last Barbara took her hands off her face.

"I'm sorry," she murmured, "I didn't want to, only . . ." She looked at Stephania as if waiting for her to finish.

"Is it Thadeus?"

"Yes."

"Did you quarrel?"

Barbara nodded.

"Oh, I see," Stephania said, with relief, almost with joy . . . because it was nothing worse, just a quarrel; and above all because now something that she had felt coming, felt hiding itself in those restless anxious visits of Barbara, something that she knew had to come, was here at last. "I see," she repeated, "but why? Was it something about his job again? Has he stopped working?"

"Yes, two weeks ago."

— Two weeks, and again she knew nothing about it. Stephania moved away slightly; she sat waiting.

Barbara understood. "I myself didn't know about it. Nothing at all, until a few days ago."

"You mean he didn't tell you?"

"Not a word. He left each morning and took his lunch with him, so . . . how could I know?"

"But why, why should he do it . . . and to you?"

"He didn't want to worry me. That's at least what he told me. I don't know if it's true. I don't know anything any longer."

"But how did you find out?"

"Just by accident. I met the engineer, the one who came to the party, you remember. He worked in the same place as Thadeus. 'What happened to your husband, did he quit the job?' he said to me. And here I stood, knowing nothing about it, just stared at him like a fool, and even said no, he must be mistaken, he was still

[ 329 ]

working every day. And then when he looked at me so queerly I began to guess something, and started telling him all kinds of nonsense, that I had misunderstood him, that of course I knew Thadeus had quit. But he could see through it, anybody could. You should have seen the look he gave me. And the way I felt, Stephania, the way I felt . . ."

"Did you tell Thadeus?"

"Yes, I only asked him, very quietly you know; I figured he must have had his reasons for not telling me, and besides I wasn't too worried, he still had hopes for that other job then, you see."

"What job was that?"

"The one for Gross."

"Oh, from Mr. Gross. Is he going to get it?"

"No, someone else got it. Gross kept calling each evening, kept telling Thadeus not to worry, it just had to take another day or two but the job was as good as his. Then all of a sudden he stopped calling. We found out through Genia he had given the job to someone else, to a cousin of his who had come from Poland. You can't imagine what it was for Thadeus; he always trusts people so much; Gross especially, he was so fond of him."

"Did he try to get anything else?"

"No, never. I don't know what happened to him then, everything went wrong, everything. People called up, Warszawska, Genia, and suggested all kinds of jobs he could try to get, gave him addresses, recommendations. But he wouldn't do anything, refused to talk to them even . . . just lay on the sofa all the day long, staring, saying nothing. First I thought he was sick; I asked him 'What's the matter with you, don't you feel well?' 'No, nothing's wrong, just leave me alone,' that was all he would say. And otherwise nothing, not even a word, as if I were not there at all." All the time Barbara's voice was quiet, almost indifferent. But now, abruptly, she turned to Stephania and whispered, "What shall I do, Stephania? You tell me." There was something childish about the way she asked, staring at Stephania, round-eyed, as if startled by her own question; but her lips remained as before — tight, bitter, old. "What shall I do?" she repeated.

That whisper, imploring and helpless, made Stephania grasp everything; made her understand what it must have meant to Barbara — that meeting with the engineer, saying, "Oh, yes, I just misunderstood you," and then listening to all those women — Genia

and Mrs. Warszawska — gossiping and feeling sorry for her. . . .
"What shall I do?" she heard Barbara saying again and again, and
to defend herself from the feeling of helplessness that had come
over her, she took out a kerchief and began to wipe off the smudges
from Barbara's face. Barbara smiled vaguely, apologetically. "I
was just in the middle of cleaning when I left and came here."
Left and came here — Stephania thought — came to me, just as
she used to come then, before Thadeus was with her, to me . . .
again. She did not know what to answer, but still she felt she had
to do something, that she could do it. "Wait, Barbara, just let me
think, I'll figure out something, I must," she said, just in order to
gain time. And already she knew, there was so much she could
do, so much. "I'll talk to Ström about some work for him, something he would like, or to Professor even, they know so many
people. They have so many connections." And when Barbara did
not answer, she went on, her voice lower and lower, a feverish
urgent whisper now: "Even if I'm here, in the hospital, I can do
something. You know I can. . . . Like that time after the war, you
remember, when you were so terribly depressed . . . I found us a
place to live and work for you . . . Just give me a little time. . . ."
   "Yes, of course, yes," Barbara nodded but her eyes remained listless and empty as if she understood nothing. And suddenly, just
as Stephania was saying she would sell her ring, so that they could
pull through the next few weeks, Barbara shook her head in dis-
agreement, in protest to something that Stephania could not understand at first, and cried, "He shouldn't have done it to me, he had
no right to treat me like that."
   He — Stephania thought, Thadeus — surprised somehow that
Barbara was still talking of him: to her he seemed so far away suddenly as if not with them any longer. "Don't you see? he can't
help being that way," she murmured soothingly. "He tries but he
can do nothing, you must understand it," she went on, feeling she
had to ask forgiveness for him, just because he was so helpless,
irresponsible, and childish, just because he seemed to matter so
little now, was not important at all. "Yes, you can't blame him
too much."
   "It's easy for you to talk," Barbara cried angrily, accusingly.
"You live so quietly here . . ."
   " 'Quietly,' you said?"
   "Yes, certainly, you have no idea of what's been going on at

home lately, of what I've been through. . . . Just look at me, the way I'm dressed." Barbara lifted her arm, showed the big clumsy patches. . . . "Do you think I enjoy it, going around like that? Other people notice it, don't think they don't; a few days ago Genia tells me, 'I've a couple of old dresses, would you like to try them on?' Do you think that was so pleasant? Still *I* can say nothing, I have no right to be depressed, it never occurs to him even that I too may be worried. . . . For me everything must be easy, going around in rags almost, and trembling at every mail that it may be a bill again, and all that work. D'you think he would ever help me at least? Never, I have to do everything myself — take care of the baby, cook, clean, shop. . . . Sometimes I feel so tired, I just can't wait for the evening to come. And he just lies there watching me, and wouldn't move even a finger to help me. . . . Don't tell me I can't blame him for that."

"Well, he just is that way." Stephania discarded Thadeus with a broad resigned gesture. What was the use of going back again and again to something that couldn't be changed? It was the plans — *her* plans for the future that they should be talking about now.

"He's that way — that's what I've been telling myself all the time. But how long can you be understanding, how long can you take life like that? And if he at least would listen to me, after all I too can think, can suggest something. But no, whatever I would say is wrong. Like with the bracelet today." Barbara stopped, turned away and without facing Stephania, said: "That was how it started today, with that bracelet . . ."

"What bracelet, what d'you mean?"

"The gold one I still have from Mother. There was not an öre at home, not a single öre. So I said to him, 'Take it and sell it, I don't need jewels now.' But he would not. For hours I pleaded with him, cried, shouted, but he just kept shaking his head, 'No,' and 'No, I won't do it.' I lost my patience, anyone would, I'm sure. 'If you won't do it then I will,' I said. I didn't even have money for the fare, had to take all the milk bottles to the store to get the ten öre. Then I went and pawned the bracelet, and really I didn't mind doing it, not at all. But later when I came back and found him lying on the sofa exactly as I had left him, something just started boiling in me. Still I said nothing; started scrubbing the floor. You know how it is with no hot water in the house, I had to drag one pail of water after another. And he saw it, he must have, and wouldn't budge, even. Then . . . then, Stephania, I said it, I just had to . . . but . . ." Barbara got up, plucked a twig, and began to tear off the leaves, one after another, crushing them in her fingers. It was all bare now and she let it fall out of her hands and sat staring at it silently.

"What happened?" Stephania felt an angry impatience rising in her.

"Let me think, Stephania, let me think. It all seems so terrible, suddenly. I thought that it was right, that I should have said it, but now . . . when I think of it again . . . I see . . . Oh, Stephania, I should never have done it to him, never. That he did not deserve, in spite of everything, anything but that . . ."

Somehow the tone of Barbara's voice, the look which she gave Stephania, absent, as if not noticing her at all, brought him, brought Thadeus back: he seemed to be right there with them, silent but insistent, accusing Barbara of something. "Whatever you said to him, you mustn't blame yourself," Stephania said fervently, trying to force Barbara to look, really look at her again. "You've been patient long enough, haven't you?"

"I know, Stephania, I know. Still I should never have said it. And his face, if you had only seen his face after that."

"What did you say to him?" Stephania cried. "Will you please tell me?"

"I don't understand how I could ever . . . I said . . . to him: 'A servant gets paid at least, but I have to do all the work and pay too.'"

"Barbara!" — So it had come to that already; but it wasn't Barbara's fault, it was his, only his. "Anyone in your place would have said the same," she exclaimed, "anyone, I know it."

"No, Stephania, I know I was wrong. And later . . . if he had hit me or yelled at me it would have been better. But he only looked at me, and said, quietly you know, 'You don't have to remind me, I know it only too well,' and he kept looking at me, not angrily, but somehow . . . I just can't tell you how. I couldn't take it and ran out, without thinking where I was going, just to get away from him. . . ."

Barbara got up abruptly, and that suddenness made Stephania feel deprived of something, alone. She looked at Barbara, trying in vain to make her stop, to come back and sit next to her. But Barbara kept pacing to and fro. Stephania said: "What's the point of all that blaming yourself, thinking over what you said and how you said it. You told him the truth, didn't you?" Stop worrying about him — she wanted to tell her, let's do something together. But there was silence around her and when she lifted her eyes she saw Barbara was walking far on the other side of the alley.

"I really have tried to be patient and understanding until now," Barbara said, coming back. "I never told him that I needed anything. Like when we go out for a walk I never stop before the store windows, so that he won't think I want something, that I would like to be well dressed like other women, like Luba or Mrs. Warszawska. I even tried to help, to do something myself, to go to work. Of course, I told Thadeus nothing about it, but I went to a children's home; they take in babies there for a whole day, even ones as young as five months old. I had almost made up my mind then. But then when I saw the place . . . it was clean and nice but still, all those strange people and the children behind the glass wall, as if they were in prison somehow . . . I just couldn't leave the baby there. I thought in a year or two perhaps I could but not now, not yet. . . . Perhaps I was wrong, perhaps I should have done it, lots of mothers do. . . . Still he would never let me do it, anyhow, so . . ."

"Barbara," Stephania cried, moving closer looking into her face. "Stop it, I can't listen to it any longer. I've tried to control myself all this time, but I can't now. . . . To leave the child among strangers just so that he could lie for hours on the sofa, and do nothing. Don't you see that he's lazy, lazy and selfish. I've seen it for a long time; still I tried not to say anything. I thought, it's your husband, your life . . . I have no right to meddle. And now since you came to me, yes, you *did* come to me . . . I thought for a while, now at last you too see it, and we shall do something together. . . . But now, all you do is reproach yourself, excusing him . . ."

"Stephania," Barbara said pleadingly. "You're too hard on him, you don't understand. He is not selfish, it's just that he cares so much for me he would like to do anything for me, give me everything. And now when he can do just so very little, he gets depressed and . . . It's like with Father during the war. . . ."

"Don't. Don't compare him to Father. That was war, everything was different then."

"Not as different as you think. He too is lost, he has no profession, no money."

"Other people are in the same boat, still they can do something, they know they are responsible for their families. And he . . ."

"He tries, don't you see? But he was used to such a different life, a first lieutenant in the army. But he has tried. It's only the last few days that he has not, but he will . . . again. And then, Stephania, you don't know, but sometimes when things just seem to be working out better, then . . ." Barbara stopped; she smiled that smile which Stephania knew so well, that smile which Thadeus had brought — soft and dreamy like her voice now, almost shameless in its complete secrecy and remoteness, "Then he can be so wonderful. Like on our wedding anniversary. He had no money then, but he borrowed some from Gross, and you know what it means to him to ask anyone for something. Still he did it and brought me a beautiful manicure set."

"A manicure set, that's just what you need, isn't it?" Stephania looked at Barbara's dress, at her shoes . . .

"But that was just like Thadeus. He would like me to have all those fancy things and so . . . That's what makes him so wonderful, don't you see?"

Stephania said nothing. Now it was she who sat crouched, her face hidden in her hands, trying by warmth of her own palms to defend herself from that feeling of complete aloneness growing vaster and vaster in her. Wonderful — maybe he was wonderful. How could she tell? She did not know those moments when he was like that, those moments at the thought of which Barbara was smiling now. Then they did not need her, then they didn't come to her. It was only when something went wrong that Barbara would come to her, not for help, not for advice even, but just to talk about him, all the time about him. . . Stubbornly she said, "I don't care how wonderful he can be. All I know is that he has no sense of responsibility and that he doesn't think of anyone but himself. He even won't help you when you're slaving by yourself all day long. You yourself said so, didn't you?"

"I did. But now when I think of it I can understand that. He feels so humiliated seeing me working so hard, he just can't face me."

"Don't give me that. That's too stupid, too ridiculous! Don't you see, don't you realize what he's doing to you?" She raised her eyes and looked at Barbara. She hesitated. Should she say it? . . . Yes, she had to for Barbara's sake, she had to open her eyes. "Look at

[ 335 ]

yourself," she said, her voice hard and accusing, "two years ago, before you got married, you were young and beautiful, and now . . ."

"Now?" Barbara nervously passed her hand over her hair, her dress. "Oh, I've neglected myself a little, that's all. The dress is old, the shoes . . ."

"I don't mean that."

"You mean that . . ." Barbara's lips moved limply, fearfully.

"Yes, I mean that you look old already; you, your face."

"No, you can't really mean that. Old . . . I'm hardly thirty now. Don't be ridiculous." And Barbara laughed shrilly, nervously. "It's just today, I don't look too well, I guess. I've been so upset, but otherwise . . ." She did not finish, but feverishly started rummaging in her purse, took out a mirror and looked. "Old? Nonsense, you make me laugh, really."

But Stephania did not answer. She kept indicating with her eyes each wrinkle, each shadow.

Barbara put on lipstick, powdered her nose, and smiled — a careful elaborate smile showing her dimples, her strong white teeth. "It's better already. I told you I was just tired."

And was it the touch of rouge, or the hair, combed, again surrounding her face by two thick golden frames, or that smile perhaps? — for now Barbara seemed changed suddenly, shining, beautiful — and young. "It's better," Stephania said, reluctantly, hastily, thinking, What should I say to her, how can I make her understand? I have to be quiet, very quiet so that she won't think it's for my own sake. . . . And lowering her voice to subdue its sharpness, unwanted but persistent she said, "Barbara, listen to me, just once, just this time . . . And then if you think I'm wrong, I promise never to talk about it again, never to interfere . . ."

"You're not interfering, just go ahead, say anything that's on your mind."

"Look, I don't want you to stop caring for him, to quarrel and make scenes. I just want you to see him clearly the way he really is, so that you can do something about it. . . ."

"You don't think I see him clearly?"

"No, Barbara, how can you? You met him, a dashing lieutenant, in uniform with medals, with a hero's halo around him. You thought he was like that, energetic, strong — oh, you know what I mean. And now in spite of all you've seen you still believe that

[ 336 ]

only some kind of a miraculous chance is needed and he'll again be . . ."

"As in the beginning I thought he was — energetic, strong, heroic," Barbara repeated slowly, mockingly.

"Yes, exactly, and . . ." Stephania looked at Barbara and fell silent. Why did she smile like that, why did she repeat those words, so strangely, so scornfully? . . . And the way she looked now, a new Barbara suddenly, one she had never seen before, a full-bodied woman with a face neither sad nor joyful, just very quiet, remote. . . . Was it, no, it was impossible, it could not be . . .

"You don't mean," she murmured, "you can't mean that you've known it from the very beginning, known he was quite different from the way he looked."

"Of course I knew."

"And still . . . you married him?"

"Why not?"

Stephania got up. "I see," she nodded, "I see." — So that was it, she thought — and here she had spent years with them, talked to them, watched them, and knew nothing about them, not even about Barbara. . . . Trying to open her eyes, to make her see him clearly, and Barbara all the time living with that knowledge, loving him in spite of it. . . . In spite? Was it in spite or perhaps just because of it, just because he was like that, weak, irresponsible, childish, just because she had so much to forgive him?

"Stephania."

"Yes?" she said wearily.

"I'm sorry, dear. I didn't want to upset you. I just had to talk to someone; things seem so much easier when you talk them over. But don't worry. We'll figure it out somehow, Thadeus and I. . . . He will get used to life here; all he needs is some more time. So don't worry."

"I won't worry."

"And thanks for listening to me. I really feel better now." Barbara glanced at the clock. "Heavens, it's almost six. Thadeus won't know what's happened to me. I better rush. And I'll explain everything to him. He'll understand, I know it. He . . ." Barbara did not finish. The bus came into the drive, and she was running, shouting from afar already, "Good-bye, dear, see you Sunday."

Stephania stood looking after her. She saw Barbara get on the bus, sit down next to the window, comb her hair. The bus moved, vanished down the drive.

Slowly she began to walk through the park, where dusk was falling, silencing the clamoring green of the trees, spreading the dense shadows further and further until everything was dark and very silent. Soon Barbara will be at home, she thought, opening the heavy hospital gate.

"Your brother-in-law called," Sister Gudrun stopped her when she was passing the hall, "ten times if not more. Asked Fröken to get in touch with him at once." In a reluctant murmur she added something about people who cannot understand that a hospital is not a private place, that one cannot be bothered constantly there. "Of course, I'm sorry," Stephania nodded, already rushing to the phone. The line was busy. She waited for a while and dialed the number again.

"Is that you, Stephania?" Thadeus' voice said.

"Yes, I heard you called me."

"I've been trying to reach you for the last two hours. Tell me, do you know where she is?"

"Who?" she said calmly, knowing only too well for whom he was asking.

"Barbara. Don't you know? I was sure she went to see you."

"She was here, but she left."

"Do you know where she's gone now?"

Slowly Stephania said: "I guess home."

"Home? Are you sure? Thank God. I was going out of my mind. How long ago did she leave?"

"About twenty minutes ago."

"So she should be back soon, any moment." He said nothing more, but somehow she could feel him, see him standing at the other end of the line, nervously passing his hand through his hair, preparing himself . . . At last he asked, "Did Barbara tell you any-thing?"

"Tell me about what?" she said, knowing she should have spared him that question; still she had to ask it, and now stood listening to how hesitantly he cleared his throat, how he said at last, "We had an argument, you see."

"Yes, she told me about . . . the argument."

[ 338 ]

"Was she terribly upset?"

"You can hardly expect her to be happy about it."

"Oh, Stephania, it was all my fault, only mine." He was talking loudly now, almost shouting in a high breaking voice. "She must have told you everything so there's no use for me to repeat. . . . I just want you to know, to understand that I didn't want it. It just happened, you see."

She said nothing.

"You understand?"

"Perhaps, I don't know," she said cautiously.

"It's so hard to explain, Stephania. Sometimes when I see her working so hard, I feel she must hate me, despise me. I can't stand being with her then, I . . ."

"I understand, Thadeus," she said, just in order to silence him, to silence that anguished piercing voice.

"You do, Stephania? I knew you would. You know, I wasn't like that before, during the war. Everything was different somehow. Perhaps I've changed, perhaps everything else has changed, but then if you weren't afraid, if you knew how to take a risk you could do anything . . . and now . . . Tell me what I can do, Stephania? Tell me!"

—Leave me alone, she wanted to cry, everything is hard enough for me, without your problems, your worries. What did they want from her, first Barbara, then he, throwing all the burden upon her and then leaving her alone with it, going back to their own life . . .

"If only once someone could help me, only once, because alone . . . I can't do anything, Stephania, I know I can't," Thadeus said.

Alone? He has Barbara, hasn't he? Or perhaps . . . sometimes Barbara wasn't enough, sometimes just Barbara could do nothing. No, it was all nonsense, why should they drag her into all this? I don't know, she wanted to say, but the receiver in her hand seemed to grow heavier and heavier. The expectant silence forced her to speak. "I'll think about it . . . I may try to talk to Ström," she said, said it without knowing why, without wanting to.

"To Ström? You think he . . . wait, the doorbell is ringing, that must be her, Barbara . . ." On the other side of the line the receiver fell down with a heavy bang. "Barbara," she heard him crying . . . then silence. For a while she stood waiting, then put the receiver down, and walked back to the room.

[ 339 ]

So now they were together, she thought, talking or perhaps standing silently, just looking at each other, until both at once would cry, shamefully and helplessly — I didn't want it, it was all my fault — No, mine.

And then everything will be fine again, for weeks, even for months; until again something would happen and again Barbara would come to her, or Thadeus for a moment only — just for a short moment. That's how it is — she thought — that's how it will always be, but somehow she did not mind it too much.

CHAPTER 25

THE HEAT CAME like the snow in the winter — unexpectedly. One day when they woke up, the sun, mild and tender until then, fell heavy and scorching upon their faces, the leaves on the trees behind the window seemed limp and withered for all their greenness, and the sky too looked faded — almost white. "It can't last too long, weather like that; after all it's only May," the patients reassured each other. But the heat remained, stubborn and unrelenting. Day after day sticky oppressive air hung over the room; sharp rays pierced through the green curtains, swallowed the last remnants of shade, made the linen on beds feel soggy and coarse. And even the nights were hot, as if the sun was still there hiding, invisible but reckless in the darkness, and the smell of acacias and lilacs streaming with the windless air through the wide-open windows was heavy with overripe sweetness.

The patients lay in their beds, hardly covered by the tousled sheets, their hair, glued with sweat, hanging in thin lusterless streaks. "Hot," they murmured reproachfully, turning the pillows, trying in vain to force them to feel cool and smooth for a while at least. They hardly ever spoke to each other, just lay half asleep, moving only to drink some of the lukewarm stale-tasting water. The silence grew deeper and more immobile than ever, and sometimes it seemed as though there was no one in the long row of white sun-flooded rooms.

But suddenly one morning strange confused noises penetrated into the rooms — the gritty sound of scrubbing brushes, brisk rushing steps. "It must be the spring cleaning," patients who had been in the hospital last year said. "So it's started already."

Yes, it began now, the great spring cleaning that each year preceded the closing of the ward for the summer. Fru Gustavsson came back, more breathless, more hectic than ever, and changed, not in her usual white coat, but in a blue duster with a red kerchief perched crookedly over her sweaty face. Maids and orderlies from other wards came with her and kept rushing from room to room bent under the piles of linen and blankets, mercilessly stripping the polka-dot curtains from the windows and the covers from beds. The rooms looked empty, strange suddenly.

And all the time beds kept rolling through the hall, as if the "great day" had come to the whole ward at once. They looked bare and desolated without the shiny whiteness of linen, the faded mattresses displaying shamefully the many spots, the tufts of hair sticking out here and there. For most of the patients were leaving, some only for the summer months, others for good. Those who stayed had been put in one large room on Fru Gustavsson's side, and waited there to be transferred to other wards. Only Thura and Stephania were still in their own room. "The year before we stayed here until the very end. It's because our room's the last in the hall, they won't clean it until much later," Thura explained, and she added quickly, "We really have nothing to worry about."

"Of course not," Stephania answered; still she felt anxious; why did Thura say that — we have nothing to worry about?

And the anxiety grew as patients kept coming into their room to say good-bye, as they said shyly, "You two are staying here, aren't you? Do you know in which ward you're going to be?" "No, we don't know, not yet," they answered, and Thura would add promptly, "But they'll tell us soon, I'm sure," until at last Stephania forcing a smile said to Sister Gudrun, "I feel we're going to be homeless this summer. No one seems to be thinking much about us." She looked at Sister Gudrun, waiting.

"Doctor Ström will tell you everything. At the beginning of next week, I guess," Sister Gudrun said, and she left.

"She's terribly busy," Thura said.

Stephania said nothing.

And now Monday was here. Early in the morning Fru Gustavs-son took Thura out on the terrace. Stephania followed them. She sat next to Thura looking at the almost empty terrace, only a few beds clinging eagerly to the small patches of shade. So they were all gone now — she thought. That time when Barbara came, it was so crowded here she could hardly make her way through all the beds and wheel chairs, and that was only two weeks ago. Strange, how long ago it seemed, that day of Barbara's unexpected visit, perhaps because so much had happened since then. First there was the tightening of the cast, then the many X-rays taken suddenly, and then Thadeus started working down in the ortho-pedic workshop. It certainly was decent of Ström to get him in there, and Thadeus seemed quite satisfied now. The work was not too bad, nor the salary either; one could more or less live on it. Still, last week he had not come to work. "He had a bad cold," Barbara had said on the phone; but that was not true, of course. It must have been too much for him again — the long hours he had to spend in the small stuffy room, the jokes of Herr Johansohn, always pointless and always the same, and the people who came there, complaining about the wooden legs that wouldn't fit, about the heavy corselets that they couldn't stand.

Still he came back at last, and now it looked as though he was going to stay. That was good, she thought, thinking about Bar-bara, quiet again, the harassed look almost gone from her face. And Thadeus? It was good for him too, he would get used to work at last. Still, she couldn't help thinking how he sat there bent among all the piles of leather and wood, the gray overall ill fitting, as if not his, the slender womanly wrists sticking out of the too short sleeves. And the way he talked, laboriously forming clumsy Swedish sentences, and smiling, as though apologizing for some-thing. It was better that way — she repeated to herself. But again and again she had to remember him — the Thadeus of two years ago — so graceful in his immaculate uniform, tossing his hair in a nonchalant gesture, laughing a free easy laugh. The remem-brance hurt, as if something had come to an end too early, too suddenly . . .

"Fröken Stephania," Thura whispered, "Doctor Ström is here. Maybe today . . ." She stopped because Ström was already standing at her bed.

"Good afternoon, Thura, how are you? Working hard on a hot

day like this?" He looked at the embroidery stretched upon wooden frames so that she could work on it with only one hand. "My, my, you are quite a master."

"Oh, not at all, Doctor."

He sat down staring at her silently. "You certainly are tanned," he said after a long while, "as if you came straight from the beach."

Thura smiled uncertainly and again there was silence.

Until he said: "The sun's good for you, Thura, you should have plenty of it. Up in Oestrsund, at your home I mean; you have a garden, don't you?"

"Yes, it's not too big, but . . ."

"That's fine, you should sit there a lot, when you're back at home."

"At . . . at home?"

Ström nodded. And then, moving closer to her as if afraid she would not understand him, he began to explain that everything had been arranged already — that Thura's mother would be waiting for her in Gävle, and that the trains were very comfortable — she had nothing to worry about. Thura stared at him, her lips opening and closing noiselessly as if she were trying to say something and could not. "You mean, you said . . . I should go home?" she murmured at last.

"Yes, Thura, you're going home. Aren't you glad about it?"

"Glad? Oh . . . oh yes," and then, very quickly, "but I'll come back here in the fall?"

Ström got up. He plucked an ivy leaf from the wall, and with the back of his hand brushed the film of dust off it. "No, Thura, you aren't coming back here."

She did not answer, only her eyes, wide open, wandered to her hand, that other hand still lifeless, lying motionlessly on the bed. His eyes followed hers. "We can do nothing more, Thura. We tried everything we could, but . . . it hasn't worked, and so . . ." And when she kept staring at him, only nodding silently, he went on, telling her how glad she should be to move one hand at least, and how you could always hope for a change, not soon, but later perhaps. "So Thursday, you'll go home, Thura," he finished.

"Yes, Doctor." She was nodding still, as if she had forgotten to stop. And only when Ström was already in the doorway, she suddenly lifted her arm. "Doctor!"

[ 343 ]

"Yes, Thura."

"But I . . . I thought . . . No, nothing, Doctor." The door closed.

Thura sat motionless. Then slowly her face grew flushed, drops of sweat gathered in the deep furrows on her forehead. Stephania looked at her; she remembered it, remembered the clenched teeth, the lips parted. . . . So Thura was trying again, forcing that other hand to move in spite of all he had said. She waited. But when the heavy panting came, she got up, put her hand on Thura's and said, "Do stop, you heard what he said."

"Yes . . . I heard." Her voice was surprised as if she suddenly remembered something. Stephania sat next to her, trying to say something, groping for words desperately and in vain. Thura too was silent, sitting erect, propped high upon the pillows, her face old and stern. And her voice too was stern when at last she said: "I don't want to go home."

"But Thura, you always said how much you wanted to go, you remember?"

"I know, but now I don't want to go."

"But don't you see? Even with one hand you can do a lot, and in a way, yes, in a way you're lucky — it's the right one, so really it doesn't make so much difference, I mean . . ."

"It makes no difference."

Stephania looked at her.

Thura said, "It's all the same, one hand or both, all the same. Makes no sense."

"But I don't understand, what do you mean?"

"Everything, don't you see, everything makes no sense at all."

"You're upset now, Thura, that's why you feel this way. And besides, you heard, didn't you, what Ström said — that there's always hope . . . ?"

"He didn't mean it, he just said it."

"But Thura, look, he never . . ." She stopped; Thura wasn't listening; she sat staring at the wall before them.

Suddenly she turned. "I can't go home," she said. "I can't, I'm afraid."

"How can you be afraid? Just think of your parents, they'll be so happy to have you back."

"No, they won't. It is better for them not to see me, not this way I am now."

[ 344 ]

"Perhaps in the beginning it'll be a little difficult for them, but then once they get used to it, it will be easy."

Thura was not listening again. For all she answered was, "No, I don't want to go back. It is not right. It is not right to be the way I am, it makes no sense."

She shook her head and fixing her eyes upon Stephania said: "I know it, I just know it now."

Somewhere a clock struck. One, two, three — Stephania counted. "Thura," she said, "I must go now . . . down . . . to see my brother-in-law. I promised him to meet him at three. But I'll be back soon." She crossed the terrace and opened the door. It slammed with a loud bang. I should open it and close it again, she thought. Still she did not do it.

Down in the park it was quiet this afternoon. They were still there, as always filling the benches, the alleys. But the too bright dresses hung flabby and crinkled, the voices seemed stifled by the dense air. She walked past them very fast, her eyes fixed high above their heads, found an empty bench and sat down.

The hospital building was right opposite her, and there on the top was the ivy-covered wall, the terrace, and she — Thura. What was she doing now? Embroidering perhaps, quietly watching the chubby flowers grow with each stitch. Had she only not been so quiet; the way she had said it — "I don't want to go back" — and then — "It makes no sense, I know," calmly and easily, as if she had known it for a long time, always perhaps. And even if she did go back, even if she was there in her home in Oestrsund seated in her wheel chair, uncomplaining, smiling shyly and gratefully, even that would not matter much. Because all the time, she would know that it all made no sense, that it was not right to be like that.

"Pardon me, do you mind if I sit here?"

She raised her head. The face before her was pretty, a small mouth painted skillfully in a heartlike shape, blond curls piled high above the forehead. But then she saw it — the neck bent as if in a gesture of exaggerated humility, the body under the bright cotton twitching and wriggling.

"Not at all, do sit down."

The girl stepped forward, stumbled, moved back, and now she stood with her hands clenched, trying to enforce obedience upon

[ 345 ]

the wilful discordant limbs. At last groping and grasping in the empty air, she sat down. "It's a bit hard." The girl smiled apologetically. She started opening her book, the pages evading her maliciously, the fingers pursuing them with eager helplessness until they held them — bent, clawlike — triumphant.

What could be wrong with her? Cerebral palsy, probably or whatever the name for it was. . . . They always found some fancy name for it, so that you would not really know what it meant to be like that — contorted, shaking, struggling for each step, each gesture. And it was that, yes, that kind of life they were trying to force upon Thura; all of them — Ström, Professor, and she herself, Thura's great friend, she above all.

A life like that?

No, it was worse, incomparably worse. Never, not even in her boldest dreams, could Thura hope to become like that twisted, wriggling creature, like the rest of them here. They here were the chosen ones, the élite of the cripples; that was why they had been granted the privilege of coming here. They could still move, no matter how clumsily; their hands could work at least. But Thura had to go home, there was nothing that could be done for her.

And all that time the people here had appalled and frightened her. How could they stand it? she kept asking. But it had never occurred to her to wonder how she, Thura, could stand it. As if Thura was fine, as if Thura had nothing to worry about. Of course she had known it, known from the day she came here, how it really was with Thura. But she managed to pretend to herself that she knew nothing; she stayed with Thura day after day, as if not noticing that she was always tied to her bed, not able to take so much as a step. It was all lying — lying and pretending, all the time.

And now again she did it, the very same thing. How could she ever have told Thura that it would be wonderful to go back home, back to those people who were afraid of her, pitying her. A fine life waited for her there, just glorious — with nothing to do, nothing to wait for. Stuck — like a fly in marmalade.

Stuck, and nothing changing, never. Even her going home was no change at all. The room perhaps would be different, the faces around, but otherwise all would be the same, exactly the same as it had been here, during all those years. A good year, wasn't it, that Thura and she herself, too, had spent in Room Five? Nothing ever to worry you, because nothing ever really happened; it was just a blank, that year here, something shapeless and senseless, and living through it was like wading through thick sticky glue day after day, month after month. You did not have to exert yourself at all; you did what? — eat and sleep, not because you were hungry or tired but simply because it helped to kill time. Killing time — that was what that year amounted to. And if one lived just for that, one might as well do it efficiently, wholesale. Thura was right — it made no sense, no sense at all. And if she had any honesty left, she would get up now, go back to Thura and tell her that. But of course, she was still sitting here quietly, as if she could figure out something.

But was it possible? Was there nothing in all those years, or at least in that year they had been here together? Hadn't there been moments at least, when it stopped — the constant glancing at the clock, the waiting for lunch, for dinner, for the evening to come at last?

Perhaps — she hesitated, not knowing yet what it meant, that thought, vaguely rising within her — yes, perhaps the nights, they were different, those nights when they talked. . . . Then they forgot about the clock, about Ström's visits; then it was gone, the futile languid waiting.

No, she shook her head angrily, how could they mean anything, those nights? Different? Certainly, they stopped being bored then when they kept dragging out all the filth, all the emptiness of their lives. So no wonder it was interesting, that washing of dirty linen in public, a nice tickling sensation sometimes even slightly tinged with sex. A better way to kill time, that was all, nothing to get lyrical about.

Still, could it be that only? Because there was also that feeling — she almost could sense it again now — a great quietness, almost the same that comes after a long day when at last you lie in the cool soft linen, and the weariness leaves your body in lazy streams, until at last it comes — the ease, the relief. Relief — that was the feeling of those nights. It came first on that night after Fröken Nilsson's "great day," when she started talking suddenly, still half in the morphine-sleep. And one felt it — not because time was moving faster at last, no, that could not have been the reason. . . . It was because . . . yes, just because Fröken Nilsson could talk like that, could sob it out: "I've lied to you," and, "It has always been wrong, always." Somehow it seemed that these words had been hidden not within her only, but within you, too; had stuck in your throat, and now at last you were freed from them. That was why it came — the relief. And it grew as Fröken Nilsson went on talking, as she threw it all in their faces — it grew as the words came easier, as her voice stopped groping fearfully.

She bent and hid her face in her hands, trying to chase away those thoughts, persistent, unwanted. It was all nonsense, bluff. There was a better name for that relief: masochistic joy; yes, that put it much clearer. She simply enjoyed herself listening to Fröken Nilsson, because here at last was someone whose life was as bad a mess as hers, or even worse. Obviously she had to follow each word with such relish — it made her feel so much better, pure, lily-white by comparison.

"Pardon me." The girl got up and walked off, hovering in a joyless abandoned dance, her stumbling feet raising a dense pillar of dust. She watched her disappear behind the trees, and then sat motionless, the sun hot and drowsing on her face. Her eyes closed, she felt very tired suddenly. What had she been thinking of? Thura, Fröken Nilsson: there was no use worrying about it, no use worrying about anything. And it felt good to sit like that, unthinking, quiet, to rest for a moment at least.

But somehow thoughts kept coming, vague and confused now — pictures, voices: the room dark, only the light above the door spreading webs of narrow veins upon the walls; then the smells — eau de cologne, ether, and something sickly sweet — was it blood? And she herself sitting on the edge of her bed, trying to move closer to the vague shape opposite her, listening. . . . No, it was not really listening either; it was as if everything Fröken Nilsson was talking about was happening all over again, right then. First the mother — what was it she said — paralyzed, like a clog of wood . . . always thirsty. . . . And you saw her; the old gray-faced woman, stretched upon the untidy bed, mumbling all the time, hoarsely, and with anger; sucking greedily the seltzer right out of the bottle, and the water trickling down the sunken jaws, the chin . . . And Fröken Nilsson next to her, watching her, waiting, always waiting for the end to come at last.

Then Kale — "He was so short I was ashamed to show myself with him on the street." And again they were there, Fröken Nilsson huge, monstrous, looking around furtively, and he shrunk and withered, hanging at her arm, and bald, "bald as a knee." Even the night, yes, that too you had to see, though you at first didn't want to, it was too much: the cats sneaking on the cracking stairs, then the cockroaches swarming in the glare of the bare bulb, then the bed. . . . It must have been terribly filthy, the bed and the sheets torn, holes everywhere and the mattress sticking through them, greasy, scratching the body. . . .

The more she talked the more senseless it all grew, that whole life of Fröken Nilsson's — and she herself too, a liar, and foolish, and greedy. Still you didn't mind it, it didn't matter somehow and if it did, then in a different way. It was as if before you saw glimpses only . . . Fröken Nilsson stuffing herself with food, Fröken Nilsson saying, "He is so interested in me, Doctor Liliencrona," or screaming with fool's cruelty: "You foreigners have everything!" But then, that night you saw it all, and everything seemed to fit together, the lies, the stupidity, Kale, Doctor Liliencrona and the mother that wouldn't die. You knew it was all wrong, you knew Fröken Nilsson should have tried to do something, should not have let herself be pushed around by everybody, should not have gone to bed with the first man she ran into. Still, all the time you knew also that — that it had been hard for her, so hard that you could not judge her, never, could not even blame her much.

The sound of voices came to her, heavy stamping, and giggles. "There's plenty of room here, now hold my crutches, Lasse, come on, don't knock me down."

Three of them came and sat down right next to her. She got up and started walking the sand, dry and hot rustling softly under her feet.

And even if they had listened, what good had it done? Certainly it did not help Fröken Nilsson much, their lying there without saying a word to her, so that she could forget or feel better at least. But what was there to say? Could she have pretended that it all did not matter, Kale and the night with him, so pitiful, so shabby, could she tell her that from now on everything would be better in spite of the bandages bulging where her leg once was? Thura, in the beginning, had tried to console her, but Fröken Nilsson would not even listen, and got angry as if Thura were laughing at her. She felt that Thura was lying, in order to console her, but still lying.

[ 349 ]

No, it somehow never worked when people tried to make you feel better and had to lie because there was no other way to do it. Like Barbara, that time before the party. "You look so lovely, Stephania," she said, "in that dress one can hardly notice anything." And even if you knew Barbara meant it well, you could not answer, you had to walk out of the room. Was it anger? No, it was something else — shame. For you knew why Barbara lied: because she was ashamed of her own beauty, of her health; ashamed she could do nothing for you. And her shame made you feel guilty, because it was you had caused it: and also it made you see clearly, terribly clearly, how different, how much better Barbara felt than you. Her shame made you worse. No, that kind of consolation could never work.

So perhaps it was better, after all, only to listen. The silence in a way meant that they could take what Fröken Nilsson was saying, meant they did not feel themselves better than she. It was as if by saying nothing they actually were telling her, Go on, Fröken Nilsson, don't you see? we're not ashamed, so you don't have to be either.

Yes, Fröken Nilsson must have understood it somehow, for she had told them everything, all the truth about herself. For the first time in her life she did it. It must have felt good to speak it out at last, to hear said out loud all that had been growing more and more frightening in the silence within her. She herself had felt it too, then, when she told them about Father. Not that it made you feel better, less guilty, when others agreed to listen; still . . . it made you feel less alone perhaps. You thought if they could take it, if they still did not change toward you, then perhaps they had some kind of faith in you in spite of everything. They knew now what you were like and still could be with you.

She must have felt it too, Fröken Nilsson. For even if soon she was her old self again, lying to herself and to others, foolish, ashamed of what she really was, still, when she did not know what to do about Willy she came to them. "I almost ran away when I saw him crawling like that," she said; she knew they would understand, would try at least. And they did. It was Thura who really understood, who knew what to say this time. "If you care enough for him," she had said to Fröken Nilsson, "you won't run away." That helped, perhaps.

That was strange, she thought suddenly. How could Thura know what to say then, she who had never lived, who had never yet learned what it meant; the fear, the shame that forced one to run away, the guilt one felt afterwards? Still she understood, as if just by listening, just by watching in that quiet way of hers, she had lived through it, had learned. . . .

Thura — now she was still there, on the terrace, waiting for her to come back. And she had nothing to tell her. Unless . . . yes, unless that had meant something, the nights, the year here. It seemed different, the year, once you remembered those nights; not easier, it was still a hard, a bitter year; but nevertheless it acquired some kind of shape, of sense of its own. Now you could say, This happened before the night when Fröken Nilsson talked, that after it. And the "before" and the "after" differed from each other, as if something had happened in the meantime, as if things had been changing, changing even if you were always in the same room, enclosed in a cast or struggling on crutches, or even . . . yes, even if you always were tied to bed. . . .

She stood at Thura's bed watching her hand sticking the needle into the piece of linen, the flower on it so much bigger now than it was when she had left.

Thura spoke first: "How's your brother-in-law, Fröken Stephania?"

"Fine, thank you."

"That's good." Again the needle moved; the thread in it was many colored, passing from purple to white, and she stared at it, wondering if the next stitch would be red, or pink perhaps.

"Is he satisfied with his work?" Thura asked.

"Yes, he is." She stopped, moved closer to her. "Thura."

"Yes, Fröken Stephania?"

"I did not see him."

"Oh, you missed him, isn't that a pity?"

"No, I didn't miss him, I . . . didn't go to see him, didn't mean to."

"Oh." The needle hesitated and then moved on imperturbably.

"I just walked around trying to think about what we were talking of, what you said." And when Thura was still silent she sat down, very close to her. "I thought I could figure out something, Thura. You can't go home and think the way you do now, don't you see, you just can't. There must be some way that it would make sense somehow. I don't know what myself, but there must be, Thura."

[ 351 ]

The needle stopped at last. And now Thura was looking at her, comprehending in a careful and exacting glance Stephania's body, her legs, her hands. Stephania moved away. "No," she said, "Thura, I know what you mean, I know you think I have no right to talk, that I'm so much better off, but . . ."

"You are, aren't you? And soon you will be operated on and then . . ."

"Yes, but . . ." She stopped because it was the first time she had said it aloud, knowingly, and that startled her. "But I too, I don't know what's going to happen — it doesn't seem so simple now, Thura."

"I'm sorry, Fröken Stephania, I shouldn't have said it. But it's because of everything that has happened today, it all came so suddenly."

"I know, Thura, I really do. But look; when I was thinking, trying . . ." She stopped again; what was it that she had to tell her? something about the year and the three of them, but she remembered nothing, she had nothing to tell her. . . . And desperately looking at Thura, afraid that at any moment she would again pick up the needle and turn away, Stephania blurted out, blindly, not understanding herself what she was saying: "I really don't know what to say, Thura. I really don't only — only, don't you see — we are going to miss each other, aren't we, Thura?"

"Yes, Fröken Stephania, you know I'm going to miss you, but . . ."

"You see, I don't quite understand it myself, but look: if we could, can mean so much to each other, we two and then Fröken Nilsson too, then that shows something; it must. It means that it was not just senseless, that year in here, not just doing nothing, but there was something, not much, but enough to bring us together, to make us feel the way we feel now."

"Perhaps, Fröken Stephania. I don't understand quite what you mean."

"It's hard to explain it, Thura. Only I think that it must be something like a hint, a sign that there too at home you'll find some people — not many perhaps but some still — You remember you said that there must be another way. And maybe that . . ."

"Yes, I did think so once. But now . . . it all seems so hard, so terribly hard, Fröken Stephania."

"It is, Thura, I know. But you must try, you must do that at least. Try to see if perhaps there's another way. I'm not promising you anything; maybe there's none. But we don't know, and so you just have to try."

"Perhaps . . . perhaps a little later, when I get used to being the way I am. Then I will. Because," she smiled, both apologetically and a little mockingly too, "because what else can one do, after all?"

"Yes," Stephania said, "what else but that — try."

Fru Gustavsson came in, Thura's dress, the dress in which she had come, which had been for three years in the storage room, in her hands. "Here, Fröken Stephania, would you mind helping her? I'm in such a rush."

No, Stephania did not mind.

She took the dress and looked at it. It was dark blue with a white collar and on the sleeve there was a darker spot as if the place had been once covered by something.

"You know, Fröken Stephania, that's my high-school uniform and here," Thura pointed to the darker spot, "was a ribbon with the name of the school; Saint Mark's High School, that was it. It feels funny to put it on again, the dress."

"Yes," Stephania said, "I guess it must feel rather funny."

Thura took the comb, stared at it for a while, then said, "If you don't mind, I'd like you to comb my hair, Fröken Stephania."

Stephania understood. She combed the brown soft hair carefully, sprinkled some of her eau de cologne on the dress to overcome the smell of moth balls. "Now you are ready, Thura," she said.

"Yes. I guess so." And then they sat, silent; only from time to time, smiling uncertainly, they would look at each other.

Until at last Sister Gudrun came in, and Fru Gustavsson, and the orderlies. Stephania, seated on her bed, heard vaguely how they said the ambulance would be here soon, yes, the ambulance; it would be more comfortable than a cab, and that the orderly had the ticket, that the train left at 11.45.

"That means in one hour," Thura said. Again she looked at Stephania.

Fru Gustavsson left, came back panting, exclaiming that the ambulance was already here. And now the door opened again and the dark uniformed men came in. "Here she is," Sister Gudrun pointed to Thura, and turning to her: "Now you say good-bye to Fröken Stephania, and we go."

Stephania got up. "Good-bye, Thura." She stood looking at the uniformed men bustling around impatiently, at the others watching curiously.

"Good-bye, Fröken Stephania."

And only in the door, when the others were already in the hall, Thura turned and said, "Thank you, Fröken Stephania, thank you for everything."

"Thura," Stephania began, but the door was closed already.

She sat staring at the empty room. Something white was lying on the floor. She picked it up. It was Thura's embroidery. Stephania smoothed it out carefully and put it back on Thura's table.

CHAPTER 26

DOCTOR STROM closed the door softly as if trying not to wake up someone quietly asleep. Stephania sat unmoving, waiting for the sound of his steps. No, she heard nothing; was he still here? But the room was empty; only in the chair where he had sat the cushion was crumpled still. Then the footsteps came, brisk and resounding. So he was gone. She moved cautiously and raised her hand, the fingers rigid and pointed in an effort to pierce through that something around her, something which pressed upon her, forced itself into her mouth, and choked her breath. No, the hand could do nothing. She balled it into a fist, then looked at it; it felt moist and sweaty.

Hot — it was terribly hot here. Still her whole body shivered and the feet were numb and cold as if she had been standing in snow. Slowly she crept under the blanket, pulled it high over her head. And only then when everything around grew dark and soft she remembered — He had said, yes, now she could even hear it; he said, "We can't do it, Stephania." No! It could not be . . . still . . . she buried her head under the pillow, but the unrelenting voice was still there — "Try to understand." What should she understand . . . no chance, not even one chance? Then — and why hadn't she listened to him? There was something about his waiting as long as he could, about the X-rays, and the cast . . . The cast? Yes, he said it did not work. . . . But it hurt, Doctor, hurt all the time, so it must have done something. . . . It was not enough, Stephania, it was nothing, try to understand. . . . She tossed the blanket off; it slid down on the floor dragging the pillow after it. . . . She leaned out, trying to lift it, but the blanket seemed very heavy suddenly. She gave it up, and lay trembling all over. But later, when he kept on talking but she could not understand any more, then he must have said something. She must have misunderstood him, that was all. Perhaps if she tried she could still catch up with him and tell him that he had promised. . . . Promised — no, she had told him that, and . . . No, I promised nothing, I just agreed to try, he said. But something must be done, Doctor. Something must be done. First to get up, if you get up then it might be easier to breathe. She grabbed the railing, staggered, stood up and started walking to and fro, faster until she was almost running, stumbling over the chairs, the beds, stopping before the walls that blocked her way. The window, yes; the window may be good, open, full of air. She stopped and tried to breathe deeply but something sharp and heavy had blocked her throat, the air gathered in her mouth grew stale there, nauseating like food chewed too long. And again walking, to and fro, to and fro. Someone was coming; Ström perhaps, Ström coming to tell her that she had not understood, that he had not meant it. . . . She stopped, and the footsteps stopped too. It must have been her own steps she heard. Ström was gone, the chair was empty. First when he came in he was standing. It was when he sat down that he said, "I've tried everything, I consulted others, doctors in the Karolinska Hospital, everybody. They all said the same thing, there's no use. . . ."

She could not stand it, that voice coming out of an invisible mouth, and then the smell that was still there, faint but distinct — cigarettes, ether. Where was the door? Right here. But her hands, numb and frozen, would not move. She pushed the door with her whole body, staggered, rushed out.

There were no walls to block your way in the hall. You could just run and run; that was good. Then something fell on the floor with a soft floppy sound — a basin full of water. She stopped, staring at the gray pool spreading wider and wider, felt something warm and sticky touching her legs and again started walking. The elevator; no, she did not want to take the elevator, here were the stairs. She walked down, came back again, through the vestibule, through the hall, until she stood before the operating room.

— No, not later either, we just can't do it, try to be sensible. Sensible? She pulled at the doorknob; the door was closed. Her hand touched it — the wood felt good, so smooth and cool. Never, he had said, and then looked at her, waiting. For what? Did he think she would cry? No, no crying for her; what for? There were other things one could do, so many of them. She had to think it over, but not now, later, because now it was still there, the block choking her breath, and the dumbness. But if you kept walking you did not feel it too much, just to keep on walking fast, very fast.

The banister was firm and when you touched it you could feel your hands again, know they were there grasping, holding it fast. That made everything easier somehow. But the stairs came to an end, the hall again, and there on the other side was the room. No, she did not want to go back to the room; not yet, there was so much else she wanted to do. To talk, yes, that was it, she wanted to talk; not to Ström, but to someone else, to anyone, so that the silence would not be there, around her and within. To hear a voice; that was what she wanted. Thadeus? No, Thadeus would not do either; Barbara, yes, of course, how could she forget — she wanted to talk to Barbara.

The phone booth was at the other end of the hall. She walked toward it, repeating with each step the number 8-9654. The door; this time it was easy to open it. But to dial the number — that was hard again; her fingers seemed swollen, she could not fit them into the holes of the dial. Now at last. She stood waiting, listening to the ringing. And what if Barbara was not at home? The cold returned, the numbness; no, she had to be in, she *had* to answer. But here it was, the jerky clicking of a lifted receiver. Soon it would come, the voice, she thought.

Hallo, she tried to say, but no sound came. She cleared her throat and tried again. This time it went fine.

"Hallo," Barbara's voice answered. "Is that you, Stephania? How are you?"

Slowly, as if she had not spoken for many days and now her tongue had grown unused to words, stiff, she said: "I . . . am . . . fine, Barbara, fine. And you?"

"As usual, busy but fine." And then when Stephania said something, "What's the matter with the phone? Speak louder, I can hardly hear you."

"Yes, it must be the phone." She listened to her own voice triumphantly, the words came so easily now, loud and distinct. "And how is the baby?"

Barbara was saying that the baby was fine, and then something about a cold, it was better now, he was just sneezing. . . . He? . . . Who? . . . The baby, of course. Stephania said, "I'm glad he's better."

"I was a little worried at first; on Monday I even wanted to call a doctor. But now there's nothing to worry about."

Monday . . . Thura had left on Monday, and today . . . today Ström had said . . . The receiver seemed very heavy suddenly, she had to hold it in both of her hands. Barbara — she wanted to cry, help me, I can't go on any more, I can't take it! No, that wasn't what she called her for, she wanted something from her. Now she couldn't remember it, but she would . . . soon. . . .

"How is Thadeus?"

And while Barbara was saying that he too was fine, that he was getting to like his work, she suddenly remembered clearly what it was that she wanted from Barbara, and that now once she had said it, everything would be simple, easy and simple.

"By the way," Barbara said, "Thadeus told me Ström wants to talk to him. He is seeing him in his office tomorrow."

"Is that so?" If you held the receiver in one hand for a while and then in the other, then it was not so heavy at all. "I guess it must be something about me, Barbara," she said.

"What is it, Stephania? Any news?"

"About . . . about my operation, I guess."

"Oh, Stephania, is he going to do it soon? How wonderful!"

"He decided . . . just today. I don't know the date exactly. But it's going to be pretty soon, I guess. He is very encouraging." Encouraging, that was a good word.

"Oh Stephania, I'm so happy."

"So am I of course." That was well done, she had to do it, and this other thing also had to be said cautiously, skillfully. Because

[ 357 ]

Barbara had changed and she might have refused otherwise, she certainly would refuse. Just to gain time she added, "He's been extremely nice to me lately, so outgoing. . . ."

And now she knew exactly what to say, and how, as if someone was standing next to her, dictating each word, even the tone of voice. "He hasn't much to do now, when most of the patients are gone, so he comes and talks to me. Thura's gone, you know," she added without knowing quite why.

"Thura? I don't think I . . ."

So Barbara did not remember Thura. That seemed funny somehow, but did not matter too much. "Thura; the paralyzed girl, you know; anyhow . . . he comes to see me quite often now, and we have long talks. And yesterday, yes, yesterday it was really funny, you know. I must tell you about it. Are you very busy?"

"No, not too much, I have to feed the baby soon, but not for a couple of minutes."

A couple of minutes: that was enough. "We talked about the war, it has a strange fascination for him; he feels guilty, I guess, or something like that . . . And I told him how everybody was buying cyanide, for any price." Now after that word had been said all would be easy, fine.

"Oh, Stephania, can't you stop dragging that out?"

"It doesn't do me any harm. And it was so funny, just a scream." She even managed to laugh, a short jerky laughter. "He wouldn't believe me. It was impossible, he said — and that I was making it all up. So I said I'll show it to you, Doctor, I still have it, it's like a souvenir for me. . . . Anyhow, if it's not any trouble for you, of course, could you bring it here? It's in the — in the small gilt box with rosebuds on it."

— Yes, the box with rosebuds. Mother used to keep rouge in it. And that was the only thing of hers she still had now; not because she cared so much for it, but because that was in it, the white powder, just a pinch wrapped in a piece of tissue. What was his name? Yes, Birnbaum, that old chemistry professor who had sold it to her. Three thousand *zloty* he took for it, the old scoundrel . . . could charge anything he wanted because everybody wanted to have it. Mother said, "We could have had twenty loaves of bread for all that money," but she told her, "This is more important than bread."

And then when she was holding it in her hand at last, that

[ 358 ]

feeling of joy, of lightness because now everything was up to you, because now they could do nothing to you, nothing at all. And it did not hurt much even, and it took only half an hour. That was true; it wasn't even that much with Mania, that woman from downstairs. She gave it first to her children when she heard them coming, then she took it herself. She was a good mother, that was all everyone said after that, and they did not even watch when she was carried out. No one made much fuss about things like that then, it was all so simple. She started, amazed that it had taken her so long to understand how simple it was. Just a few minutes. But here people kept talking and fussing about it. Like Thura, and she too in a way, as if it were God only knows what a big thing.

Barbara was saying something about the box, asked why didn't she answer.

"I'm sorry, someone was talking to me, I couldn't hear you. What was it you were saying?" And when Barbara was silent she said quickly, her voice dry and hoarse suddenly. "If it's a great trouble for you, don't bother."

"I don't have it, Stephania."

"Oh . . . I see. You . . . you lost it?"

"No. It was Thadeus, it got on his nerves, he said, to have something like that at home. So I threw it out. I knew you didn't believe in all that childish talk, you know what I mean, and anyhow since everything was going fine . . . So I threw it out."

"Oh, you did?"

"Did you say something, Stephania?"

"No, nothing." So, she threw it out. Because of Thadeus, of course . . . It got on his nerves, so how could anything else matter? Childish talk — Barbara would soon see what it meant, that childish talk.

Barbara said, "I'd better hurry now, Stephania. The baby may wake up any minute."

"Yes, why don't you?"

"Good-bye then, dear. See you soon, Sunday."

"Yes," she answered slowly, "I'll see you . . . soon."

Strange how tired she felt, her hands, each finger, and the lips hurting almost from fatigue. But it was nice to be moving again; standing in one place was wrong, but as long as you remembered to move . . .

Here was the room. But no, that wasn't the right place to go. She wanted to go somewhere else. . . . The telephone booth? That was done. The kitchen; certainly that was it — the kitchen. And suddenly she felt quiet and rested, until it was almost as if a strange joy, strong and powerful, was rising within her. The kitchen — that was a good place. Never put off until tomorrow what you have to do today, a proverb said. Proverbs were fine things, the wisdom of the people. And the kitchen would be empty now.

And wasn't it actually lucky that Ström had waited so long? Before, there had been people everywhere, but now you could do anything you wanted undisturbed. Not a soul in the hall, nor in the living room; no one would come into the kitchen to make coffee or put milk in the icebox. As if everything was especially prepared for you. One could almost believe in Providence. Yes, Providence clearly had a hand in it.

Just as she had thought; the kitchen was empty. And a key in the door; what luxury, complete privacy. Please do not disturb, busy on an urgent appointment. If Fru Gustavsson came she would think Sister Gudrun had taken the key. And if Sister Gudrun . . . She had not seen her around. What was it today, Wednesday? Yes, Wednesday was Sister Gudrun's day off. The finger of Providence, here it was again.

And a chair was there too, right in the corner. They certainly were stingy here; a plain wooden chair, without even a cushion. If you had to sit too long it might get uncomfortable. But that did not matter, you couldn't have everything in life, after all. And the stove had four burners; that was fine, two would have taken too long, but four . . . Funny how they hissed as if exasperated that there was no flame. . . . .

Now, breathe deeply . . .

You certainly were lucky in many respects, like not having to worry about anybody. No one would be terribly upset. . . . Barbara perhaps for a while, and not too much either, she had so many other things to do. Thadeus, oh no, not he. And the others? There were no others. Providence had taken care of them too. Only, yes, only Thura perhaps . . . she might feel badly about it . . . might even try to do it herself, after all. How would it be in a wheel chair and with only one hand? Kind of difficult to reach the key, but if she tried really hard . . . Tried . . . that certainly was a lot

[ 360 ]

of nonsense she had told her then, but now it did not matter.

And now it was starting, first getting a little dizzy and a sweet taste in the mouth, like black coffee with saccharine. Terrible stuff, saccharine. But that was even worse, made you feel all upside down, as if you were getting sick. Next time you do it, you should remember not to eat before; empty stomach like on the "great day." Next time — there would be no next time. And the dizziness was not so bad after all. Nothing to be afraid of.

Strange how some people would do it the hard way. Like jumping out of the window, from the tenth floor even, and the falling down; that must be quite something. You fall and fall and there is no stopping even if you want to. Gas is better. Give me gas and I'm satisfied, though it certainly rustles and hisses like a waterfall or like wind. And everything around whirling and turning, round and round. Better close your eyes and wait, wait . . . .

Steps? Yes, someone is coming, but the door is locked so there is nothing to worry about. Quick steps clicking. It must be the orderly, the handsome one with the very shiny eyes, and teeth white and sharp like a puppy's. Handsome . . . Isn't he singing? If you can still hear it, if you recognize the song, that means it hasn't begun yet, not really. Oh yes, "Roses in Bloom in Picardy" . . . Where's Picardy — in France, in Italy?

And now it's gone — the steps, the song . . .

If you hold fast to the chair then the falling will stop perhaps. Falling, why should it be? it was only gas, gas, not the window . . . But now . . . falling down and down with something hard and dark underneath coming closer and then far away again. And the air — hot, heavy, striking into the face; tearing out everything from within the body, sucking it out, hotter and hotter . . . Yes it was the window, and now they are everywhere, black, shiny windows. If you grasp hold of them, burst through, then you can stop that — the falling. Try — but no, they slip out, melt away into something sleek and sticky. The railing, sharp teeth sticking out, grasp, not that, it will hurt, it hurts already deep inside, terribly. And again the air slashing, and the falling. Stop, you can stop it, it wasn't the window, it is the gas. TURN IT OFF.

— Hands, where are they, the hands, why don't they move? Try once more, now here is a switch, another, how many are there? Now the hissing stops, now everything is quiet, except for a faraway pounding. . . .

[ 361 ]

She sat trembling all over, her hands on the switches, her eyes wide open. The smell was still there, sticking to her tongue, to her whole body, mixed with cold sweat. She tried to get up, groped around, sank back. And suddenly she was coughing, choking with a deep, slimy cough, as if she had to free herself from the smell, had to spit out everything within her. Until at last she got sick and it was everywhere, the dense sticky slime, clinging to her face, to her hands. . . . Still she could not get up, sat watching. . . . But the smell . . . she forced herself to move, to rise from the chair, and walk to the sink. The water did not smell, it was cold and clear. She filled her hands with it, splashed it over her face, her neck, felt it running in icy streaks underneath the cast. Now it was better, if she only could open the window . . . She turned, looked. . . .

The big window stood wide open, branches of trees peering through it, air streaming in, fresh, clean . . . She stood staring, felt herself grinning at last. Efficient, what? . . . the window open all the time, while she . . . No wonder it hadn't worked. Still, once she knew she could try again. Turning, she glanced at the stove. The smell seized her, nauseating saliva filled her mouth. Try again? No, never. And groping blindly she rushed toward the door. . . .

But there she stopped and looked at the freshly polished floor, then at the gray slimy pond. They would come in, Sister Gudrun or Fru Gustavsson, and would start sniffing around asking who had been in the room, when, why . . . ? No, she couldn't leave it like that. Carefully circling the stove, hardly breathing to escape that smell that was still pressing upon her, she walked to the closet and opened it. Frantically, her hands trembling, she began to rummage in it: jars, pots, fell out; then piles of neatly folded paper, an old cookbook, jars again, they must have been storing that junk for years, but no rag, no rag of course. Furiously she slammed the closet door and walked out.

From the other end of the hall came the sound of scrubbing brushes. She walked toward it and opened the door. Thank God, it was the other maid, not Fru Gustavsson, who was in there. For a while she stood watching the bulky woman crouched on her knees, the brush spreading wide circles of gray soapy water, the fat buttocks shaking with each movement.

"Excuse me," she said at last.

"Yes," the maid snapped back, without lifting her head.

[ 362 ]

"I wonder . . . I would like to borrow the mop and the bucket, just for a moment."

"What for?" the reddish hand reached out, splashed more water out of the bucket on the floor.

"I spilled something, not much, in my room."

"I'll clean it. Fröken will leave a mess anyhow, then I'll have to hear from Sister Gudrun."

"No, I can do it, I really can."

"I told Fröken, I'd rather do it myself." The maid got up heavily, looked at Stephania, stepped back startled. Stephania murmured something, snatched the pail and mop and rushed out. Breathlessly she ran through the hall and back into the kitchen, locked the door and stood listening. No, no one was coming. She breathed with relief, and suddenly started laughing, noiselessly at first, then louder and louder until tears came into her eyes. And laughing still, she began to mop the floor, holding onto the chair and the walls, panting heavily.

Now it was done at last. She walked back, opened the door, and just putting her arm through it, sneaked the pail and mop inside. She stopped, hesitated. — What now? The room — yes, she wanted to go back to her room.

"Can't you people watch out, for Heaven's sake?"

She looked up. "I'm sorry, Fru Gustavsson."

"It's all right, Fröken Stephania, I thought it was that orderly again." Fru Gustavsson's head emerged from behind a pile of blankets. "But what's the matter? You're all wet, and as pale as a ghost?"

"Wet? Oh yes, I spilled some water. I . . . I don't feel too well; a cold coming on, I guess . . . No, I don't think so, it must be the heat, I guess."

"Yes, it certainly is hot. And in the cast, poor thing, it must be hard on you. High time they took it off, isn't it?"

She looked at her, said slowly: "They're going to take it off."

"Really? Isn't that wonderful. Is Ström going to operate on you?"

"No, I'm leaving."

"Oh," Fru Gustavsson said, then again, "oh. Let me help you back to your room, Fröken Stephania."

"Please don't, I can walk all right."

[ 363 ]

Still she felt grateful for that arm around her, supporting her gently, carefully. But then she stopped. "I really don't need help, Fru Gustavsson, please go back to work," she said. Because suddenly everything within her grew warm and soft and she wanted so much to put her head on Fru Gustavsson's plump shoulder and cry. But the time for it had not come . . . not yet. "Please, let me go."

"Take care of yourself, Fröken Stephania."

"I will."

The door to the room was half open. Someone must have been in there; she could hear impatient steps and then the sound of a chair pushed aside. Noiselessly Stephania opened the door and looked — it was Ström. So he had come back after all. Had he changed his mind perhaps? No, Ström never changed his mind, not he. Still it was good to know that he had come, good that now for once it was he who had to wait for her, impatiently too, because his fingers kept drumming on the windowpanes. She watched him, prolonging for him this moment of waiting, and feeling how suddenly something was solidifying within her — deliberate, malicious anticipation. With carefully measured steps she walked toward him. Ström heard her and turned away from the window. For a moment she stood silent, not certain yet what to say. But again, as before when she had talked to Barbara, her voice as if of itself chose the right pitch, cold and overpolite. "Hello, Doctor, are you waiting for me?"

"Yes . . . I . . . Stephania." She felt he was trying in vain to say something, and that made her quieter still, almost joyful. Her eyes squinted as she looked at him, at the shining white coat, at the immaculate bow tie, then at his face, calm again, the eyes behind the horn-rimmed glasses watching her patiently. So here he was, the great Doctor Ström, always quiet, always dignified; but soon it would happen, soon she would rob him of that dignity, of that complacency. And slowly sounding her words she said:

"It's unusually nice of you, Doctor, to come to see me, to show so much interest in me still."

"There's nothing unusual about it, Stephania. After all, you've been my patient and so . . . ."

"Still, it *is* unusual," her smile deepened into a grin, "because if I may be frank, Doctor . . ."

"Yes, I want you to be frank . . ."

[ 364 ]

She glanced at him distrustfully. "Don't expect any great revelations, Doctor. All I wanted to say is that after all that's happened you must dislike me intensely."

"If I disliked anybody, it would be myself, in the first place," he smiled, pulling up a chair for her.

"Oh no, Doctor," she said sitting down, "don't be so hard on yourself. After all it was me who got you into this embarrassing mess. I actually blackmailed you into it, didn't I?"

"No, Stephania," he shook his head, "you blackmailed me into nothing. I wanted to try, and . . ."

"And you failed." She managed to smile amiably. Then slowly she lifted herself higher in the chair, so that the bulging hunch was right before him, and glancing appreciatively at his well-proportioned body she began to pass her hand over the cast — to and fro, to and fro.

Ström said nothing, but she could feel his eyes upon her, soothing, pleading almost. So that was why he came; he felt sorry for her. Fine; he would find out soon that she was not a good object for that professional kindness of his. And looking at the empty beds, at the gaping frames, she said: "It certainly is sad you had such bad luck in this room, Doctor. First Fröken Nilsson, chopping off her leg after she had been here for over two years. Then Thura, carried out on a stretcher, and it was three years for her." She stopped. "No, I must be wrong, Doctor, it couldn't have been that long."

"Yes, Stephania, it was that long. Still, it all depends on how one looks at it. After all, Fröken Nilsson could walk when she left, Thura did move her hand."

So he was still quiet, still dignified. Softly she said: "So you're satisfied, Doctor, with your . . . your accomplishments? To me they're rather doubtful, but you know better of course. Still in my case there's no doubt. I am a clear-cut failure. I leave this place just as I came, untouched, in the virginal state, so to speak." She shrugged. "Not that it matters much, Doctor; please don't ever worry about me."

He came closer, bent over her. "Look here, Stephania, what's the use of bringing all that up again? Not that I mind, but it happened, nothing can be done about it. I came here to find out what your plans are, that's what's important now. Are you going to live with your sister?"

So he had found a new role already . . . wanted to take paternal care of her. "With my sister?" she repeated. "Certainly not, Doctor. I like my freedom, you see, and besides . . . the apartment is too small." She paused. "There's no room for both of us to move around here" — when had Barbara said it? Yes, after the party. "Much too small," she repeated, "just one room and the kitchen. And I, Doctor, don't like to sleep in the kitchen; it smells of gas no matter how careful you are," and she looked at him challengingly.

"I might help you to find a room, my wife knows a family . . . "

"Oh no, Doctor, how could I ever bother your wife?"

"It wouldn't be a bother; still, if you prefer to look for it yourself . . . but . . . " He hesitated. "There's another thing that I wanted to mention to you. I hope you won't mind, Stephania. If you ever need help, you know what I mean, please do feel free . . . because I'll be glad . . . " He smiled awkwardly.

"You're most kind, Doctor. But I have all I need, and besides — " She paused again. "Besides, I don't take money from strange men. Especially since any reciprocal services are excluded." And again her hand in a caressing gesture passed over the cast.

"Well, I just want you to remember, in case . . . " He took out cigarettes, offered her one and lit another for himself. She inhaled, once, but suddenly the smoke brought it all back again — the dense sweet taste, the hollowness in her stomach. She put the cigarette away and tried to suppress the cough, but it burst out of her, rasping and choking until her whole body shook and her face was covered with sweat.

"What's the matter, Stephania?"

"Nothing," she tried to say, but the cough choked her words. Ström got up hastily and filled the glass with water. She drank slowly. The cough stopped at last. Panting heavily she turned to him and said drily: "Don't look so concerned, Doctor. Nothing dreadful happened, something got stuck in my throat, that's all." But when he still stood bent over her, she added, her voice breaking with anger, "Have you found out all you wanted to know, Doctor? If so I see no point in my keeping you here."

"There's one thing more, Stephania. Have you thought about the kind of work you would like to do later?"

Work — that was just like him to bring it up now, to remind her of the endless walks from office to office, of the startled faces,

of shame-filled voices saying, "Sorry, but there are no openings."
But her voice was very quiet when she answered, "I can do anything, Doctor. Since I know nothing — exactly like my brother-
in-law, it runs in the family as you see — I have unlimited choice,
boundless opportunities." Her hand moved in a rounded spacious
gesture.

"For instance what, Stephania?"

"Well," she hesitated, playing with the extinguished cigarette.
"By boundless opportunities I mean some kind of work in an office.
Not as a secretary of course. That would be reaching much too
high, a secretary must be aesthetically pleasing, Doctor. And I . . .
I may easily scare the clients away. Still, I can find something in
a small office, someplace where they could hide me in a corner."

"Perhaps my idea is better then, Stephania. Do you remember I
once suggested you should work in the children's ward? I still think
it is a good idea. The training could be easily arranged, and Fröken Haagen, personnel director, said they would love to have you."

"So you have it all figured out, Doctor. Thank you ever so
much, but you could have saved yourself the trouble."

"Wouldn't you like to try at least?"

"There's no use trying. I told you I have no maternal instincts,
and besides . . . besides, I hate doing what is useless."

He came up to her so abruptly that she was startled. "Useless?
You may not want to work here, but don't call it useless. Have
you ever seen the children there? Unable to move, in casts for
years? Still they're children, they want to play, they're curious and
want to learn. Don't you understand, a good therapist is as important as the doctor."

"Is that so?" She stopped but only for a moment, for already
she knew what to say, knew what it was that she had tried to tell
him all that time. "So you feel important, Doctor? A helper of
suffering mankind, a savior. But has it ever occurred to you that
in reality you may be nothing but — a cobbler?"

"I don't quite understand what you mean?"

"Exactly what I said. Cobblers all of you, from intern to Professor, the big fish and the small. And not even first rate — third
rate only, fixing old trash, good for nothing but a junk yard." Furtively she glanced at him; his face was quiet, just mildly attentive.
And so she got up and walked to the window. He followed her.
Fine, that meant he understood, even if he pretended not to.

[ 367 ]

Silently she looked at the densely filled benches, with her eyes choosing the most deformed figures, pointing them to him with a glance. "You see, that's what I mean — a junk yard."

"You have no right to say that." With relief she listened to the anger that at last came into his voice. "No right, d'you understand? They're ugly, I agree; they can hardly move. Still, in spite of all that they're like other people. They are learning here and when they leave they'll start working just like everybody else."

"Working? Isn't that wonderful, Doctor? As seamstresses, as typists, hemming dresses, typing business letters for eight hours a day, and then going home — to what, Doctor, tell me, to what?"

"There's some use for that kind of work too. Many whom you wouldn't call trash do it. And besides, they do have families, friends."

"Families? Old parents who are afraid of them, afraid and ashamed. And friends? Companions from the School for the Handicapped at best. I've seen the announcements in the paper you put out here. 'All handicapped come to the great Christmas dinner'; or 'Basketball game, all in wheel chairs invited.' What fun! Always together, like lepers."

He turned away from the window and sat down. She followed him, grinning, feverishly expectant. But when he started his voice was quiet again, very cold. "It's hard on them, Stephania, I know it. Still it's not so humiliating, so disgustingly hopeless as you are trying to make it. It's true they do certain things together, it's easier for them that way. But look at all those people who come to see them here. They have friends everywhere."

"Aren't you overoptimistic, Doctor?" She paused, gave him a prolonged look, and then as though to herself said, "Yes, even you, Doctor, even you . . ."

"What about me?"

"Even you would be ashamed, Doctor, of 'friends' like them, like me."

"I hope not, Stephania."

"Are you sure? Let me ask you a question. Would you ever take me to a dance, Doctor, to a big formal dance? But be frank."

"I'm going to be frank, Stephania. Probably not."

For a long while she was silent, then said laboriously, "Thanks for proving my point, Doctor."

"I proved nothing, Stephania. I wouldn't take you probably, but

[ 368 ]

not for the reasons you have in mind. That would be one of the situations in which you could not be as good as the others. It might be hard for you, not for me, that's all I meant."

"Oh, only for me, never for you, Doctor. But that's not true. After all I can still dance, pretty well too. All you'd have to do would be to put your arm slightly lower, under the hunch, I mean. But otherwise . . . still you would never take me. Because you'd be ashamed, Doctor. What would people think? Here's Doctor Ström, such a handsome man, couldn't he have found someone better? Don't you see? we're the damaged goods, the refuse. And being with me would cast a reflection upon you, as if you were not good enough either. Someone like me makes people ashamed, terribly ashamed."

"Some may be ashamed, I admit that, Stephania. But I think I would not, and I know there must be others who wouldn't either."

"There are? Strange, I've never been fortunate enough to meet any of them. Of course, I've known some who tried, out of nobility, you know; out of Christian self-sacrificing spirit. Even here in Stockholm, when I lived in the boardinghouse, there was a whole group of them. They were so nice, came around every day, brought me books. I had never been so intellectual in my life. And they too enjoyed themselves, in the beginning at least; felt so good, each of them a Florence Nightingale, the lady with the lamp. Only sometimes, Doctor, sometimes all that nobility grew a little embarrassing. They would try very hard to cover it up, their embarrassment I mean. Still I could smell it. We'd be sitting together and suddenly someone would say, 'Wasn't that a nice evening last Sunday when we had cocktails together and then dinner and the dance — the dance was really fine.' And then they would all look at me, because you see I hadn't even been told about the cocktails, the dinner, and the dance. And someone very fast would start talking about the last book by Sartre, just to break the silence, you know. So that I wouldn't find out I was good enough only up to five o'clock in the afternoon, but not later. Never later, Doctor," she repeated softly. "But then when they knew I did find out they stopped coming. Petered out, one after another, men and women. Men of course have a harder time with creatures like me, they're afraid . . . you know, 'hunchback or not, she still may get some unreasonable ideas. . . .' But even women . . . It's too much for them, that's all."

[ 369 ]

She sat, her fingers drumming upon the back of the chair, waiting for him to answer. And when he was still silent, she started again, her voice nonchalant and smooth, only occasionally rising to a high pitch and then breaking suddenly. "D'you know I'm getting an idea and I really think I'm putting my finger on something. I had an interesting experience this year, and it suggests something to me. Christian love doesn't work too well, Doctor, but a drink might, even if not for too long. You're drunk and you forget, you forgive even the crutches, even the hunch or whatever it may be. Like a man I met at the party my sister gave in my honor. He was one of those who believe that only the soul matters, and oddly enough he discovered I happened to have one. So we had fun together in a soulful and also a not too soulful way. But the next morning, when the hangover came, probably, he must have discovered that the soul was not enough after all. He was supposed to call me, we had a real luncheon engagement, but he never did. Still, as I said, the evening was fun. So perhaps if people, people like you, I mean, drank more, there would be some bright moments in store for us. But that is not too probable and so . . ." she bent toward him, "it all makes very little sense, none at all as a matter of fact. Unless — " There was a knock on the door.

"Come in," Ström called. It was Fru Gustavsson. "Oh, here you are, Doctor," she said staring at them curiously. "I've been looking for you everywhere. Docent Skarin is on the phone, he wants to know if Doctor would come to look at Fru Hakelund's X-rays."

Stephania listened, her eyes passing from Fru Gustavsson to Ström, expectant, mocking. So now he would leave; he would just grab the chance to run away. Already she could hear him murmuring shamefully, I'm sorry, but I really have to go. Of course, you should go, she would answer, and, This was a most enjoyable visit . . .

"Tell Docent I'm busy right now, I'll look at them later," she heard Ström's voice saying.

The door closed.

Why did he stay? she thought. And to deafen the restless feeling rising within her she said: "You should have gone with her, Doctor, you must not let me take so much of your time. And besides you've heard everything I had to tell you."

"Are you sure? Because if there's anything else . . ."

So he had not had enough yet. "Let me see, Doctor, let me see. Yes, perhaps there's something more. A suggestion it has just occurred to me, but it seems fine. The Spartans, do you remember how well they solved the problem?"

"Yes . . . I remember. What about it, Stephania?"

"They used to expose cripples — as soon as they were born. They didn't even let them grow up, you see. Fine people the old Spartans, Doctor, honest. . . ." She glanced at him — was he smiling? It was hard to tell; still she said: "I'm not joking, Doctor, I've never been so serious in my life. Here, just listen, I have it all figured out, with details. We must try to find supporters, patrons of the Spartan Revival Society. A good name, isn't it? We could also use a subtitle to make it clearer, you know — For Exposure of All Crippled and Disabled. There must be even now a few unsentimental, realistic people. Even the government might be interested, who knows? Just think of all the expense saved, all the trouble, and the embarrassment, the embarrassment above all. Exposure may be a little old-fashioned, but after all we live in the twentieth century. Why not utilize some of the great German inventions? I saw them working, extremely efficiently, believe me, ten thousand people at once. And exposure could be only symbolic — it has such a nice mild sound, you see." She stopped and looked at him. Why would he say nothing, why was he just staring at her? "Don't look so worried, Doctor," she said through her teeth. "You would still be able to make a living. Mending ankles of pretty girls, sprained at a dance — it will only increase your prestige, that kind of work. At least then you'll be a first-rate cobbler, don't you see?" She grinned again, but her hand when she passed it through her hair trembled.

He sat bent slightly, nodding his head as if he were talking to himself. Then he took off his glasses and started wiping them off carefully. The sudden silence raised again the restless feeling within her, and she said very loudly: "Do you agree, Doctor? You seem to have nothing to say."

He started. "Agree with the Spartan revival idea? No, Stephania, certainly not. But I was thinking about something else you said, about me being a cobbler. You're right there, Stephania. Only you told me nothing new, I've known it for a long time. Because Thura was not the first one I had to send home on a stretcher; there were many like that before her, and there will be more still.

But I've no choice, Stephania. I try to cobble — that's the only thing I can do."

"No, Doctor, I told you clearly, that's not the only thing."

"What else is there?" His voice was low but insistent, hard. "Tell me what else? I couldn't save Thura from getting polio, I couldn't prevent those people in the park from becoming cripples. So what should I do? Leave them just as they are, in pain, in fever, unable to even move? Don't you see? I agree to do what I'm doing just because I understand that I am only a cobbler, just because I know I can't do more, and so I have to do the little I can."

"What for, Doctor? Don't you see what you are doing to them?" she cried. "It's not only that they are crippled, crawling, but . . . but it's that they have to be alone." Her voice lapsing into a whisper she repeated, "Do you understand? Always alone. Always. That's why nothing can make sense for them."

Again he was silent. Staring straight into his face she said shrilly: "Come on, Doctor, say something. You don't have to be ashamed that you have a lovely wife."

"Yes, Stephania, I'm married, happily married, I guess. I know that perhaps I have no right to speak; still it seems to me it would be impossible, just absurd that everything should make sense for two together and no sense for those who are alone. If each of them alone has nothing, then what would they share, what would they have together? It would be like saying that zero and zero makes one. But it doesn't. It is harder, much harder, if one is alone but even then, it all must make some kind of sense, because otherwise it would be too absurd, just too absurd."

The softness of his voice frightened her. She wanted to get up, to move far away from him, but could not. And without looking at him she said: "It is harder. It is so much harder that one can't take it." Her voice rose to a scream, but she forced it down again. "The Spartans, Doctor, the Spartans; they had the only answer."

"The answer for all the people out there, what?"

"Yes, for all."

"Try it then. Go out into the park and ask them one after another if they want it."

"Them?" she shrugged.

"Yes, them. Or don't they count at all, don't they have anything to say?"

"No." She got up, stood face to face with him, no longer knowing that she was screaming. "They don't count! Of course they want to go on, but why, have you ever asked yourself why? It is out of cowardice, out of habit, don't you see?"

"And who's to judge what it is, cowardice, habit or something else? Who, you or me?"

"Yes, you or me, anybody who has eyes and can see. Look at them. It's wrong, it is too humiliating to let them crawl on like that. You know it so you can judge, you must!"

"I? D'you think that I really know why I'm going on? I don't, Stephania, I don't think I ever will. When I stop and start weighing it all, the losses, the futility, the failure, on one side; the few good moments I've had on the other, then it all makes very little sense to me."

"To you?"

"Yes, you may believe it or not, to me, too. Still each time I decide to go on. Why? Don't ask me. But it's not because I keep waiting for something, not because I still hope it all will change suddenly." He fell silent. "No," he murmured, "no, I just don't know." Slowly he raised his hand, clenched it, and strangely grinding each word said: "It's only that I feel it, Stephania, no matter what I do and think, I feel it . . . that I and all of us cling with whatever strength we have to something, as if to a piece of rock with nothing round it. And the more difficult, the more impossible it is to do it, the more you feel you've got, you've just got to stick it all out. . . . Because . . ." he looked at her, "because at least, no matter how much I don't know, I feel this at least; the strength, I know I *can* do it."

He shrugged. "I guess it all means very little, all that I'm saying; but still," he raised his voice again, "still, don't you see that I too have no proof? I too . . . I am here, I feel I have to be, and that feeling, that is my only proof. So what right do I have to tell anyone it is not worth while for him? They are here, crawling I agree, but they are here, and that means they too feel it, they too decide they have to stick it out no matter what. Their proof is the same as mine, so how can I dare to tell them it is less good, how could I give less credit to their decision, when it is all the same thing? All I can say is that they need much more of it, of the strength, because it is so much harder for them. That's all. But to run away from them, to leave them alone as you want to do, just because they have it harder . . . no, I can't see that."

[ 373 ]

She seemed not to have heard him. She sat with her head bent, and murmured haltingly, "What . . . d'you mean, what did you say?"

"Nothing very important. Only that one must not run away and leave them alone just because they have it so much harder."

She crouched as if all her strength was gone suddenly. "Maybe, Doctor, maybe," she whispered, "I never thought of it that way. But I don't know . . . I . . ." Her face hidden in her hands she said, "I need rest, Doctor, plenty of rest."

And then she started crying noiselessly, her whole body shaking with sobs. Ström sat next to her, his hand awkwardly stroking her hair.

"Good-bye, Fröken Stephania," Sister Gudrun's hand feels bony and cool; then its grasp tightens; "take good care of yourself."

"I will, Sister."

"Good-bye, Fru Gustavsson"; again a hand in hers, plump and soft this time.

"Best of luck, Fröken Stephania."

"Thanks, Fru Gustavsson."

Ström is standing farther aside. She walks toward him, smiles faintly.

"Here I am, Doctor."

"Let me take you to the door, Stephania."

She hesitated. "Please don't bother."

"It's not a bother; I want to."

They walk silently. In the vestibule he stops, searches in his pocket. "Please take this, it's my address and phone number." She hesitates again, then takes the card. "Thank you, Doctor."

"If I am not at home, try to get me in the hospital. And be sure to leave a message if I'm not here either." He speaks very fast without looking at her. And only when suddenly, unexpected to herself, she turns to him and repeats chokedly, "Thank you . . . thank you very much, Doctor," he raises his eyes and says: "Just don't keep me waiting too long, Stephania. I want to hear from you, remember."

For a long while he holds her hand in his and then opens the door. Stepping outside she hears it slamming with a reluctant bang.

— It is cooler today. The sun touching her cheeks feels tender, cautious somehow, and the air is mild, too; — May air again. A breeze rises, sways the branches of the trees, whirls her dress. She stares at it, at the black silk with gaudy flowers, then at her shadow sharply cut out on the white asphalt; then again, quickly, at the trees.

It must have rained in the night. Round transparent drops hang from the leaves, and the driveway, where the sun has not yet reached, is dark and shiny — moist. The park is empty still, very quiet; only the leaves rustle and sometimes a bird's voice calls; shrill, far-resounding in the clear air. Then another sound comes, the rhythmical clapping of a carpet beater. "Fröken Stephania!!"

She turns; Fru Gustavsson is leaning over the balcony railing, waving at her with the beater. "Good-bye again." Her kerchief has loosened, it flutters bright-red around her smiling face. "Remember, do come to see us."

She raises her head, says slowly, "I may, Fru Gustavsson." The beating starts again, brisk and even. She hears it as she walks down the driveway, then it grows fainter and fainter, merges with the confused noise of the city — with the rattle of trains, the tooting of horns, with the jerky clinking of streetcars. Once more she stops, looks at the red brick building, at the many windows gleaming in the early sun. I may come back, she thinks — yes . . . later . . . I may.

And then she walks on.